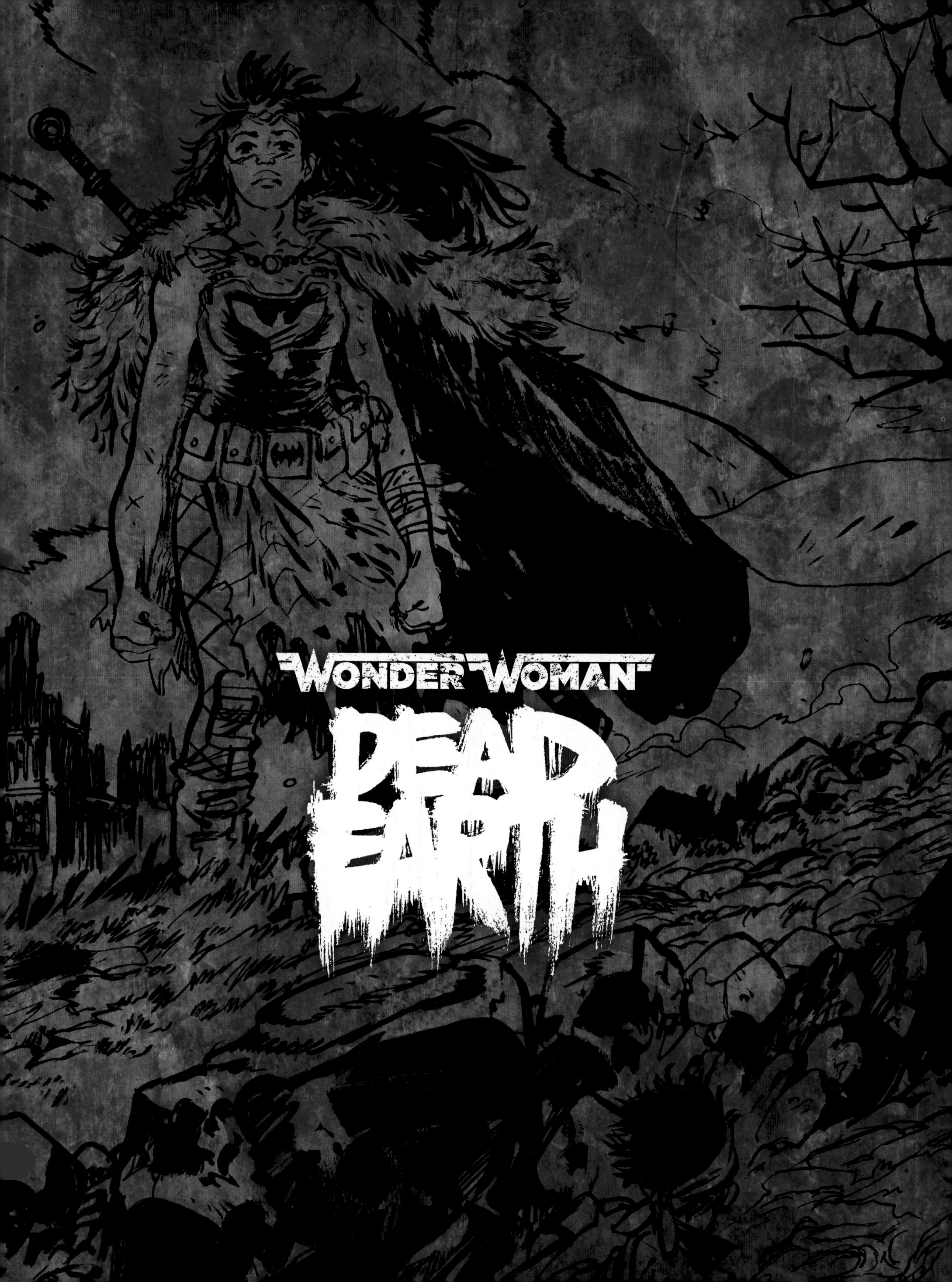
WONDER WOMAN
DEAD EARTH

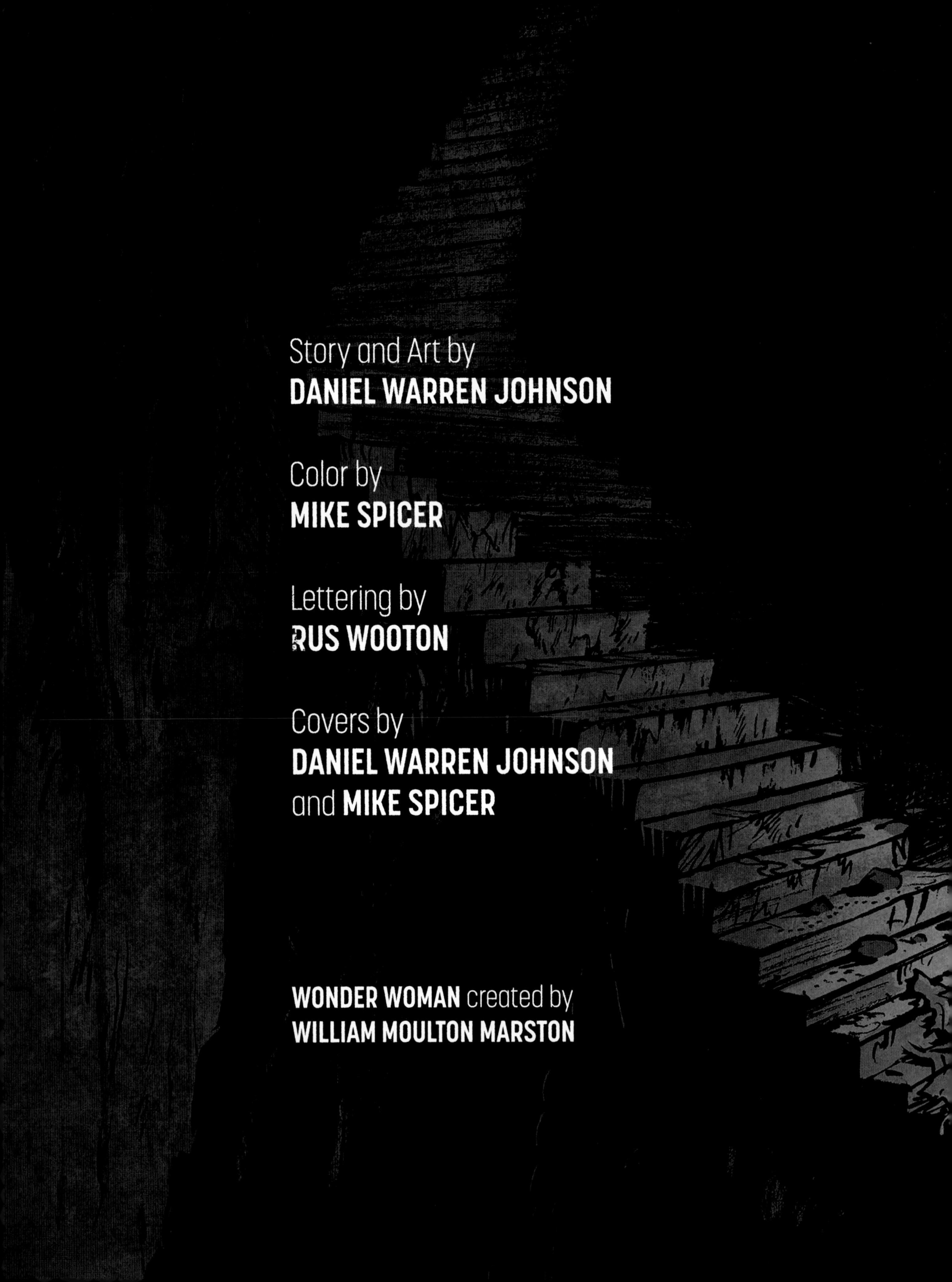

Story and Art by
DANIEL WARREN JOHNSON

Color by
MIKE SPICER

Lettering by
RUS WOOTON

Covers by
DANIEL WARREN JOHNSON
and **MIKE SPICER**

WONDER WOMAN created by
WILLIAM MOULTON MARSTON

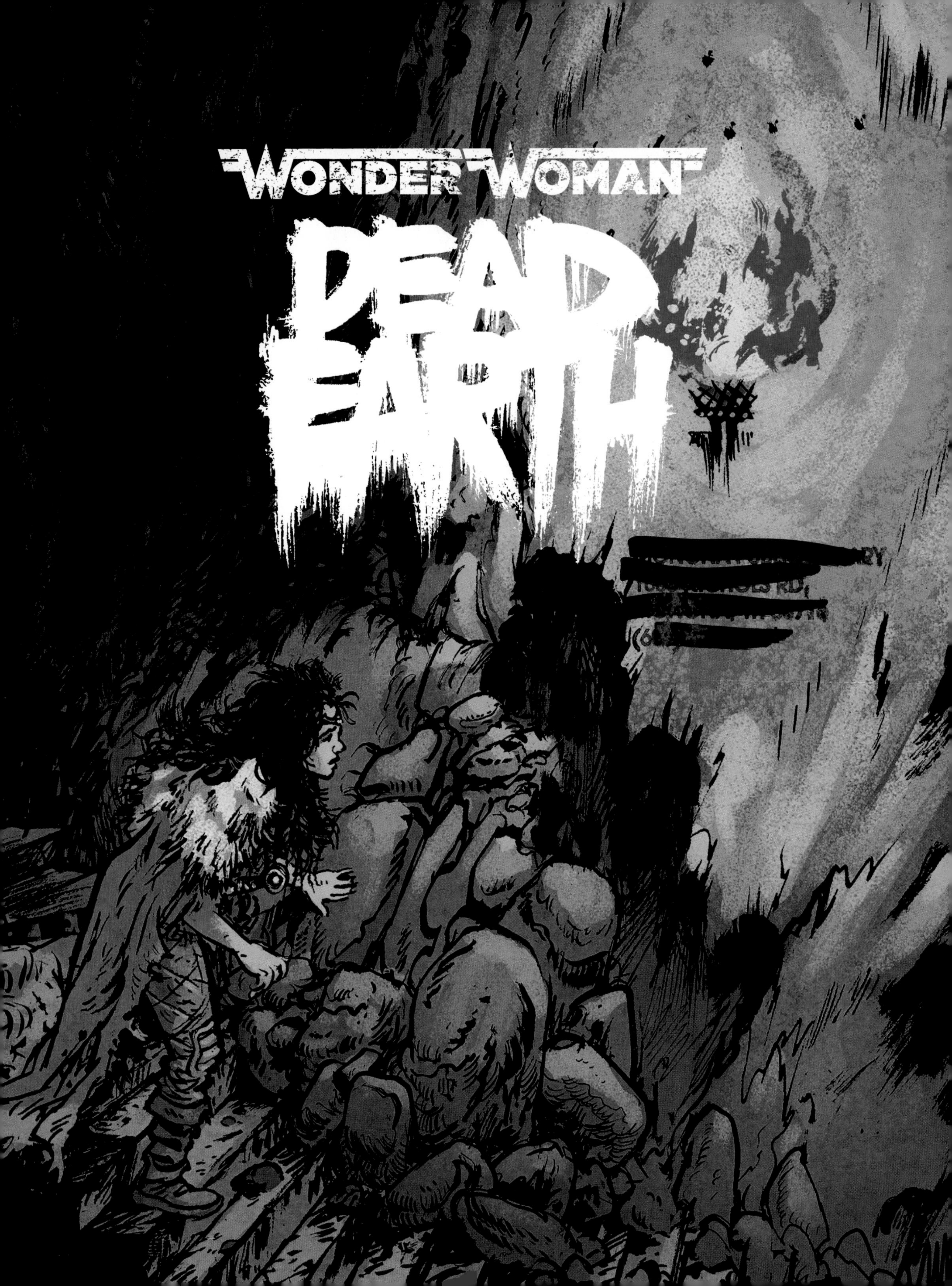
WONDER WOMAN
DEAD EARTH

ANDY KHOURI   Editor - Original Series
MAGGIE HOWELL   Associate Editor - Original Series
JEB WOODARD   Group Editor - Collected Editions
ROBIN WILDMAN   Editor - Collected Edition
STEVE COOK   Design Director - Books
    & Publication Design
SUZANNAH ROWNTREE   Publication Production

BOB HARRAS   Senior VP - Editor-in-Chief, DC Comics
MARK DOYLE   Executive Editor, DC Black Label

JIM LEE   Publisher & Chief Creative Officer
BOBBIE CHASE   VP - Global Publishing Initiatives & Digital Strategy
DON FALLETTI   VP - Manufacturing Operations & Workflow Management
LAWRENCE GANEM   VP - Talent Services
ALISON GILL   Senior VP - Manufacturing & Operations
HANK KANALZ   Senior VP - Publishing Strategy & Support Services
DAN MIRON   VP - Publishing Operations
NICK J. NAPOLITANO   VP - Manufacturing Administration & Design
NANCY SPEARS   VP - Sales
JONAH WEILAND   VP - Marketing & Creative Services
MICHELE R. WELLS   VP & Executive Editor, Young Reader

WONDER WOMAN: DEAD EARTH

Published by DC Comics. Compilation, cover, and all new material Copyright © 2020 DC Comics. All Rights Reserved. Originally published in single magazine form in *Wonder Woman: Dead Earth* 1-4. Copyright © 2020 DC Comics. All Rights Reserved. All characters, their distinctive likenesses, and related elements featured in this publication are trademarks of DC Comics. The stories, characters, and incidents featured in this publication are entirely fictional. DC Comics does not read or accept unsolicited submissions of ideas, stories, or artwork. DC - a WarnerMedia Company.

DC Comics, 2900 West Alameda Ave., Burbank, CA 91505
Printed by Transcontinental Interglobe, Beauceville, QC, Canada. 10/23/20. First Printing.
ISBN: 978-1-77950-261-2

Library of Congress Cataloging-in-Publication Data is available.

PEFC Certified

This product is
from sustainably
managed forests and
controlled sources

PEFC/01-31-106   www.pefc.org

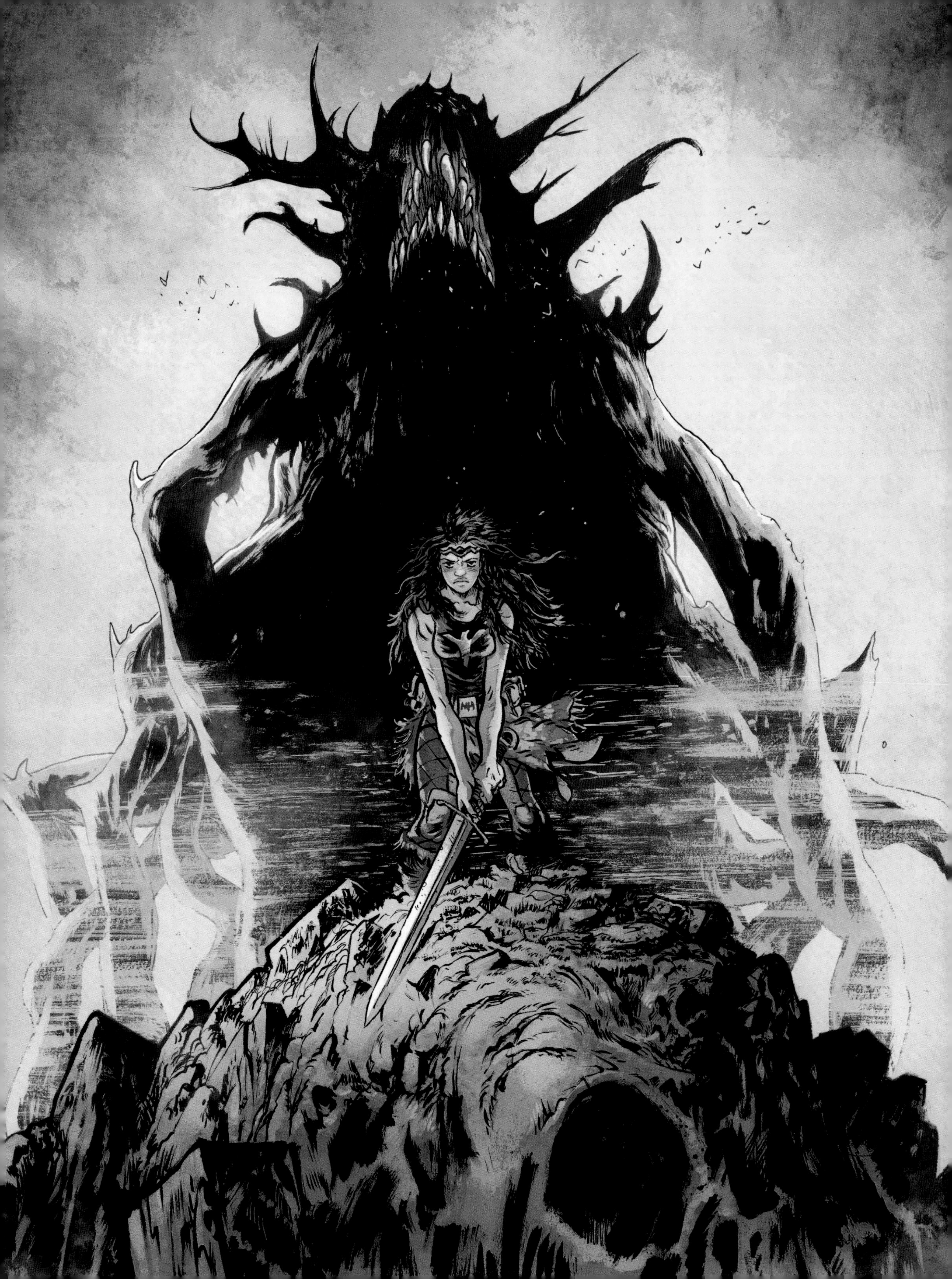

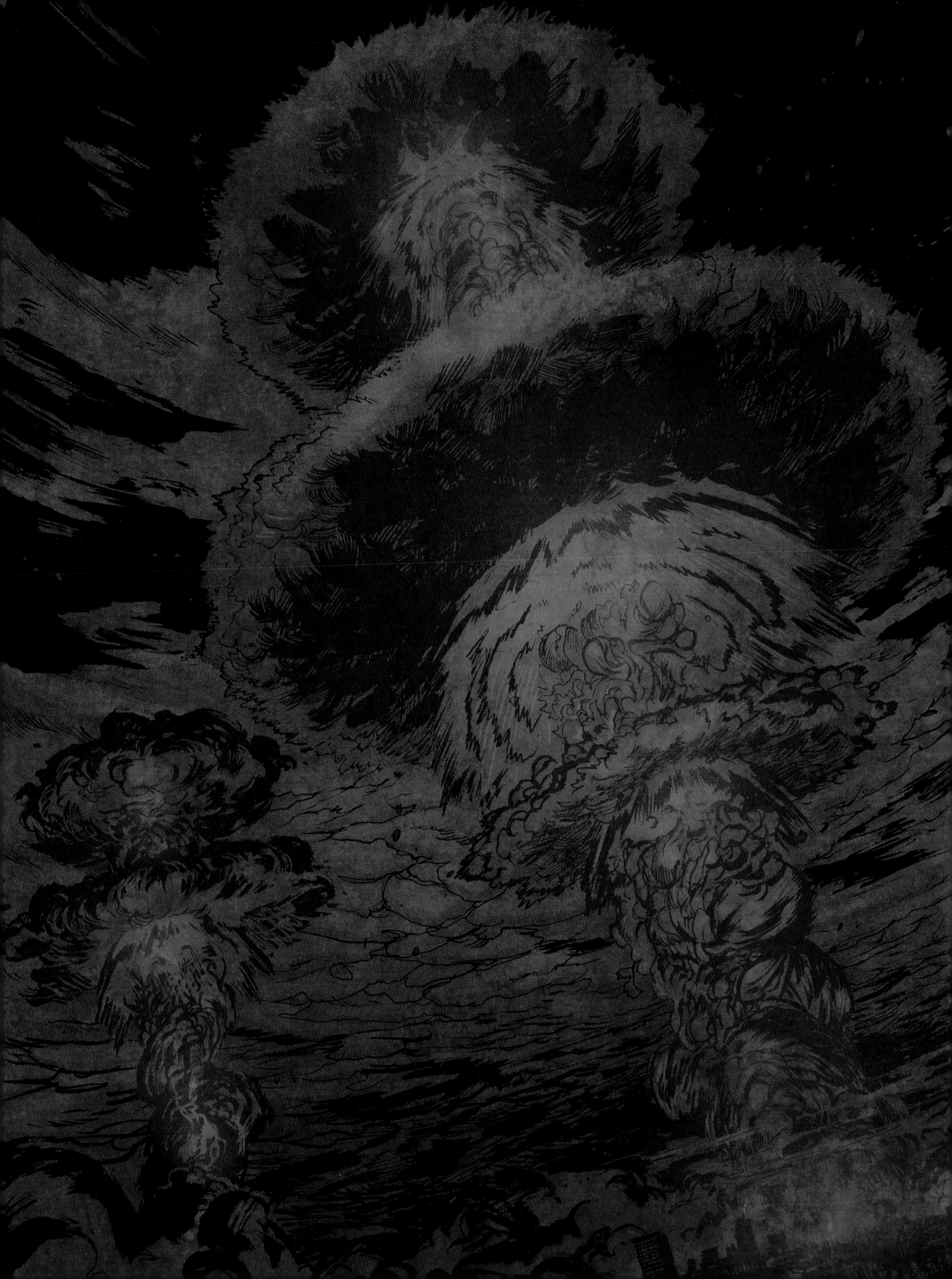

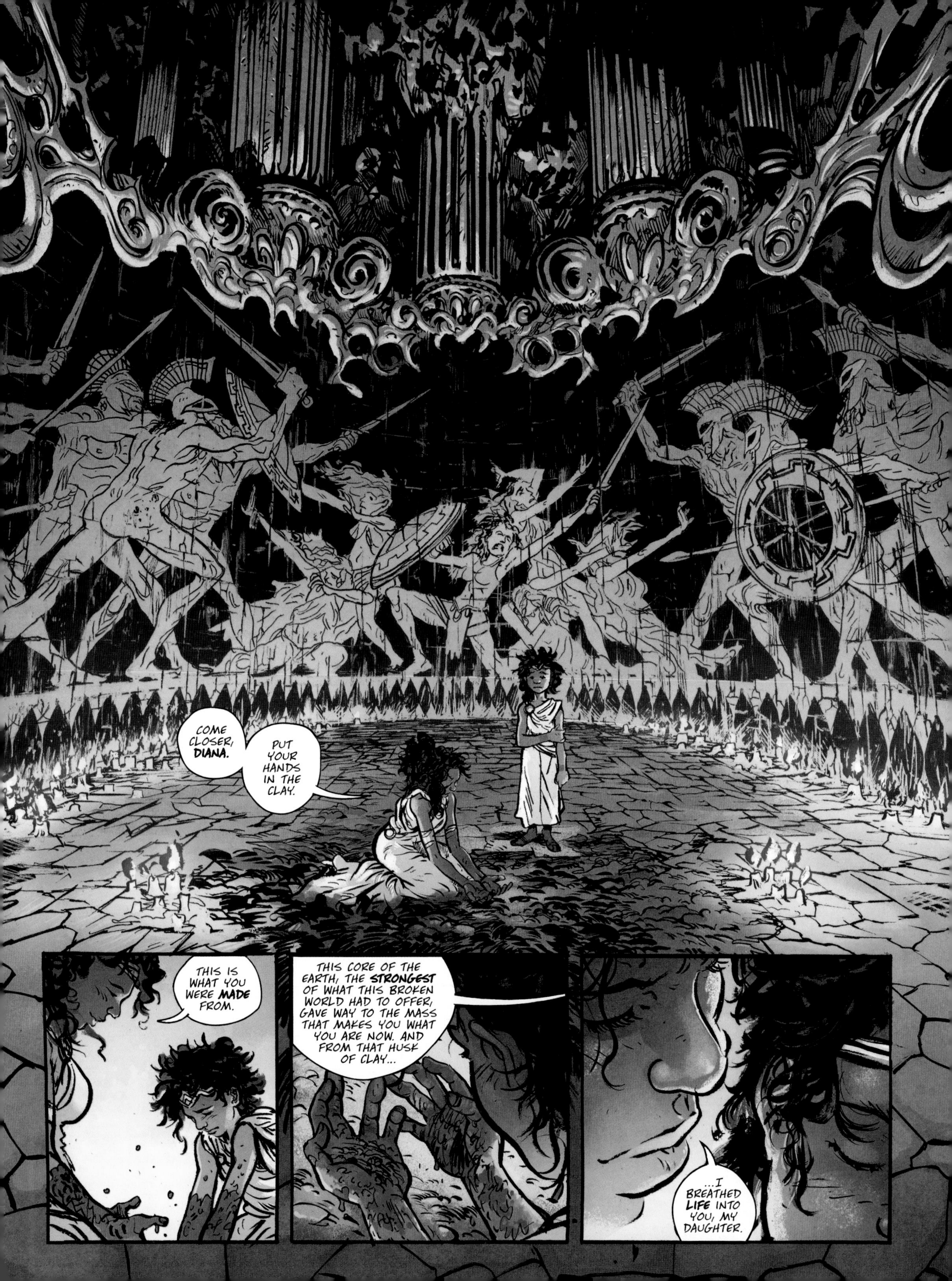
COME CLOSER, **DIANA.**
PUT YOUR HANDS IN THE CLAY.
THIS IS WHAT YOU WERE **MADE** FROM.
THIS CORE OF THE EARTH, THE **STRONGEST** OF WHAT THIS BROKEN WORLD HAD TO OFFER, GAVE WAY TO THE MASS THAT MAKES YOU WHAT YOU ARE NOW. AND FROM THAT HUSK OF CLAY...
...I BREATHED **LIFE** INTO YOU, MY DAUGHTER.

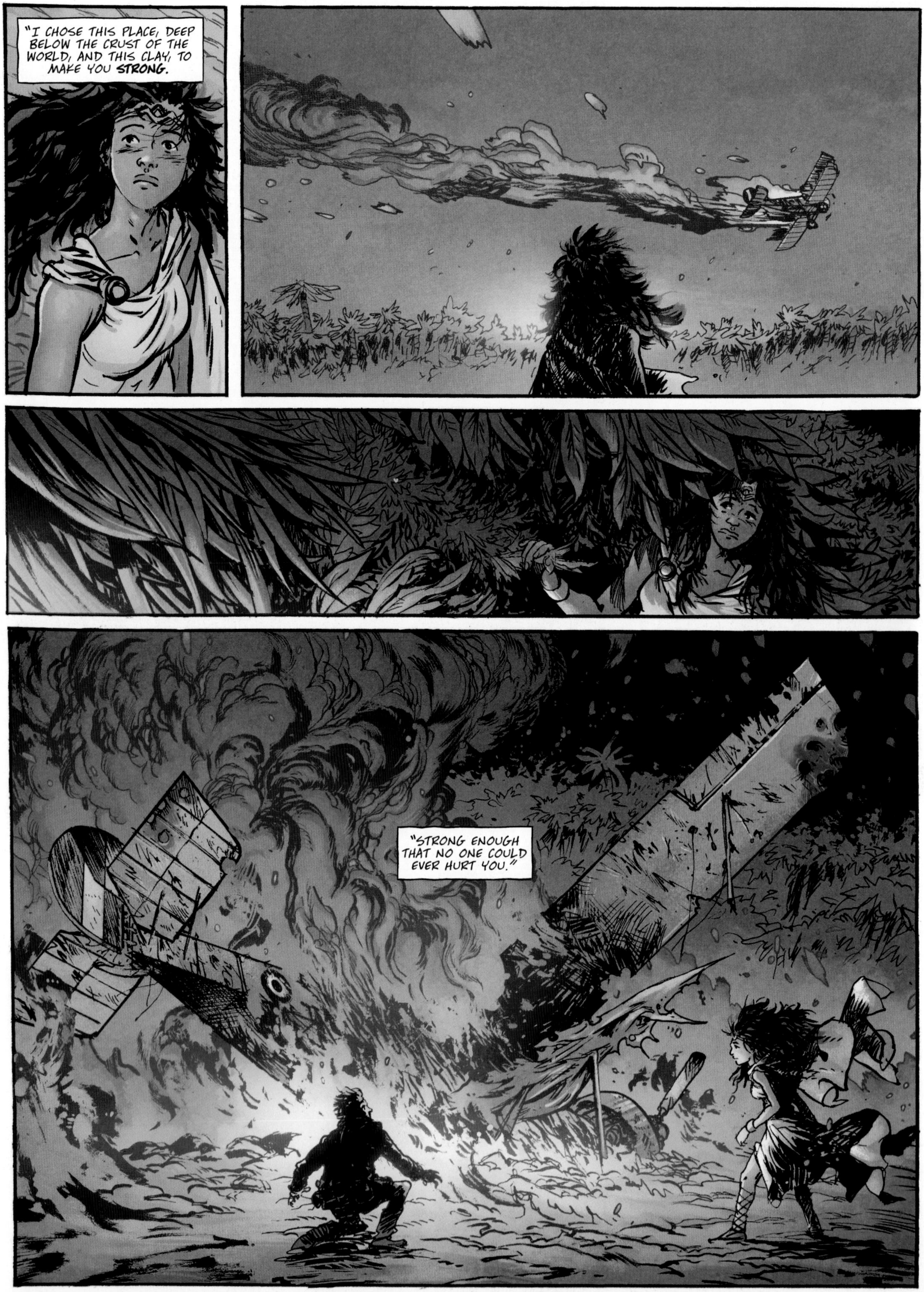

"I CHOSE THIS PLACE, DEEP BELOW THE CRUST OF THE WORLD, AND THIS CLAY, TO MAKE YOU **STRONG**.
"STRONG ENOUGH THAT NO ONE COULD EVER HURT YOU."

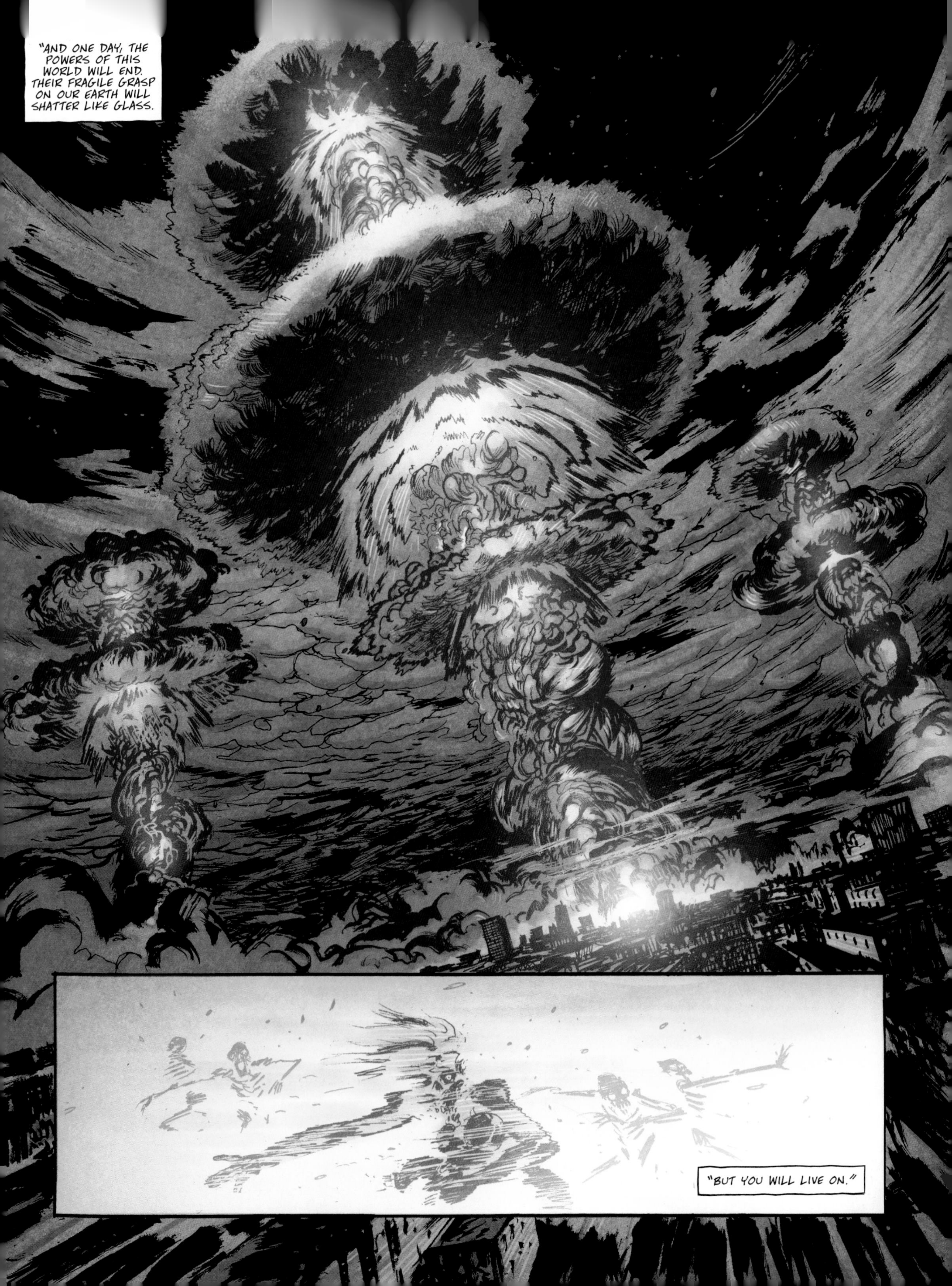
"AND ONE DAY, THE POWERS OF THIS WORLD WILL END. THEIR FRAGILE GRASP ON OUR EARTH WILL SHATTER LIKE GLASS.
"BUT YOU WILL LIVE ON."

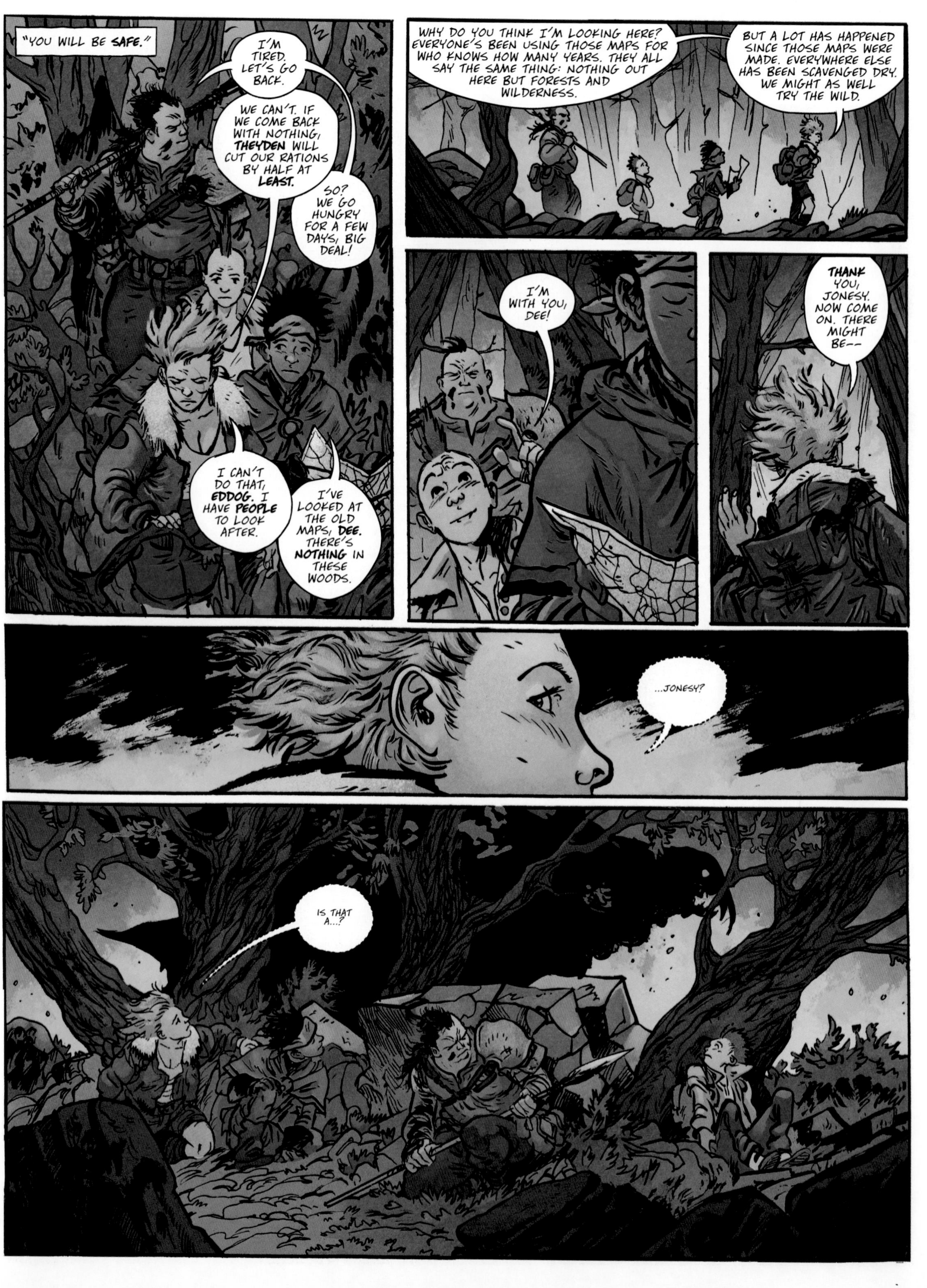
"YOU WILL BE SAFE."
I'M TIRED. LET'S GO BACK.
WE CAN'T. IF WE COME BACK WITH NOTHING, THEYDEN WILL CUT OUR RATIONS BY HALF AT LEAST.
SO? WE GO HUNGRY FOR A FEW DAYS, BIG DEAL!
I CAN'T DO THAT, EDDOG. I HAVE PEOPLE TO LOOK AFTER.
I'VE LOOKED AT THE OLD MAPS, DEE. THERE'S NOTHING IN THESE WOODS.
WHY DO YOU THINK I'M LOOKING HERE? EVERYONE'S BEEN USING THOSE MAPS FOR WHO KNOWS HOW MANY YEARS. THEY ALL SAY THE SAME THING: NOTHING OUT HERE BUT FORESTS AND WILDERNESS.
BUT A LOT HAS HAPPENED SINCE THOSE MAPS WERE MADE. EVERYWHERE ELSE HAS BEEN SCAVENGED DRY. WE MIGHT AS WELL TRY THE WILD.
I'M WITH YOU, DEE!
THANK YOU, JONESY. NOW COME ON. THERE MIGHT BE--
...JONESY?
IS THAT A...?

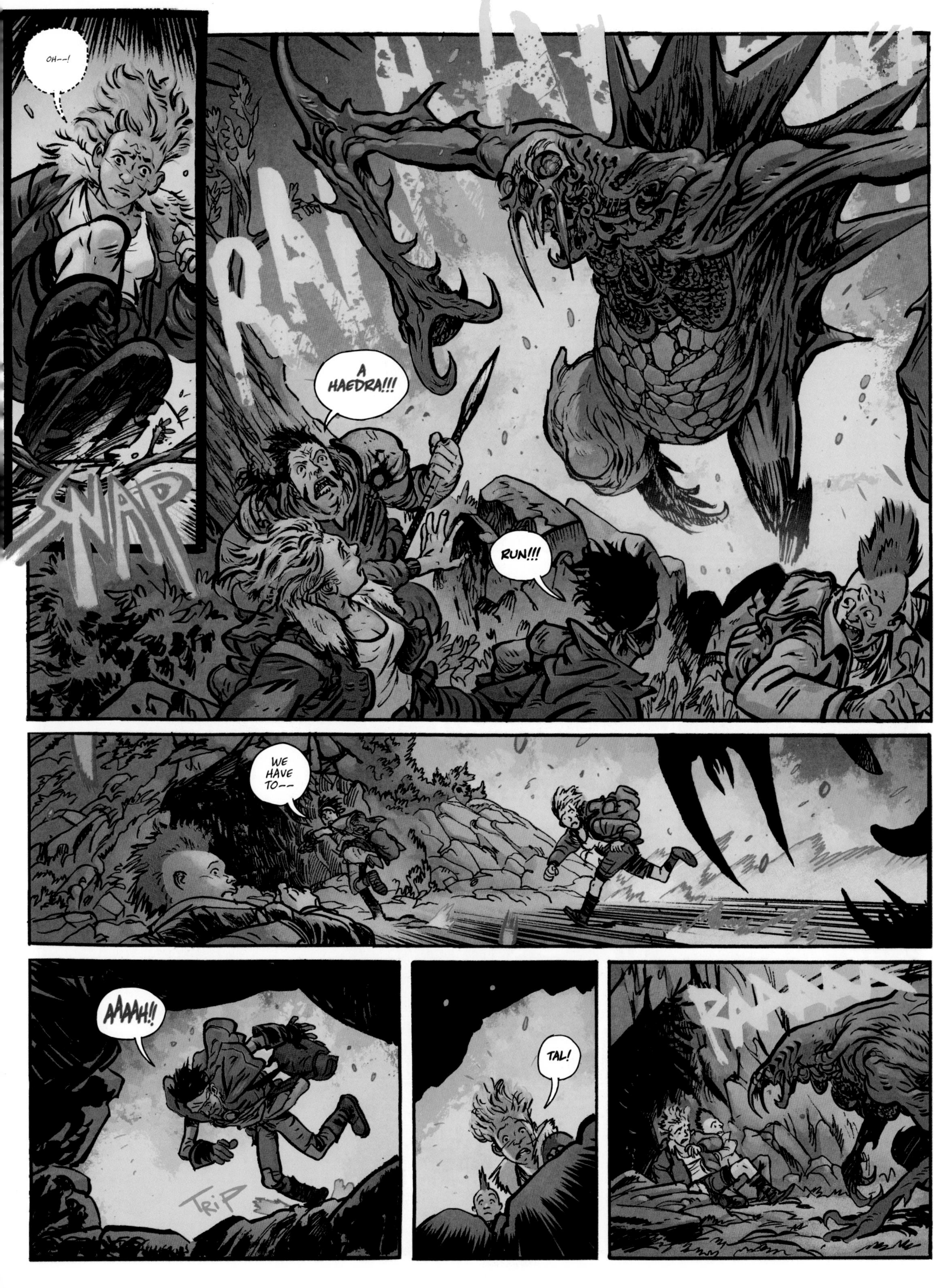
OH--!
SNAP
RAH
A HAEDRA!!!
RUN!!!
WE HAVE TO--
AAAAH!!
TRIP
TAL!
RAAAR

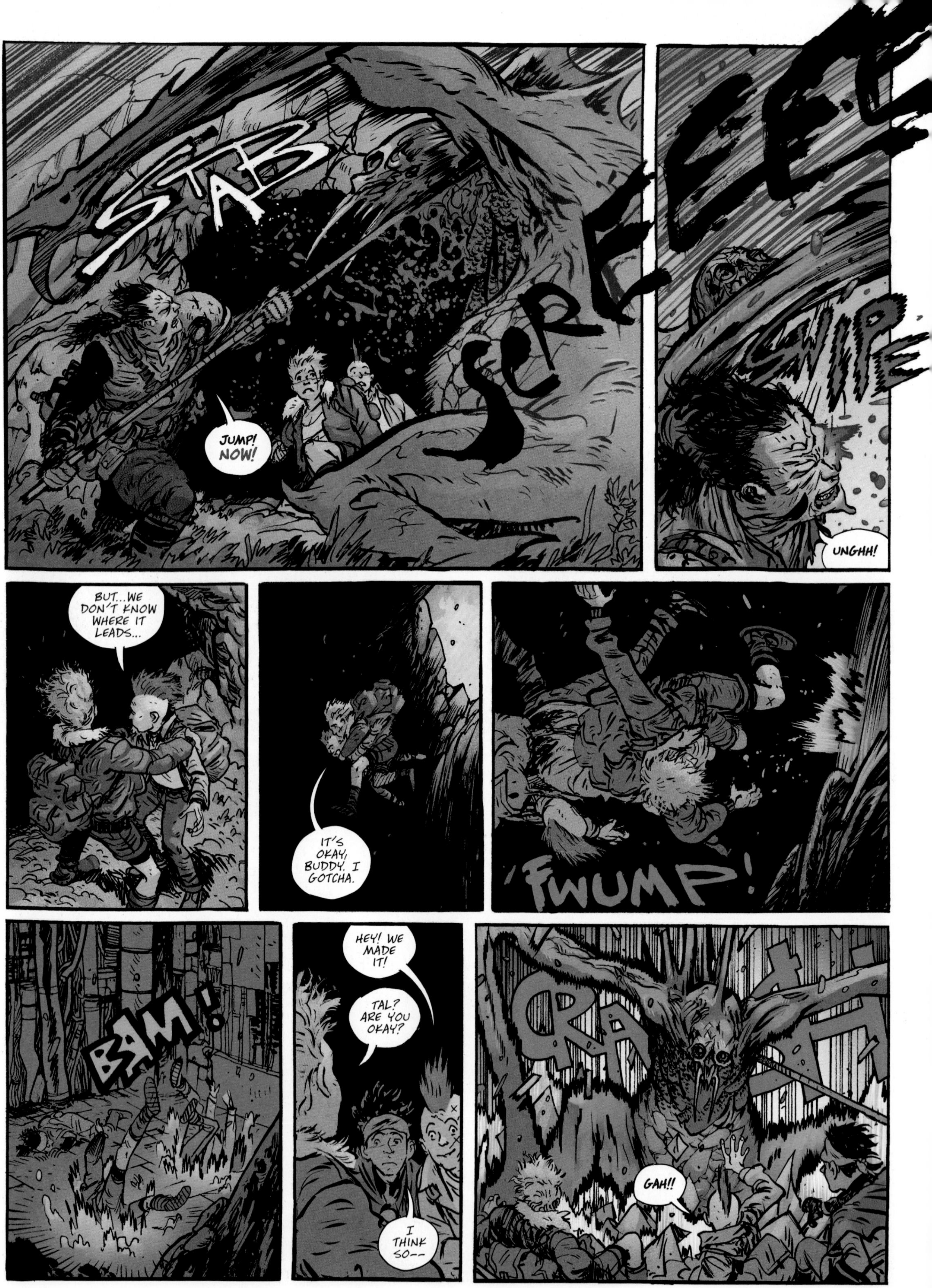
STAB
JUMP! NOW!
SCREEEE
SWIPE
UNGHH!
BUT...WE DON'T KNOW WHERE IT LEADS...
IT'S OKAY, BUDDY. I GOTCHA.
FWUMP!
BAM!
HEY! WE MADE IT!
TAL? ARE YOU OKAY?
I THINK SO--
CRASH
GAH!!

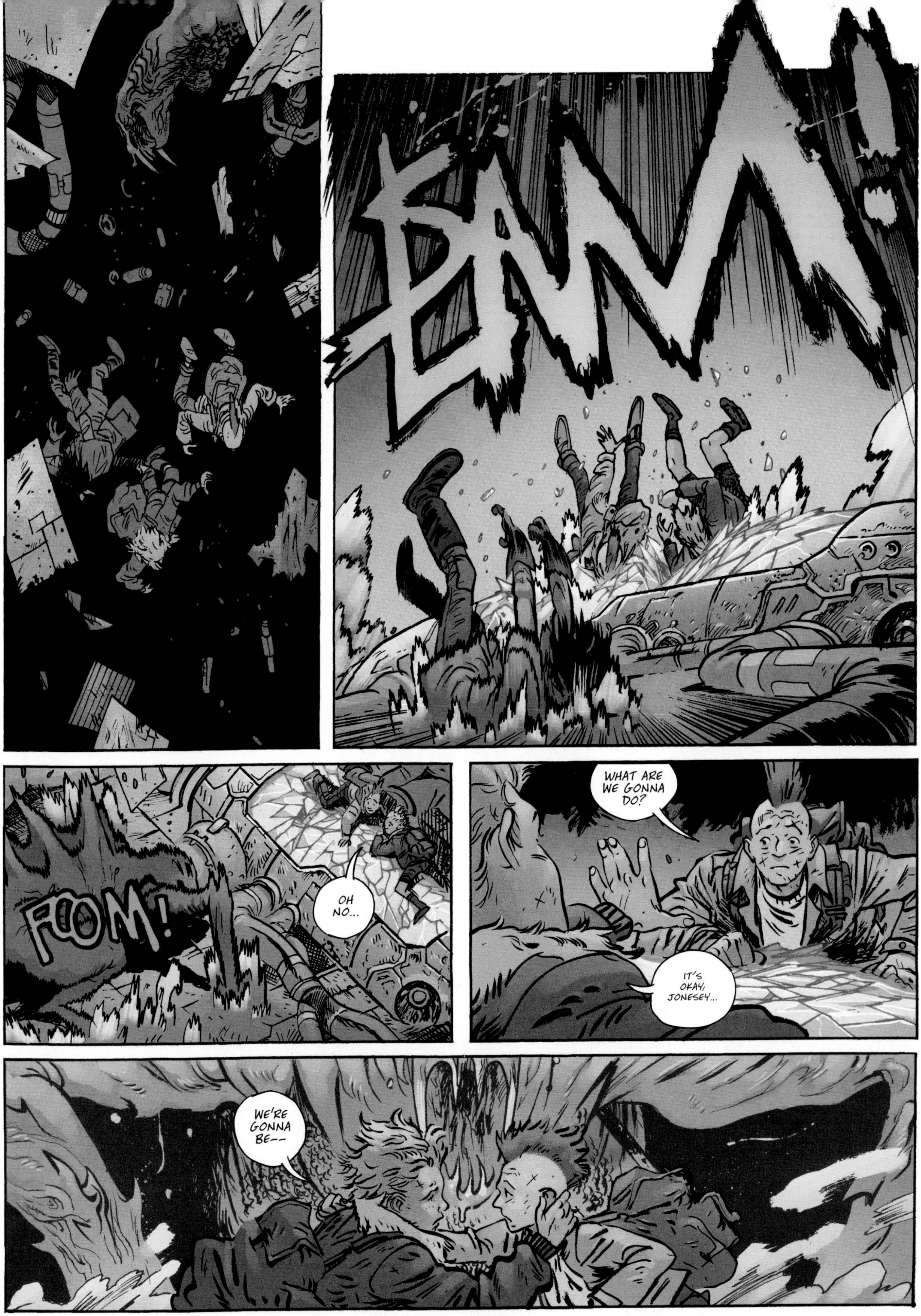
BAM!
FOOM!
OH NO...
WHAT ARE WE GONNA DO?
IT'S OKAY, JONESEY...
WE'RE GONNA BE--

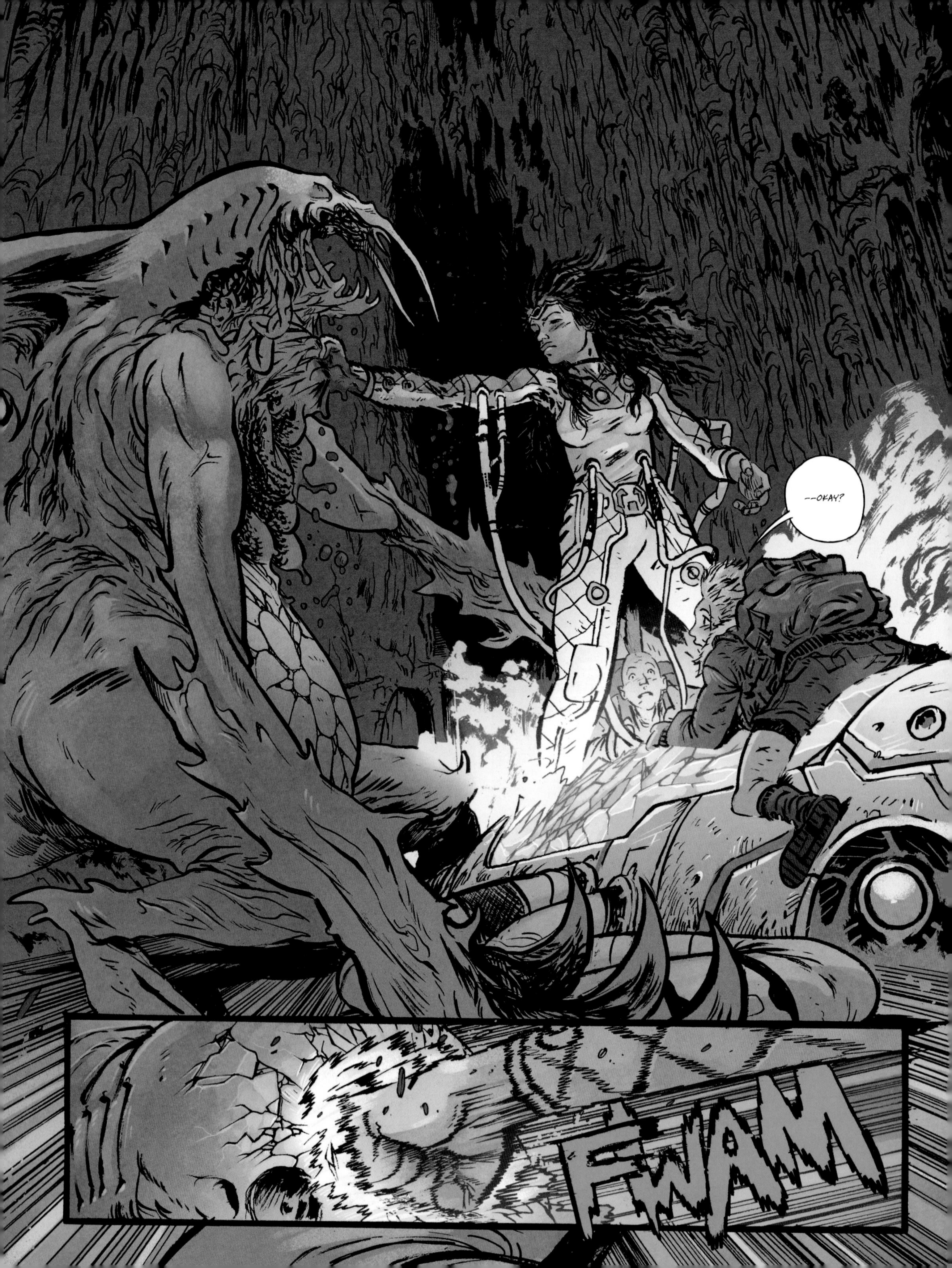
--OKAY?
FWAM

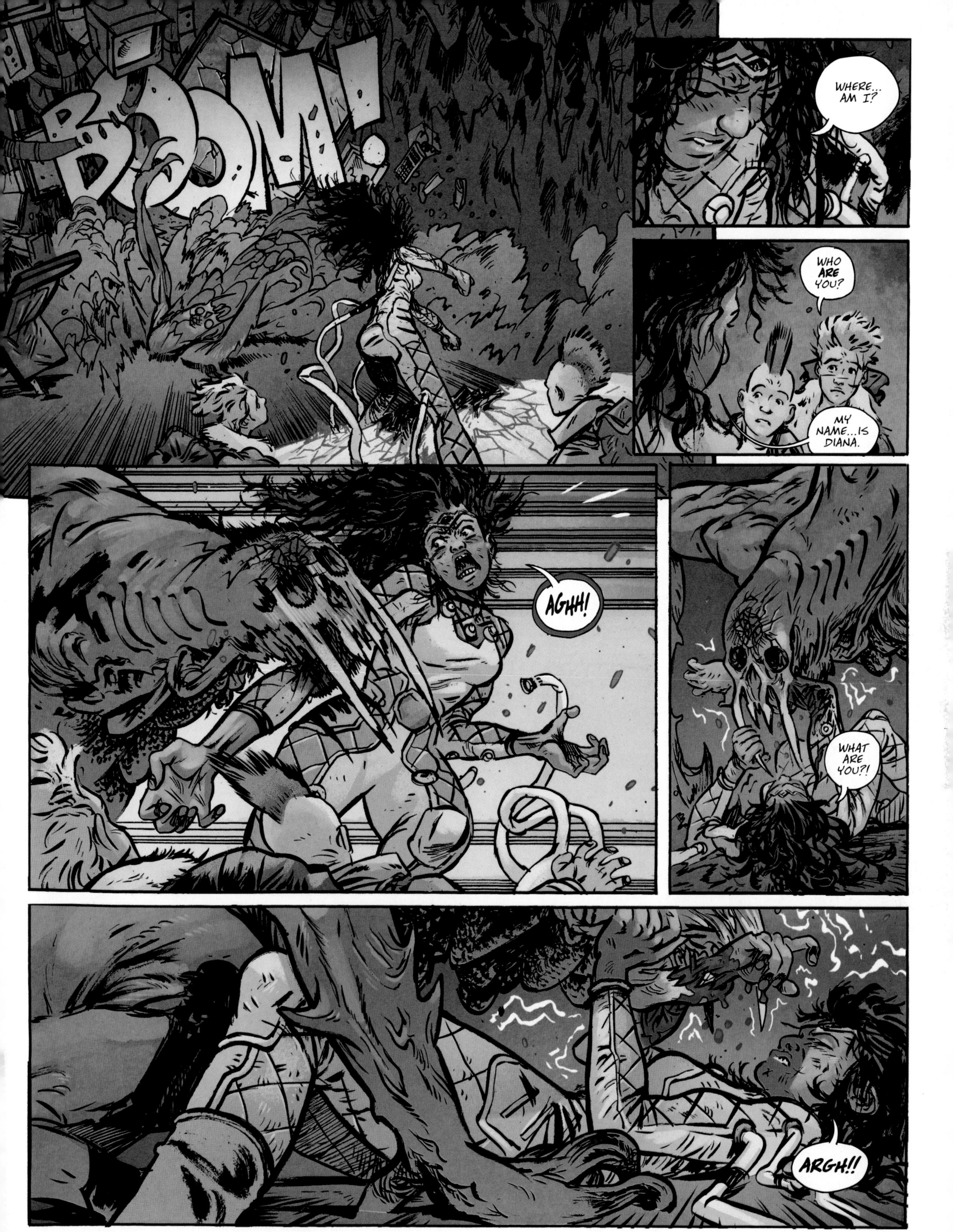
BOOM!
WHERE... AM I?
WHO ARE YOU?
MY NAME...IS DIANA.
AGHH!
WHAT ARE YOU?!
ARGH!!

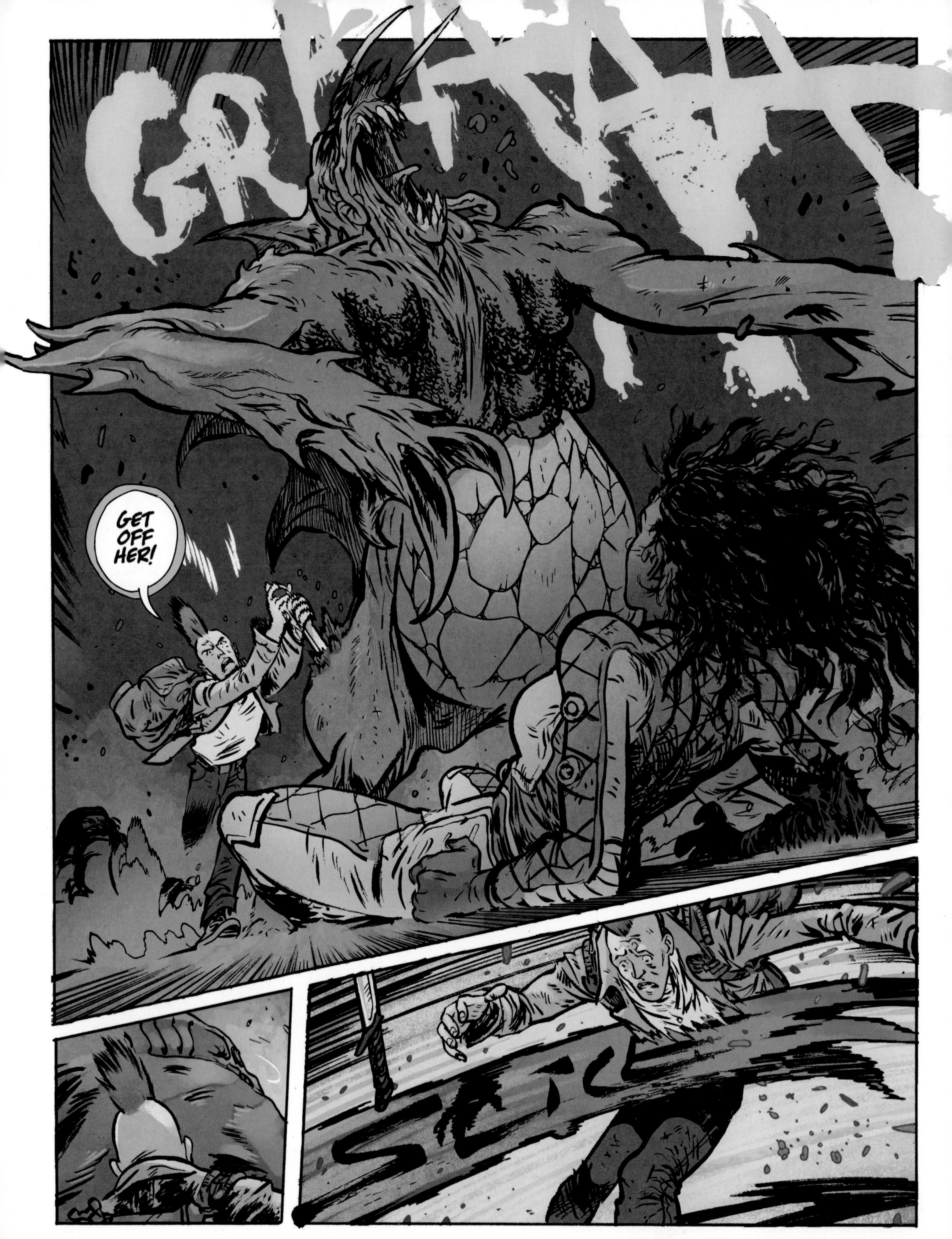
GET OFF HER!

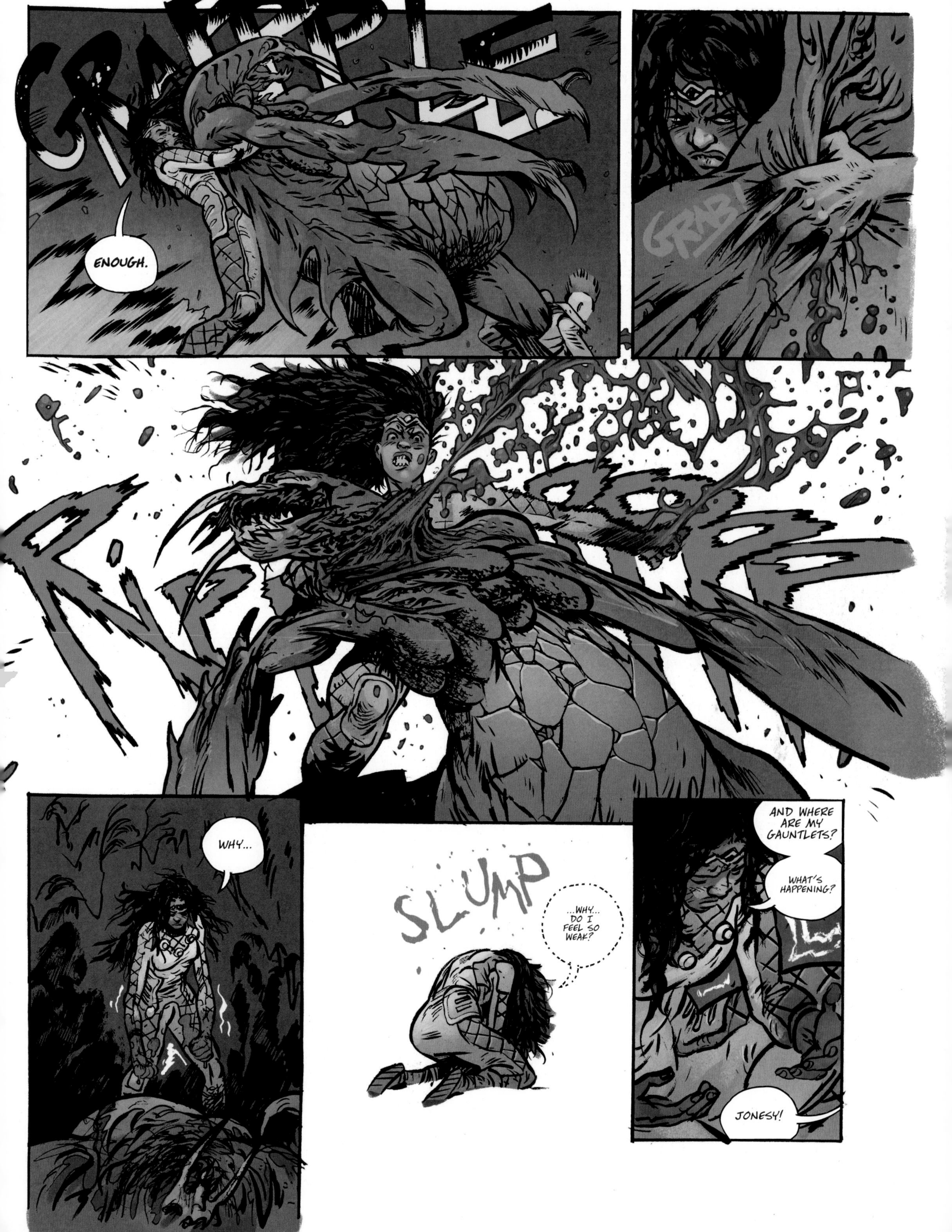
GRAPPLE
ENOUGH.
GRAB!
RIPP
WHY...
SLUMP
...WHY... DO I FEEL SO WEAK?
AND WHERE ARE MY GAUNTLETS?
WHAT'S HAPPENING?
JONESY!

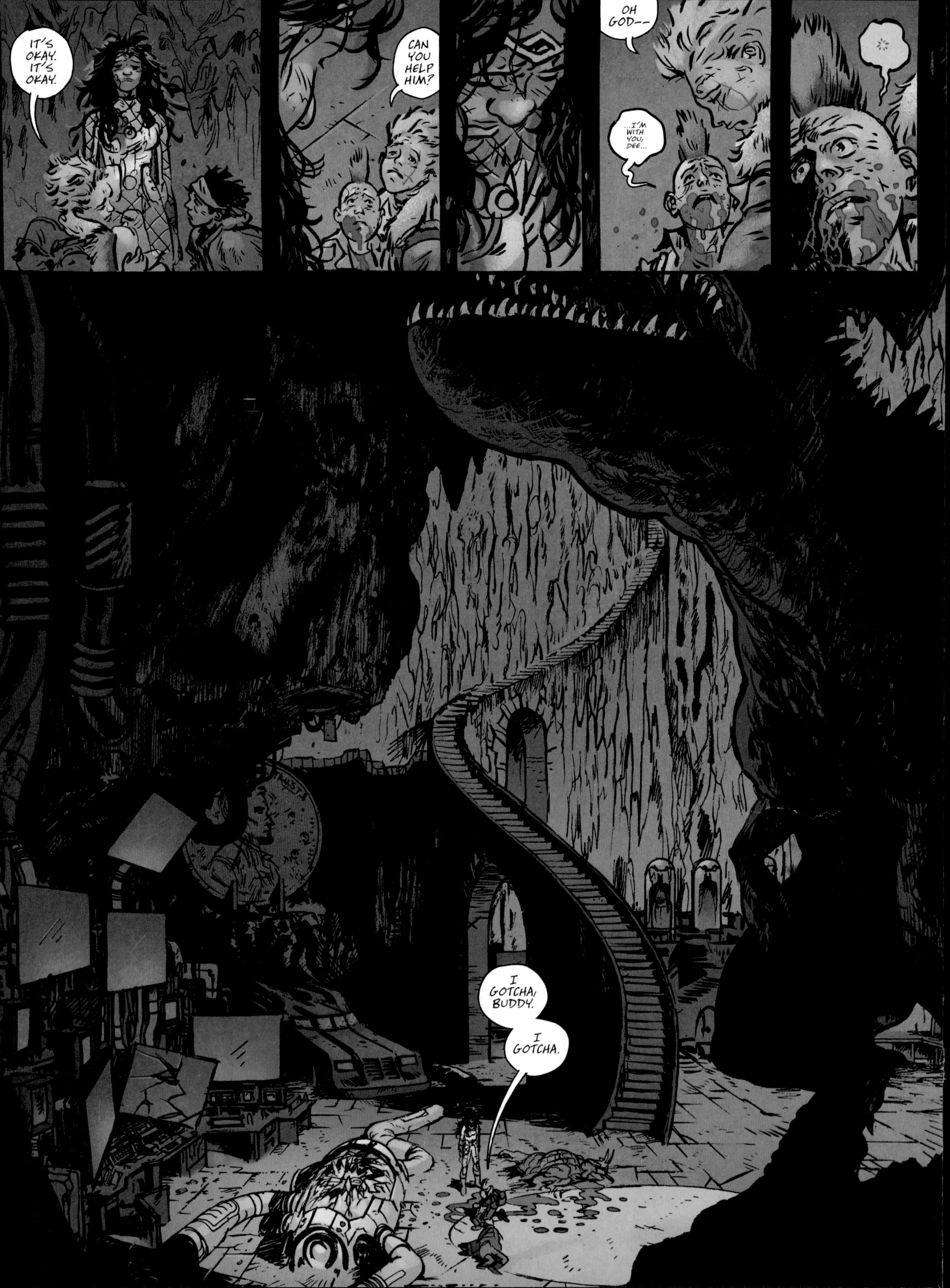
IT'S OKAY. IT'S OKAY.
CAN YOU HELP HIM?
OH GOD--
...I'M WITH YOU, DEE...
I GOTCHA, BUDDY.
I GOTCHA.

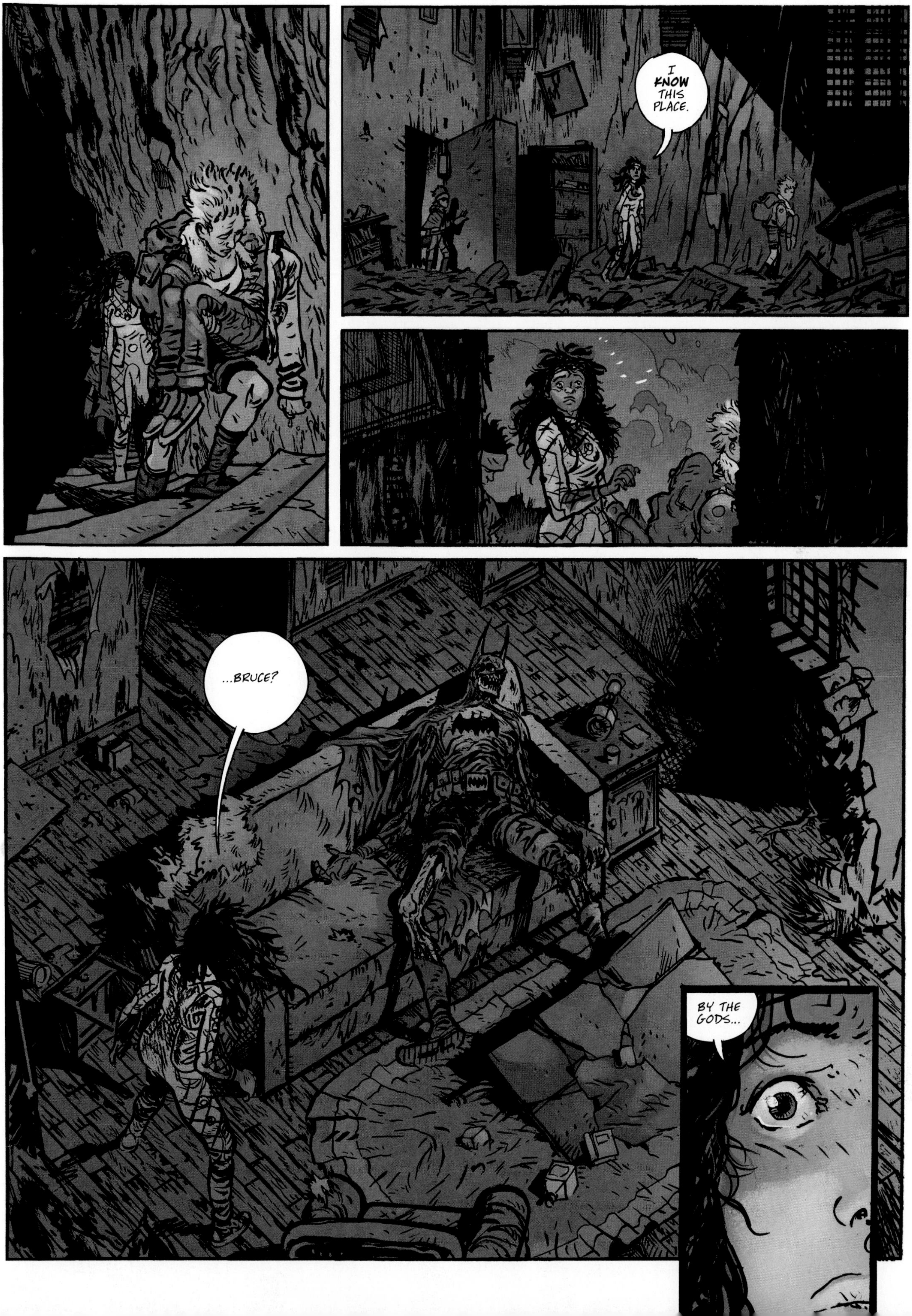
I KNOW THIS PLACE.
...BRUCE?
BY THE GODS...

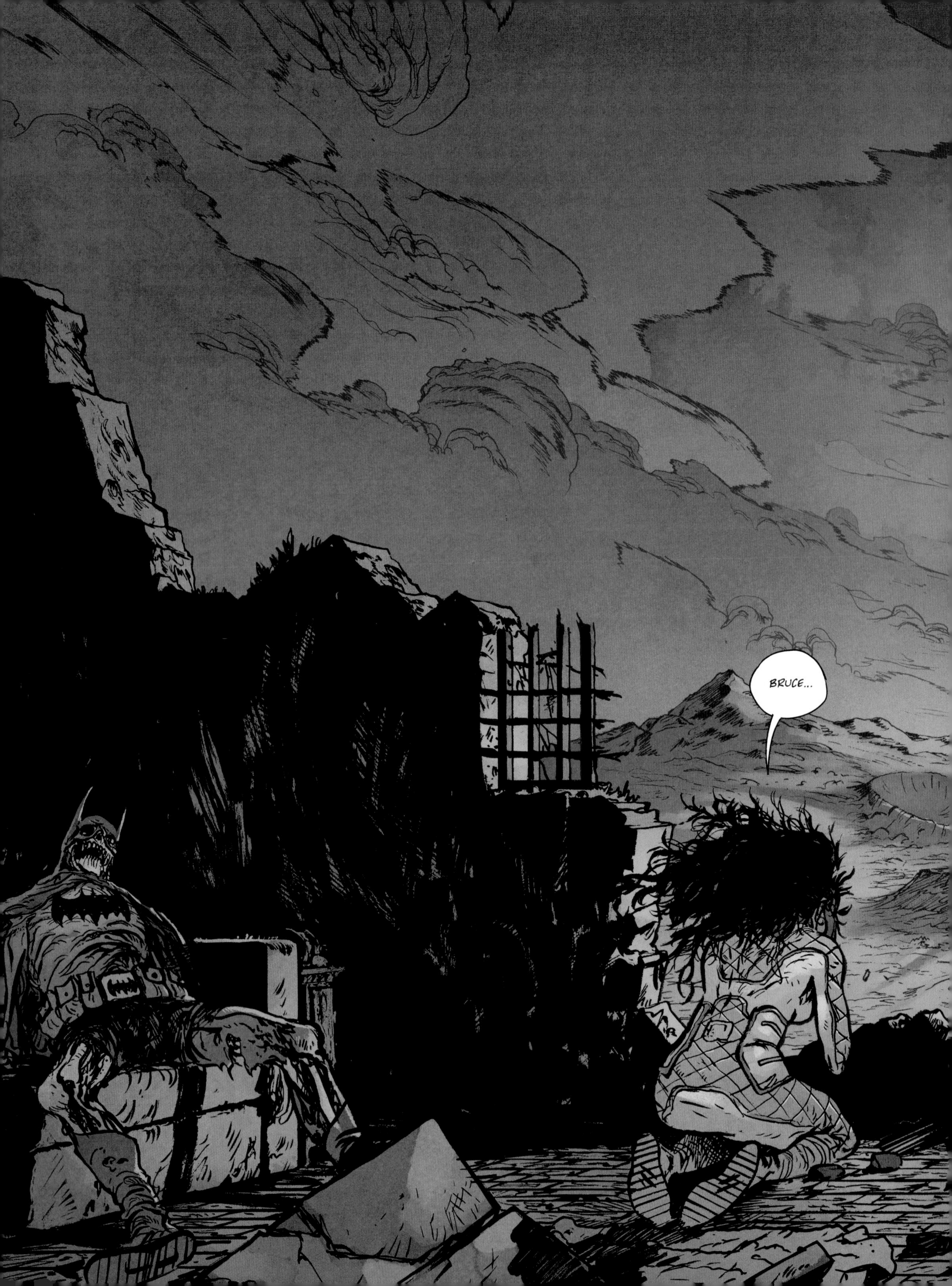
BRUCE...

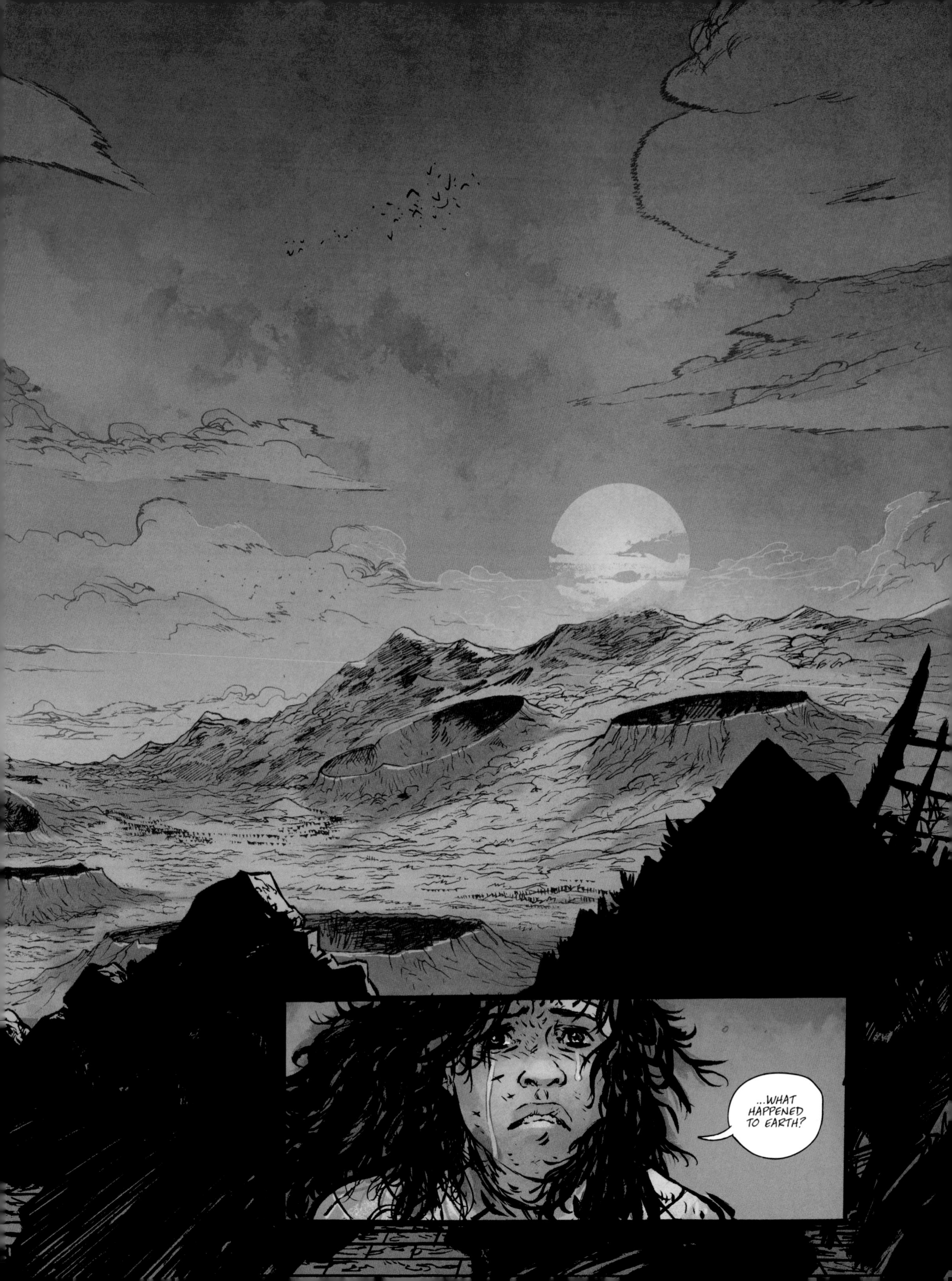
...WHAT HAPPENED TO EARTH?

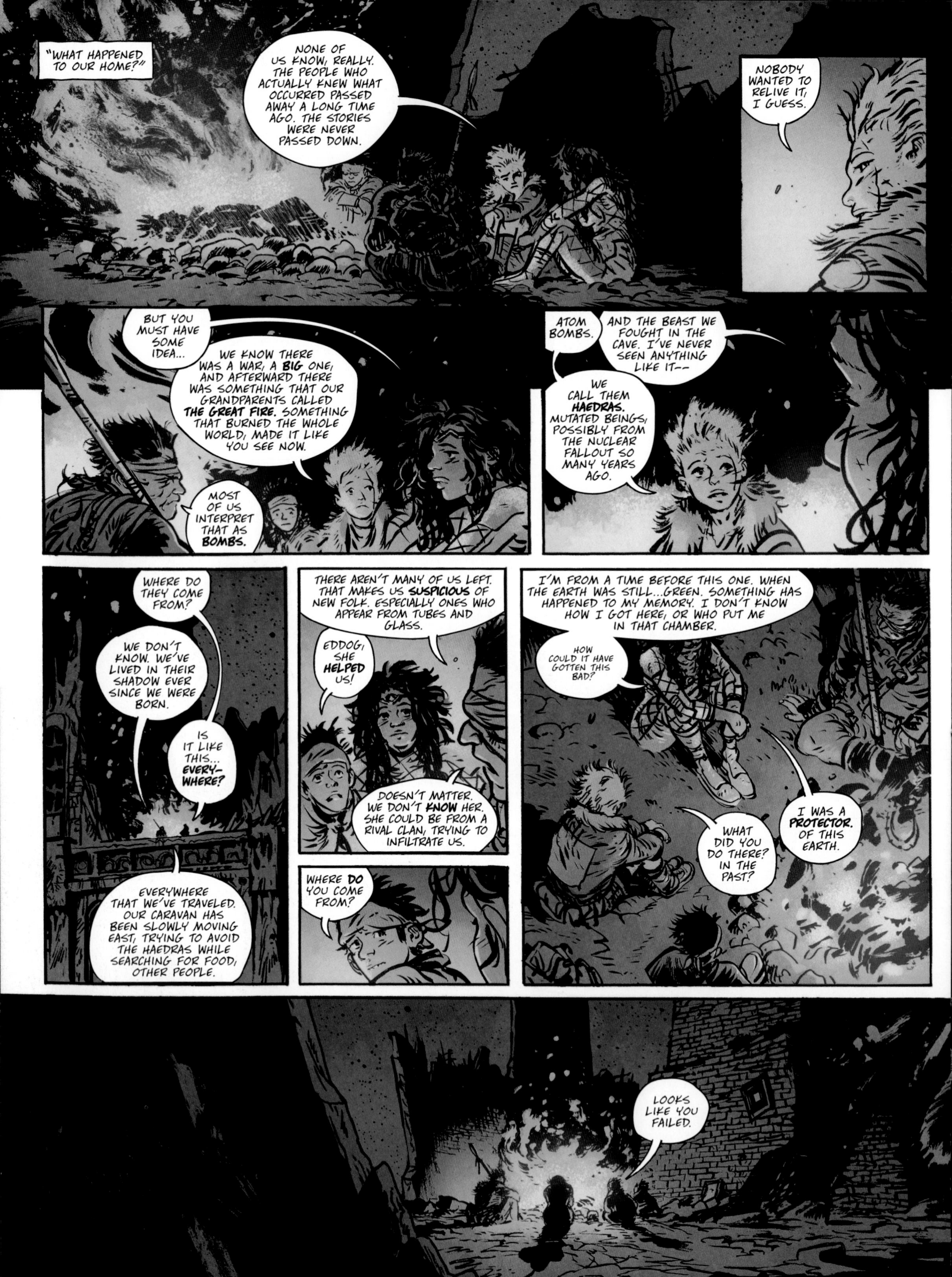
"WHAT HAPPENED TO OUR HOME?"
NONE OF US KNOW, REALLY. THE PEOPLE WHO ACTUALLY KNEW WHAT OCCURRED PASSED AWAY A LONG TIME AGO. THE STORIES WERE NEVER PASSED DOWN.
NOBODY WANTED TO RELIVE IT, I GUESS.
BUT YOU MUST HAVE SOME IDEA...
WE KNOW THERE WAS A WAR, A BIG ONE, AND AFTERWARD THERE WAS SOMETHING THAT OUR GRANDPARENTS CALLED THE GREAT FIRE. SOMETHING THAT BURNED THE WHOLE WORLD, MADE IT LIKE YOU SEE NOW.
MOST OF US INTERPRET THAT AS BOMBS.
ATOM BOMBS.
AND THE BEAST WE FOUGHT IN THE CAVE. I'VE NEVER SEEN ANYTHING LIKE IT--
WE CALL THEM HAEDRAS. MUTATED BEINGS, POSSIBLY FROM THE NUCLEAR FALLOUT SO MANY YEARS AGO.
WHERE DO THEY COME FROM?
WE DON'T KNOW. WE'VE LIVED IN THEIR SHADOW EVER SINCE WE WERE BORN.
IS IT LIKE THIS... EVERY-WHERE?
EVERYWHERE THAT WE'VE TRAVELED. OUR CARAVAN HAS BEEN SLOWLY MOVING EAST, TRYING TO AVOID THE HAEDRAS WHILE SEARCHING FOR FOOD, OTHER PEOPLE.
THERE AREN'T MANY OF US LEFT. THAT MAKES US SUSPICIOUS OF NEW FOLK. ESPECIALLY ONES WHO APPEAR FROM TUBES AND GLASS.
EDDOG, SHE HELPED US!
DOESN'T MATTER. WE DON'T KNOW HER. SHE COULD BE FROM A RIVAL CLAN, TRYING TO INFILTRATE US.
WHERE DO YOU COME FROM?
I'M FROM A TIME BEFORE THIS ONE. WHEN THE EARTH WAS STILL...GREEN. SOMETHING HAS HAPPENED TO MY MEMORY. I DON'T KNOW HOW I GOT HERE, OR WHO PUT ME IN THAT CHAMBER.
HOW COULD IT HAVE GOTTEN THIS BAD?
WHAT DID YOU DO THERE? IN THE PAST?
I WAS A PROTECTOR. OF THIS EARTH.
LOOKS LIKE YOU FAILED.

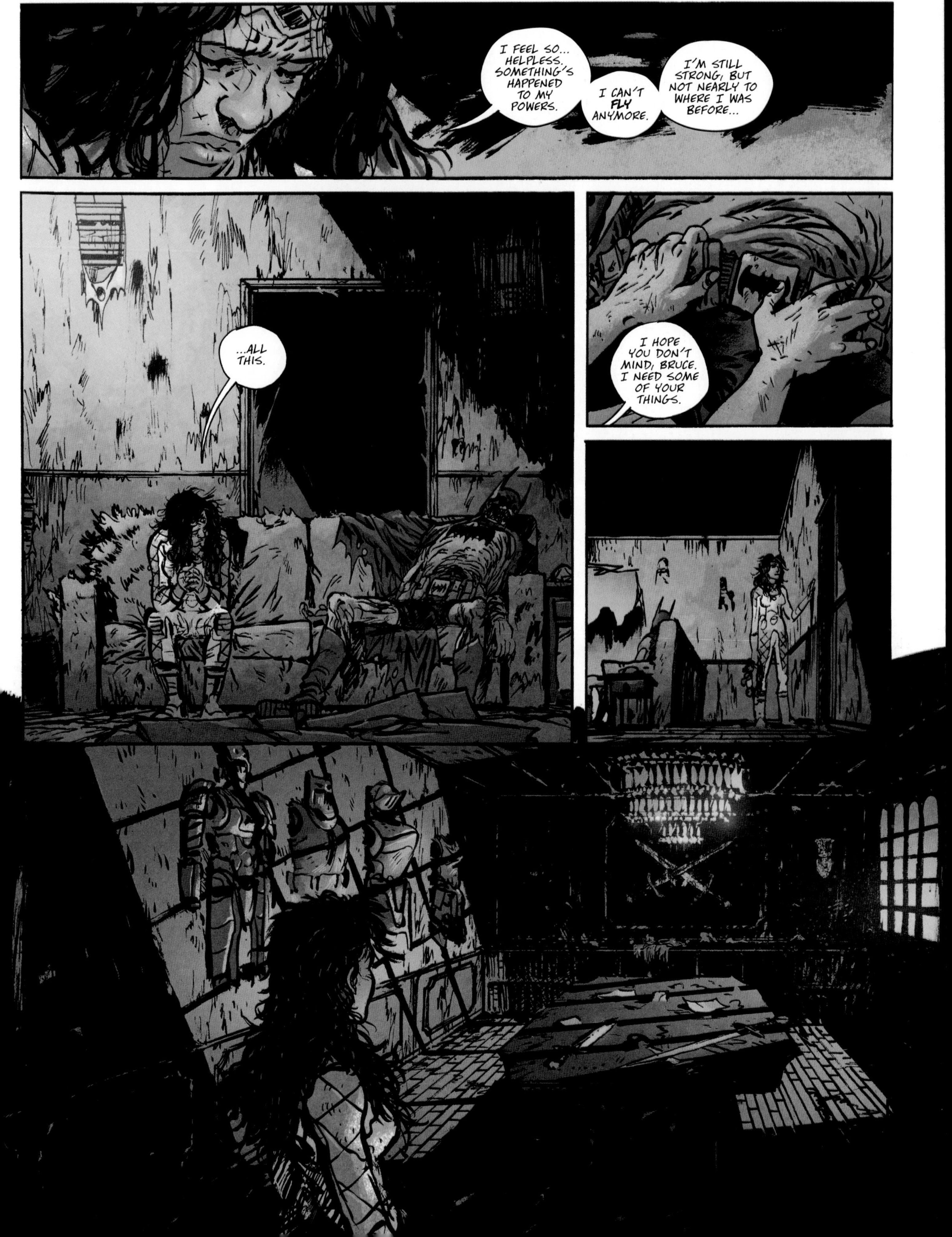
I FEEL SO... HELPLESS. SOMETHING'S HAPPENED TO MY POWERS.
I CAN'T FLY ANYMORE.
I'M STILL STRONG, BUT NOT NEARLY TO WHERE I WAS BEFORE...
...ALL THIS.
I HOPE YOU DON'T MIND, BRUCE. I NEED SOME OF YOUR THINGS.

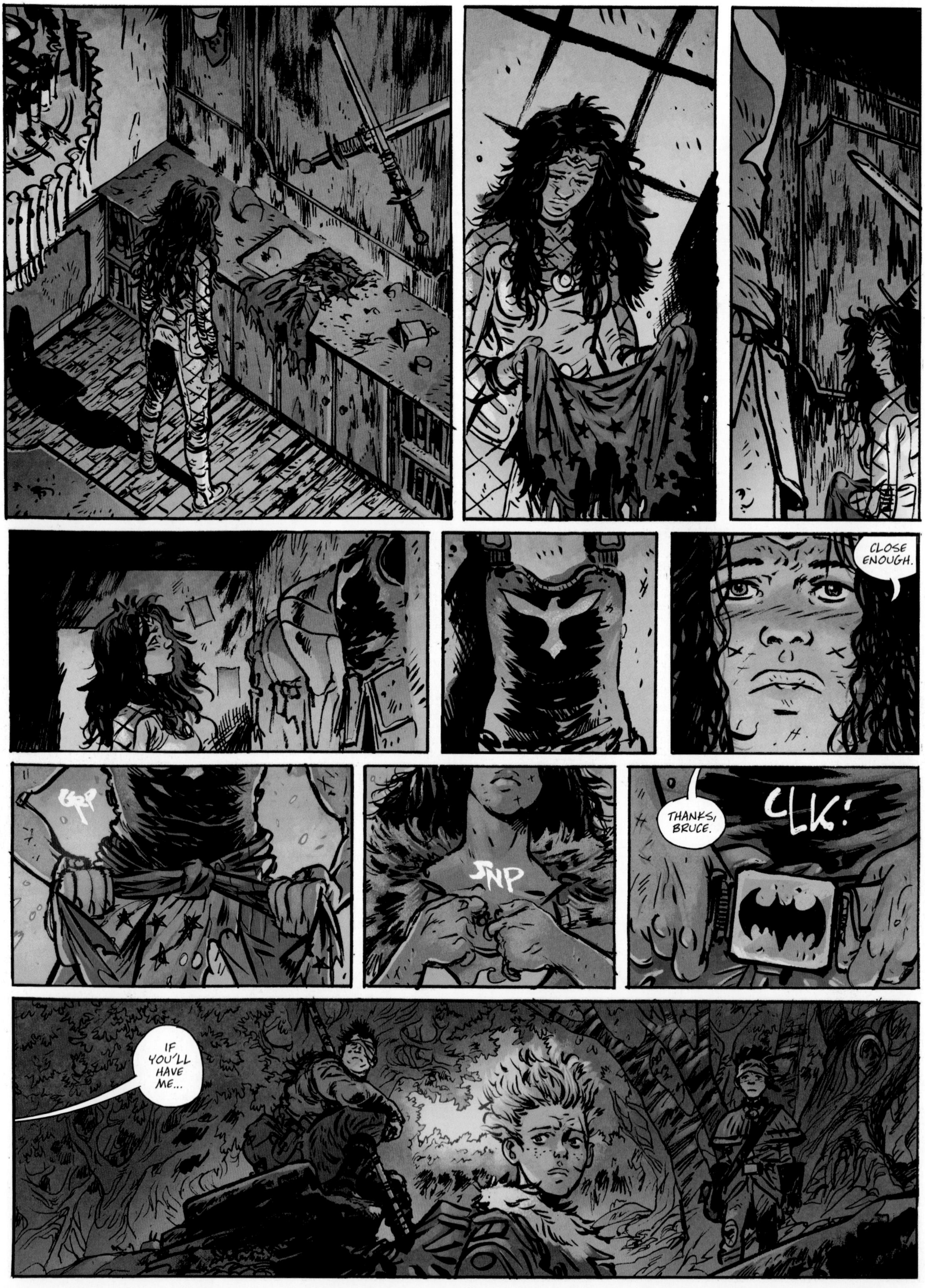
CLOSE ENOUGH.
GRP
SNP
THANKS, BRUCE.
CLK!
IF YOU'LL HAVE ME...

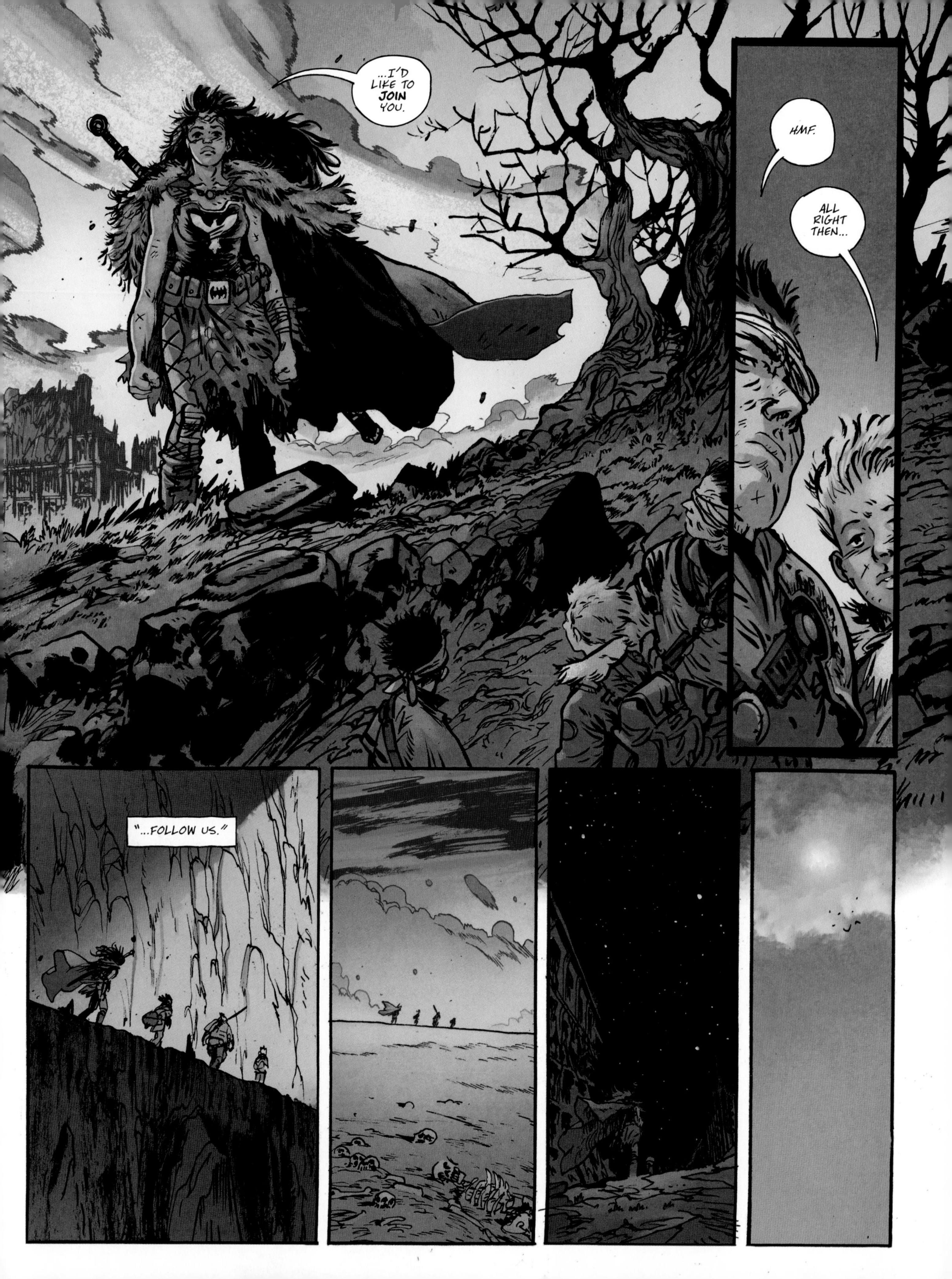
...I'D LIKE TO **JOIN** YOU.
HMF.
ALL RIGHT THEN...
"...FOLLOW US."

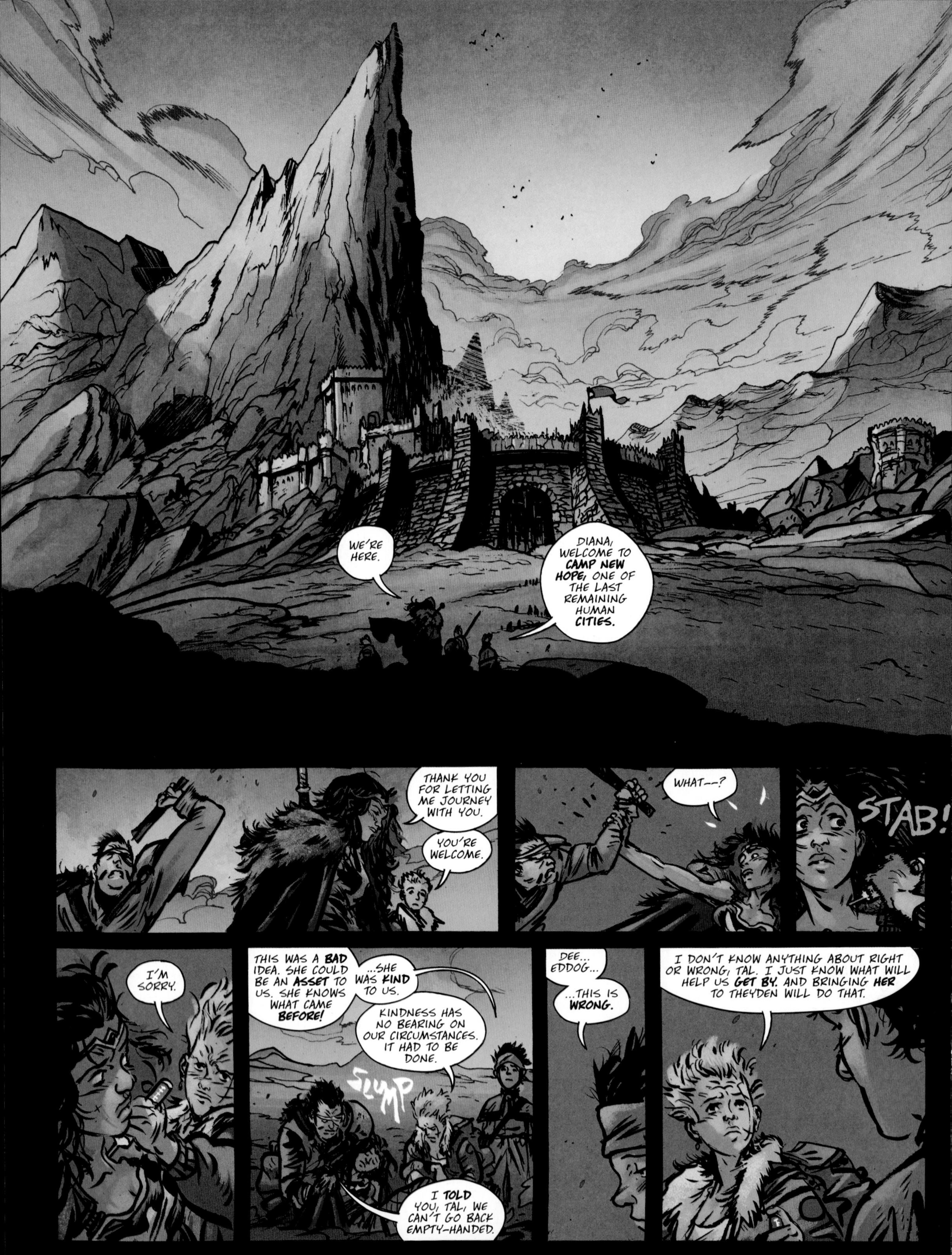
WE'RE HERE.
DIANA, WELCOME TO CAMP NEW HOPE, ONE OF THE LAST REMAINING HUMAN CITIES.
THANK YOU FOR LETTING ME JOURNEY WITH YOU.
YOU'RE WELCOME.
WHAT--?
STAB!
I'M SORRY.
THIS WAS A BAD IDEA. SHE COULD BE AN ASSET TO US. SHE KNOWS WHAT CAME BEFORE!
...SHE WAS KIND TO US.
KINDNESS HAS NO BEARING ON OUR CIRCUMSTANCES. IT HAD TO BE DONE.
SLUMP
I TOLD YOU, TAL, WE CAN'T GO BACK EMPTY-HANDED.
DEE... EDDOG...
...THIS IS WRONG.
I DON'T KNOW ANYTHING ABOUT RIGHT OR WRONG, TAL. I JUST KNOW WHAT WILL HELP US GET BY. AND BRINGING HER TO THEYDEN WILL DO THAT.

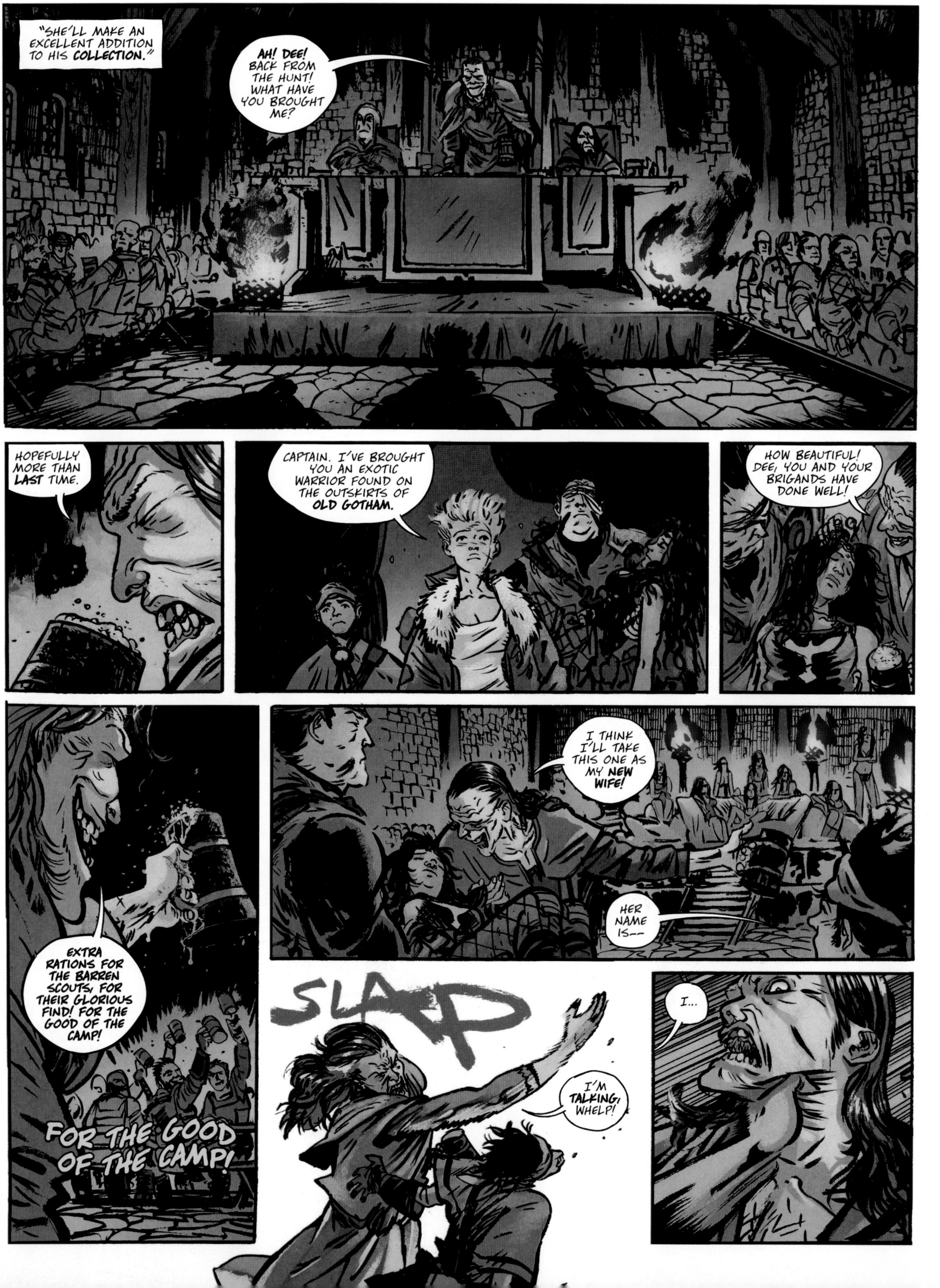
"SHE'LL MAKE AN EXCELLENT ADDITION TO HIS COLLECTION."
AH! DEE! BACK FROM THE HUNT! WHAT HAVE YOU BROUGHT ME?
HOPEFULLY MORE THAN LAST TIME.
CAPTAIN. I'VE BROUGHT YOU AN EXOTIC WARRIOR FOUND ON THE OUTSKIRTS OF OLD GOTHAM.
HOW BEAUTIFUL! DEE, YOU AND YOUR BRIGANDS HAVE DONE WELL!
EXTRA RATIONS FOR THE BARREN SCOUTS, FOR THEIR GLORIOUS FIND! FOR THE GOOD OF THE CAMP!
FOR THE GOOD OF THE CAMP!
I THINK I'LL TAKE THIS ONE AS MY NEW WIFE!
HER NAME IS--
SLAP
I'M TALKING, WHELP!
I...

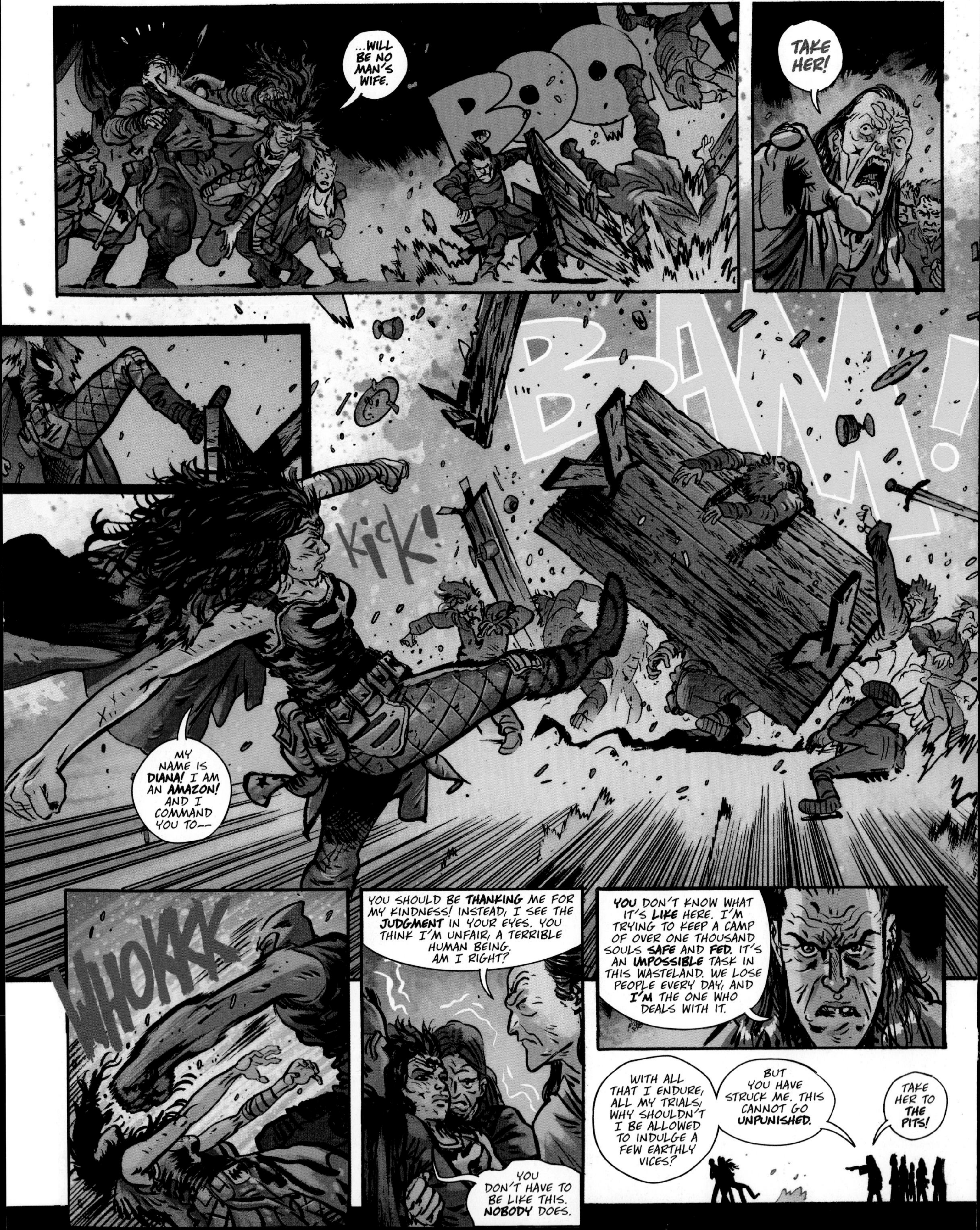
...WILL BE NO MAN'S WIFE.
BOOM
TAKE HER!
BAM!
KICK!
MY NAME IS DIANA! I AM AN AMAZON! AND I COMMAND YOU TO--
WHOKK
YOU SHOULD BE THANKING ME FOR MY KINDNESS! INSTEAD, I SEE THE JUDGMENT IN YOUR EYES. YOU THINK I'M UNFAIR, A TERRIBLE HUMAN BEING. AM I RIGHT?
YOU DON'T HAVE TO BE LIKE THIS. NOBODY DOES.
YOU DON'T KNOW WHAT IT'S LIKE HERE. I'M TRYING TO KEEP A CAMP OF OVER ONE THOUSAND SOULS SAFE AND FED. IT'S AN IMPOSSIBLE TASK IN THIS WASTELAND. WE LOSE PEOPLE EVERY DAY, AND I'M THE ONE WHO DEALS WITH IT.
WITH ALL THAT I ENDURE, ALL MY TRIALS, WHY SHOULDN'T I BE ALLOWED TO INDULGE A FEW EARTHLY VICES?
BUT YOU HAVE STRUCK ME. THIS CANNOT GO UNPUNISHED.
TAKE HER TO THE PITS!

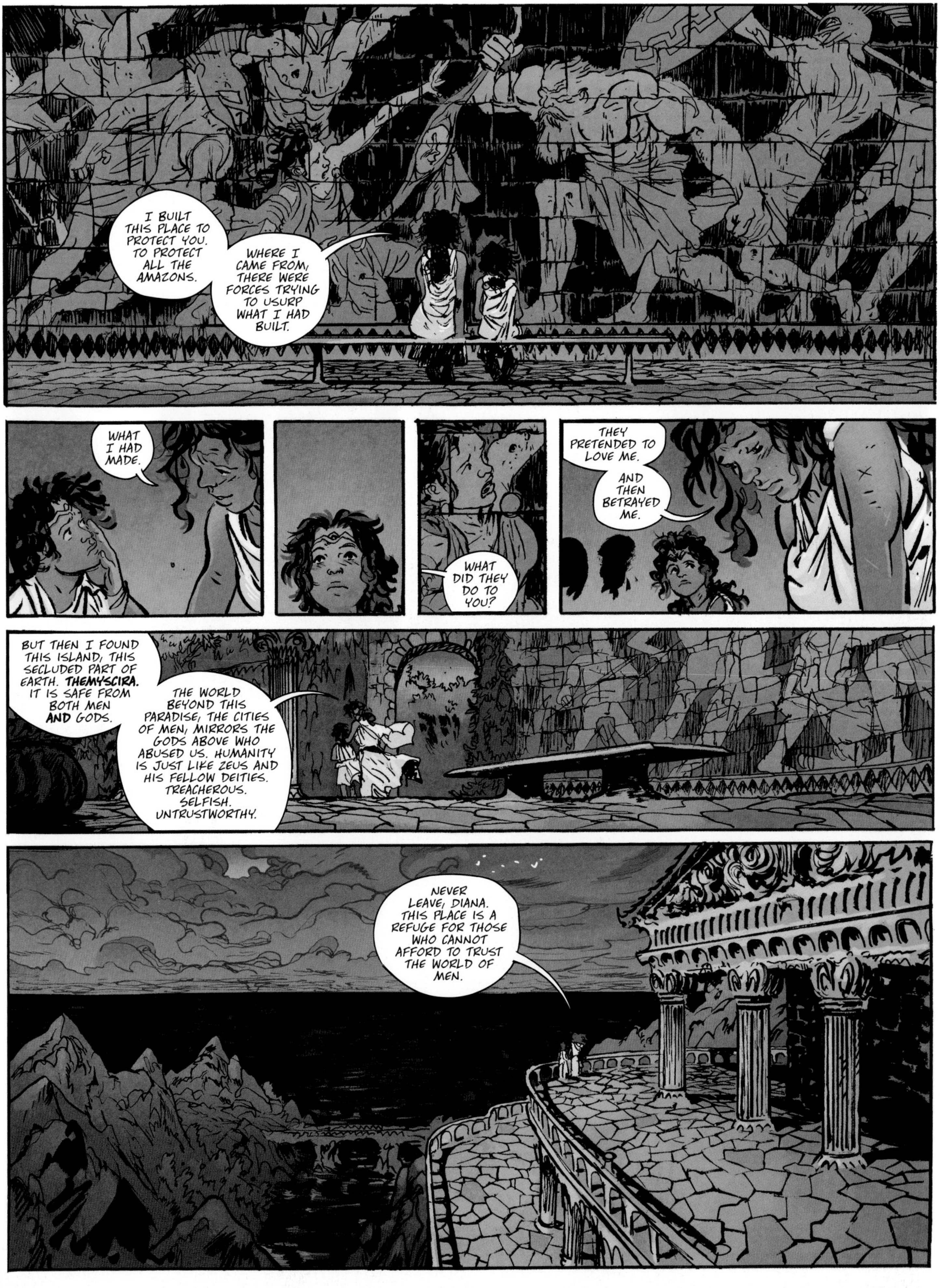
I BUILT THIS PLACE TO PROTECT YOU. TO PROTECT ALL THE AMAZONS.
WHERE I CAME FROM, THERE WERE FORCES TRYING TO USURP WHAT I HAD BUILT.
WHAT I HAD MADE.
WHAT DID THEY DO TO YOU?
THEY PRETENDED TO LOVE ME.
AND THEN BETRAYED ME.
BUT THEN I FOUND THIS ISLAND, THIS SECLUDED PART OF EARTH. **THEMYSCIRA.** IT IS SAFE FROM BOTH MEN **AND** GODS.
THE WORLD BEYOND THIS PARADISE, THE CITIES OF MEN, MIRRORS THE GODS ABOVE WHO ABUSED US. HUMANITY IS JUST LIKE ZEUS AND HIS FELLOW DEITIES. TREACHEROUS. SELFISH. UNTRUSTWORTHY.
NEVER LEAVE, DIANA. THIS PLACE IS A REFUGE FOR THOSE WHO CANNOT AFFORD TO TRUST THE WORLD OF MEN.

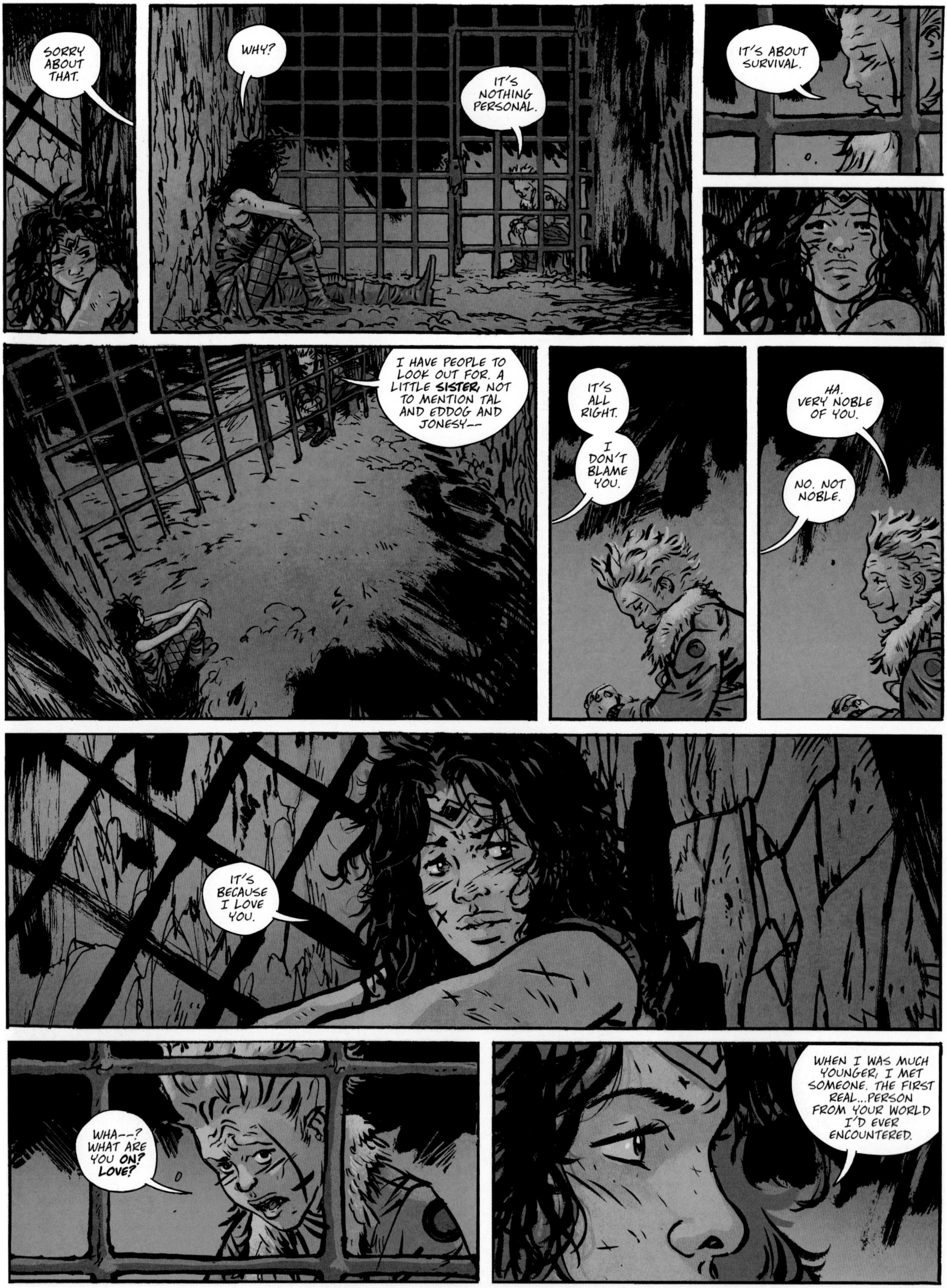
SORRY ABOUT THAT.
WHY?
IT'S NOTHING PERSONAL.
IT'S ABOUT SURVIVAL.
I HAVE PEOPLE TO LOOK OUT FOR. A LITTLE SISTER, NOT TO MENTION TAL AND EDDOG AND JONESY--
IT'S ALL RIGHT.
I DON'T BLAME YOU.
HA. VERY NOBLE OF YOU.
NO. NOT NOBLE.
IT'S BECAUSE I LOVE YOU.
WHA--? WHAT ARE YOU ON? LOVE?
WHEN I WAS MUCH YOUNGER, I MET SOMEONE. THE FIRST REAL...PERSON FROM YOUR WORLD I'D EVER ENCOUNTERED.

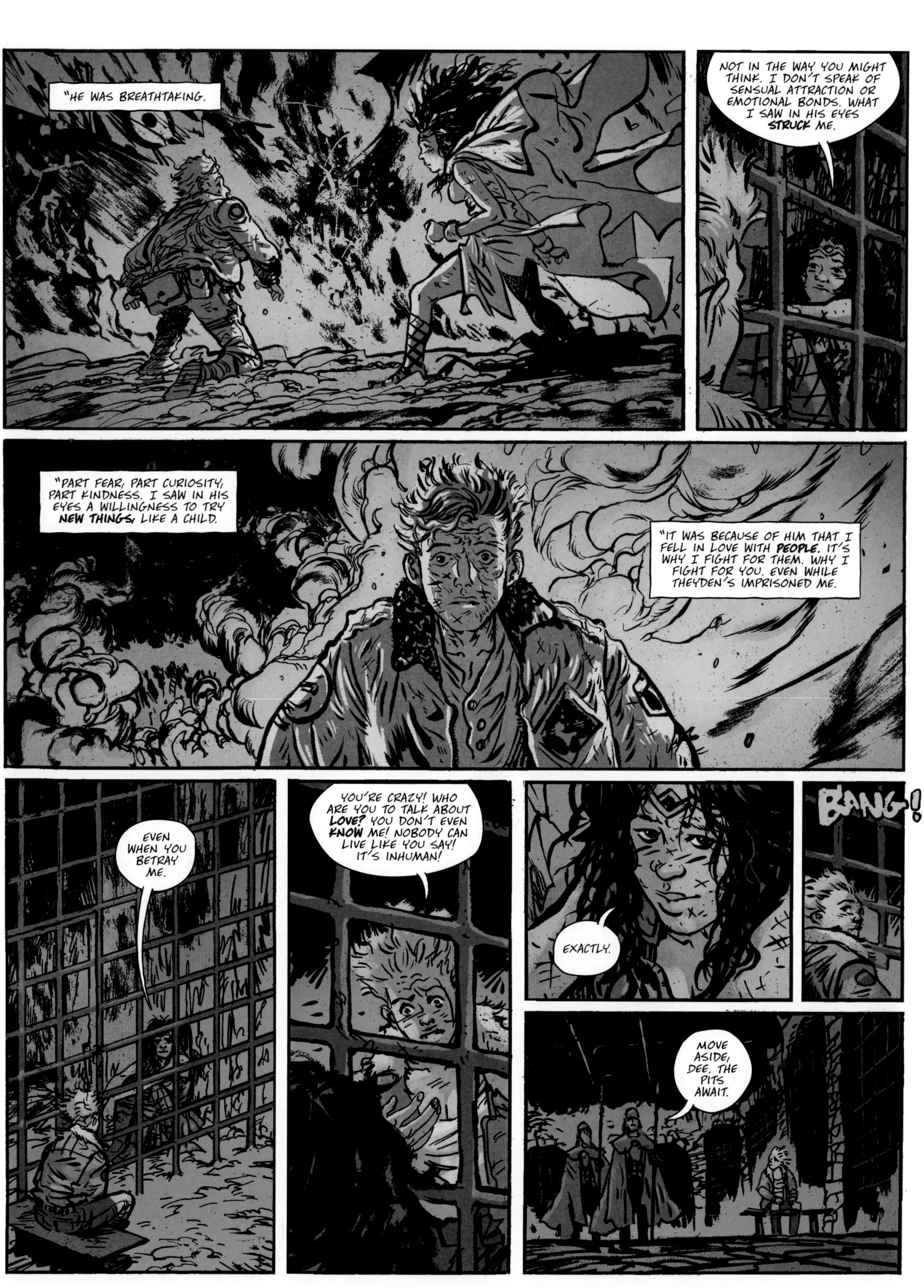
"HE WAS BREATHTAKING.
NOT IN THE WAY YOU MIGHT THINK. I DON'T SPEAK OF SENSUAL ATTRACTION OR EMOTIONAL BONDS. WHAT I SAW IN HIS EYES STRUCK ME.
"PART FEAR, PART CURIOSITY, PART KINDNESS. I SAW IN HIS EYES A WILLINGNESS TO TRY NEW THINGS, LIKE A CHILD.
"IT WAS BECAUSE OF HIM THAT I FELL IN LOVE WITH PEOPLE. IT'S WHY I FIGHT FOR THEM. WHY I FIGHT FOR YOU. EVEN WHILE THEYDEN'S IMPRISONED ME.
EVEN WHEN YOU BETRAY ME.
YOU'RE CRAZY! WHO ARE YOU TO TALK ABOUT LOVE? YOU DON'T EVEN KNOW ME! NOBODY CAN LIVE LIKE YOU SAY! IT'S INHUMAN!
EXACTLY.
BANG!
MOVE ASIDE, DEE. THE PITS AWAIT.

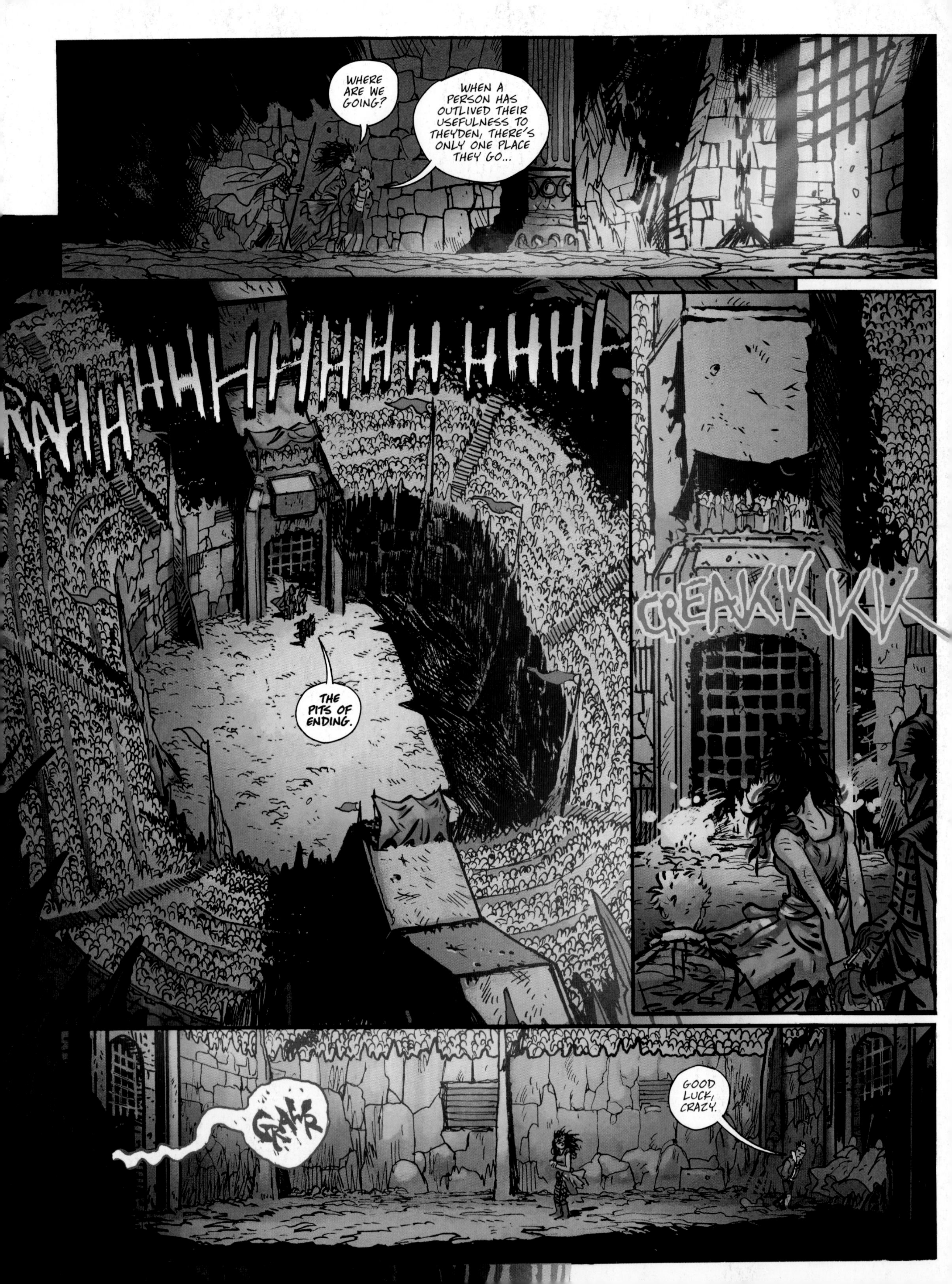
WHERE ARE WE GOING?
WHEN A PERSON HAS OUTLIVED THEIR USEFULNESS TO THEYDEN, THERE'S ONLY ONE PLACE THEY GO...
RAHHHHHHHHHHHHHHH
THE PITS OF ENDING.
CREAKKKK
GRAWR
GOOD LUCK, CRAZY.

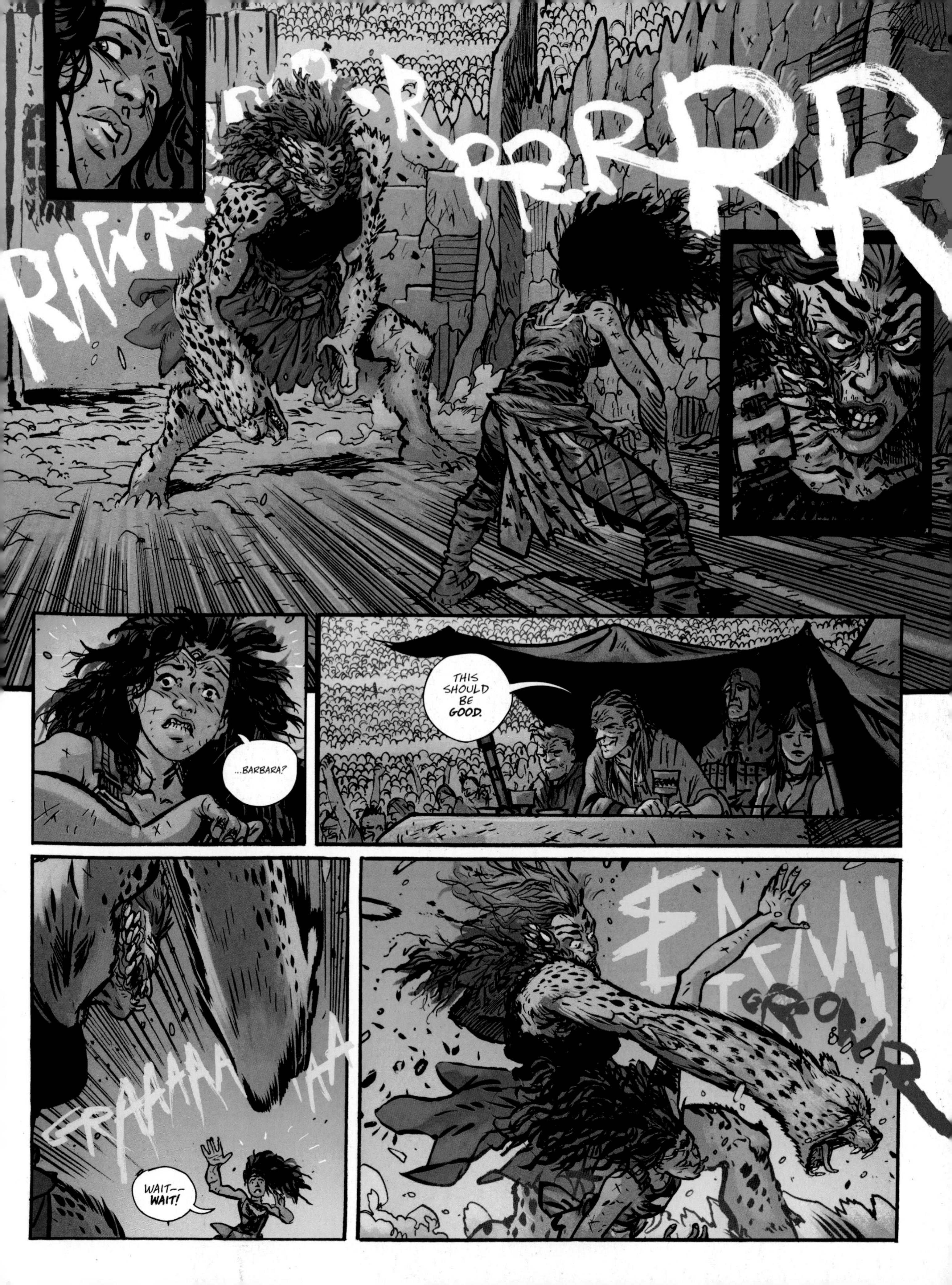
...BARBARA?
THIS SHOULD BE GOOD.
WAIT-- WAIT!

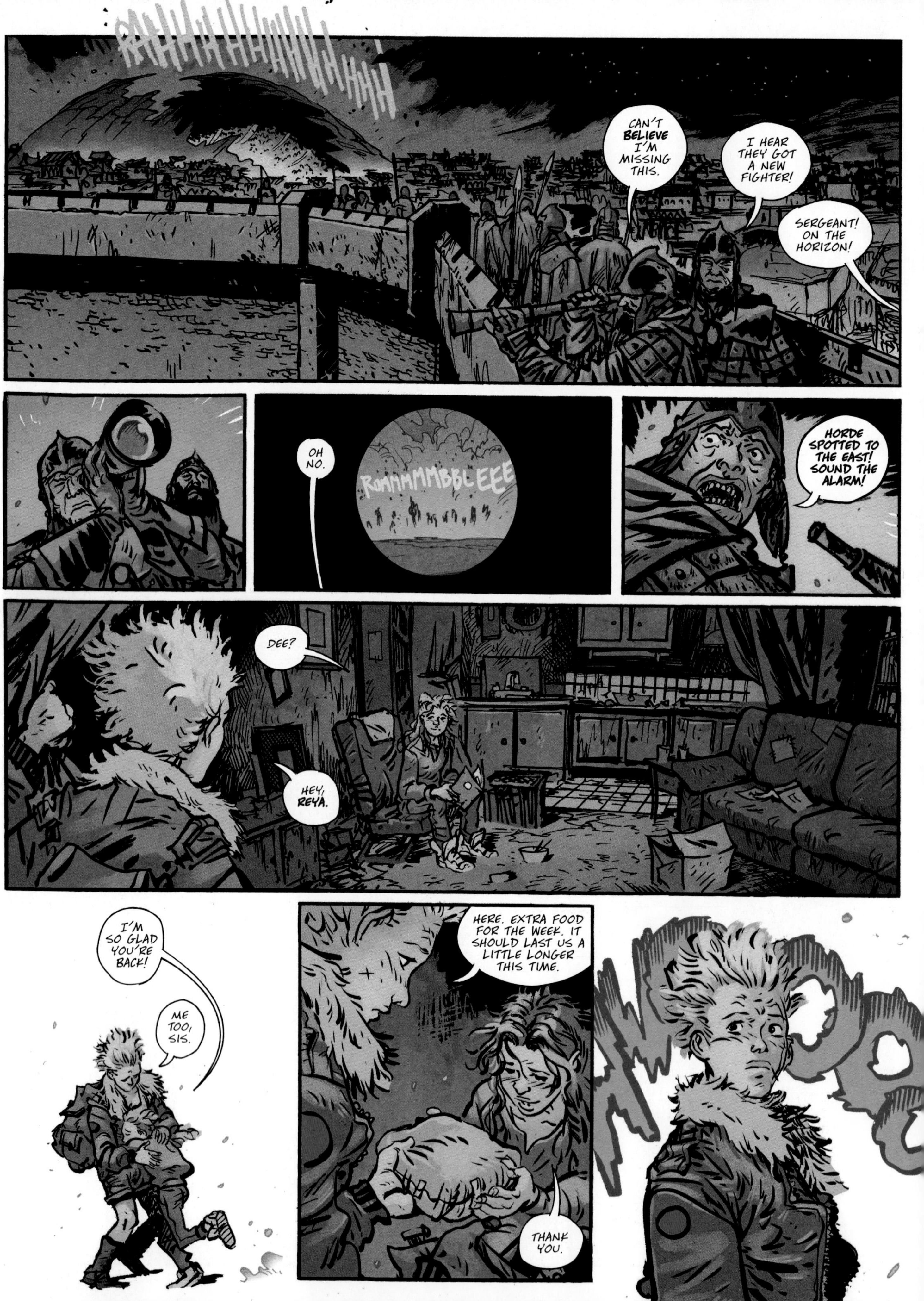
CAN'T **BELIEVE** I'M MISSING THIS.
I HEAR THEY GOT A NEW FIGHTER!
SERGEANT! ON THE HORIZON!
OH NO.
ROMMMMMBBLEEE
HORDE SPOTTED TO THE EAST! SOUND THE ALARM!
DEE?
HEY, **REYA.**
I'M SO GLAD YOU'RE BACK!
ME TOO, SIS.
HERE. EXTRA FOOD FOR THE WEEK. IT SHOULD LAST US A LITTLE LONGER THIS TIME.
THANK YOU.

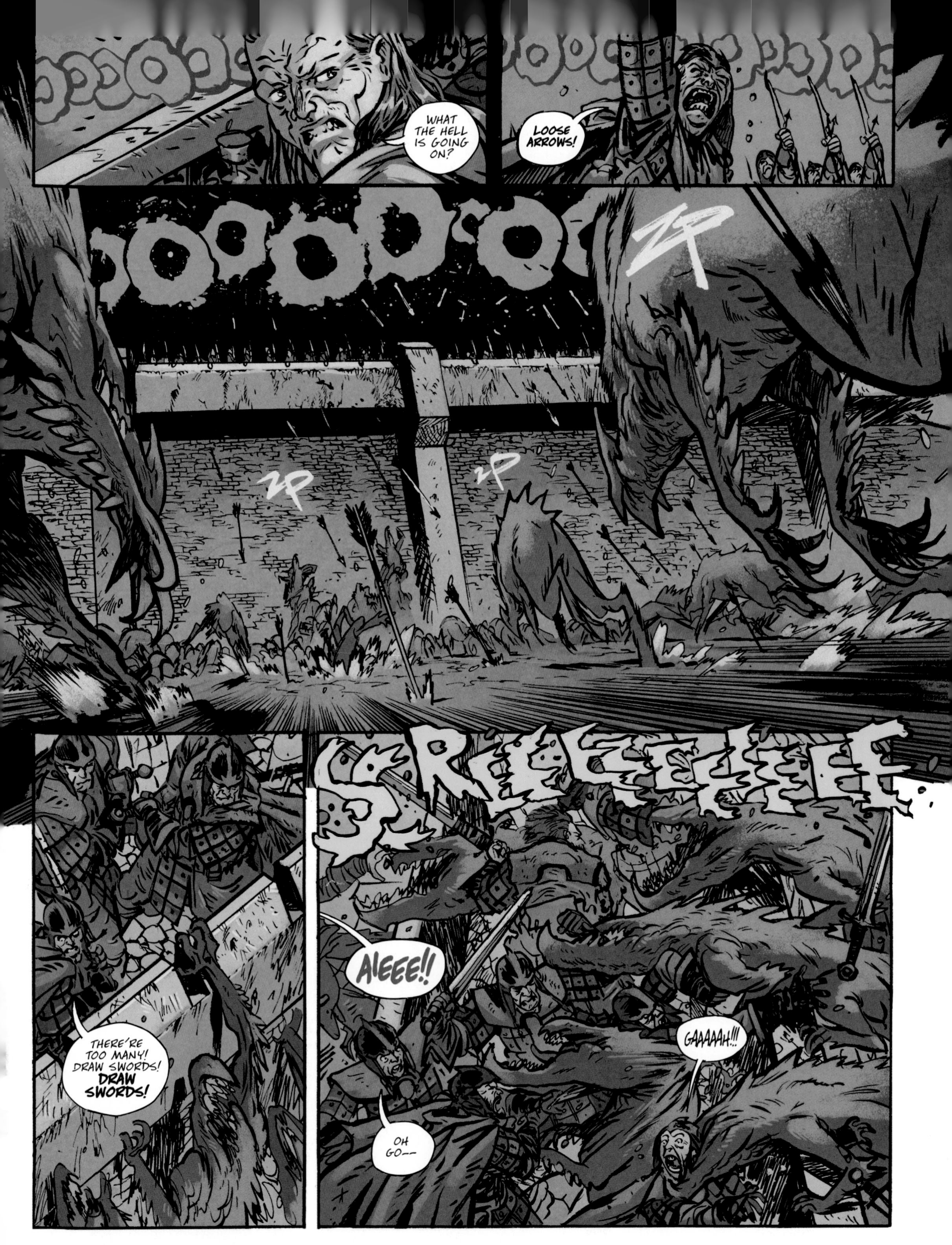

WHAT THE HELL IS GOING ON?
LOOSE ARROWS!
ZP
ZP
ZP
SREEEEEEE
THERE'RE TOO MANY! DRAW SWORDS! **DRAW SWORDS!**
AIEEE!!
GAAAAAH!!!
OH GO--

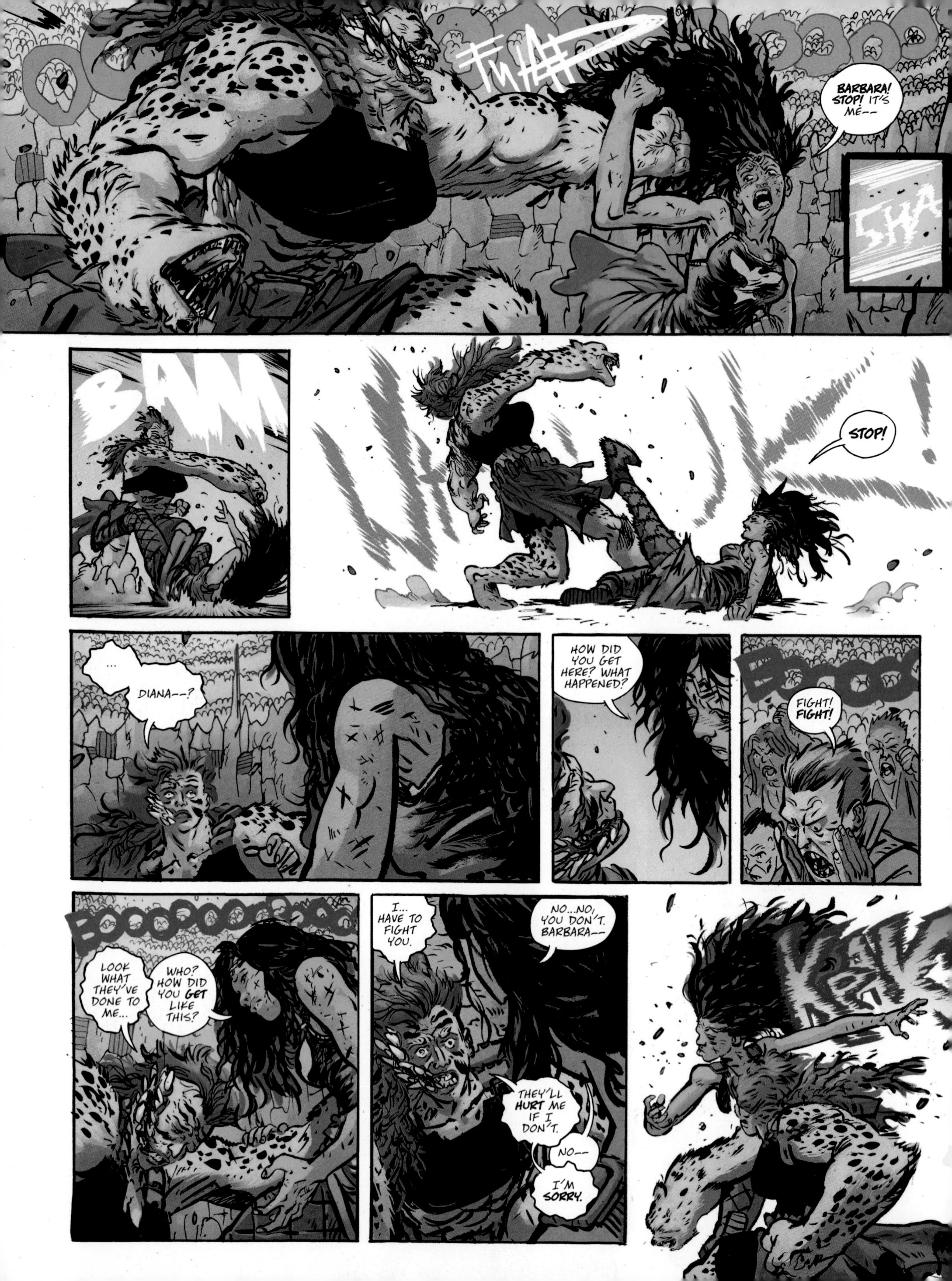
FWAP
BARBARA! STOP! IT'S ME--
SHA
BAM
WHUK!
STOP!
...
DIANA--?
HOW DID YOU GET HERE? WHAT HAPPENED?
BOOO
FIGHT! FIGHT!
BOOOOOOOOOO
LOOK WHAT THEY'VE DONE TO ME...
WHO? HOW DID YOU GET LIKE THIS?
I... HAVE TO FIGHT YOU.
NO...NO, YOU DON'T. BARBARA--
THEY'LL HURT ME IF I DON'T.
NO--
I'M SORRY.

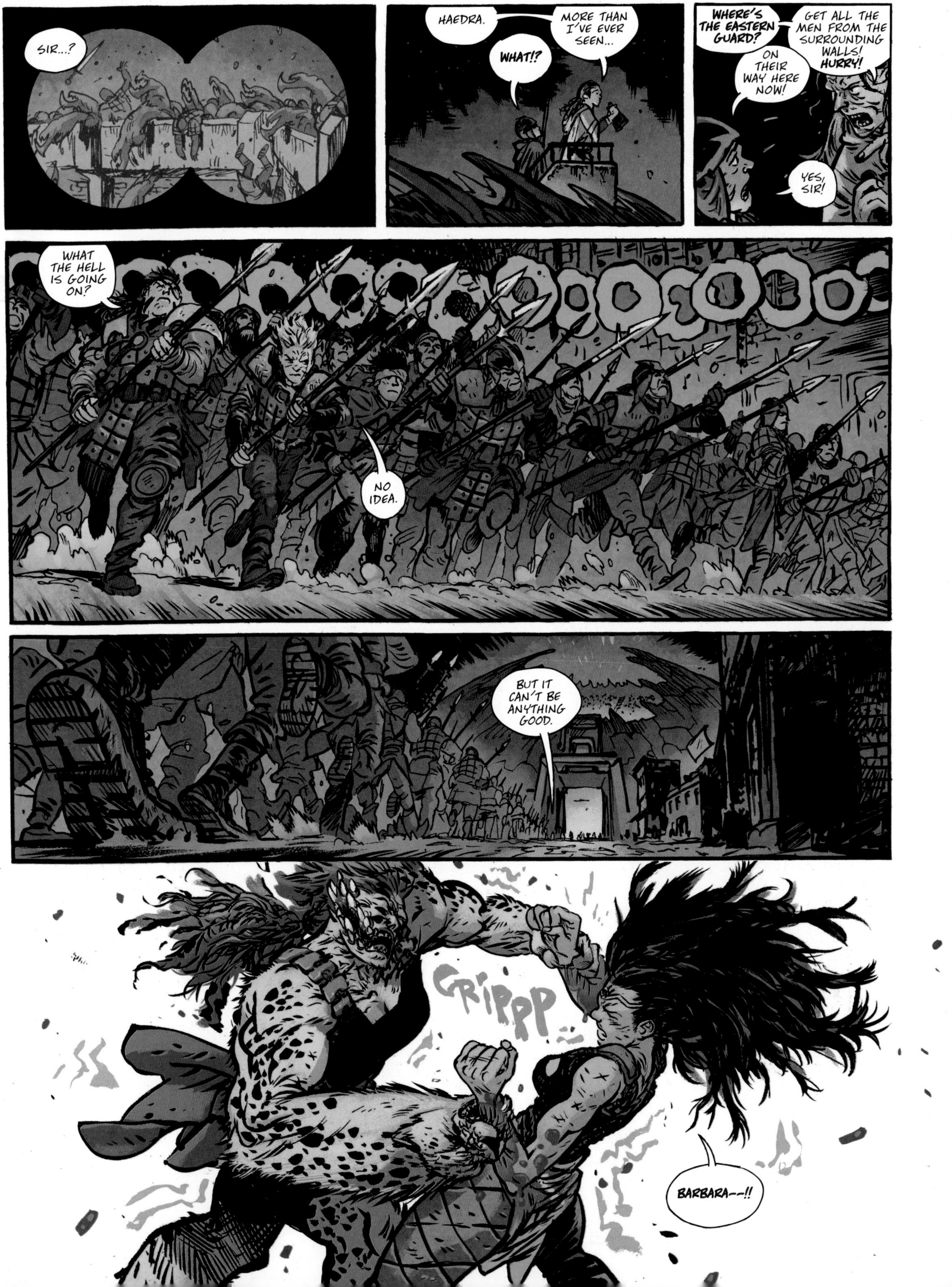
SIR...?
HAEDRA.
MORE THAN I'VE EVER SEEN...
WHAT!?
WHERE'S THE EASTERN GUARD?
GET ALL THE MEN FROM THE SURROUNDING WALLS! HURRY!
ON THEIR WAY HERE NOW!
YES, SIR!
WHAT THE HELL IS GOING ON?
NO IDEA.
BUT IT CAN'T BE ANYTHING GOOD.
CRIPPP
BARBARA--!!

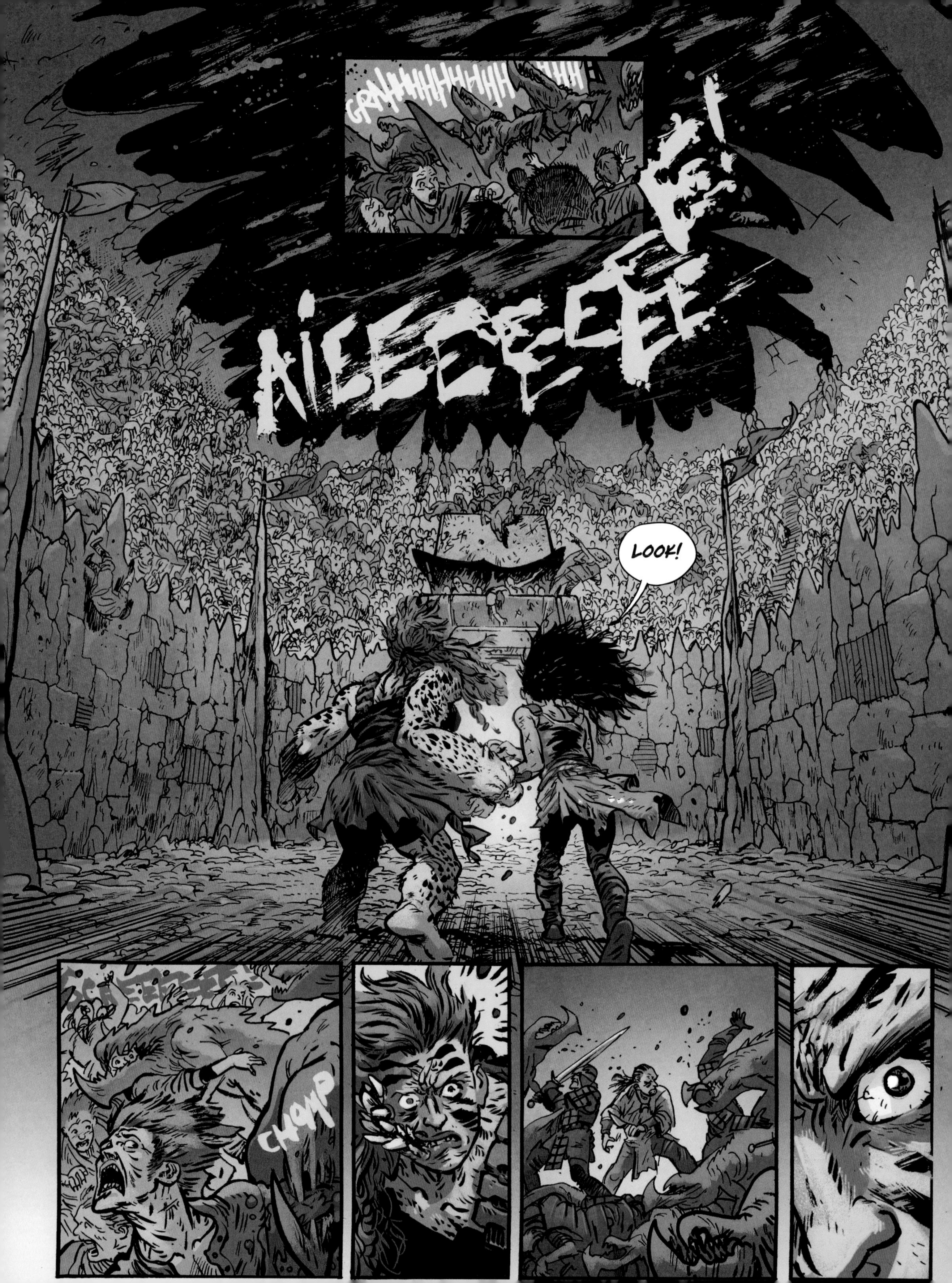
GRAHHHHHHHHHHHHHHH
AIEEEEEEE
LOOK!
CHOMP

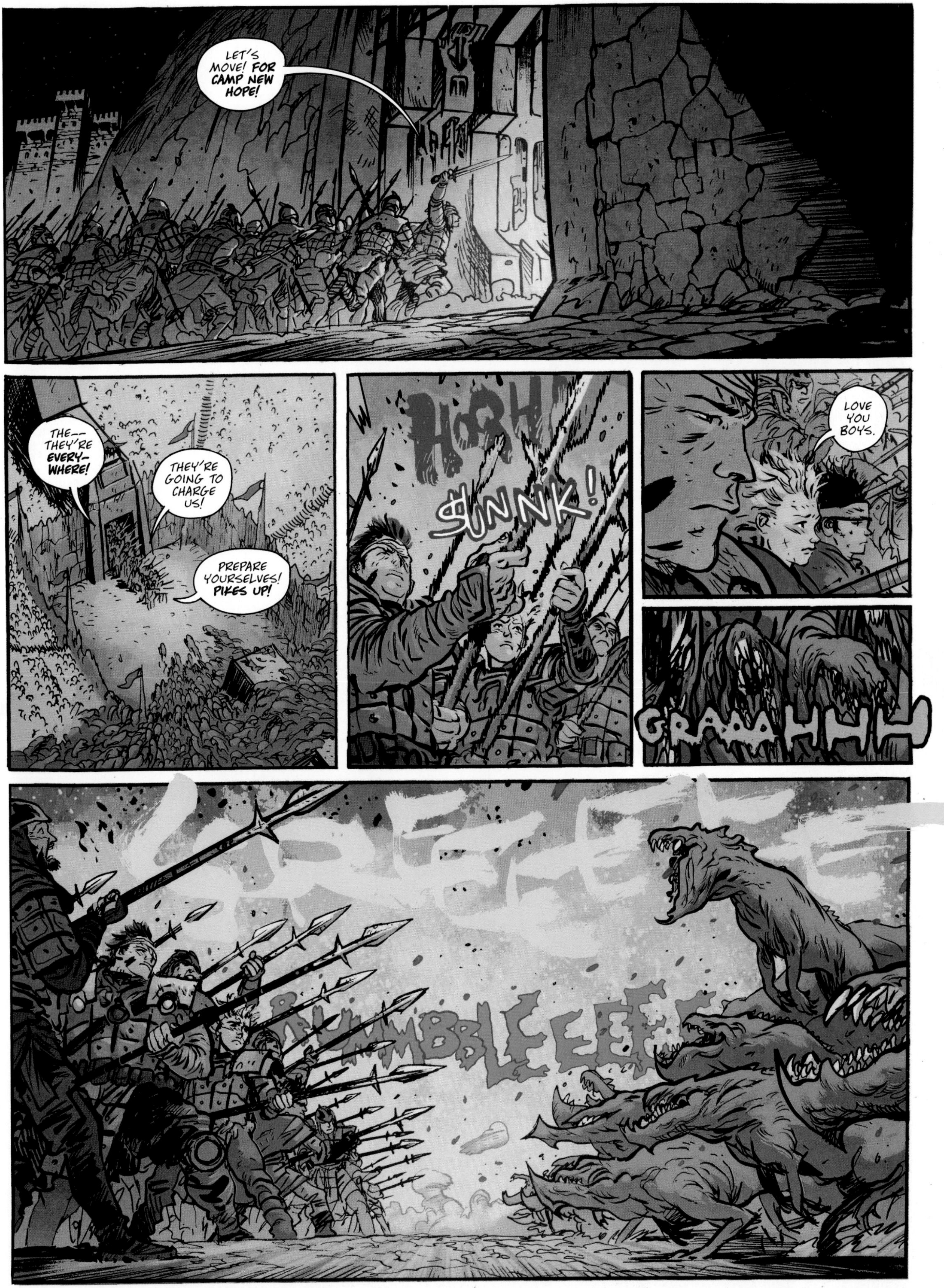
LET'S MOVE! FOR CAMP NEW HOPE!
THE-- THEY'RE EVERY-WHERE!
THEY'RE GOING TO CHARGE US!
PREPARE YOURSELVES! PIKES UP!
SUNNK!
LOVE YOU BOYS.
GRAAAHHH

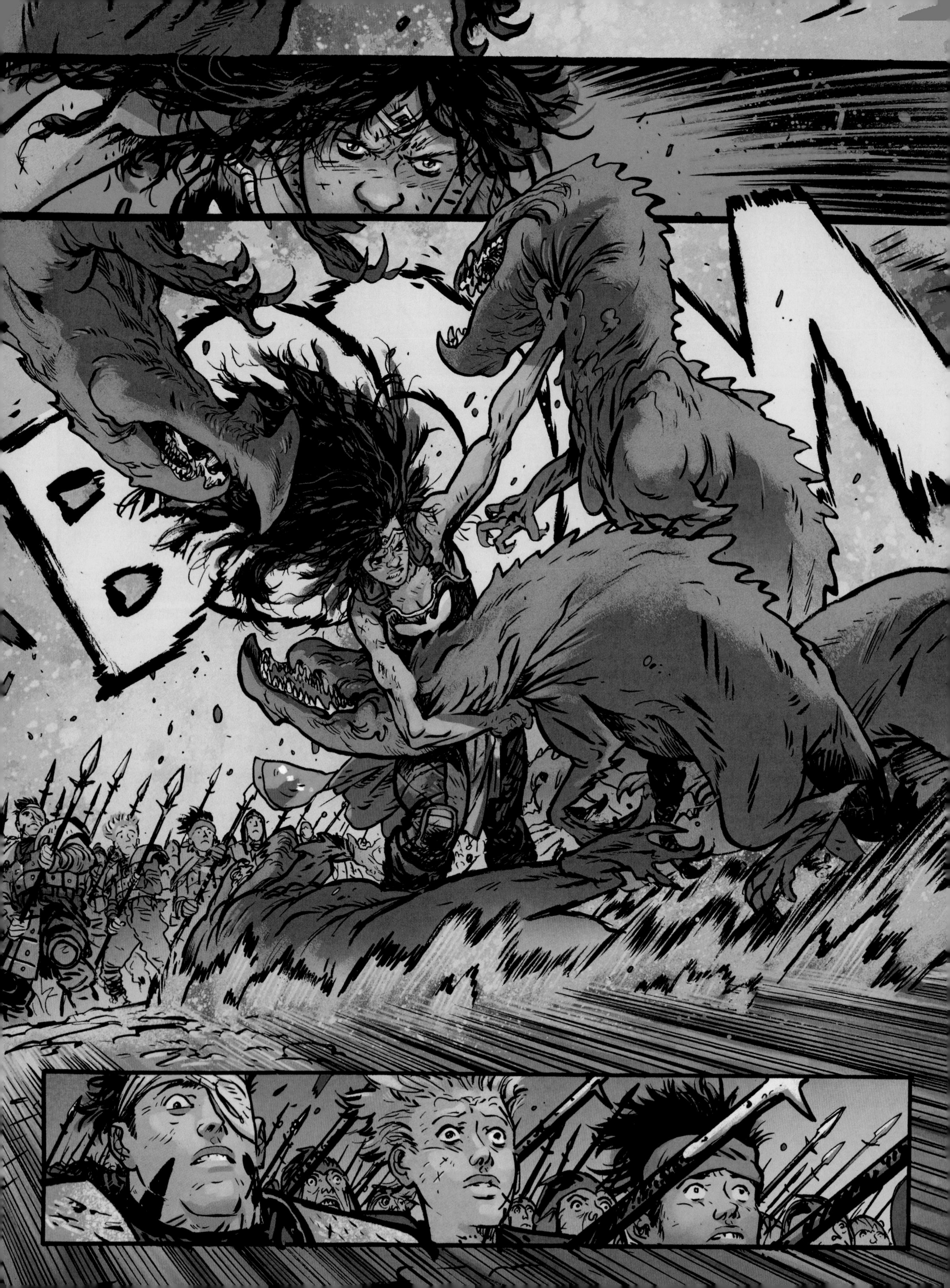

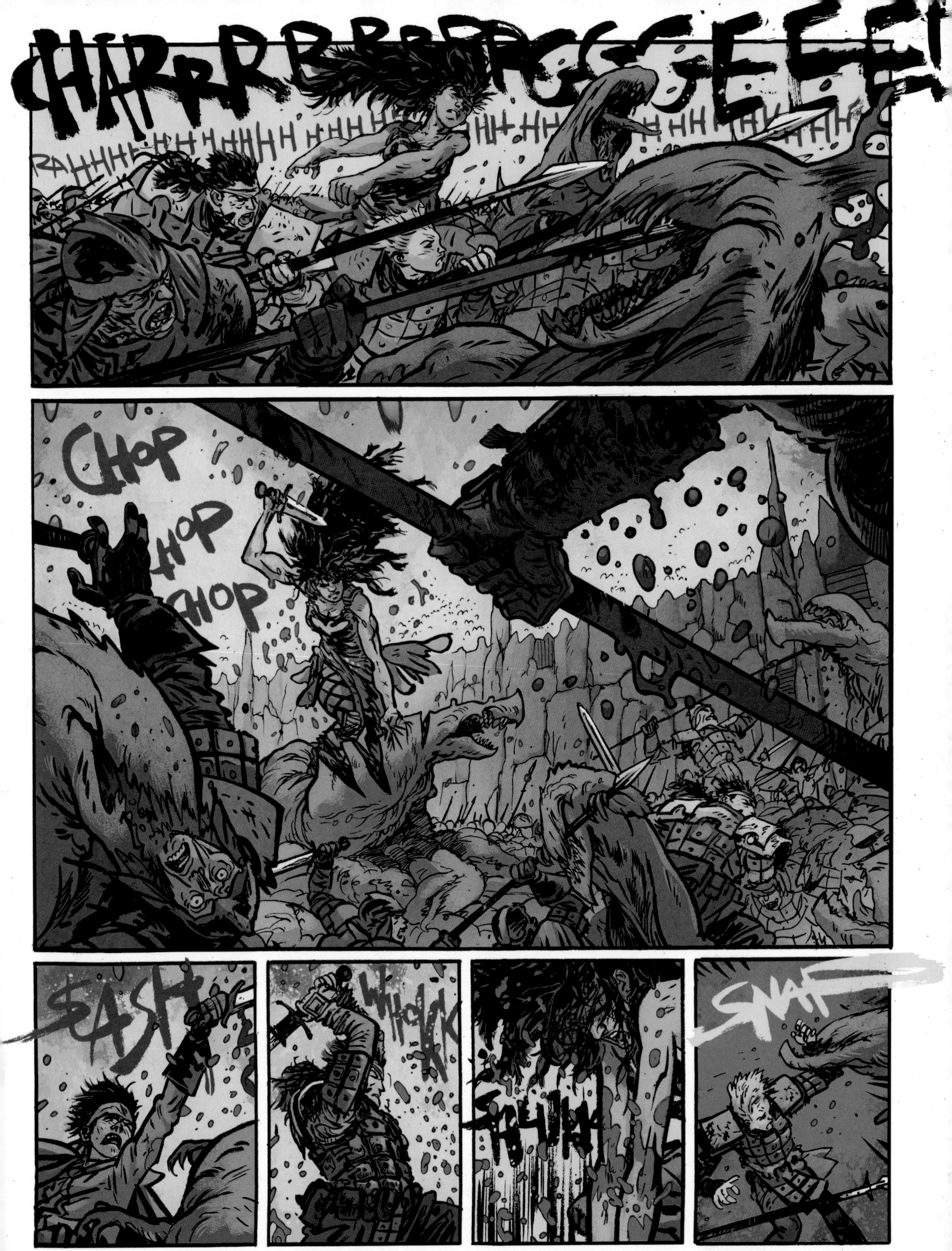
CHARRRRRRGGGEEE!
RAHHHHHHHHHHHHHHH
CHOP
CHOP
CHOP
WHACKK
SNAP

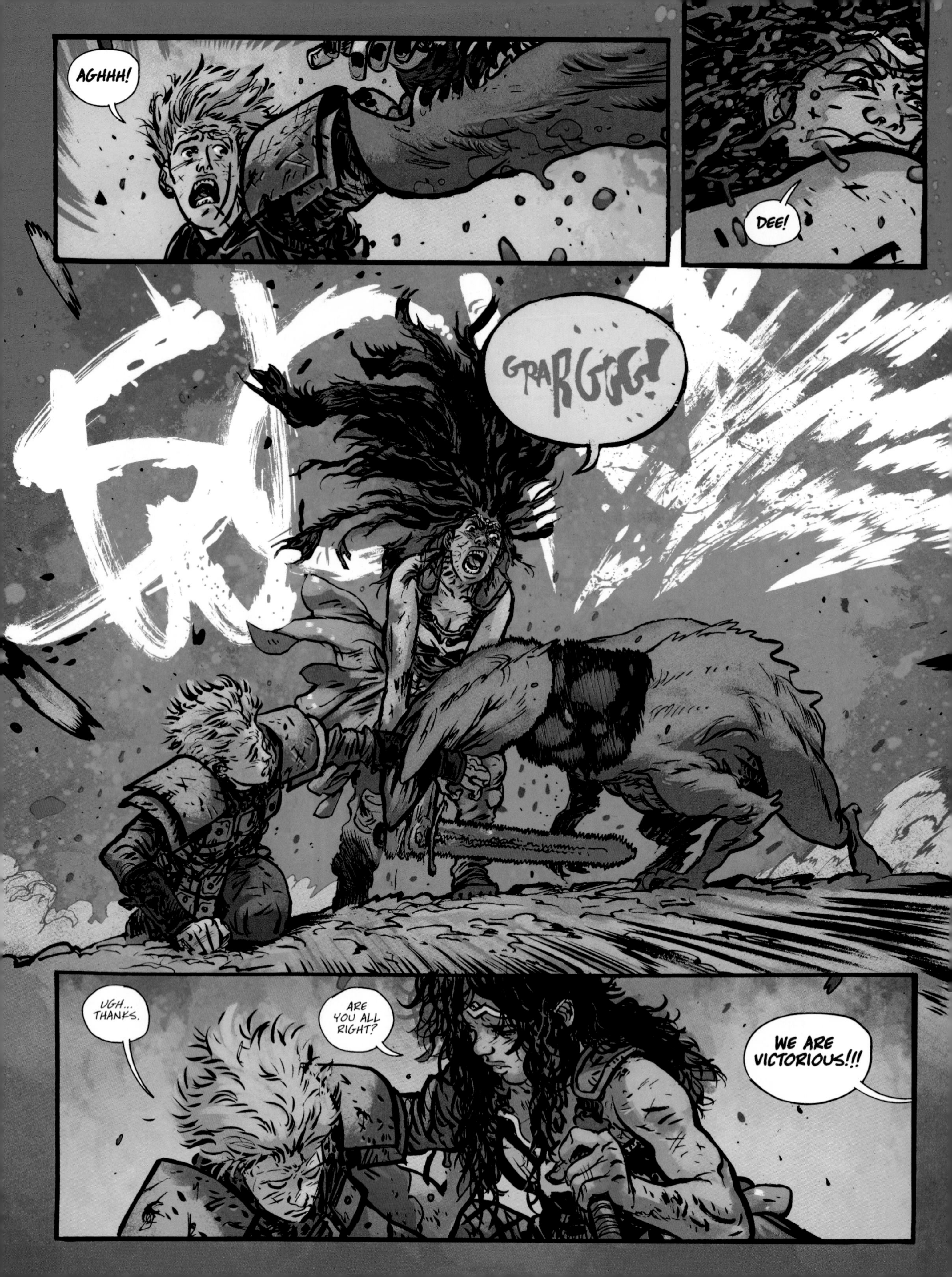
AGHHH!
DEE!
GRARGGG!
UGH... THANKS.
ARE YOU ALL RIGHT?
WE ARE VICTORIOUS!!!

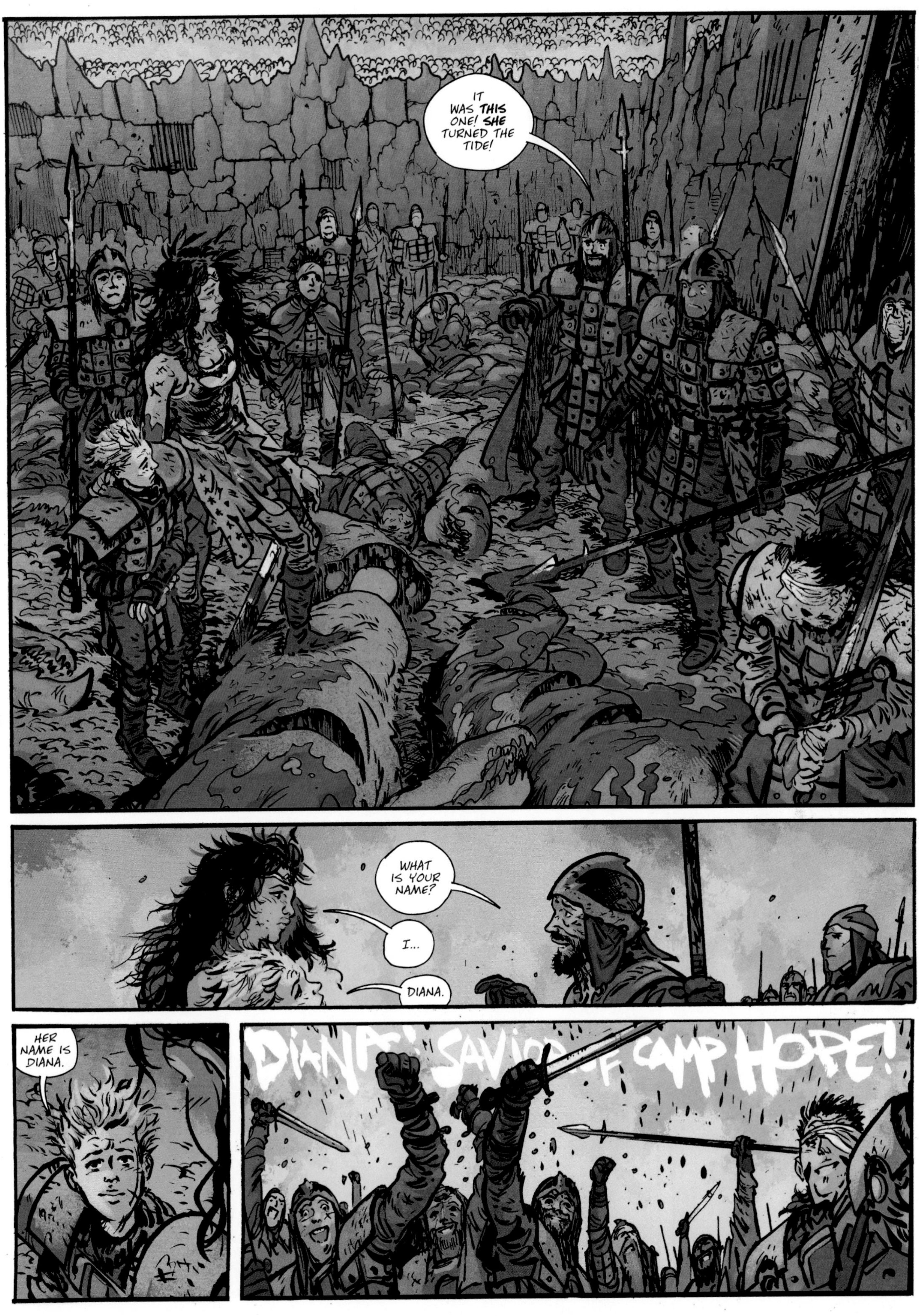
IT WAS **THIS** ONE! **SHE** TURNED THE TIDE!
WHAT IS YOUR NAME?
I...
DIANA.
HER NAME IS DIANA.
DIANA! SAVIOR OF CAMP HOPE!

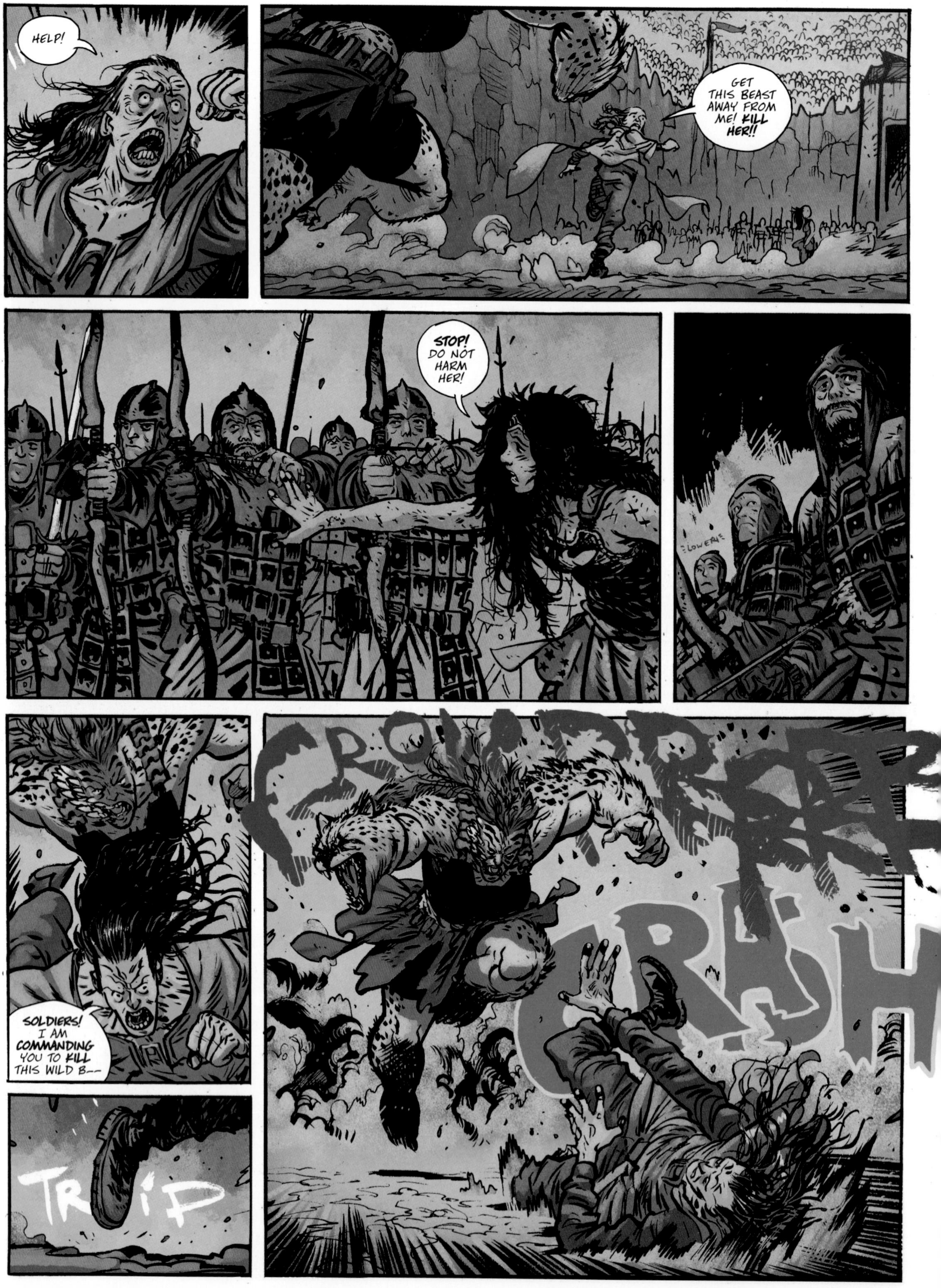
HELP!
GET THIS BEAST AWAY FROM ME! **KILL HER!!**
STOP! DO NOT HARM HER!
LOWER
SOLDIERS! I AM **COMMANDING** YOU TO **KILL** THIS WILD B--
TRIP
CRASH

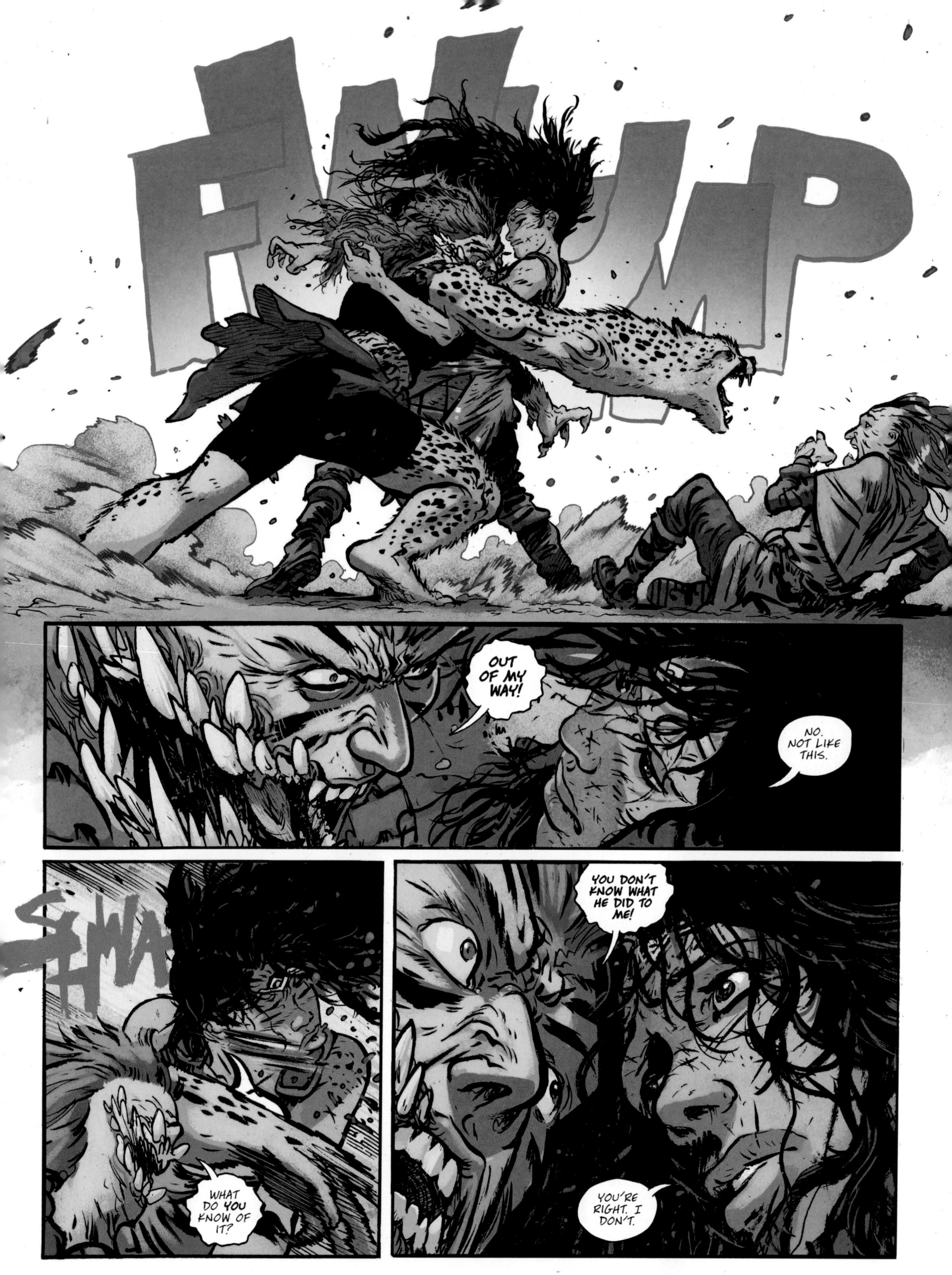
FWUMP
OUT OF MY WAY!
NO. NOT LIKE THIS.
SHWA
WHAT DO YOU KNOW OF IT?
YOU DON'T KNOW WHAT HE DID TO ME!
YOU'RE RIGHT. I DON'T.

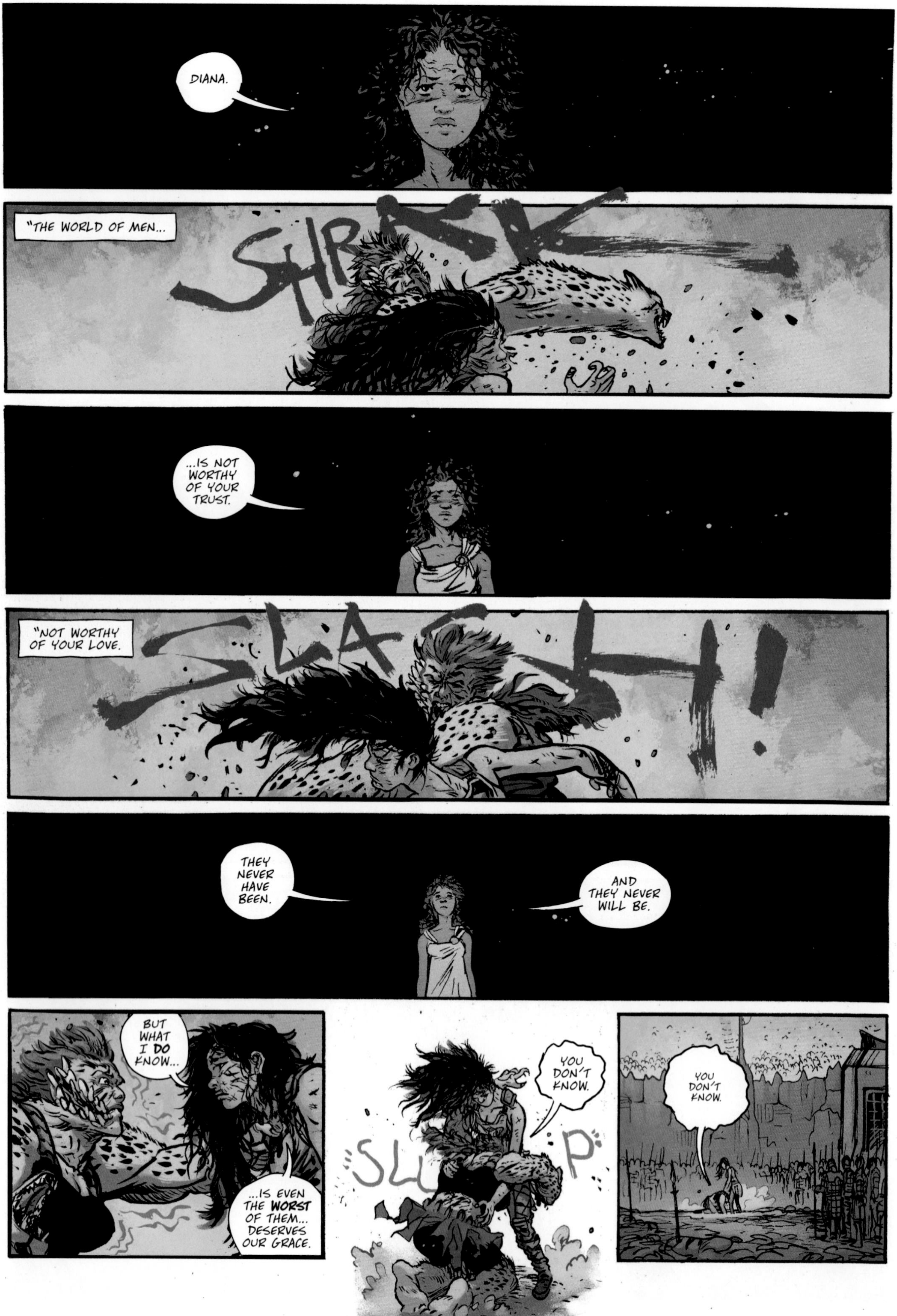
DIANA.
"THE WORLD OF MEN...
SHRAK
...IS NOT WORTHY OF YOUR TRUST.
"NOT WORTHY OF YOUR LOVE.
SLASH!
THEY NEVER HAVE BEEN.
AND THEY NEVER WILL BE.
BUT WHAT I DO KNOW...
...IS EVEN THE WORST OF THEM... DESERVES OUR GRACE.
SLUP
YOU DON'T KNOW.
YOU DON'T KNOW.

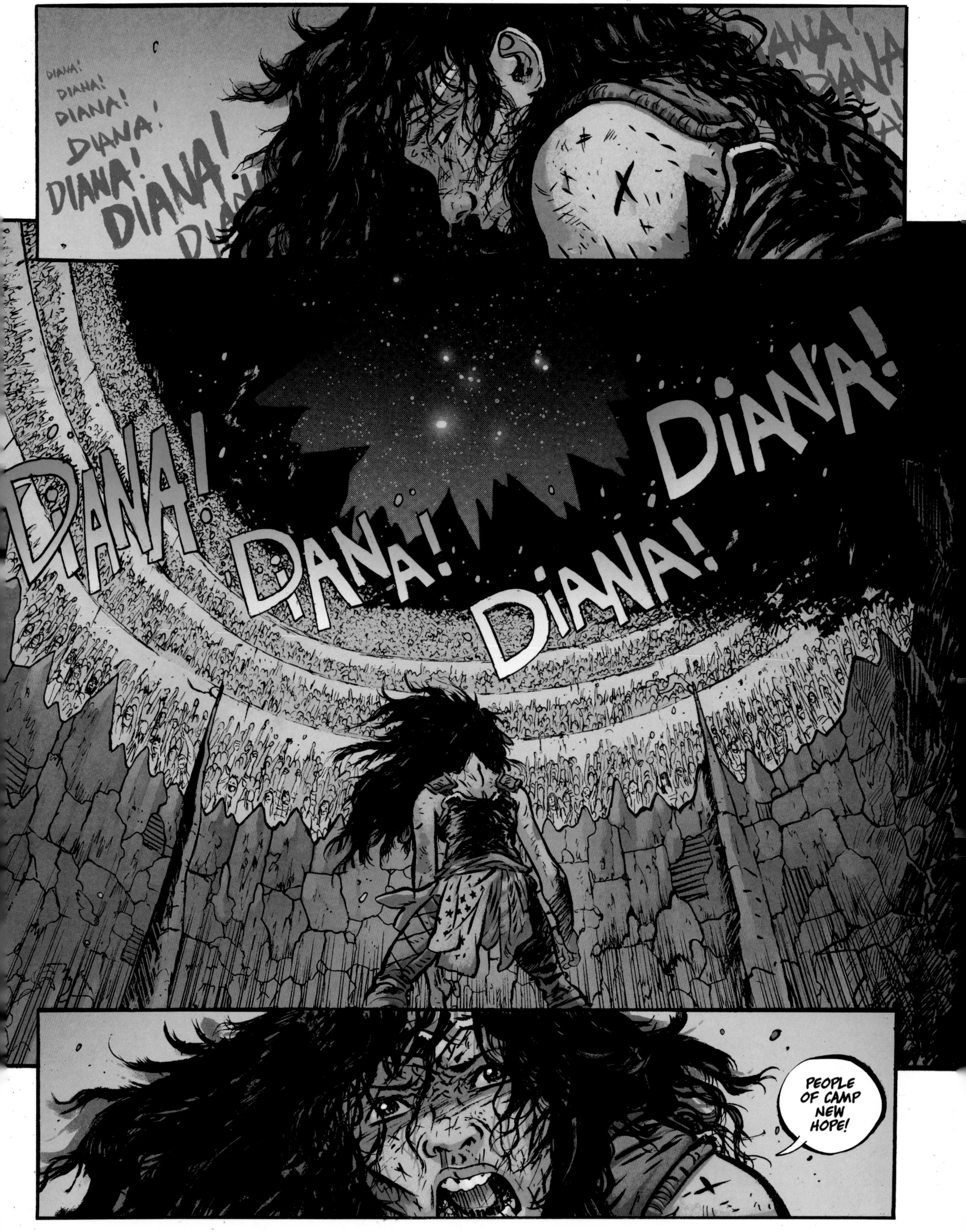
DIANA!
DIANA!
DIANA!
DIANA!
DIANA!
DIANA!
DIANA!
DIANA!
DIANA!
DIANA!
PEOPLE OF CAMP NEW HOPE!

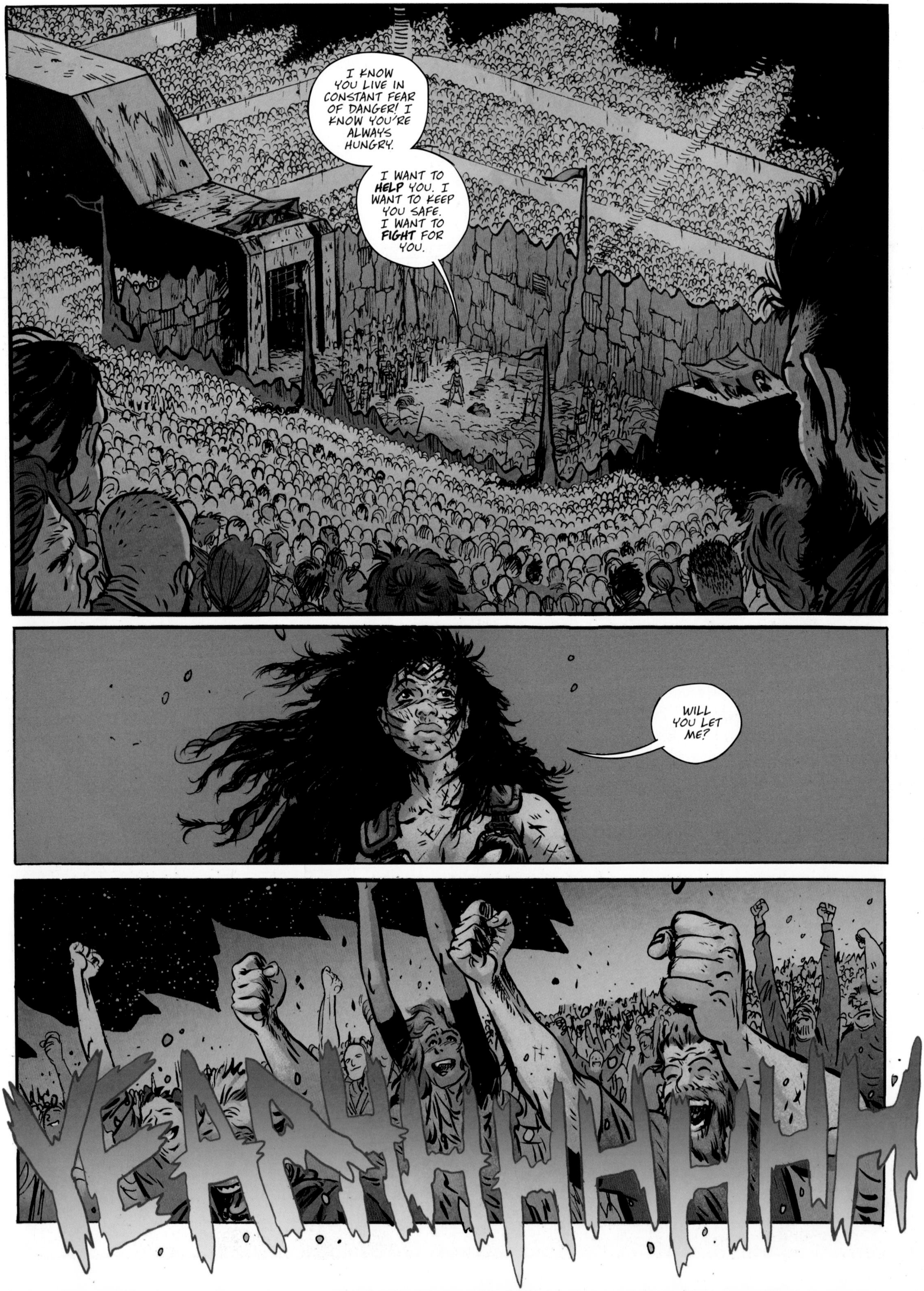
I KNOW YOU LIVE IN CONSTANT FEAR OF DANGER! I KNOW YOU'RE ALWAYS HUNGRY.
I WANT TO **HELP** YOU. I WANT TO KEEP YOU SAFE. I WANT TO **FIGHT** FOR YOU.
WILL YOU LET ME?
YEAHHHHHHHH

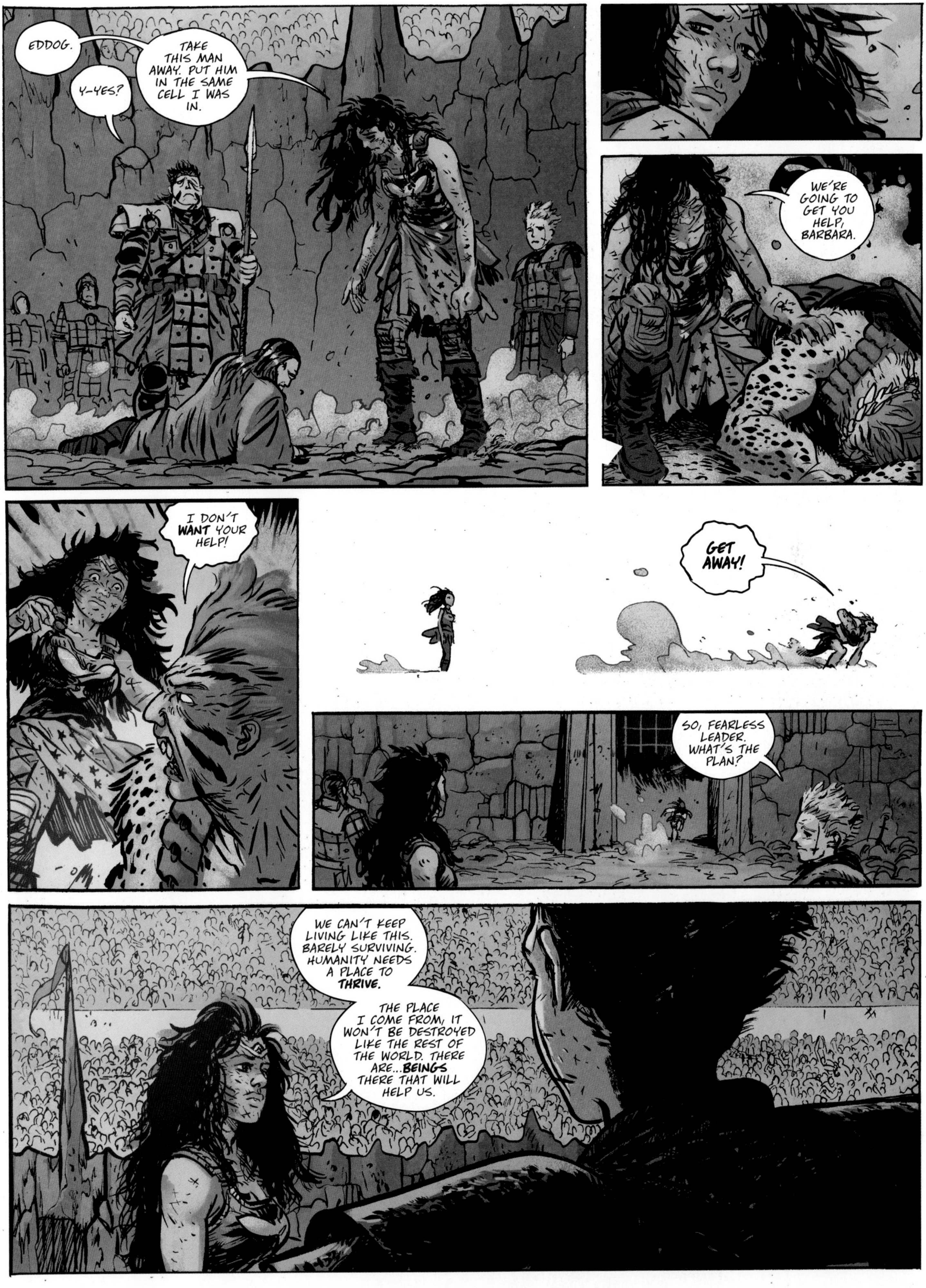
EDDOG.
Y-YES?
TAKE THIS MAN AWAY. PUT HIM IN THE SAME CELL I WAS IN.
WE'RE GOING TO GET YOU HELP, BARBARA.
I DON'T **WANT** YOUR HELP!
GET AWAY!
SO, FEARLESS LEADER. WHAT'S THE PLAN?
WE CAN'T KEEP LIVING LIKE THIS. BARELY SURVIVING. HUMANITY NEEDS A PLACE TO **THRIVE.**
THE PLACE I COME FROM, IT WON'T BE DESTROYED LIKE THE REST OF THE WORLD. THERE ARE... **BEINGS** THERE THAT WILL HELP US.

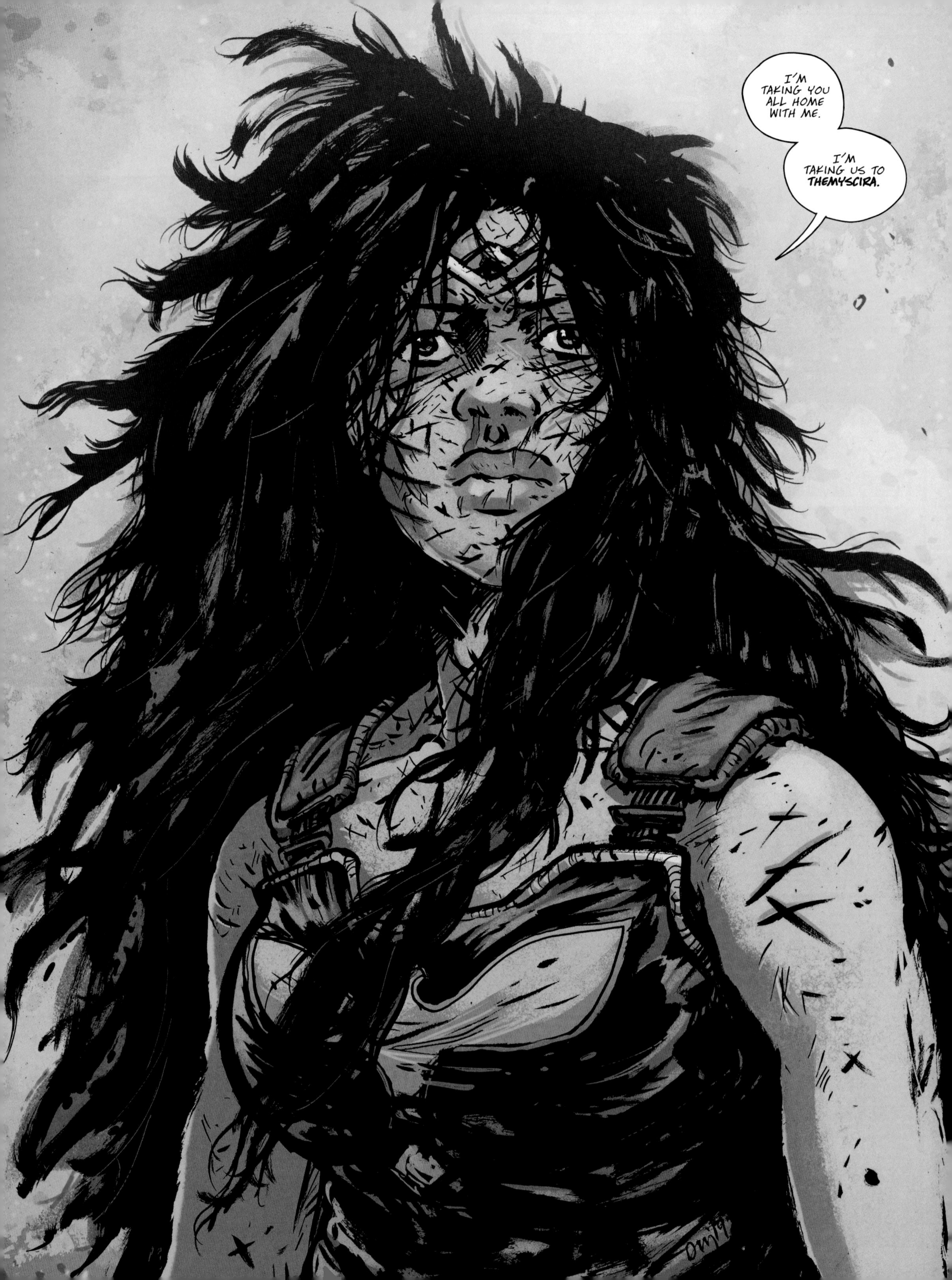
I'M TAKING YOU ALL HOME WITH ME.
I'M TAKING US TO THEMYSCIRA.

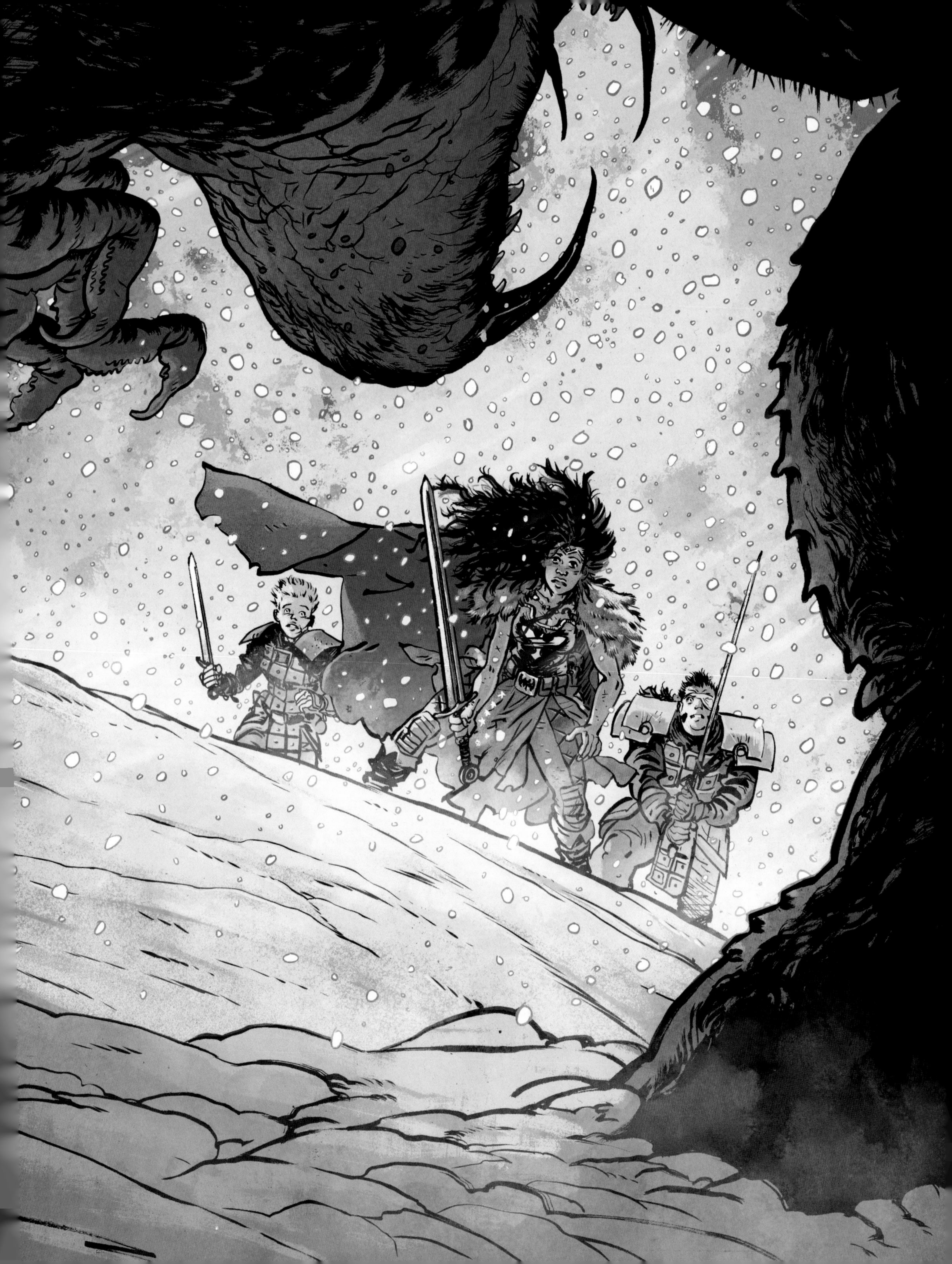

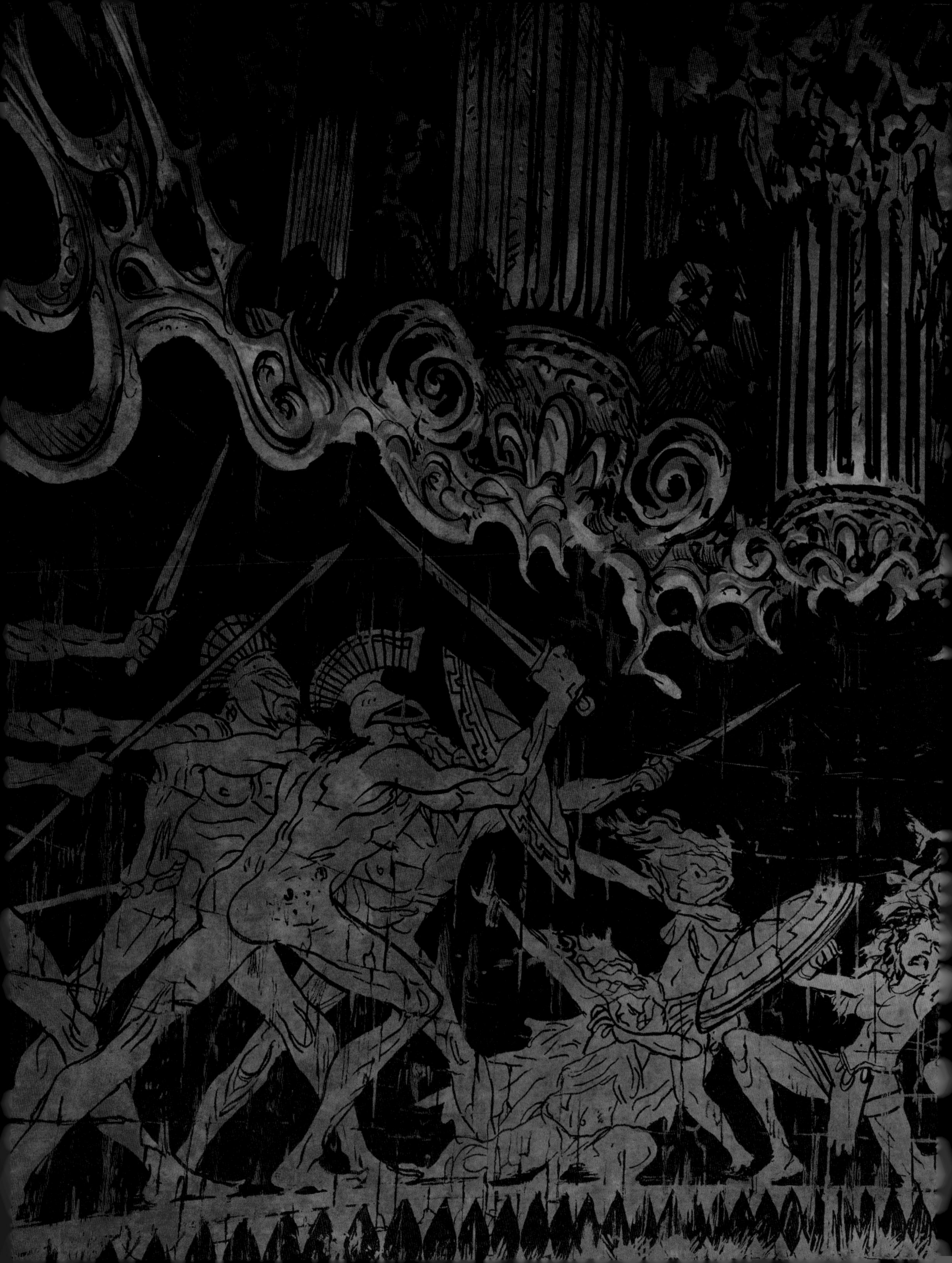

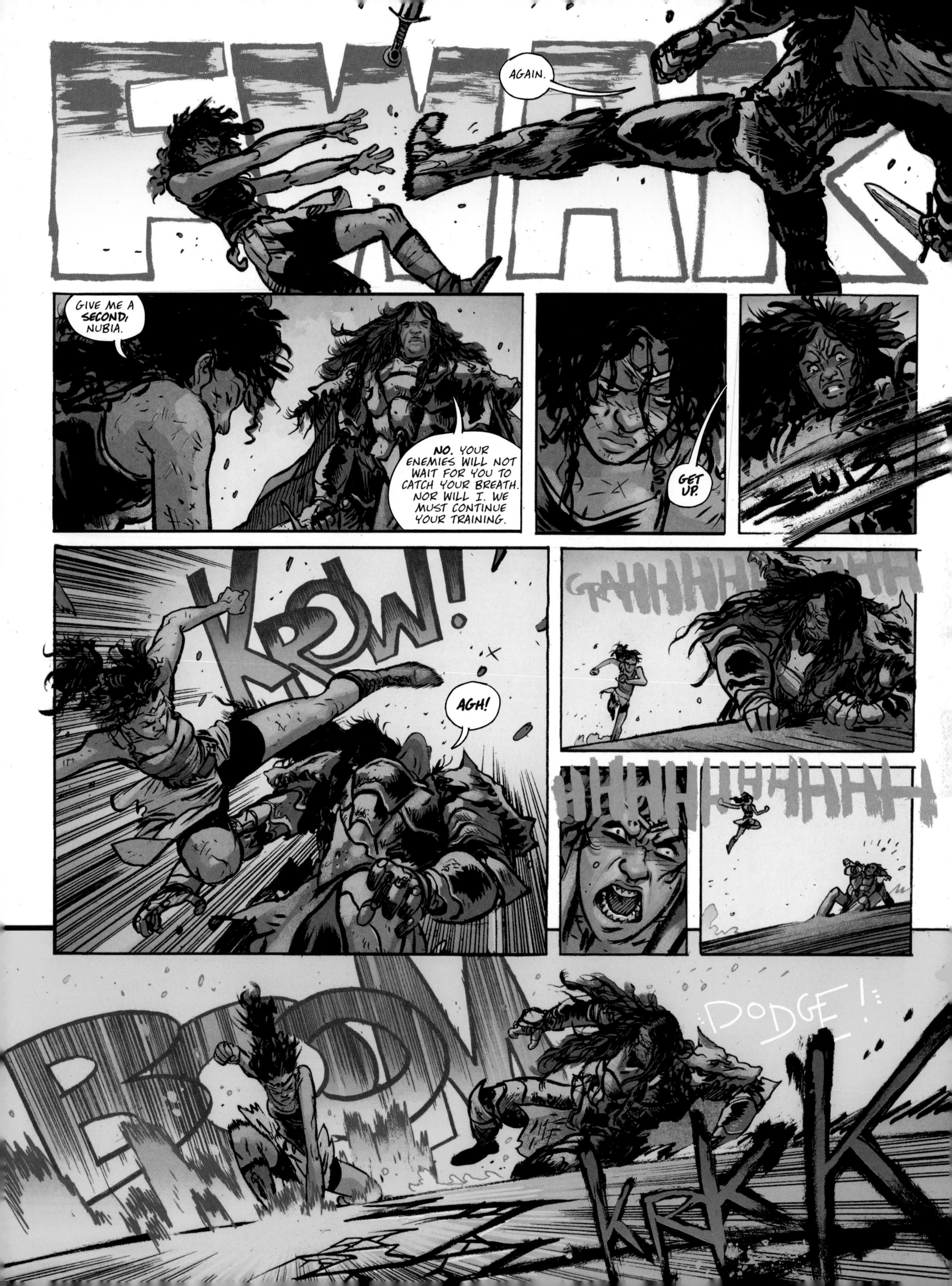
AGAIN.
GIVE ME A SECOND, NUBIA.
NO. YOUR ENEMIES WILL NOT WAIT FOR YOU TO CATCH YOUR BREATH. NOR WILL I. WE MUST CONTINUE YOUR TRAINING.
GET UP.
KROW!
AGH!
DODGE!
KRAK

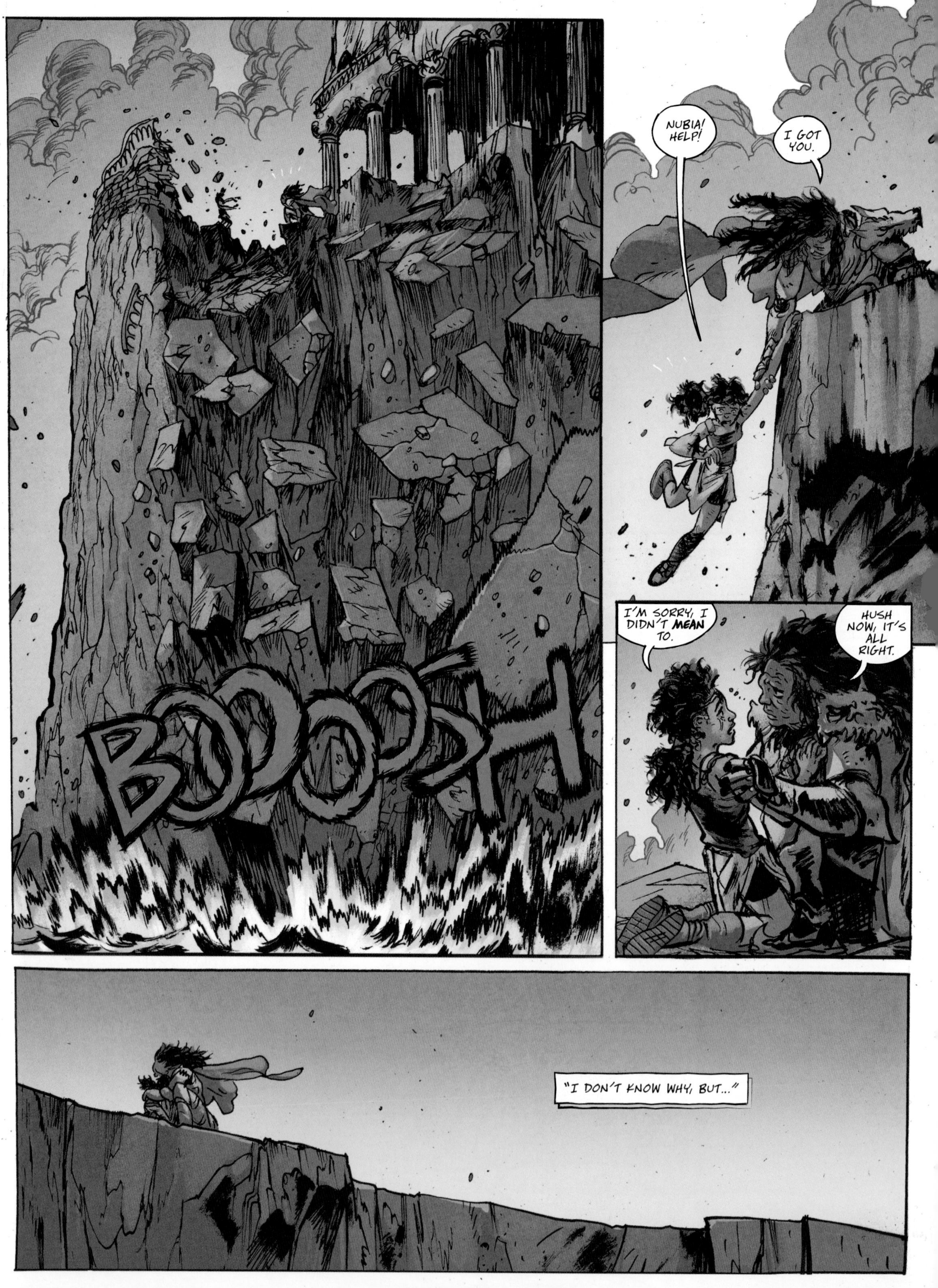
BOOOOSH
NUBIA! HELP!
I GOT YOU.
I'M SORRY, I DIDN'T **MEAN** TO.
HUSH NOW, IT'S ALL RIGHT.
"I DON'T KNOW WHY, BUT..."

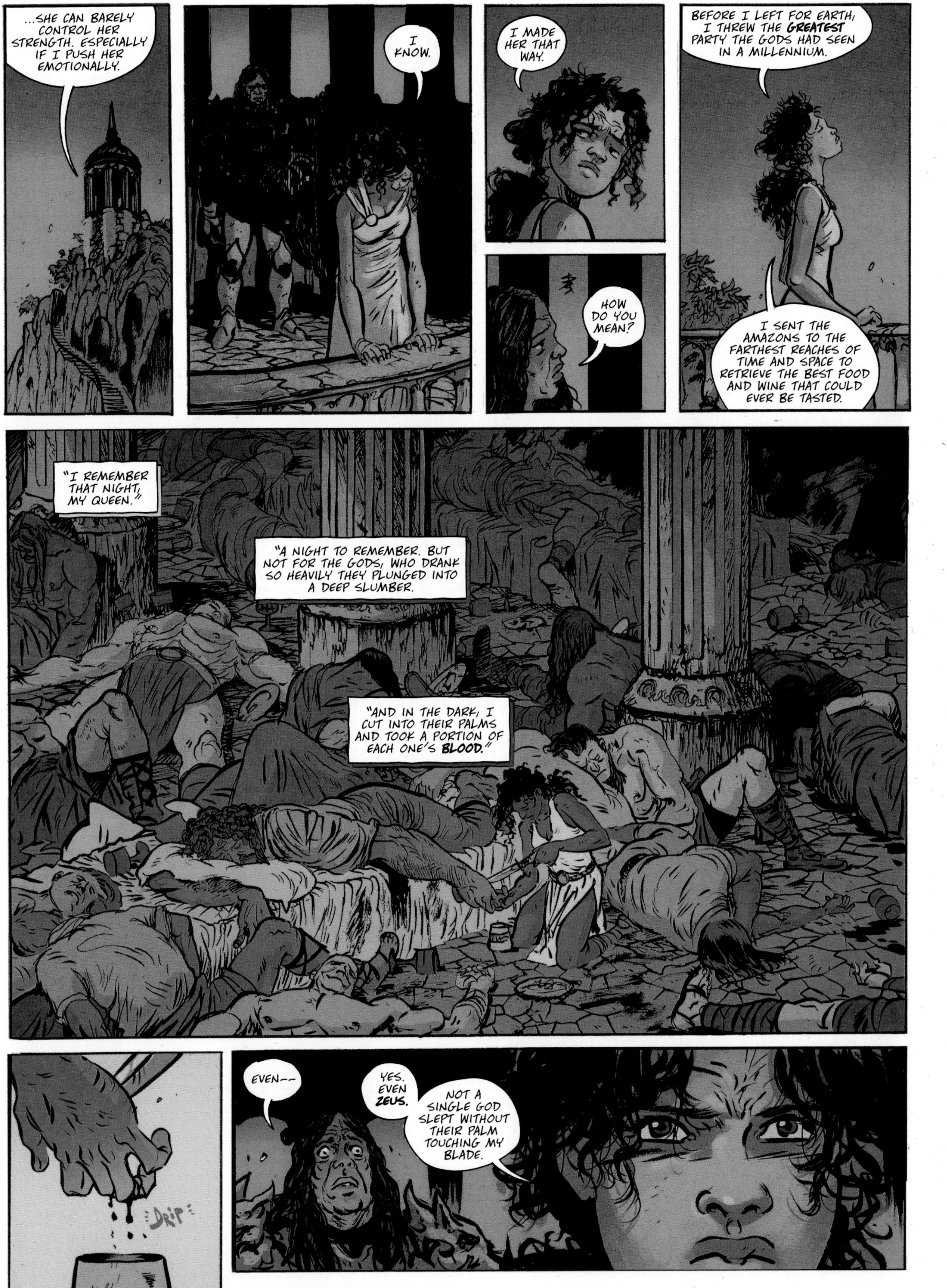
...SHE CAN BARELY CONTROL HER STRENGTH. ESPECIALLY IF I PUSH HER EMOTIONALLY.
I KNOW.
I MADE HER THAT WAY.
HOW DO YOU MEAN?
BEFORE I LEFT FOR EARTH, I THREW THE GREATEST PARTY THE GODS HAD SEEN IN A MILLENNIUM.
I SENT THE AMAZONS TO THE FARTHEST REACHES OF TIME AND SPACE TO RETRIEVE THE BEST FOOD AND WINE THAT COULD EVER BE TASTED.
"I REMEMBER THAT NIGHT, MY QUEEN."
"A NIGHT TO REMEMBER. BUT NOT FOR THE GODS, WHO DRANK SO HEAVILY THEY PLUNGED INTO A DEEP SLUMBER.
"AND IN THE DARK, I CUT INTO THEIR PALMS AND TOOK A PORTION OF EACH ONE'S BLOOD."
DRIP
EVEN--
YES. EVEN ZEUS.
NOT A SINGLE GOD SLEPT WITHOUT THEIR PALM TOUCHING MY BLADE.

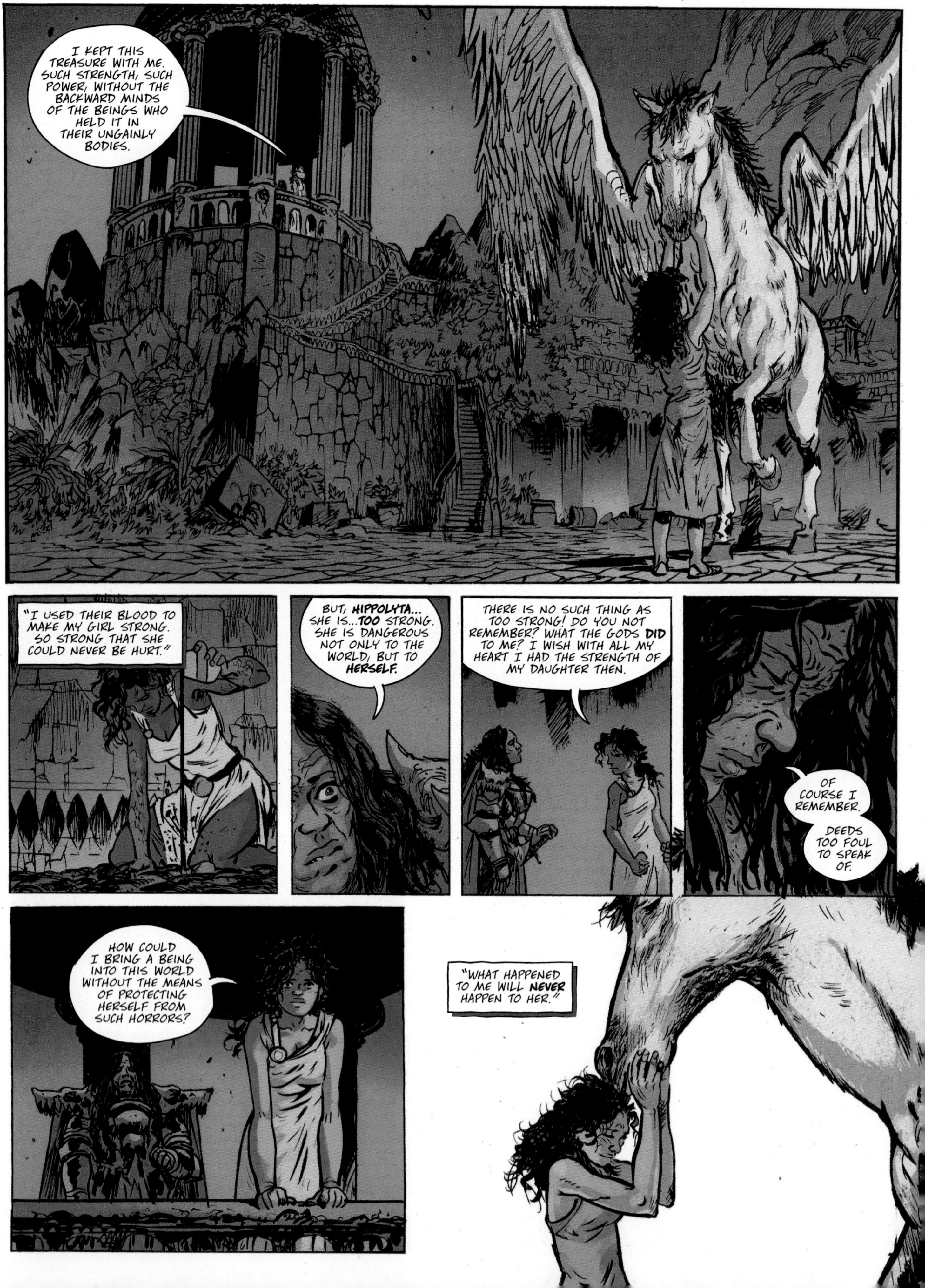
I KEPT THIS TREASURE WITH ME. SUCH STRENGTH, SUCH POWER, WITHOUT THE BACKWARD MINDS OF THE BEINGS WHO HELD IT IN THEIR UNGAINLY BODIES.
"I USED THEIR BLOOD TO MAKE MY GIRL STRONG. SO STRONG THAT SHE COULD NEVER BE HURT."
BUT, **HIPPOLYTA**... SHE IS... **TOO** STRONG. SHE IS DANGEROUS NOT ONLY TO THE WORLD, BUT TO **HERSELF**.
THERE IS NO SUCH THING AS TOO STRONG! DO YOU NOT REMEMBER? WHAT THE GODS **DID** TO ME? I WISH WITH ALL MY HEART I HAD THE STRENGTH OF MY DAUGHTER THEN.
OF COURSE I REMEMBER.
DEEDS TOO FOUL TO SPEAK OF.
HOW COULD I BRING A BEING INTO THIS WORLD WITHOUT THE MEANS OF PROTECTING HERSELF FROM SUCH HORRORS?
"WHAT HAPPENED TO ME WILL **NEVER** HAPPEN TO HER."

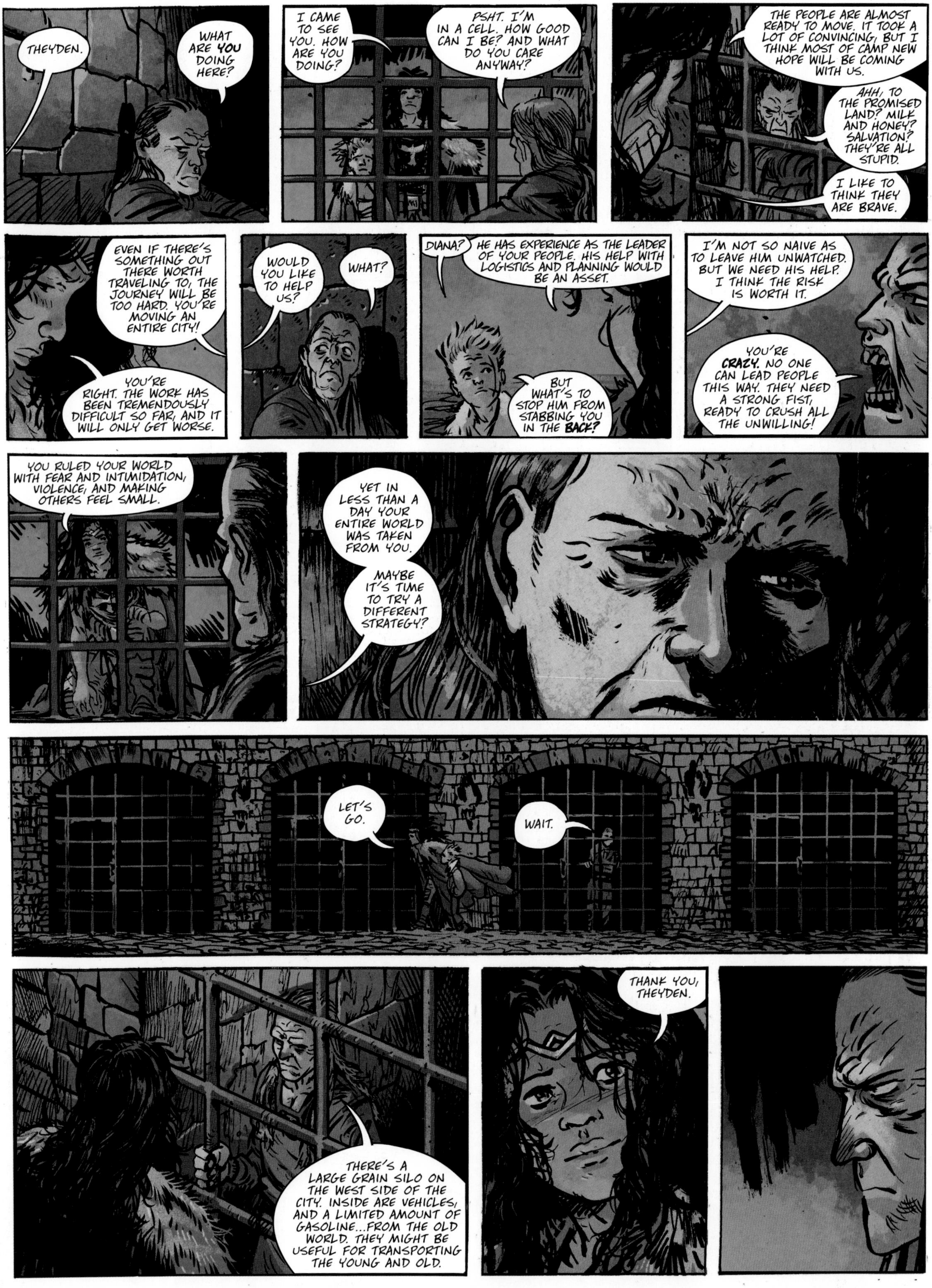
THEYDEN.
WHAT ARE **YOU** DOING HERE?
I CAME TO SEE YOU. HOW ARE YOU DOING?
PSHT. I'M IN A CELL. HOW GOOD CAN I BE? AND WHAT DO YOU CARE ANYWAY?
THE PEOPLE ARE ALMOST READY TO MOVE. IT TOOK A LOT OF CONVINCING, BUT I THINK MOST OF CAMP NEW HOPE WILL BE COMING WITH US.
AHH, TO THE PROMISED LAND? MILK AND HONEY? SALVATION? THEY'RE ALL STUPID.
I LIKE TO THINK THEY ARE BRAVE.
EVEN IF THERE'S SOMETHING OUT THERE WORTH TRAVELING TO, THE JOURNEY WILL BE TOO HARD. YOU'RE MOVING AN ENTIRE CITY!
YOU'RE RIGHT. THE WORK HAS BEEN TREMENDOUSLY DIFFICULT SO FAR, AND IT WILL ONLY GET WORSE.
WOULD YOU LIKE TO HELP US?
WHAT?
DIANA?
HE HAS EXPERIENCE AS THE LEADER OF YOUR PEOPLE. HIS HELP WITH LOGISTICS AND PLANNING WOULD BE AN ASSET.
BUT WHAT'S TO STOP HIM FROM STABBING YOU IN THE **BACK?**
I'M NOT SO NAIVE AS TO LEAVE HIM UNWATCHED. BUT WE NEED HIS HELP. I THINK THE RISK IS WORTH IT.
YOU'RE **CRAZY.** NO ONE CAN LEAD PEOPLE THIS WAY. THEY NEED A STRONG FIST, READY TO CRUSH ALL THE UNWILLING!
YOU RULED YOUR WORLD WITH FEAR AND INTIMIDATION, VIOLENCE, AND MAKING OTHERS FEEL SMALL.
YET IN LESS THAN A DAY YOUR ENTIRE WORLD WAS TAKEN FROM YOU.
MAYBE IT'S TIME TO TRY A DIFFERENT STRATEGY?
LET'S GO.
WAIT.
THERE'S A LARGE GRAIN SILO ON THE WEST SIDE OF THE CITY. INSIDE ARE VEHICLES, AND A LIMITED AMOUNT OF GASOLINE...FROM THE OLD WORLD. THEY MIGHT BE USEFUL FOR TRANSPORTING THE YOUNG AND OLD.
THANK YOU, THEYDEN.

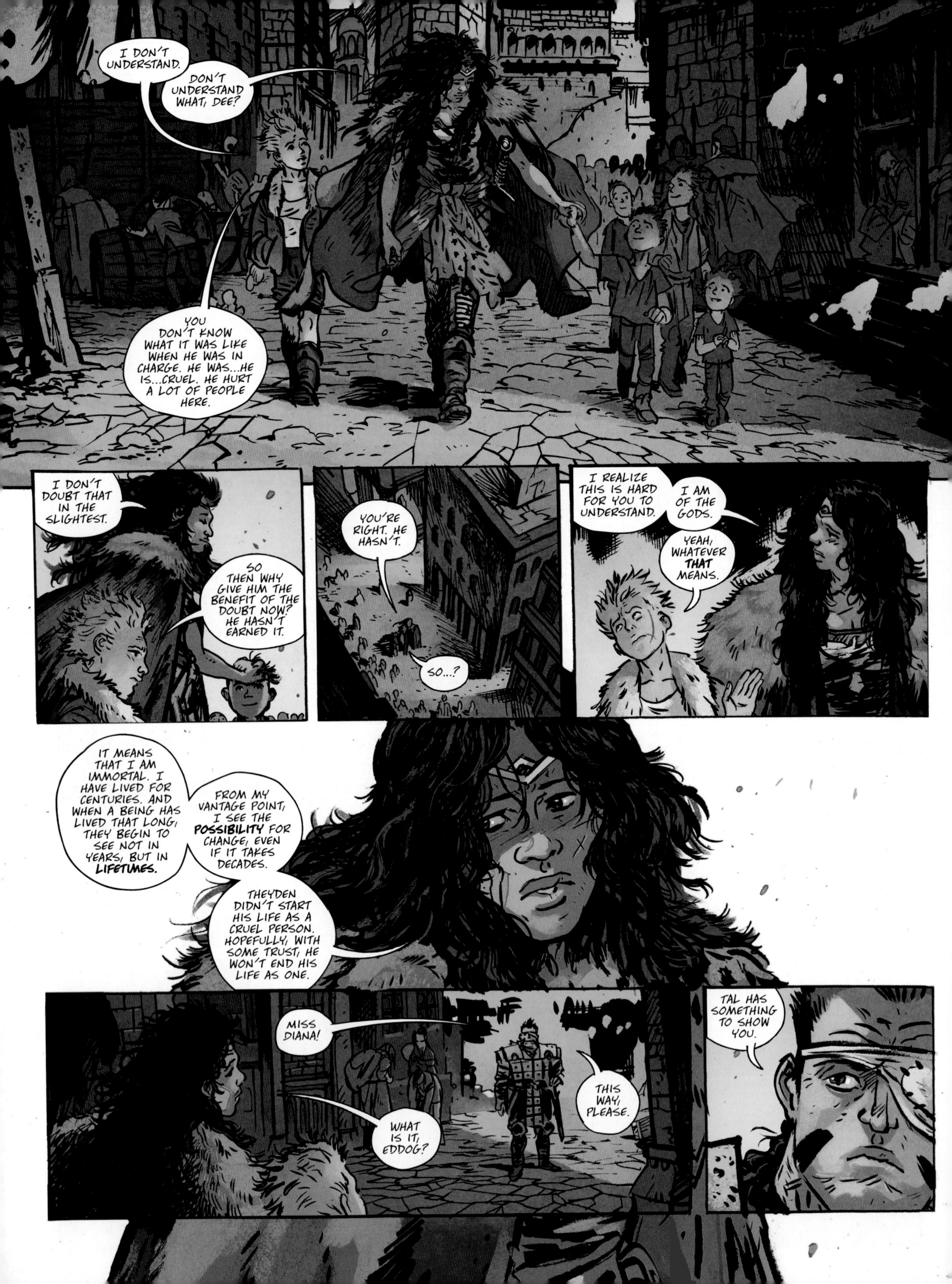
I DON'T UNDERSTAND.
DON'T UNDERSTAND WHAT, DEE?
YOU DON'T KNOW WHAT IT WAS LIKE WHEN HE WAS IN CHARGE. HE WAS...HE IS...CRUEL. HE HURT A LOT OF PEOPLE HERE.
I DON'T DOUBT THAT IN THE SLIGHTEST.
SO THEN WHY GIVE HIM THE BENEFIT OF THE DOUBT NOW? HE HASN'T EARNED IT.
YOU'RE RIGHT. HE HASN'T.
SO...?
I REALIZE THIS IS HARD FOR YOU TO UNDERSTAND.
I AM OF THE GODS.
YEAH, WHATEVER **THAT** MEANS.
IT MEANS THAT I AM IMMORTAL. I HAVE LIVED FOR CENTURIES. AND WHEN A BEING HAS LIVED THAT LONG, THEY BEGIN TO SEE NOT IN YEARS, BUT IN **LIFETIMES.**
FROM MY VANTAGE POINT, I SEE THE **POSSIBILITY** FOR CHANGE, EVEN IF IT TAKES DECADES.
THEYDEN DIDN'T START HIS LIFE AS A CRUEL PERSON. HOPEFULLY, WITH SOME TRUST, HE WON'T END HIS LIFE AS ONE.
MISS DIANA!
WHAT IS IT, EDDOG?
THIS WAY, PLEASE.
TAL HAS SOMETHING TO SHOW YOU.

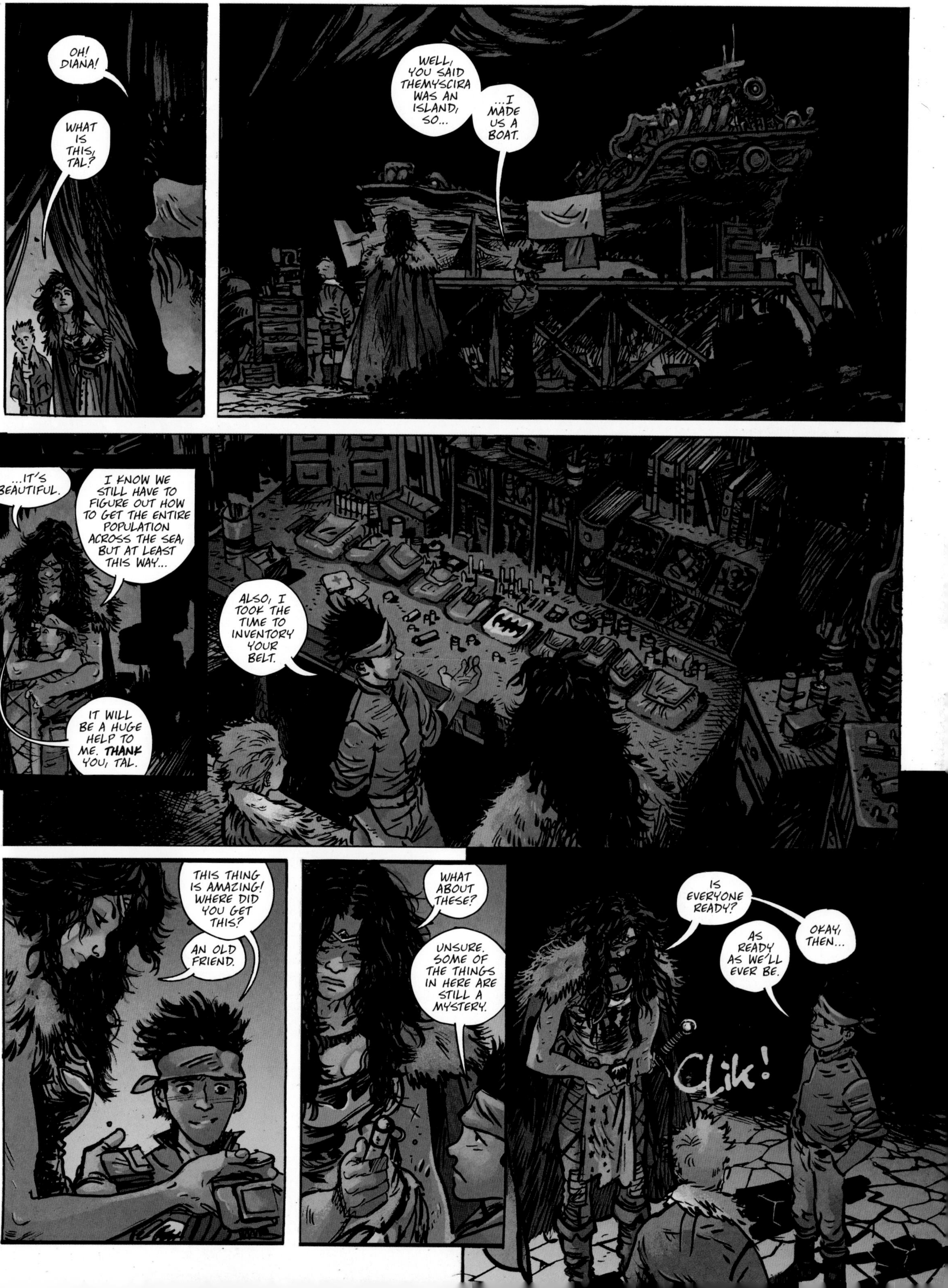
OH! DIANA!
WHAT IS THIS, TAL?
WELL, YOU SAID THEMYSCIRA WAS AN ISLAND, SO...
...I MADE US A BOAT.
...IT'S BEAUTIFUL.
I KNOW WE STILL HAVE TO FIGURE OUT HOW TO GET THE ENTIRE POPULATION ACROSS THE SEA, BUT AT LEAST THIS WAY...
ALSO, I TOOK THE TIME TO INVENTORY YOUR BELT.
IT WILL BE A HUGE HELP TO ME. **THANK** YOU, TAL.
THIS THING IS AMAZING! WHERE DID YOU GET THIS?
AN OLD FRIEND.
WHAT ABOUT THESE?
UNSURE. SOME OF THE THINGS IN HERE ARE STILL A MYSTERY.
IS EVERYONE READY?
AS READY AS WE'LL EVER BE.
OKAY, THEN...
CLIK!

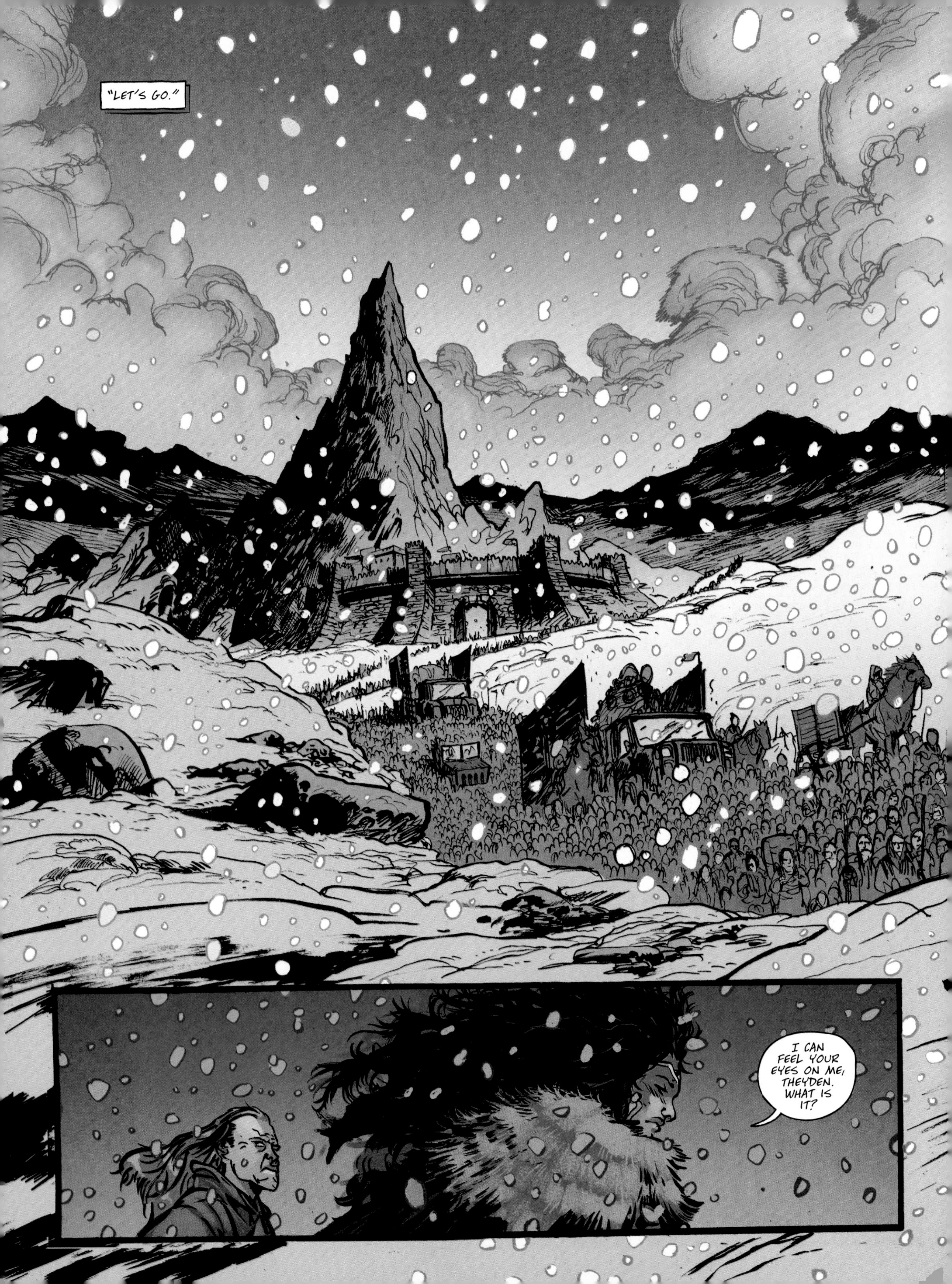
"LET'S GO."
I CAN FEEL YOUR EYES ON ME, THEYDEN. WHAT IS IT?

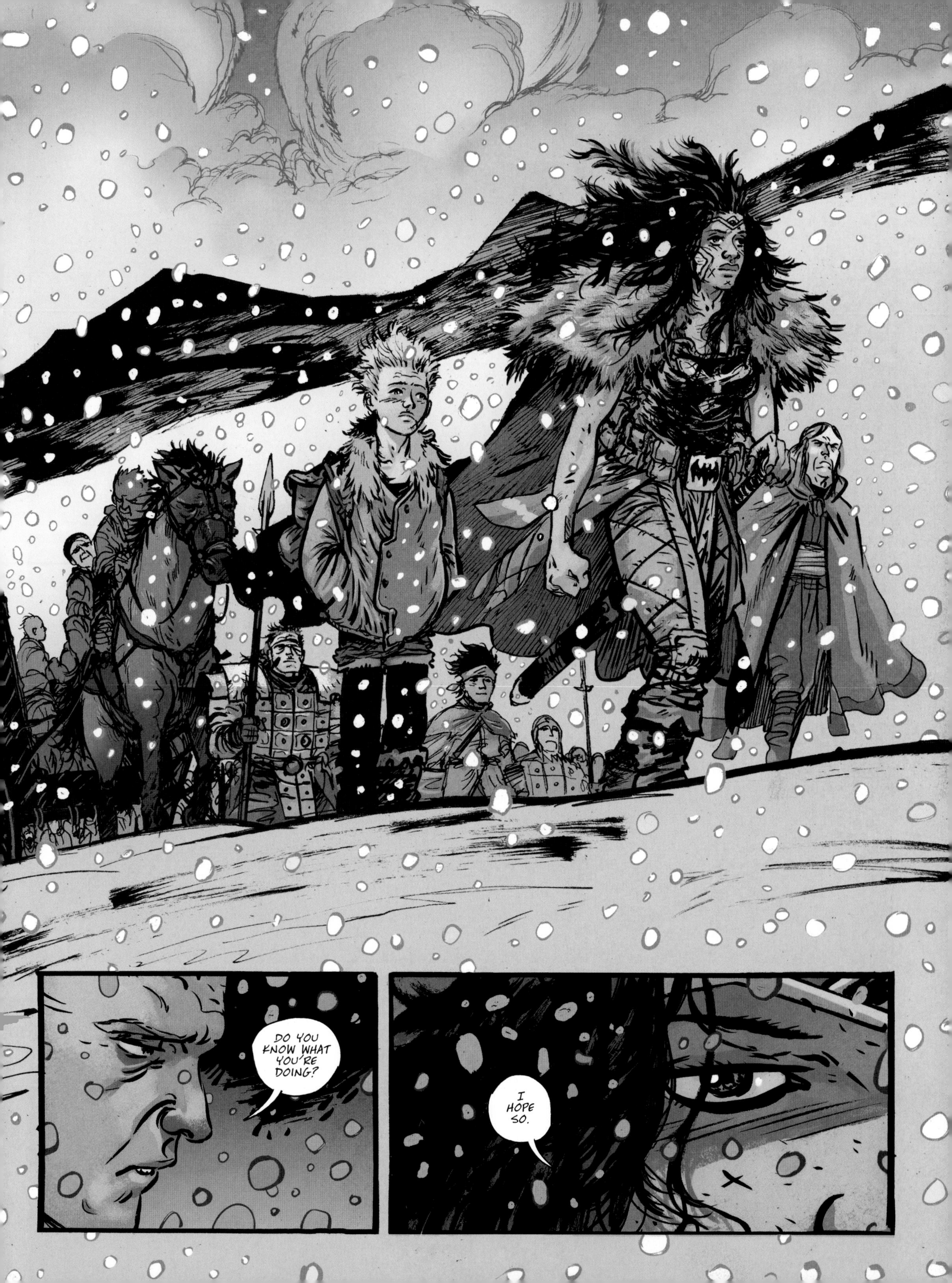
DO YOU KNOW WHAT YOU'RE DOING?
I HOPE SO.

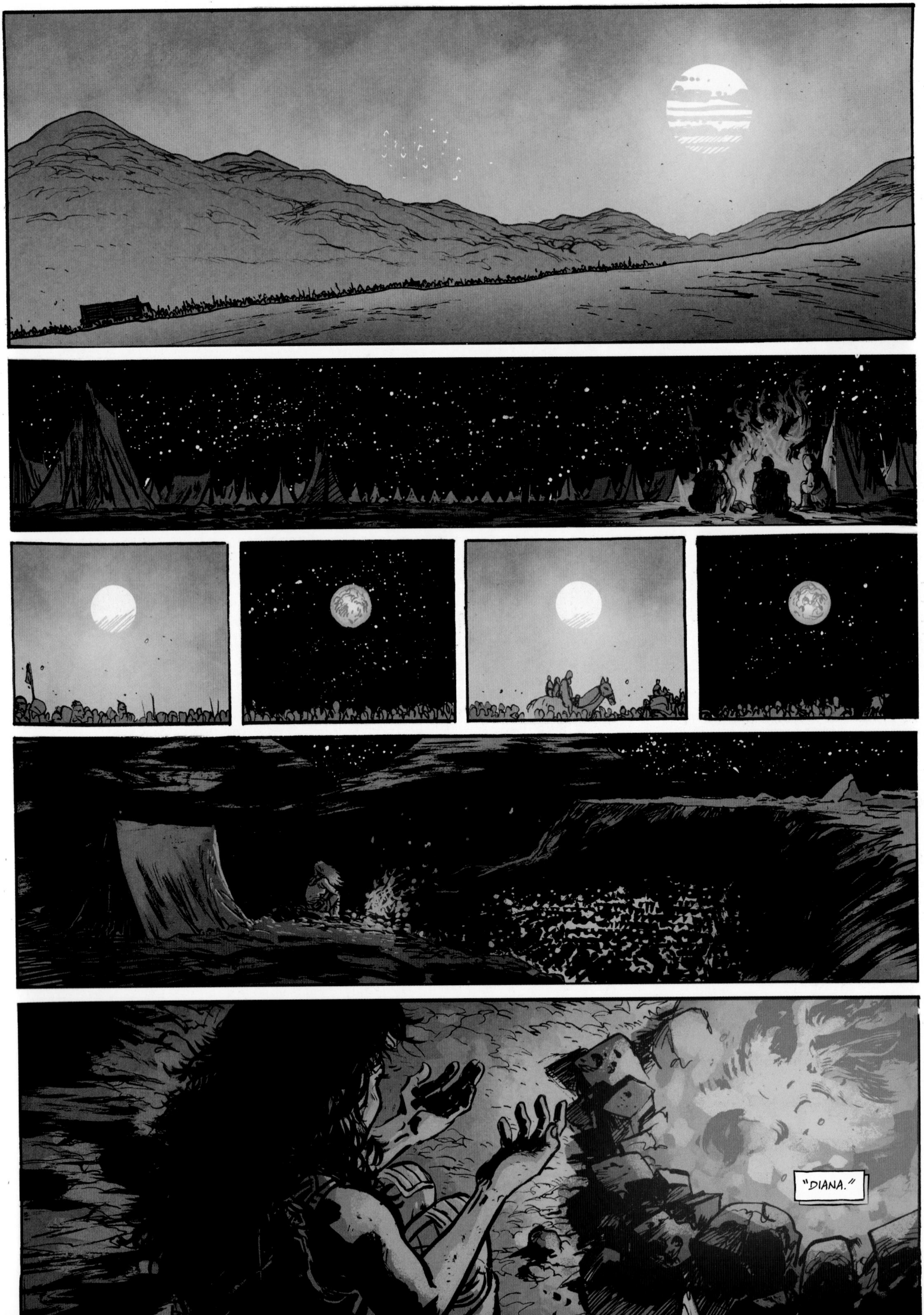
"DIANA."

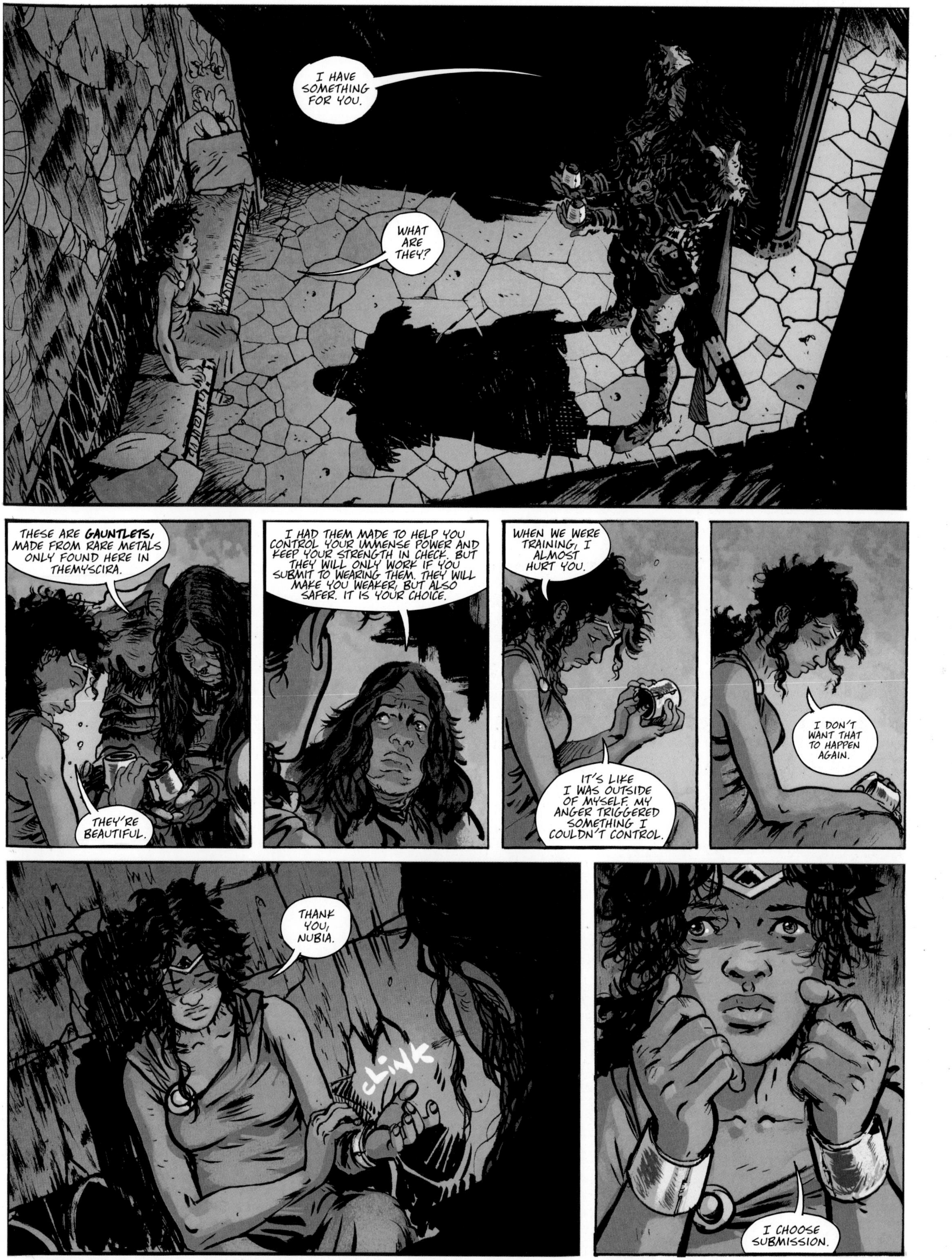
I HAVE SOMETHING FOR YOU.
WHAT ARE THEY?
THESE ARE GAUNTLETS, MADE FROM RARE METALS ONLY FOUND HERE IN THEMYSCIRA.
THEY'RE BEAUTIFUL.
I HAD THEM MADE TO HELP YOU CONTROL YOUR IMMENSE POWER AND KEEP YOUR STRENGTH IN CHECK. BUT THEY WILL ONLY WORK IF YOU SUBMIT TO WEARING THEM. THEY WILL MAKE YOU WEAKER, BUT ALSO SAFER. IT IS YOUR CHOICE.
WHEN WE WERE TRAINING, I ALMOST HURT YOU.
IT'S LIKE I WAS OUTSIDE OF MYSELF. MY ANGER TRIGGERED SOMETHING I COULDN'T CONTROL.
I DON'T WANT THAT TO HAPPEN AGAIN.
THANK YOU, NUBIA.
CLINK
I CHOOSE SUBMISSION.

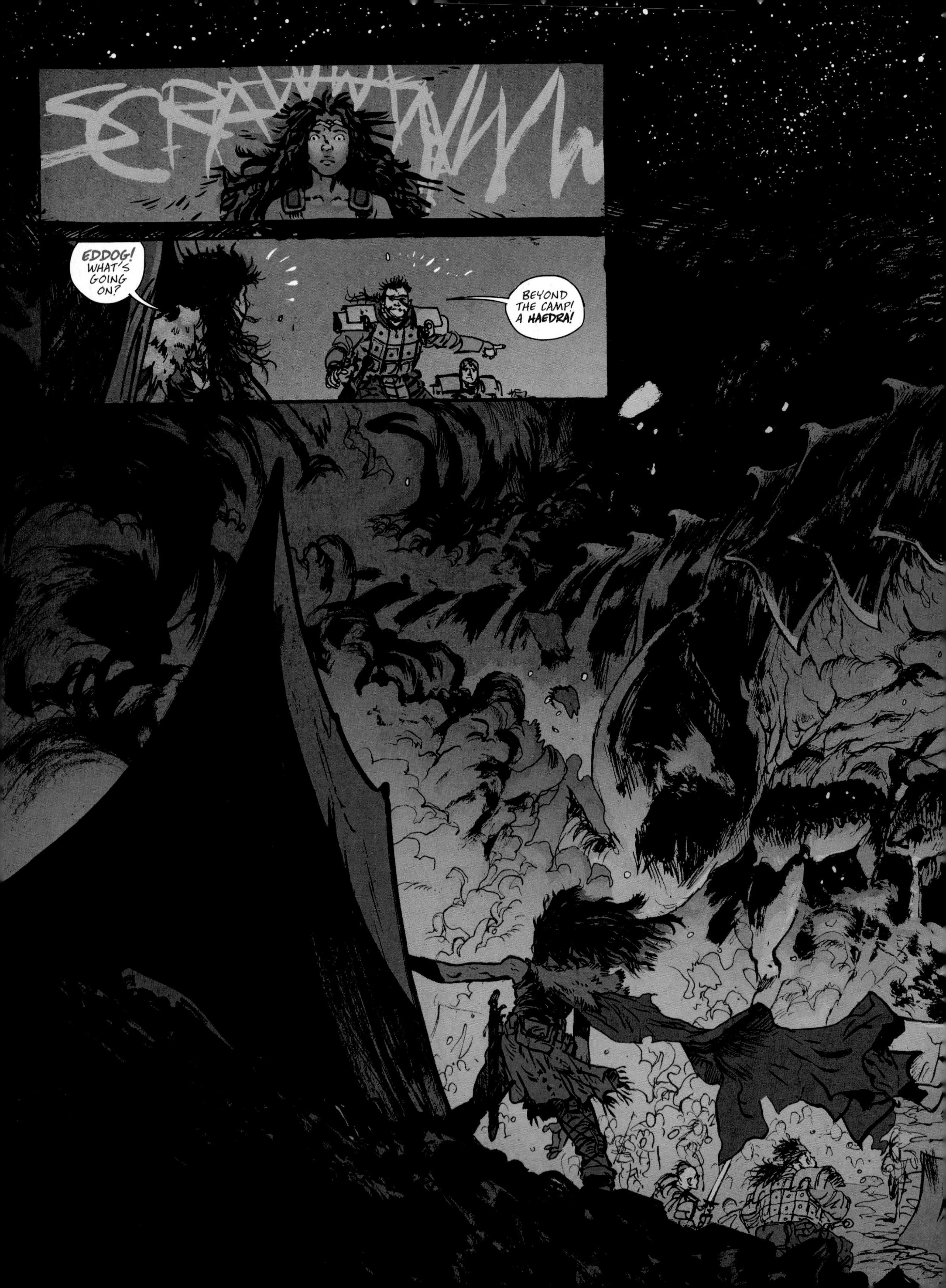
SCRAWWWW
EDDOG! WHAT'S GOING ON?
BEYOND THE CAMP! A HAEDRA!

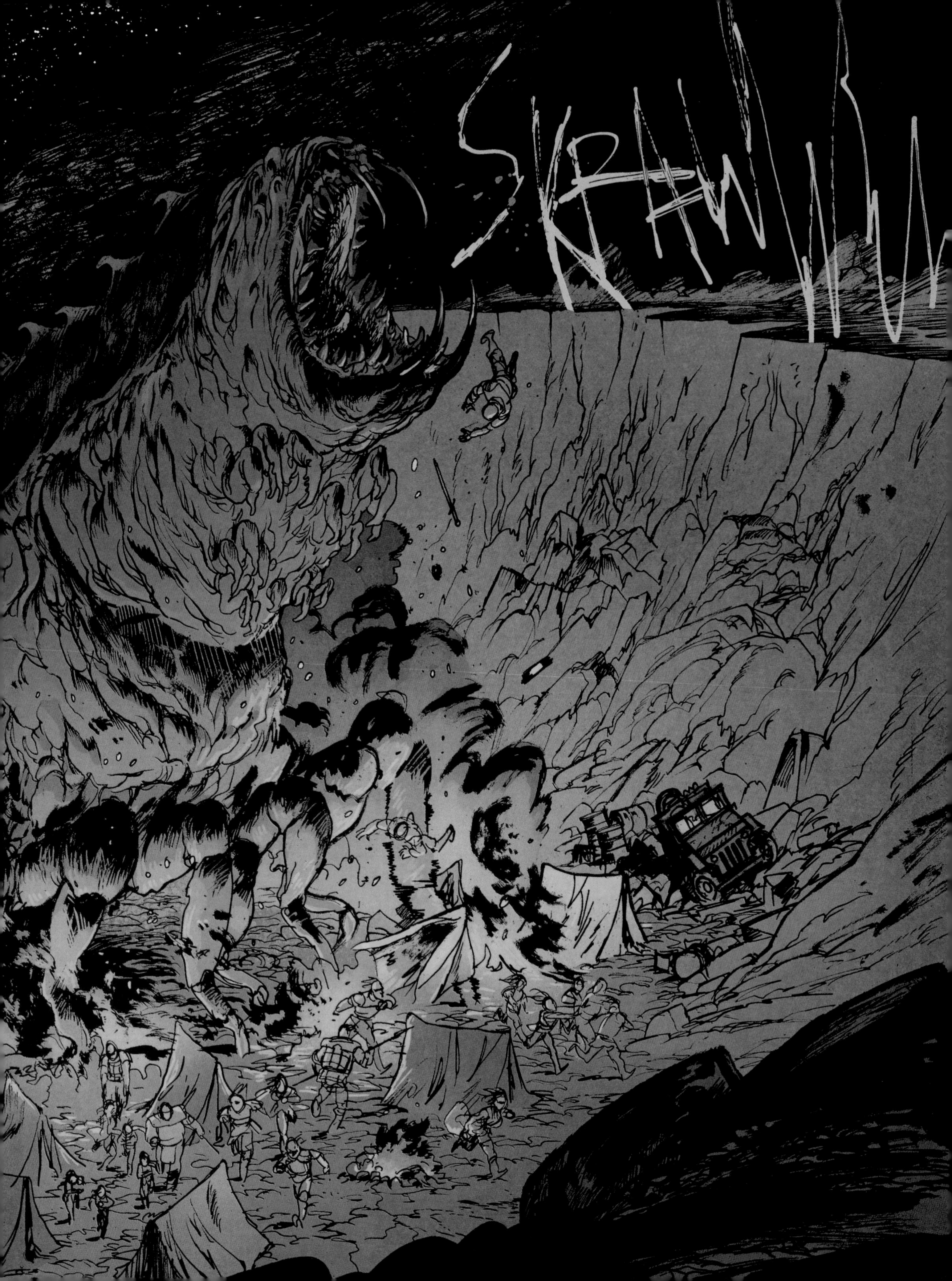
SKRAWWW

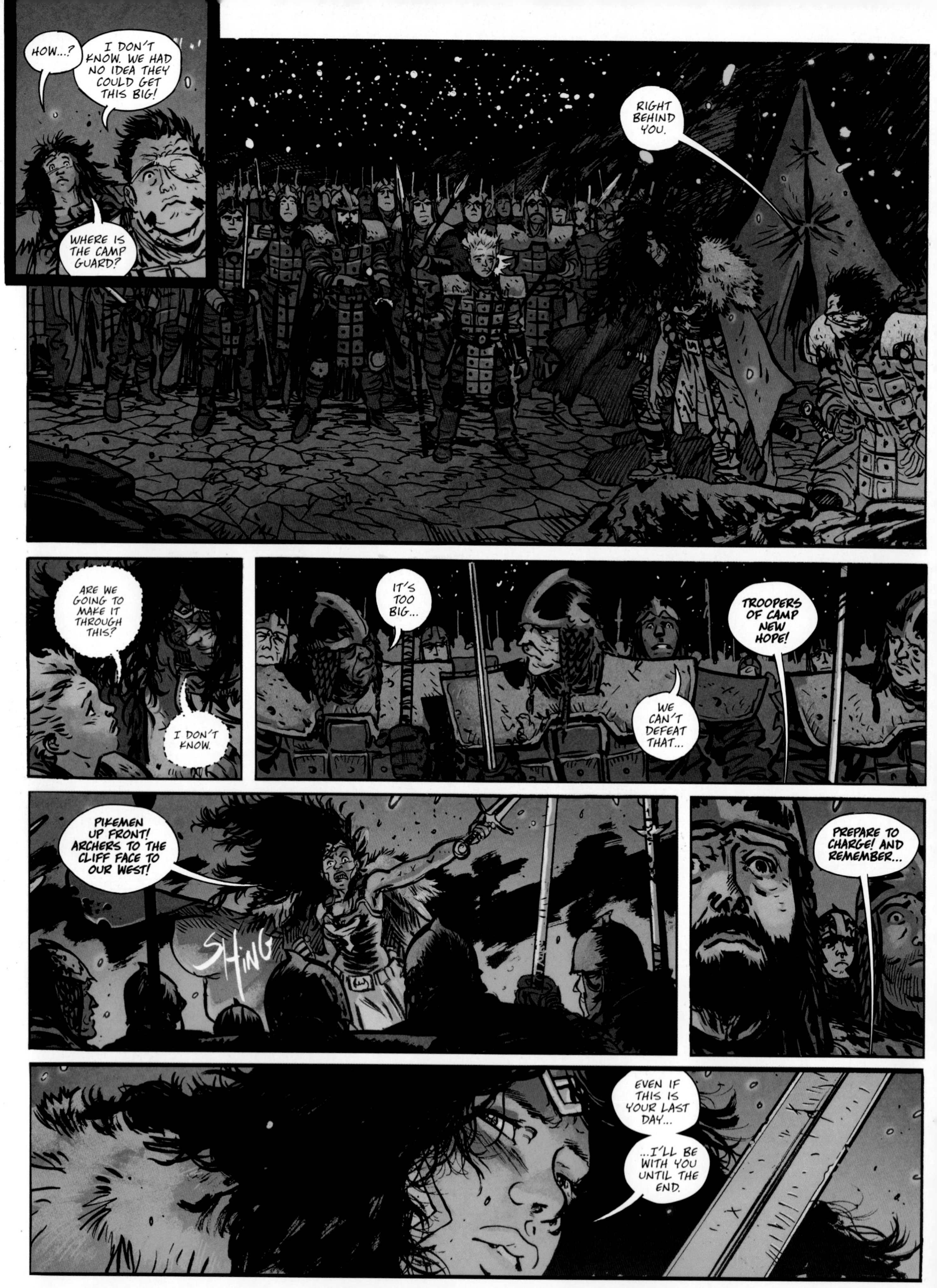
HOW...?
I DON'T KNOW. WE HAD NO IDEA THEY COULD GET THIS BIG!
WHERE IS THE CAMP GUARD?
RIGHT BEHIND YOU.
ARE WE GOING TO MAKE IT THROUGH THIS?
I DON'T KNOW.
IT'S TOO BIG...
WE CAN'T DEFEAT THAT...
TROOPERS OF CAMP NEW HOPE!
PIKEMEN UP FRONT! ARCHERS TO THE CLIFF FACE TO OUR WEST!
SHING
PREPARE TO CHARGE! AND REMEMBER...
EVEN IF THIS IS YOUR LAST DAY...
...I'LL BE WITH YOU UNTIL THE END.

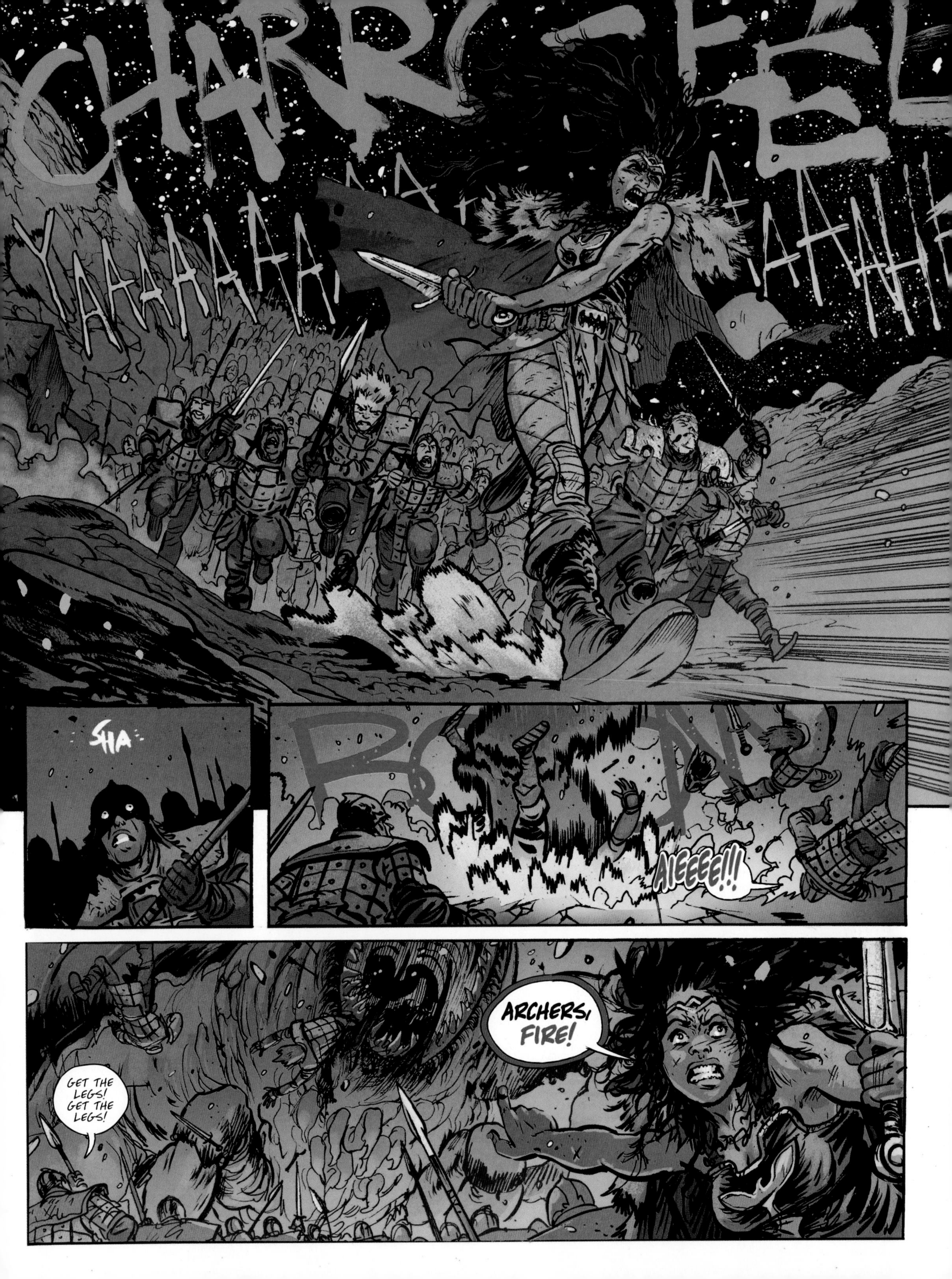

SHA
AIEEEE!!!
ARCHERS, FIRE!
GET THE LEGS! GET THE LEGS!

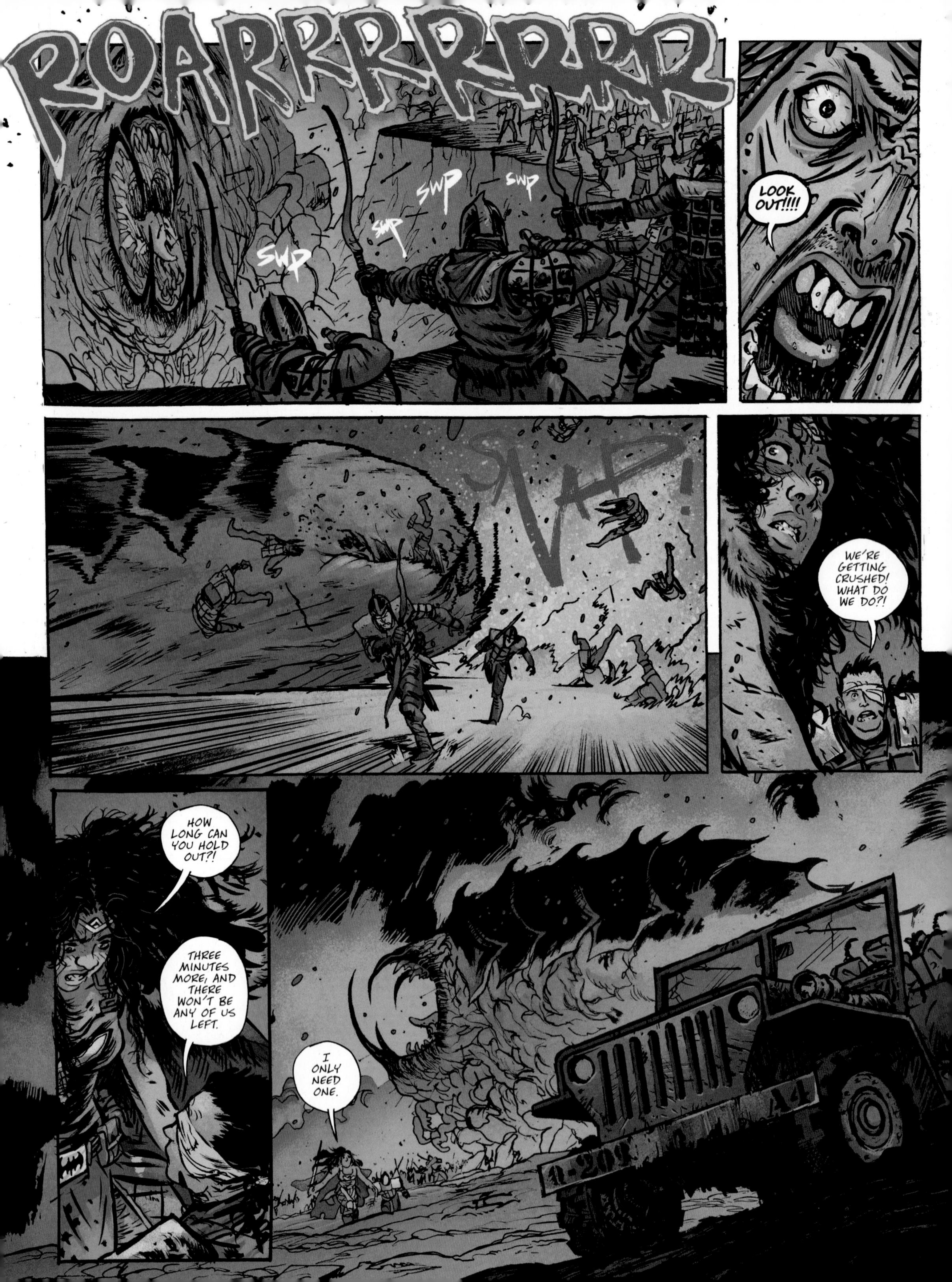
ROARRRRRRR
SWP
SWP
SWP
SWP
LOOK OUT!!!!
SWAP!
WE'RE GETTING CRUSHED! WHAT DO WE DO?!
HOW LONG CAN YOU HOLD OUT?!
THREE MINUTES MORE, AND THERE WON'T BE ANY OF US LEFT.
I ONLY NEED ONE.

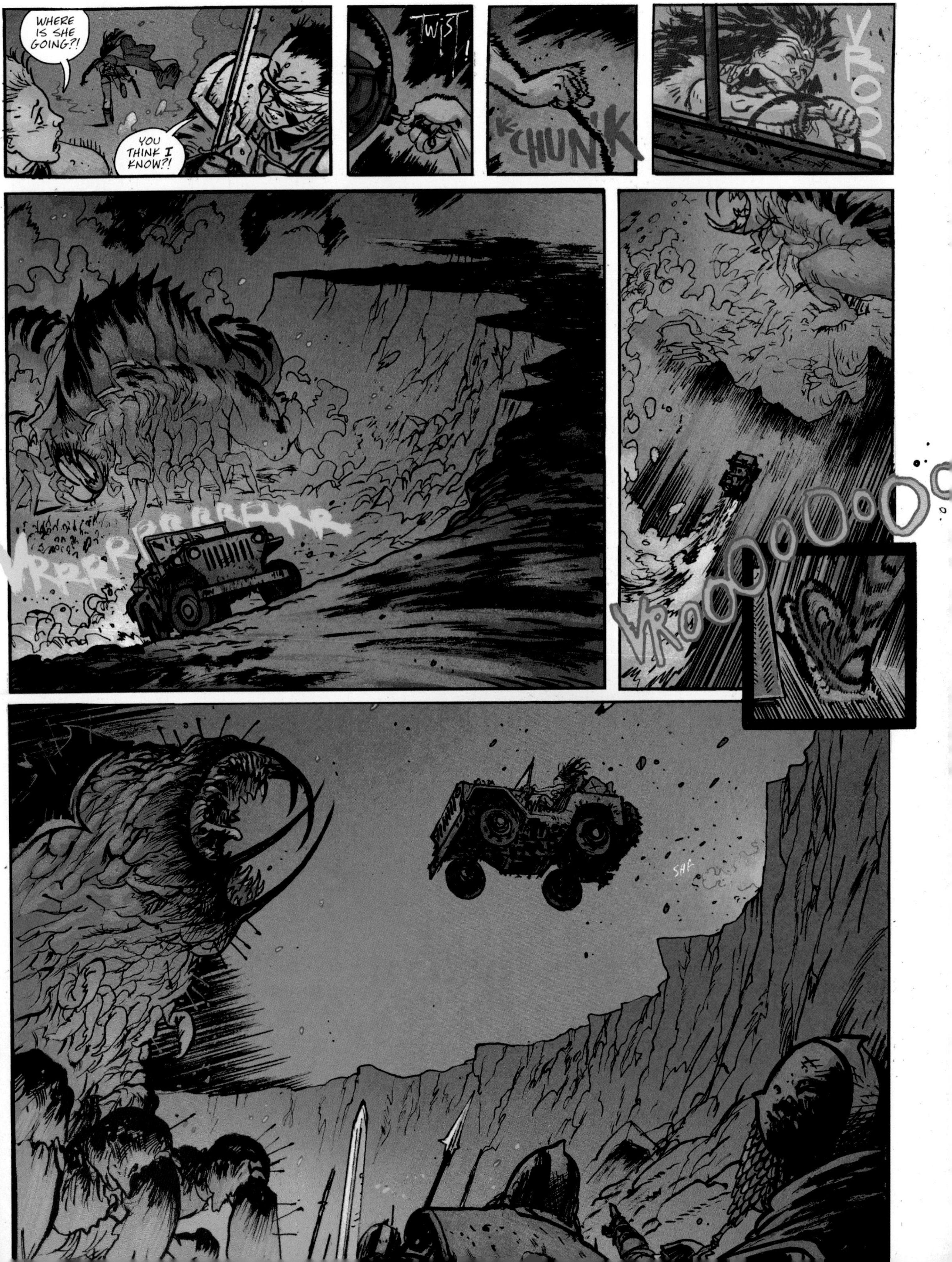

WHERE IS SHE GOING?!
YOU THINK I KNOW?!
TWIST
K-CHUNK
VROOO
VRRRRRRRRRRRR
VROOOOOOOOO
SHA

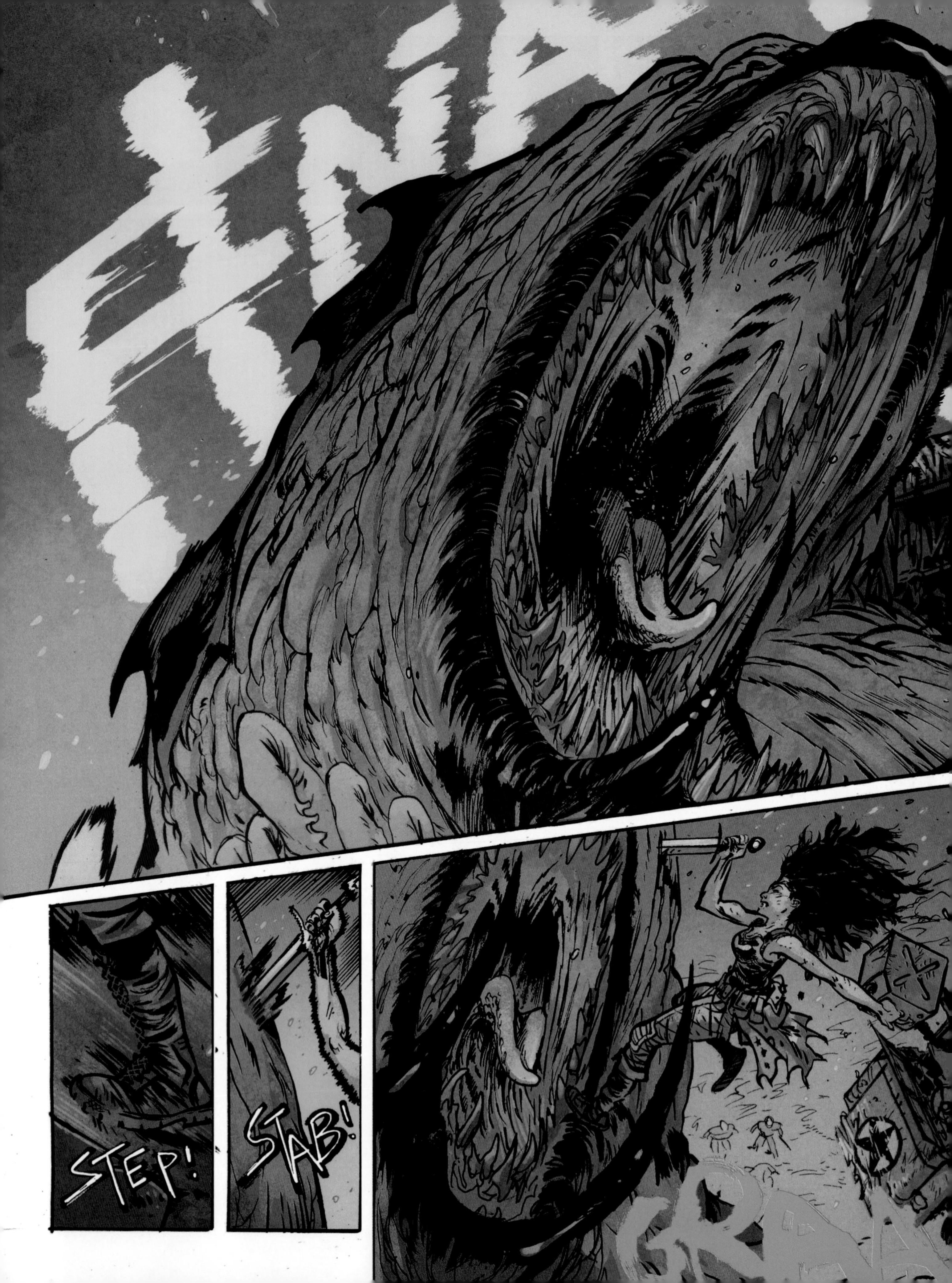
STEP!
STAB!

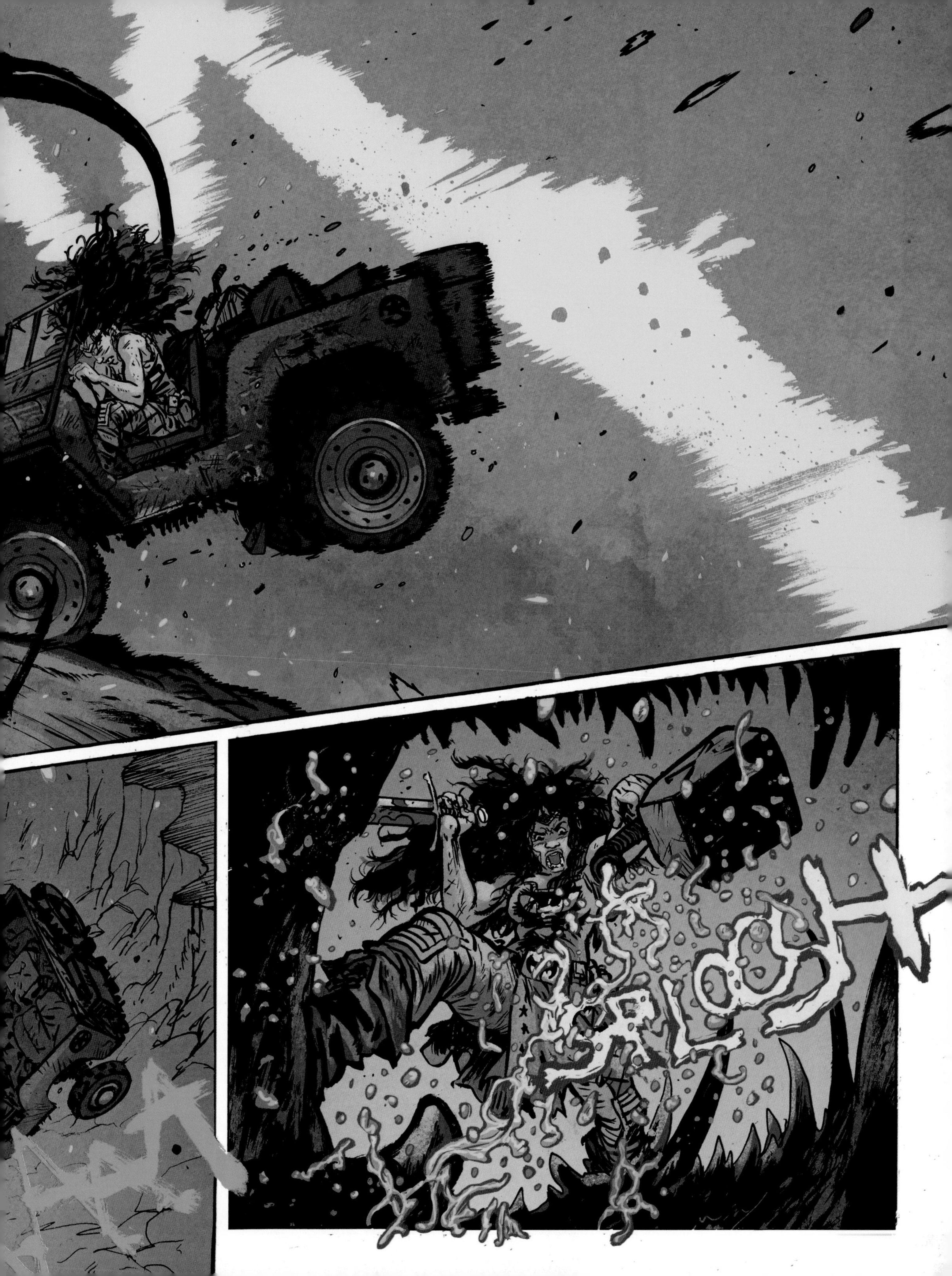

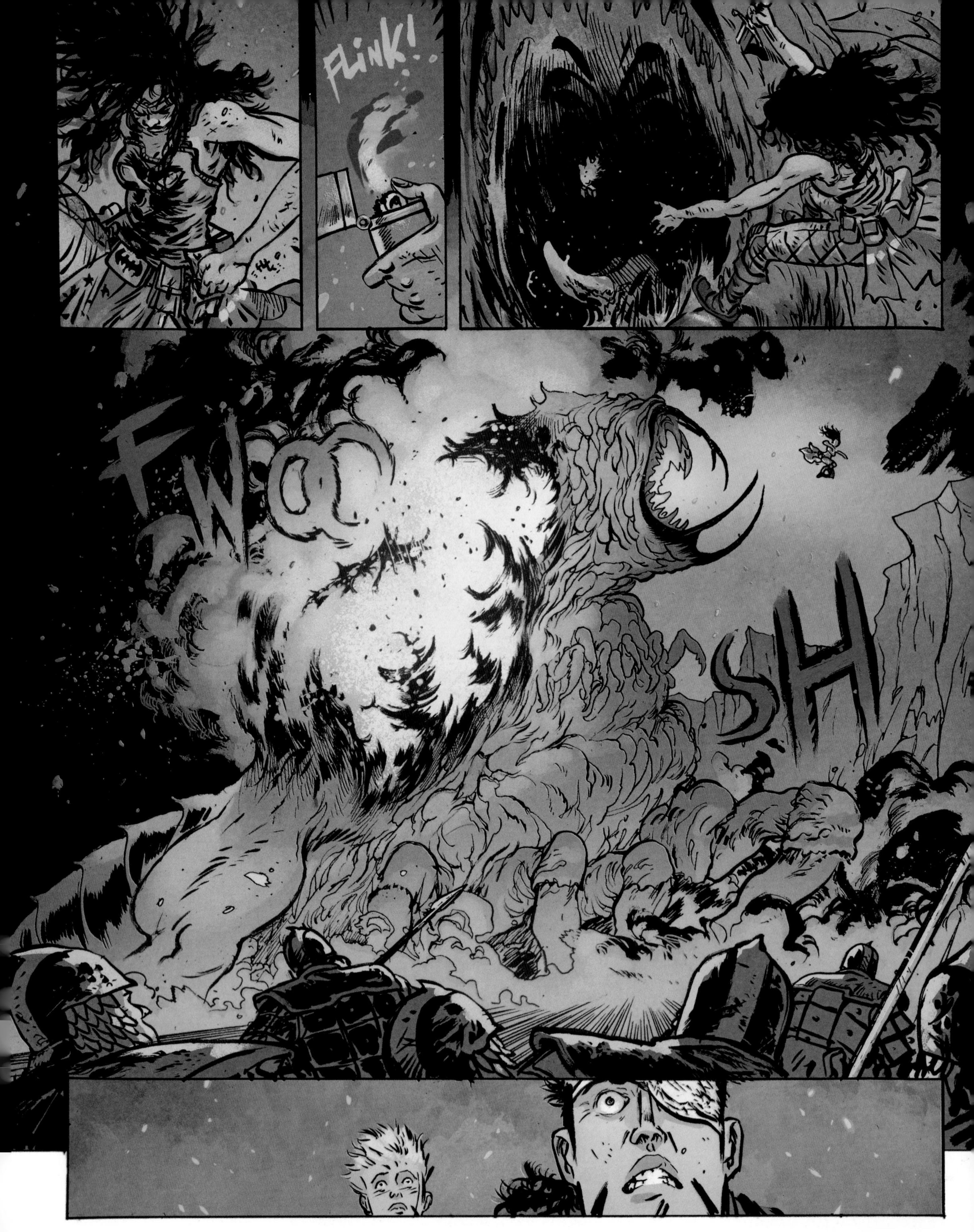
FLINK!
FWOOOSH

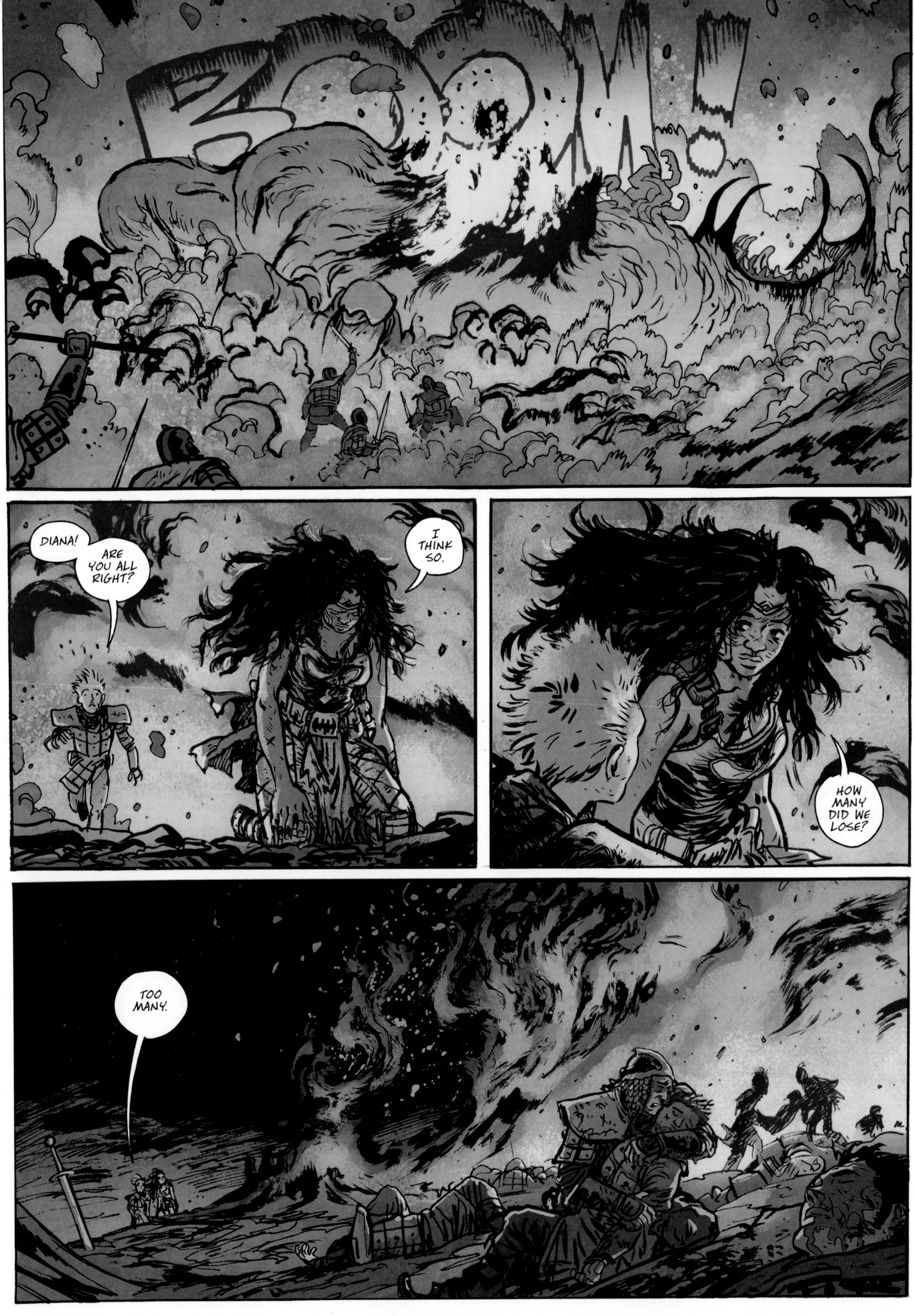
BOOM!
DIANA!
ARE YOU ALL RIGHT?
I THINK SO.
HOW MANY DID WE LOSE?
TOO MANY.

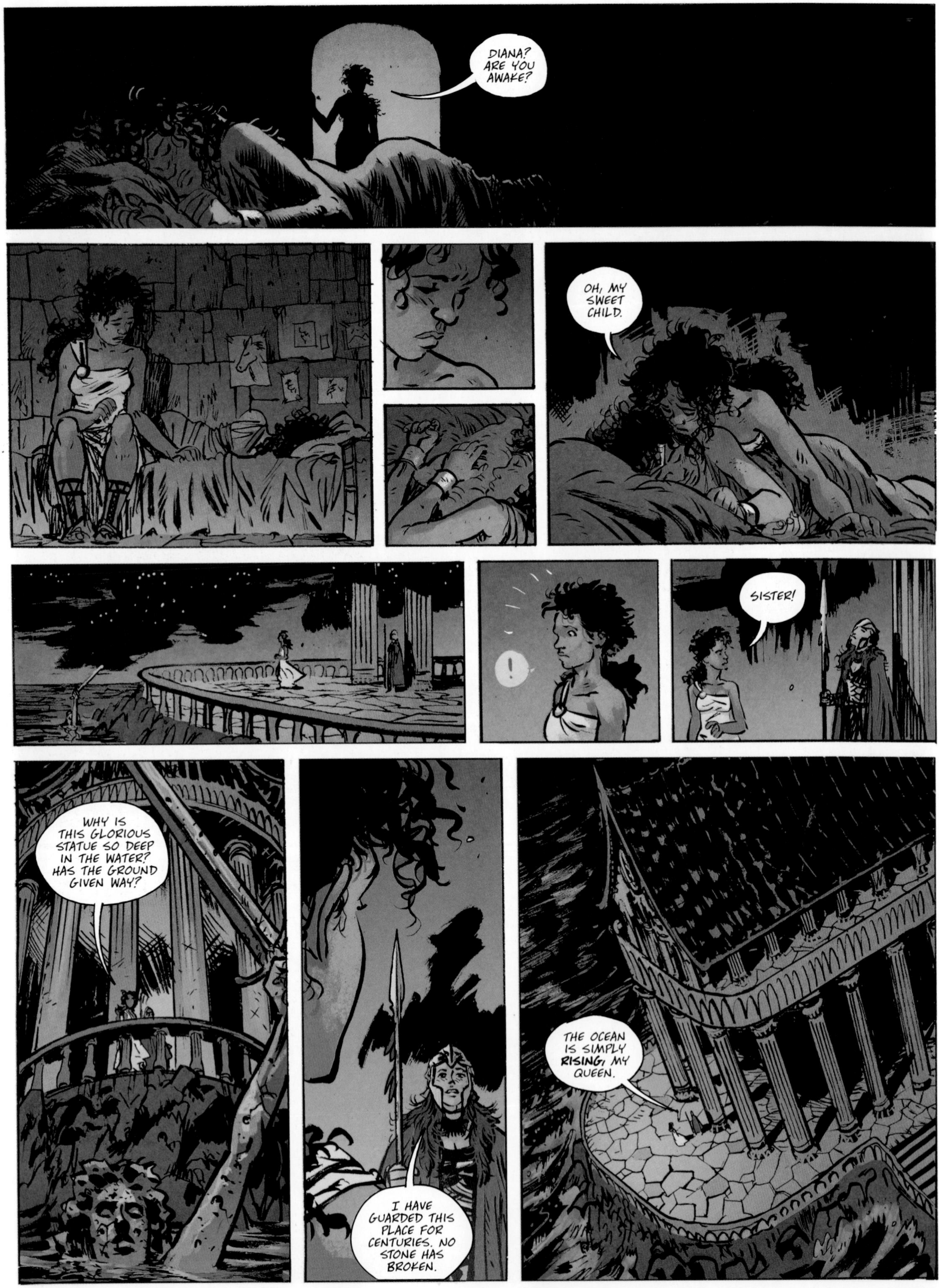
DIANA? ARE YOU AWAKE?
OH, MY SWEET CHILD.
!
SISTER!
WHY IS THIS GLORIOUS STATUE SO DEEP IN THE WATER? HAS THE GROUND GIVEN WAY?
I HAVE GUARDED THIS PLACE FOR CENTURIES. NO STONE HAS BROKEN.
THE OCEAN IS SIMPLY **RISING**, MY QUEEN.

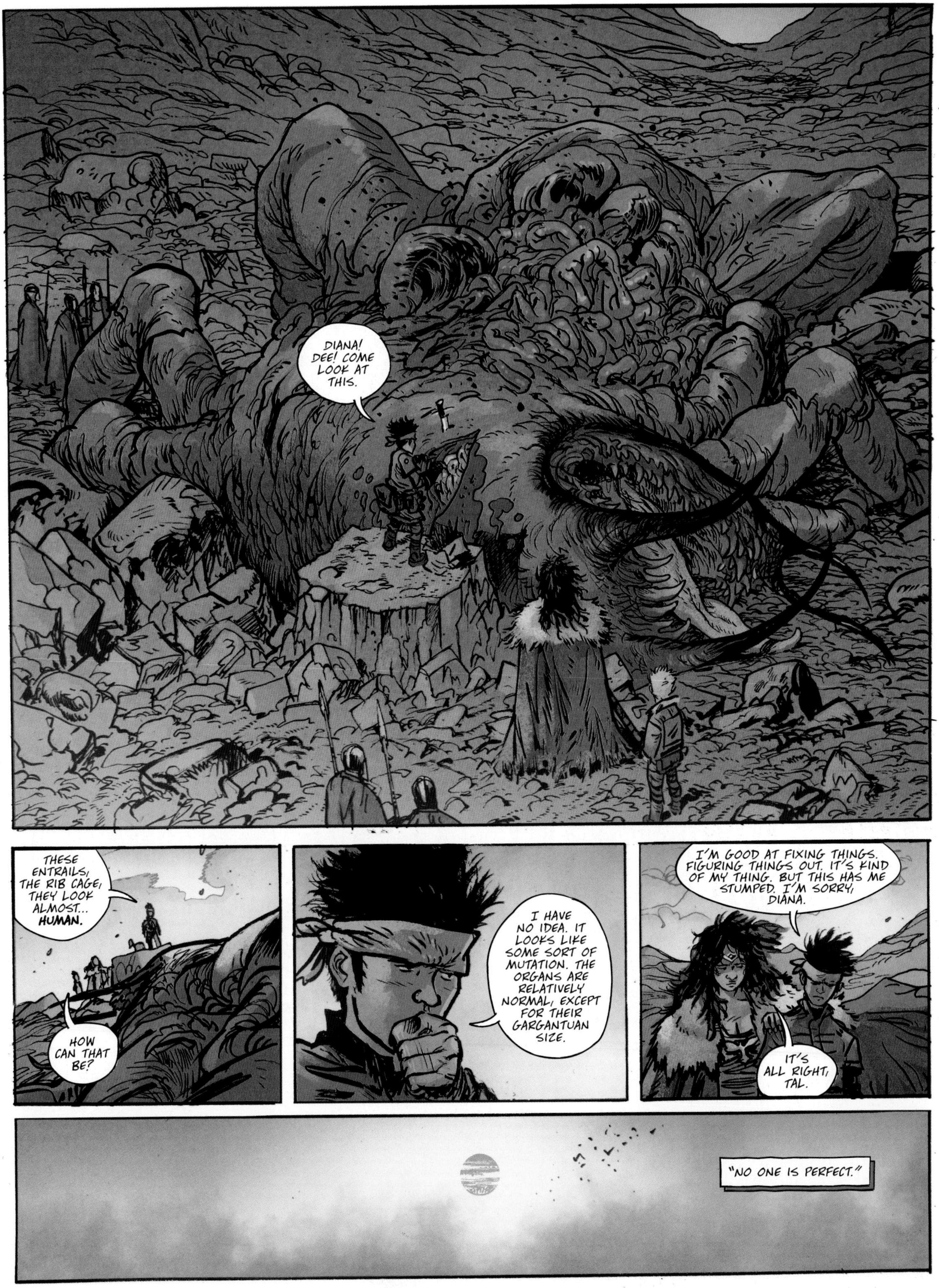

DIANA! DEE! COME LOOK AT THIS.
THESE ENTRAILS, THE RIB CAGE, THEY LOOK ALMOST... **HUMAN.**
HOW CAN THAT BE?
I HAVE NO IDEA. IT LOOKS LIKE SOME SORT OF MUTATION. THE ORGANS ARE RELATIVELY NORMAL, EXCEPT FOR THEIR GARGANTUAN SIZE.
I'M GOOD AT FIXING THINGS. FIGURING THINGS OUT. IT'S KIND OF MY THING. BUT THIS HAS ME STUMPED. I'M SORRY, DIANA.
IT'S ALL RIGHT, TAL.
"NO ONE IS PERFECT."

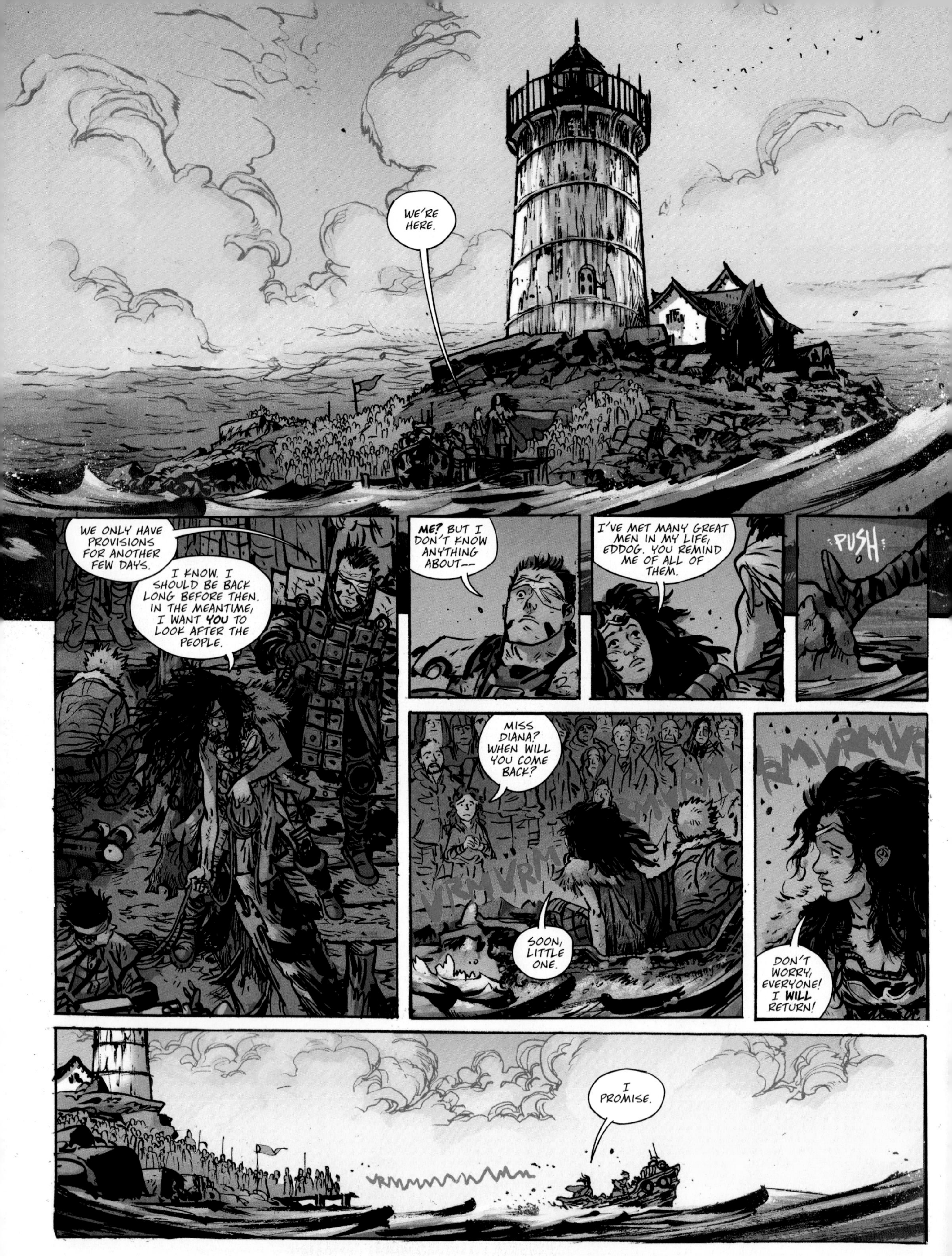
WE'RE HERE.
WE ONLY HAVE PROVISIONS FOR ANOTHER FEW DAYS.
I KNOW. I SHOULD BE BACK LONG BEFORE THEN. IN THE MEANTIME, I WANT **YOU** TO LOOK AFTER THE PEOPLE.
ME? BUT I DON'T KNOW ANYTHING ABOUT--
I'VE MET MANY GREAT MEN IN MY LIFE, EDDOG. YOU REMIND ME OF ALL OF THEM.
PUSH
MISS DIANA? WHEN WILL YOU COME BACK?
VRMVRM
SOON, LITTLE ONE.
VRMVRM
DON'T WORRY, EVERYONE! I **WILL** RETURN!
I PROMISE.
VRMMMMMMMMM

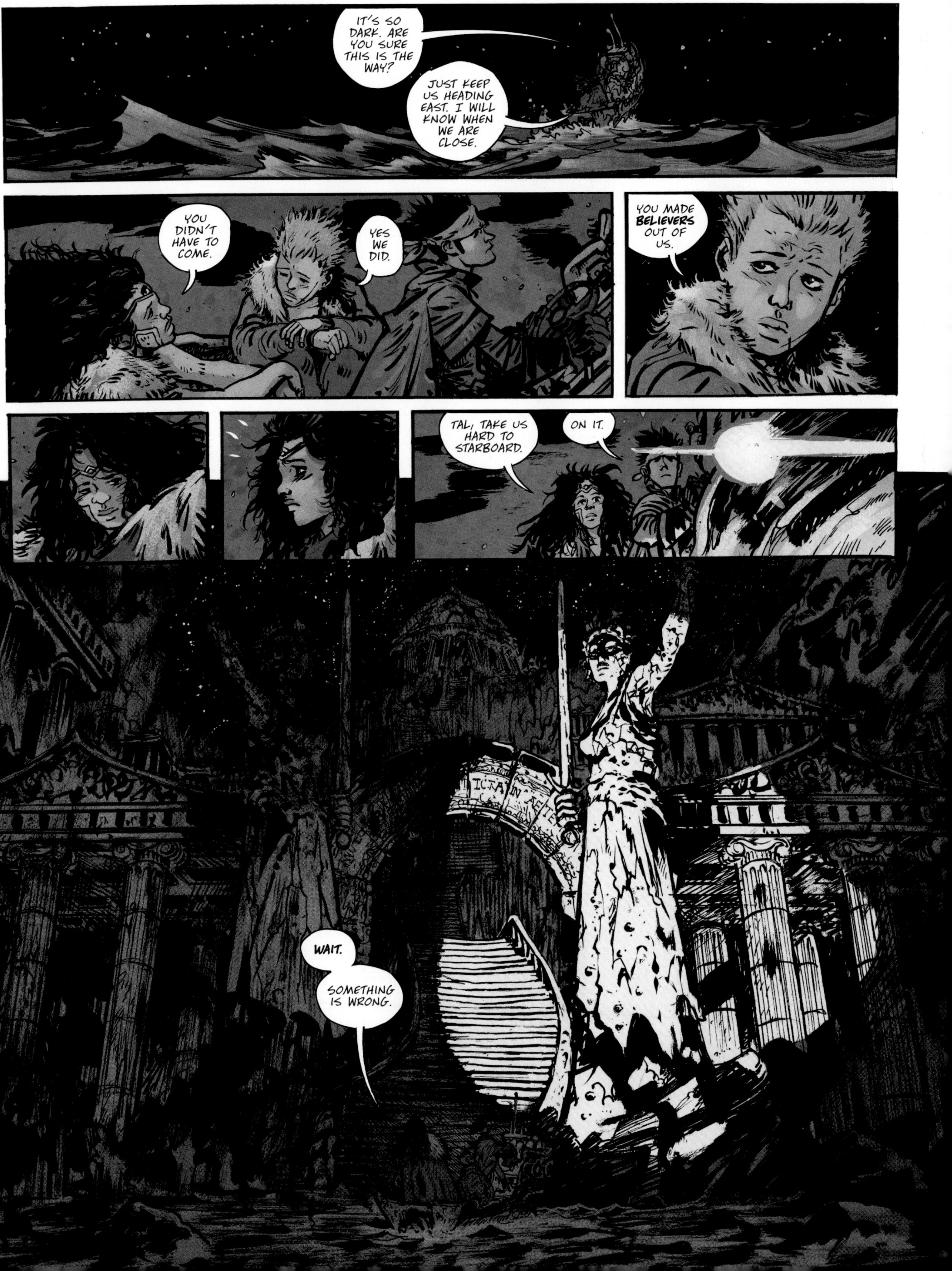
IT'S SO DARK. ARE YOU SURE THIS IS THE WAY?
JUST KEEP US HEADING EAST. I WILL KNOW WHEN WE ARE CLOSE.
YOU DIDN'T HAVE TO COME.
YES WE DID.
YOU MADE **BELIEVERS** OUT OF US.
TAL, TAKE US HARD TO STARBOARD.
ON IT.
WAIT.
SOMETHING IS WRONG.

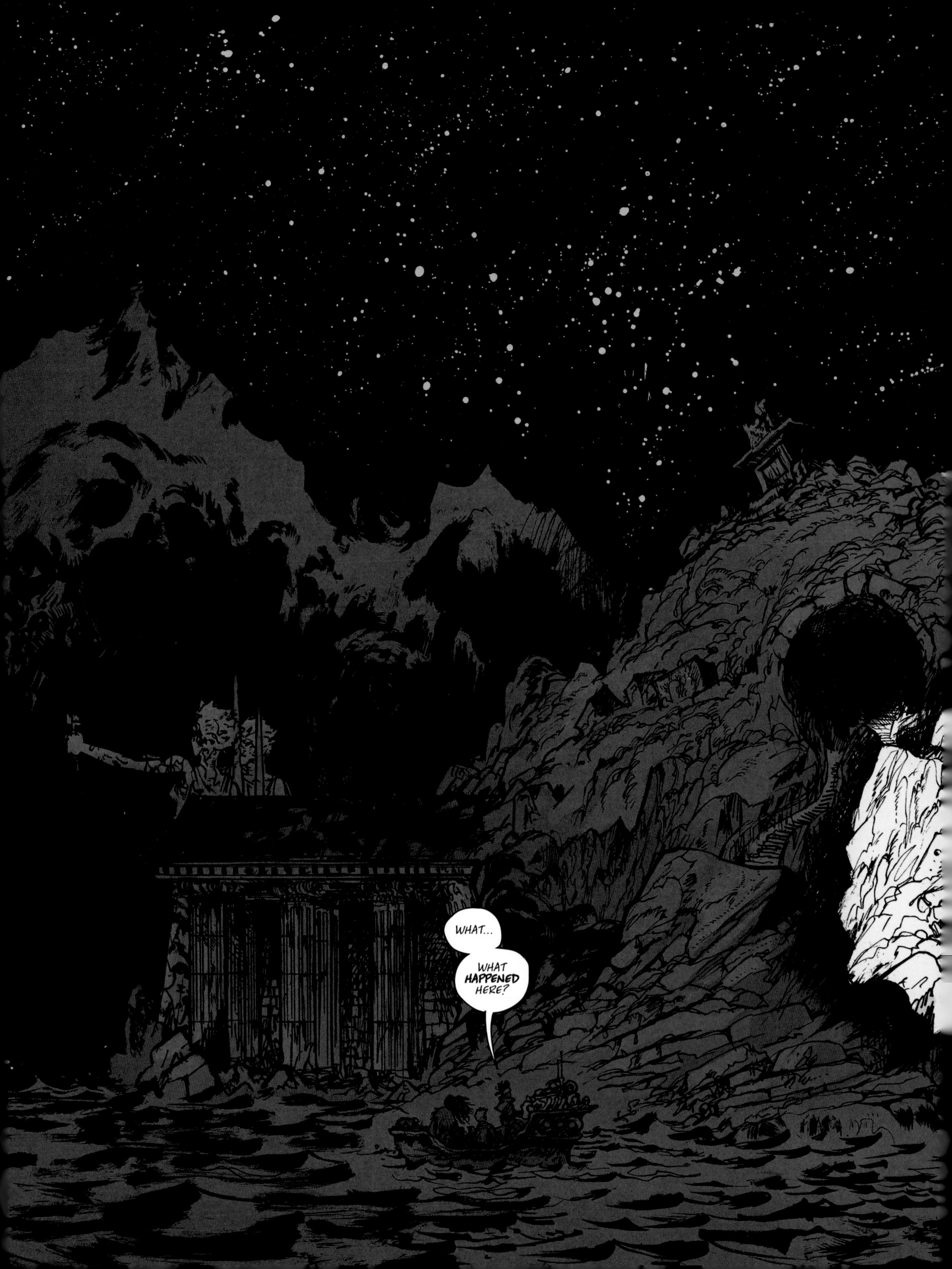
WHAT...
WHAT HAPPENED HERE?

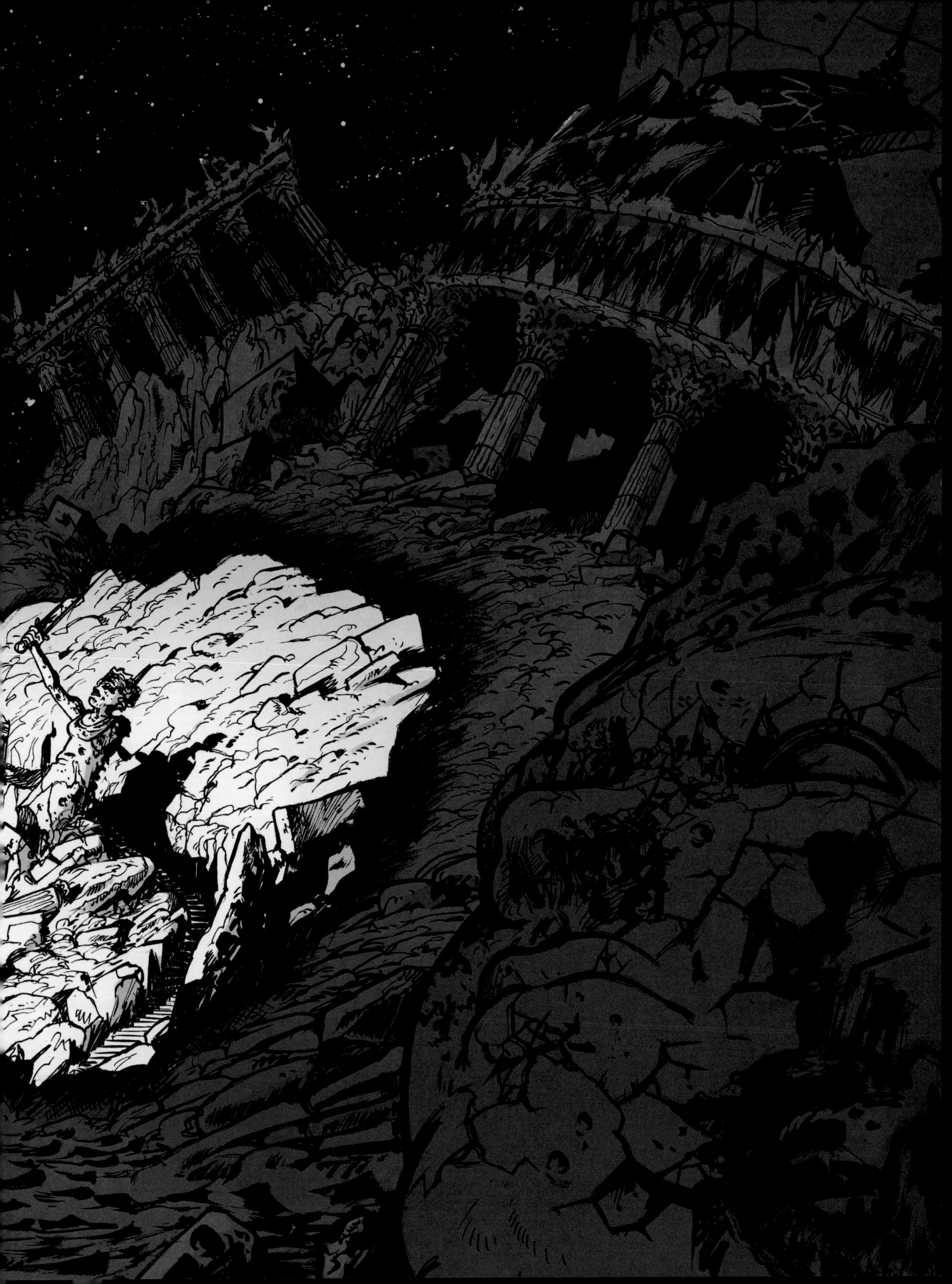

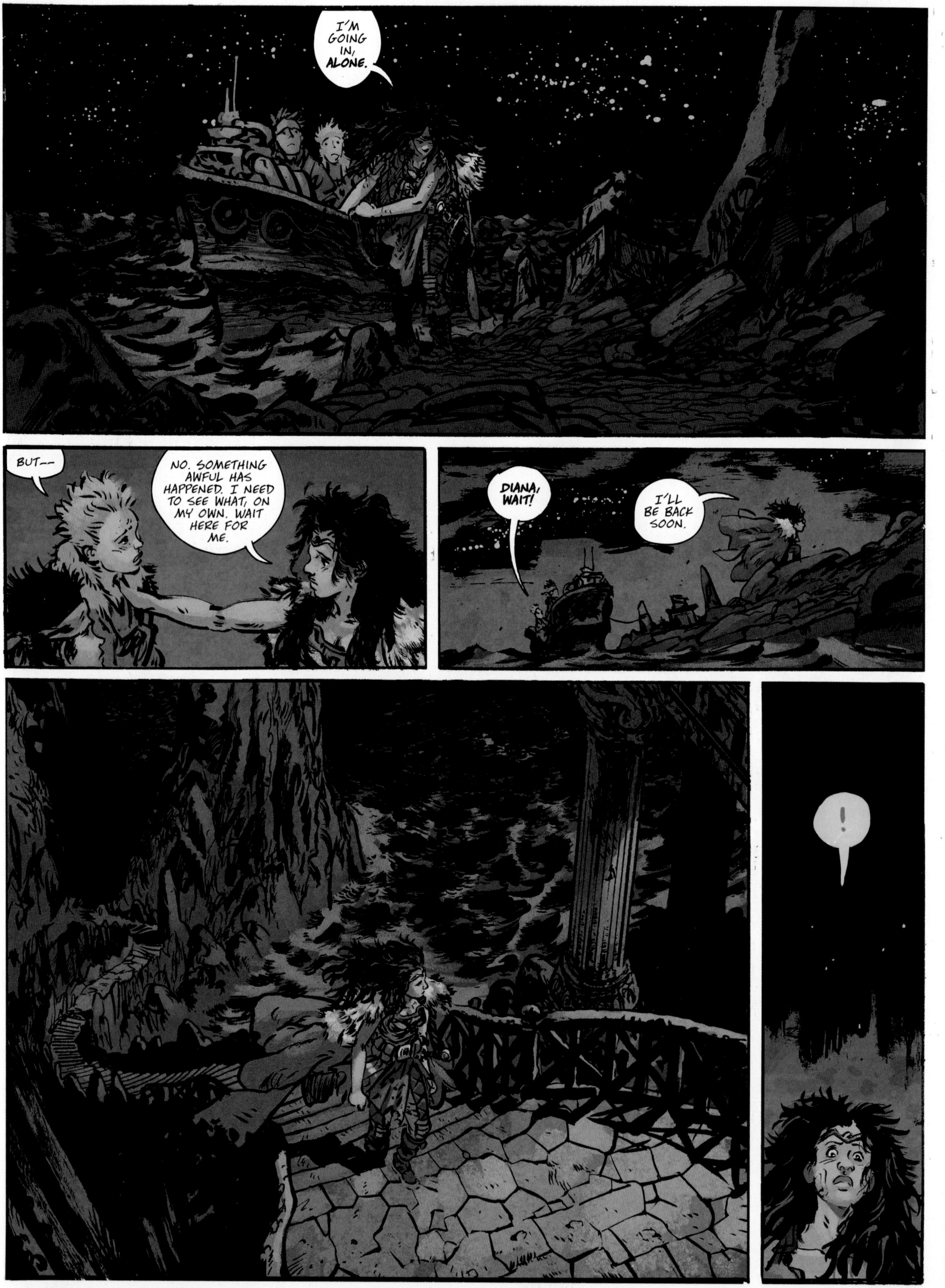

I'M GOING IN, ALONE.
BUT--
NO. SOMETHING AWFUL HAS HAPPENED. I NEED TO SEE WHAT, ON MY OWN. WAIT HERE FOR ME.
DIANA, WAIT!
I'LL BE BACK SOON.
!

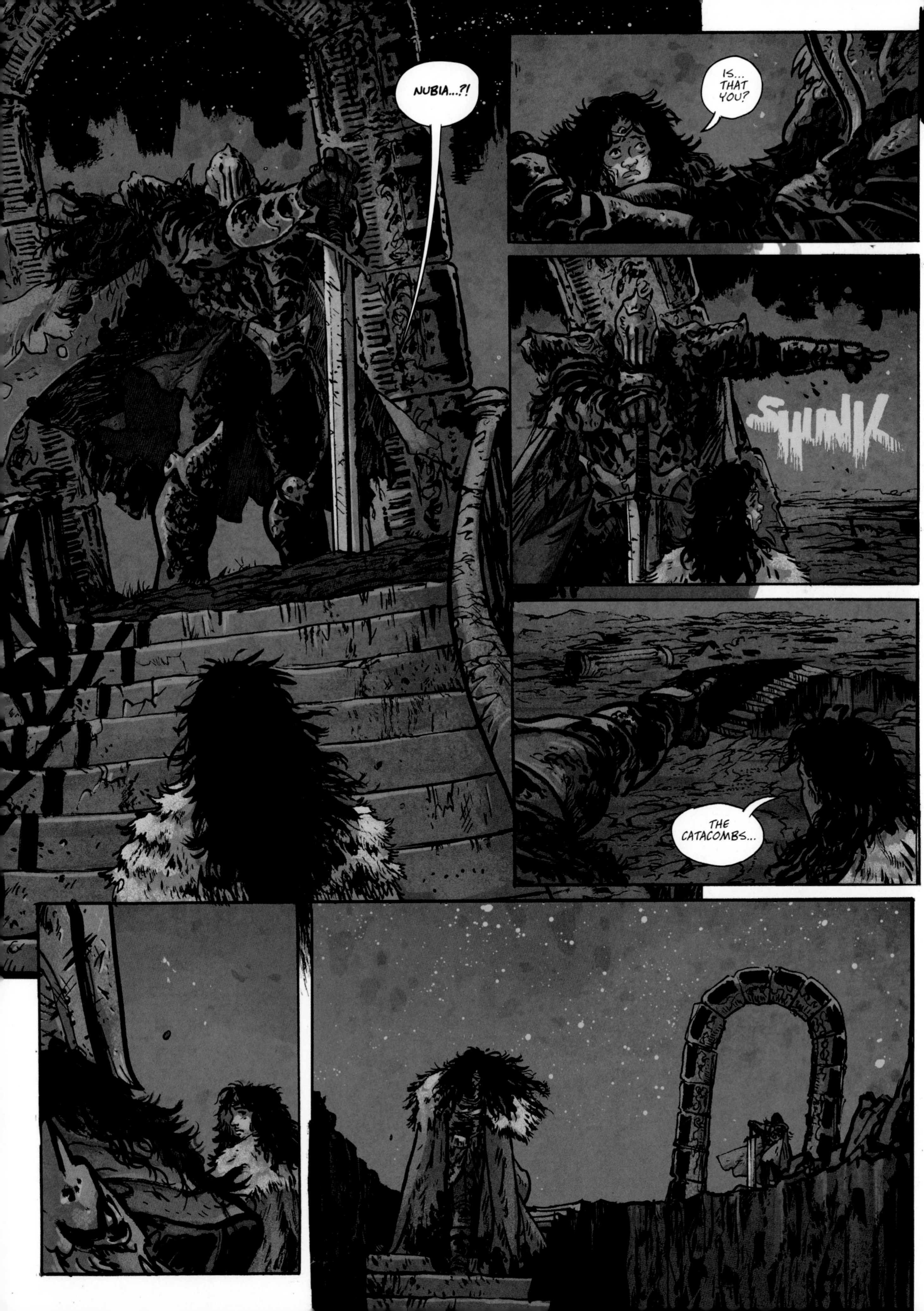
NUBIA...?!
IS... THAT YOU?
SHUNK
THE CATACOMBS...

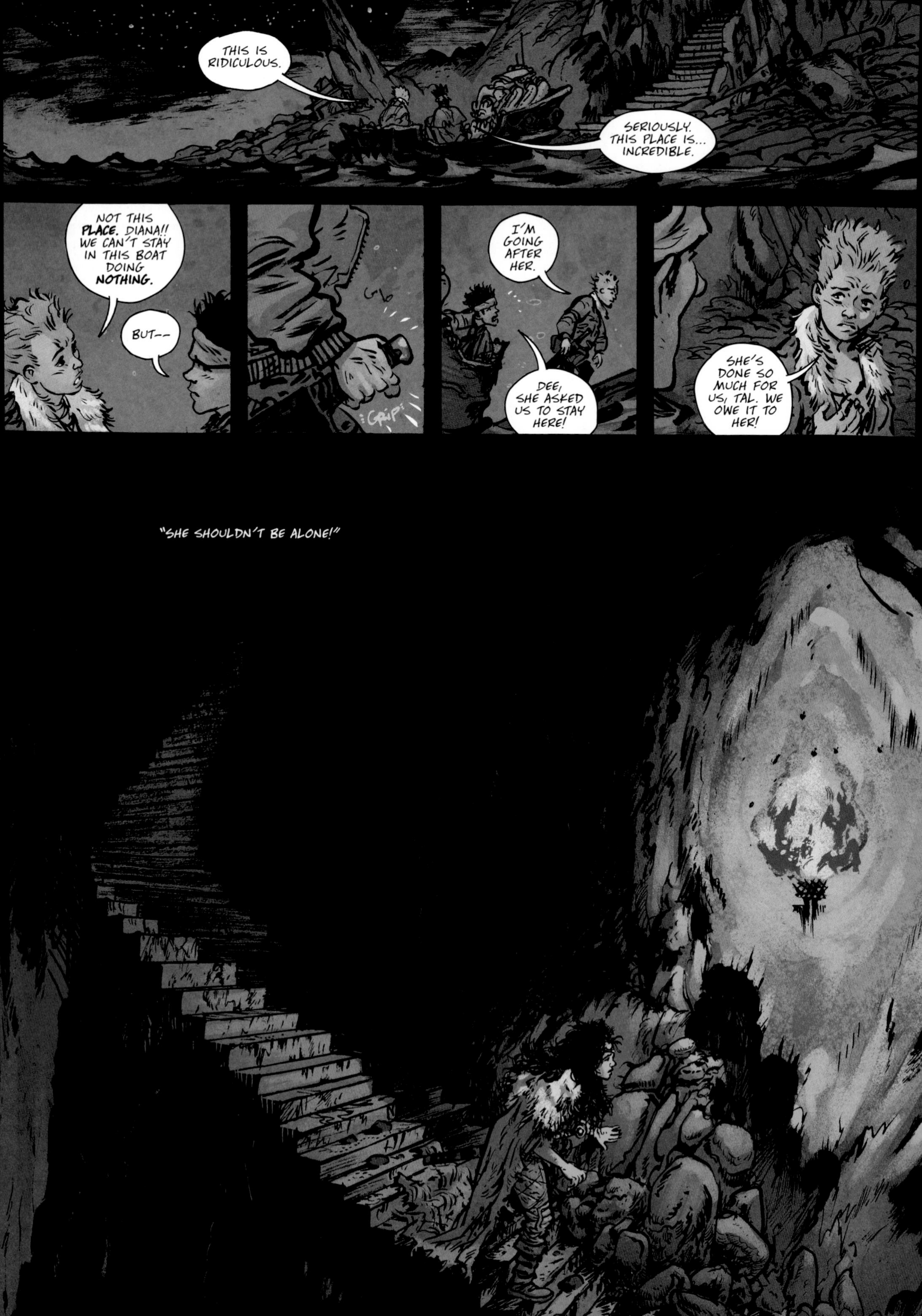
THIS IS RIDICULOUS.
SERIOUSLY. THIS PLACE IS... INCREDIBLE.
NOT THIS PLACE. DIANA!! WE CAN'T STAY IN THIS BOAT DOING NOTHING.
BUT--
GRIP
I'M GOING AFTER HER.
DEE, SHE ASKED US TO STAY HERE!
SHE'S DONE SO MUCH FOR US, TAL. WE OWE IT TO HER!
"SHE SHOULDN'T BE ALONE!"

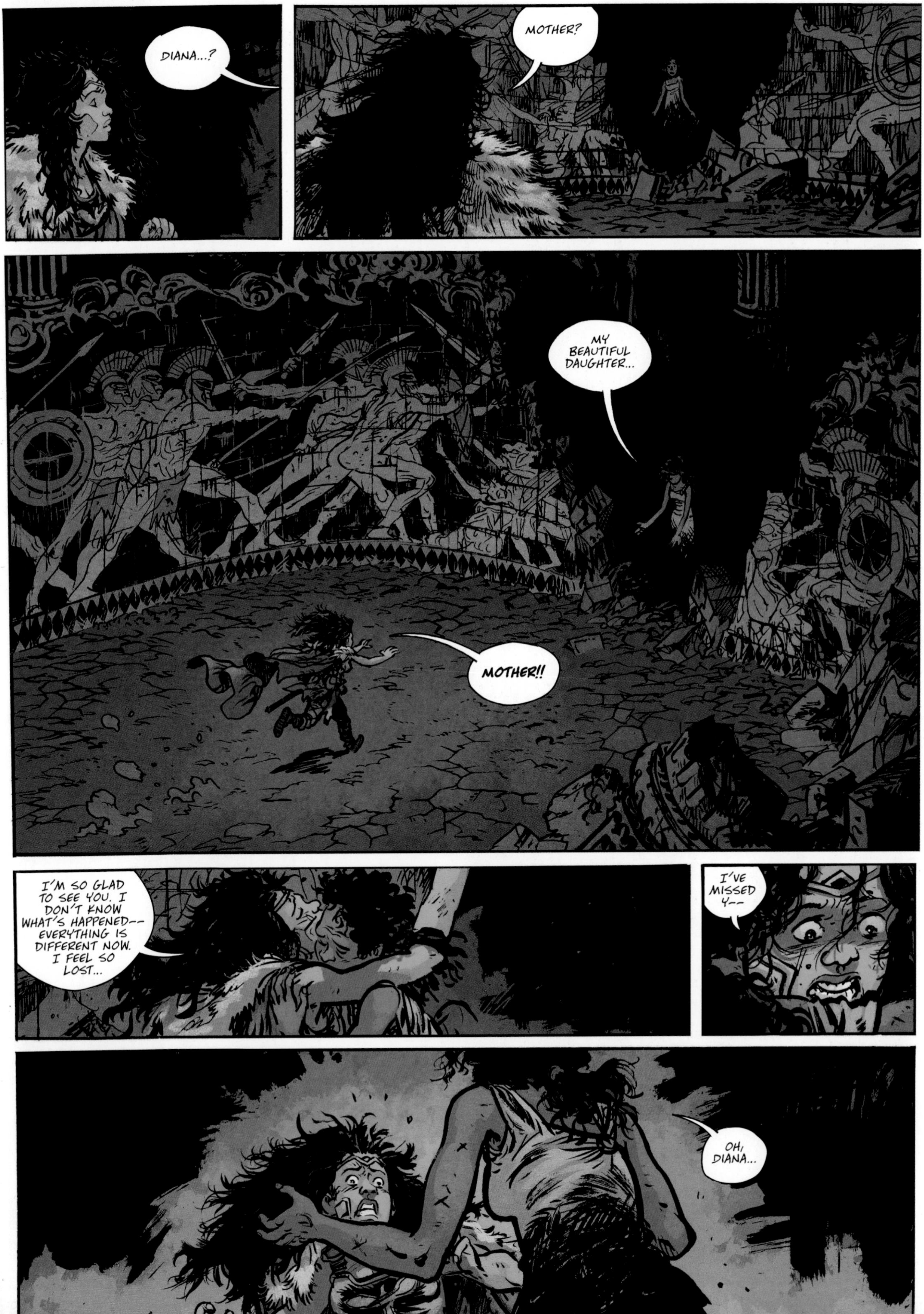
DIANA...?
MOTHER?
MY BEAUTIFUL DAUGHTER...
MOTHER!!
I'M SO GLAD TO SEE YOU. I DON'T KNOW WHAT'S HAPPENED-- EVERYTHING IS DIFFERENT NOW. I FEEL SO LOST...
I'VE MISSED Y--
OH, DIANA...

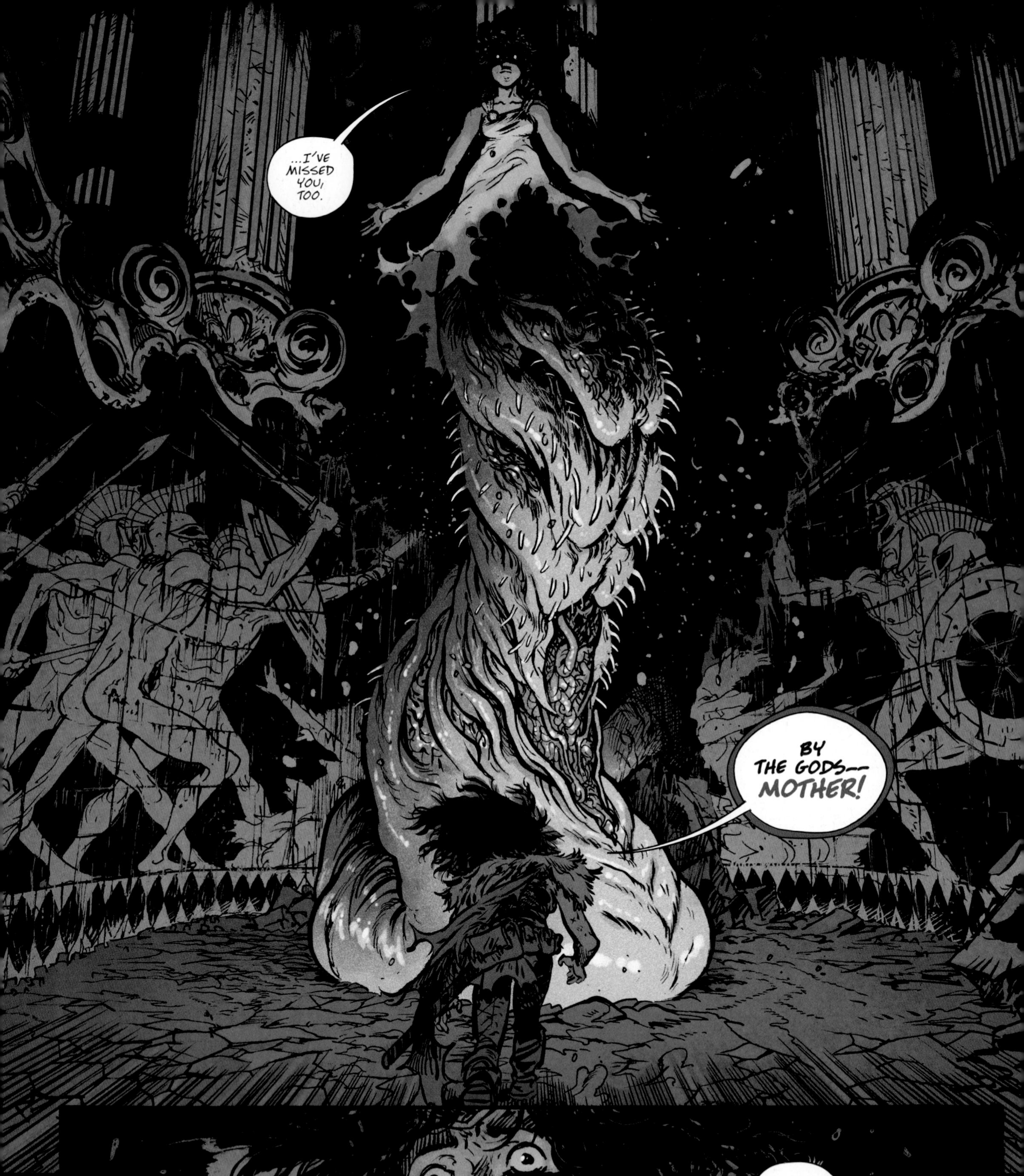
...I'VE MISSED YOU, TOO.
BY THE GODS-- MOTHER!
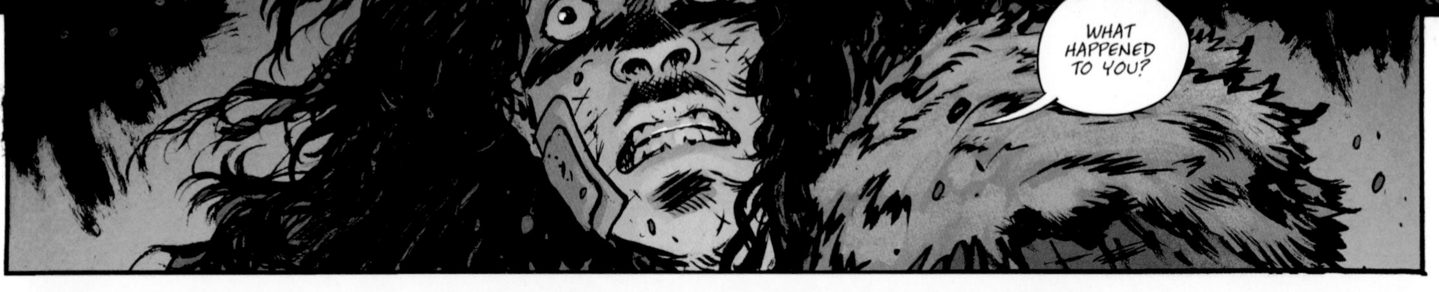
WHAT HAPPENED TO YOU?

LET ME SHOW YOU, MY LOVE.

"THE HUMANS YOU LOVE SO MUCH...

"THEY **BOMBED** US.

"SO HARD AND SO MANY TIMES, THERE WAS ALMOST NOTHING LEFT.

"BUT THE HUMANS FORGOT WE WERE OF THE **GODS**. NUCLEAR BOMBS COULD NOT **KILL** US.

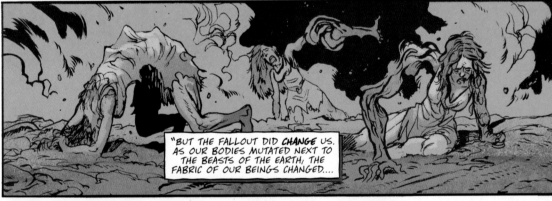

"BUT THE FALLOUT DID **CHANGE** US. AS OUR BODIES MUTATED NEXT TO THE BEASTS OF THE EARTH, THE FABRIC OF OUR BEINGS CHANGED....

"...INTO SOMETHING AWFUL.

"THE BEAUTIFUL AMAZONS...

"...MUTATED BY THE HUMANS.

"THE GREAT RUINERS."

AND EVER SINCE THEN, I HAVE BEEN SENDING OUR MUTATED GODDESSES INTO THE WILDERNESS OF HUMANITY. TO RECLAIM OUR HONOR. TO SERVE CONTINUAL PUNISHMENT TO THE BEINGS THAT DID THIS TO US.

BUT, DIANA...

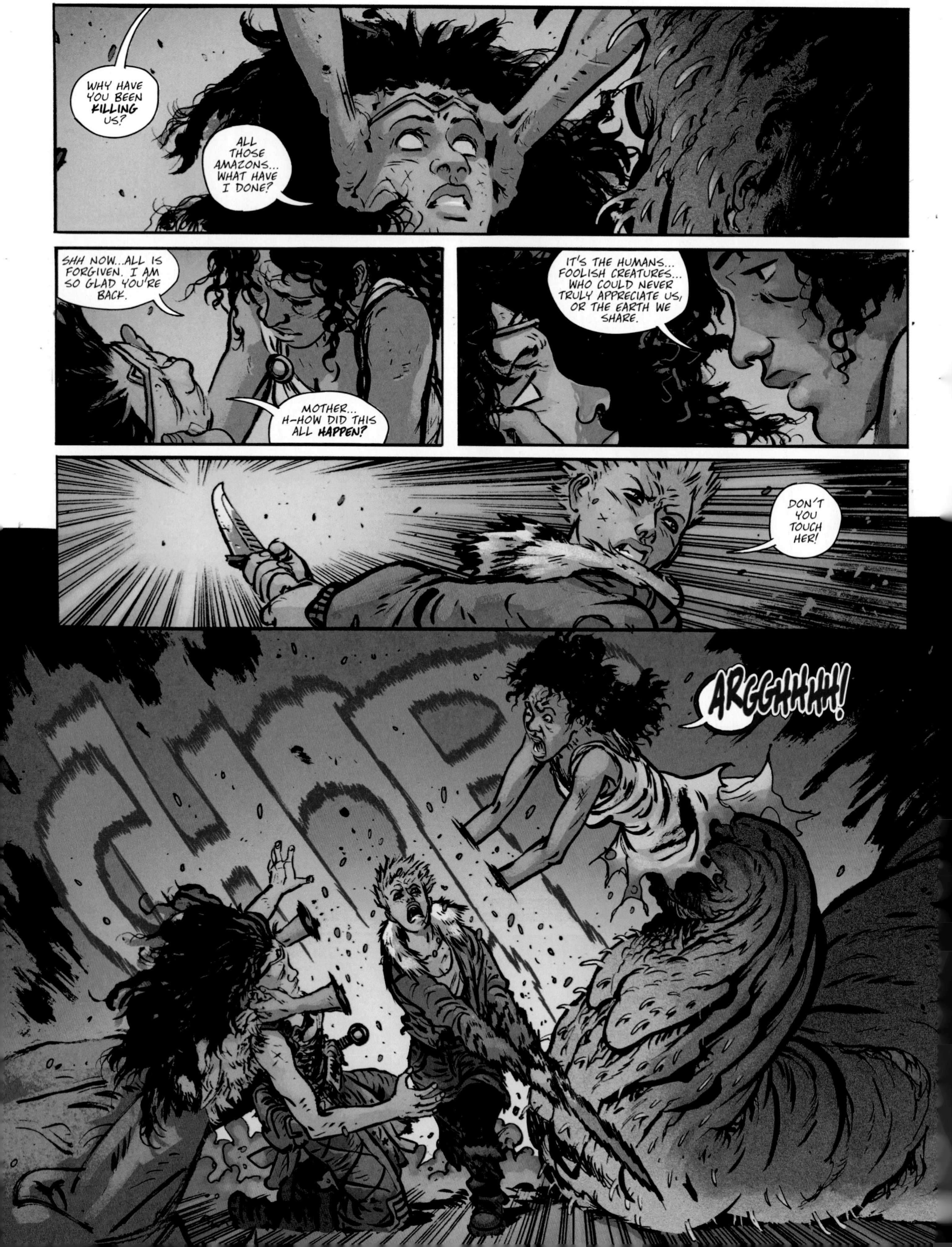
WHY HAVE YOU BEEN KILLING US?
ALL THOSE AMAZONS... WHAT HAVE I DONE?
SHH NOW...ALL IS FORGIVEN. I AM SO GLAD YOU'RE BACK.
MOTHER... H-HOW DID THIS ALL HAPPEN?
IT'S THE HUMANS... FOOLISH CREATURES... WHO COULD NEVER TRULY APPRECIATE US, OR THE EARTH WE SHARE.
DON'T YOU TOUCH HER!
ARGGHHHH!
CHOP

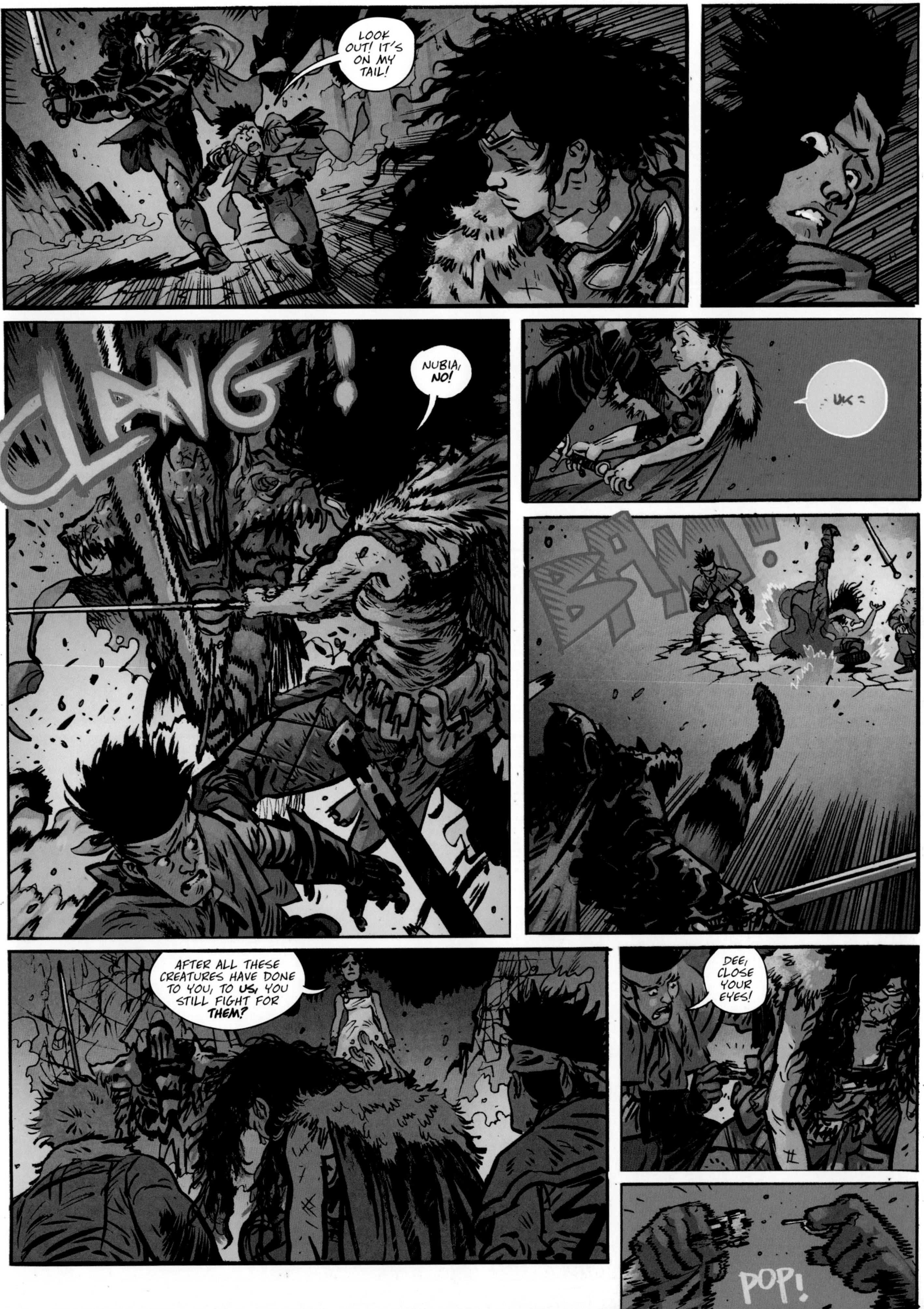
LOOK OUT! IT'S ON MY TAIL!
CLANG!
NUBIA, NO!
UK
BAM!
AFTER ALL THESE CREATURES HAVE DONE TO YOU, TO **US**, YOU STILL FIGHT FOR **THEM**?
DEE, CLOSE YOUR EYES!
POP!

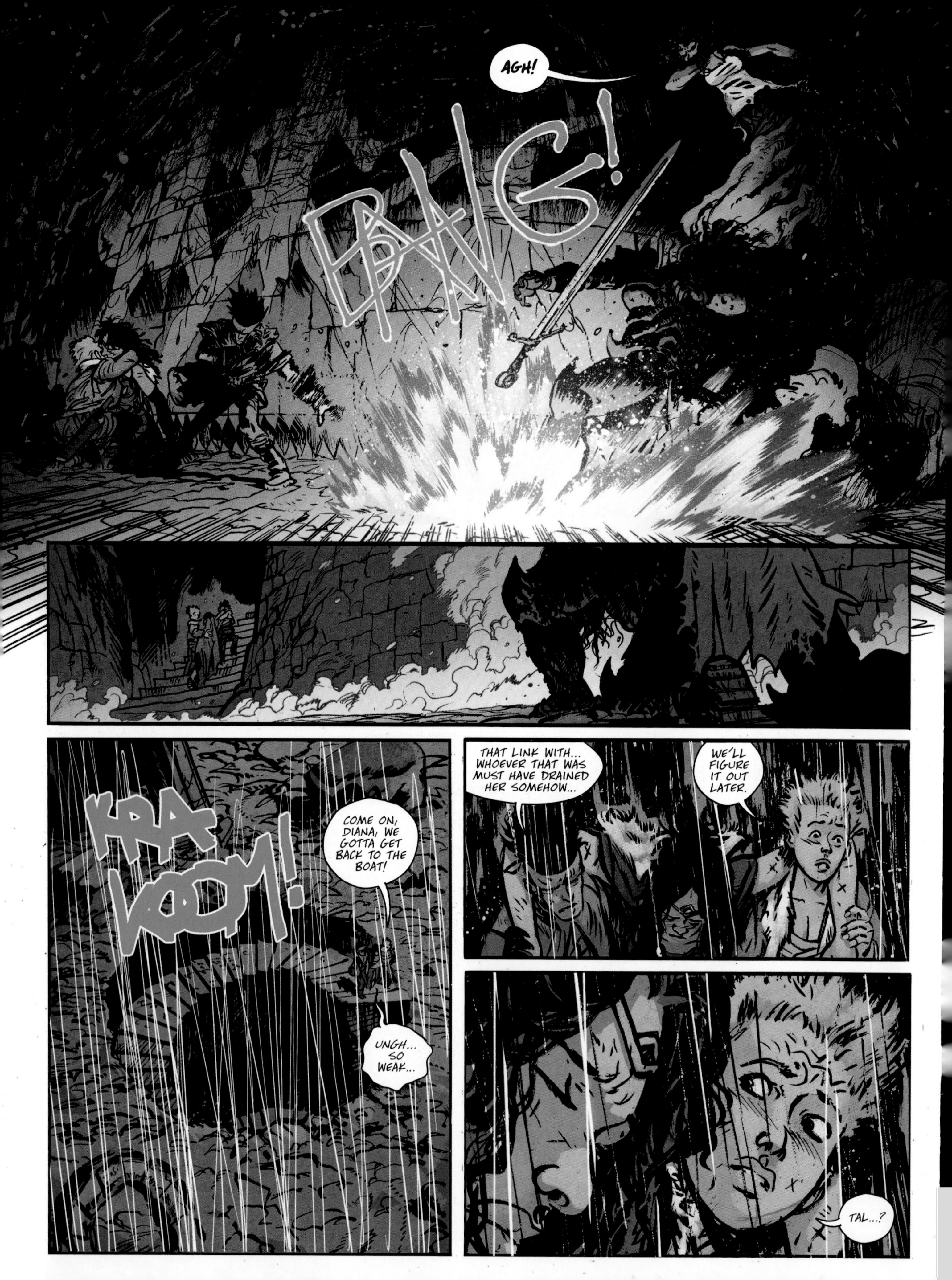
AGH!
BANG!
KRA KOOM!
COME ON, DIANA, WE GOTTA GET BACK TO THE BOAT!
UNGH... SO WEAK...
THAT LINK WITH... WHOEVER THAT WAS MUST HAVE DRAINED HER SOMEHOW...
WE'LL FIGURE IT OUT LATER.
TAL...?

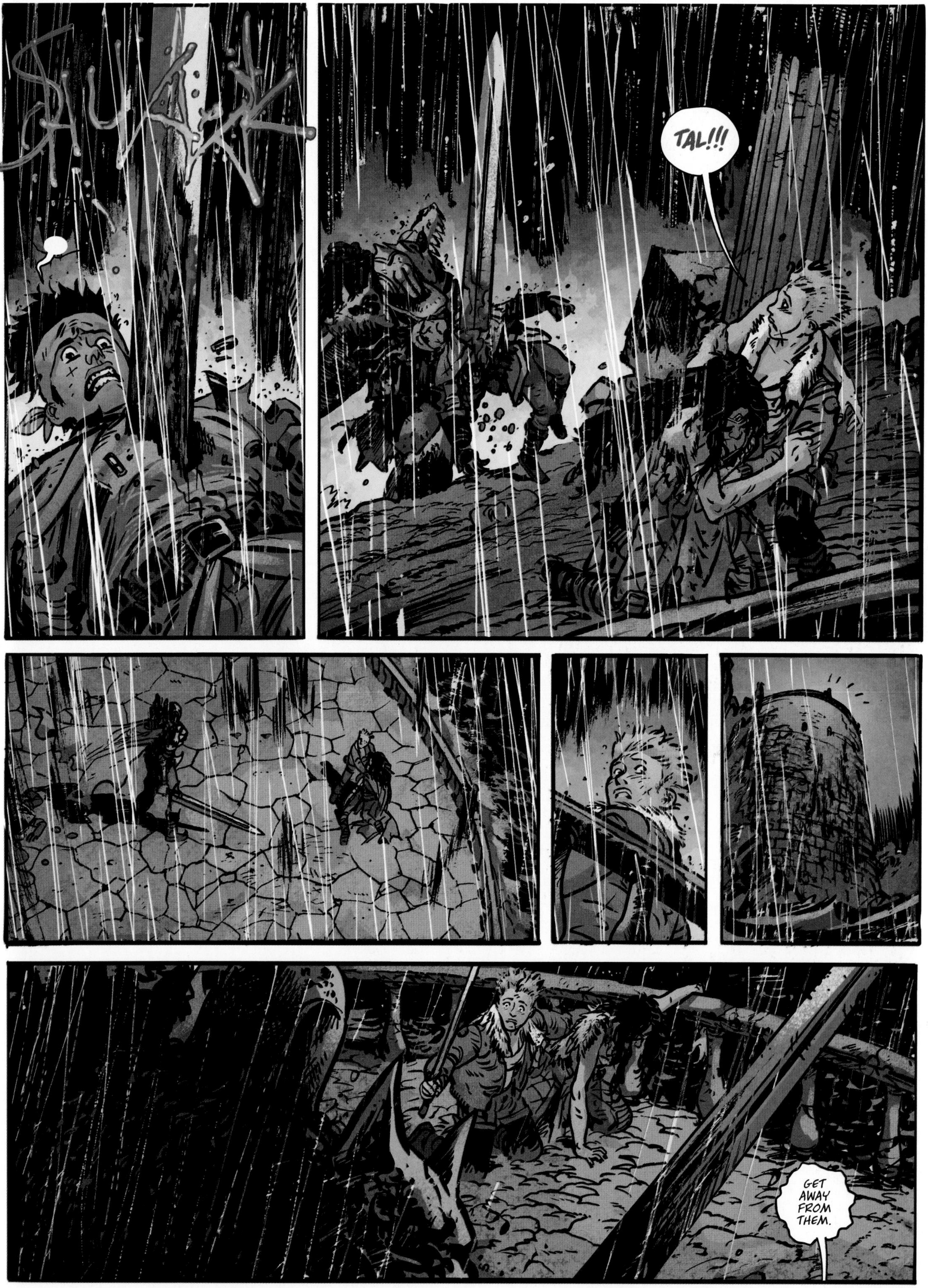
TAL!!!
GET AWAY FROM THEM.

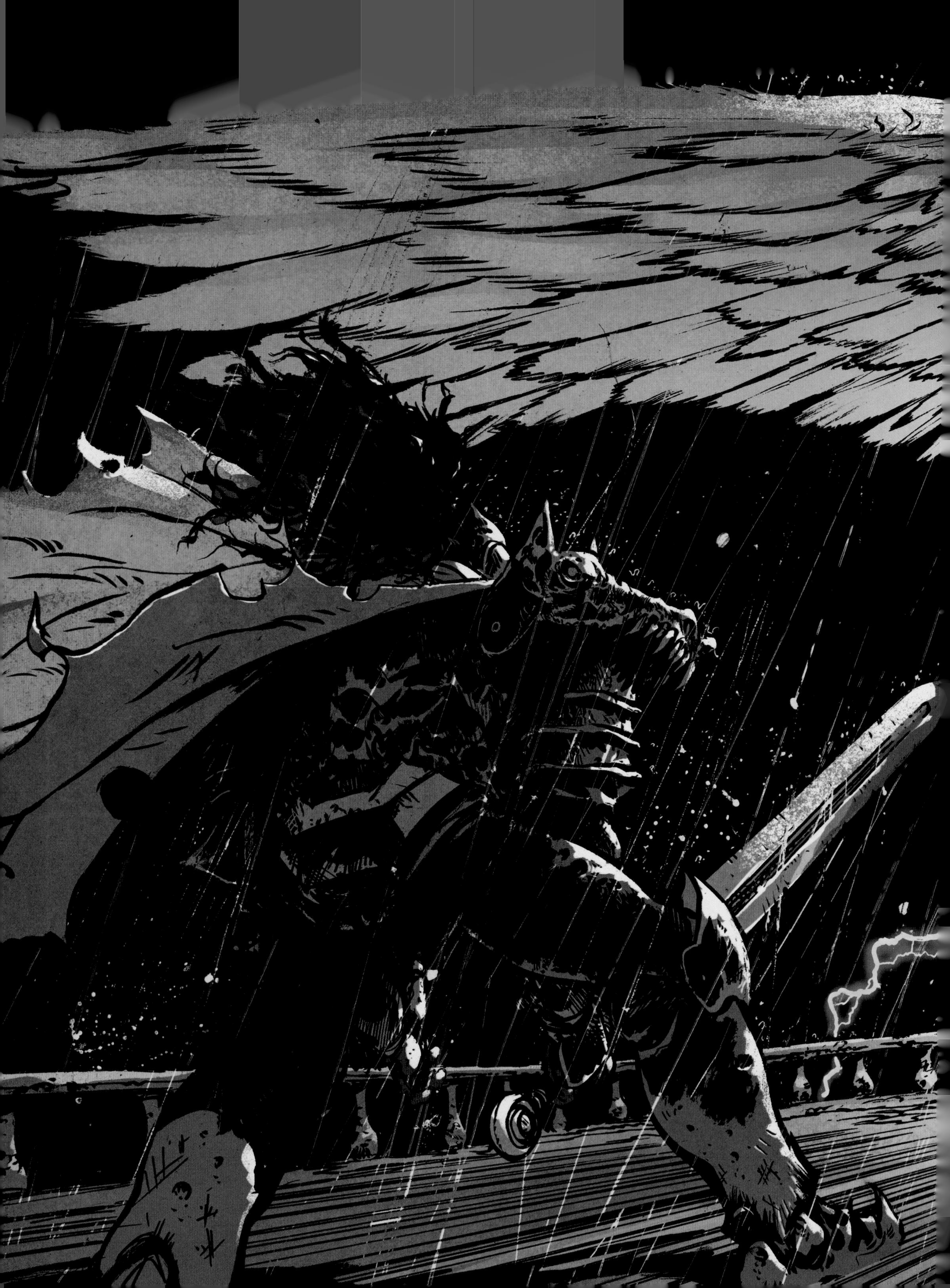

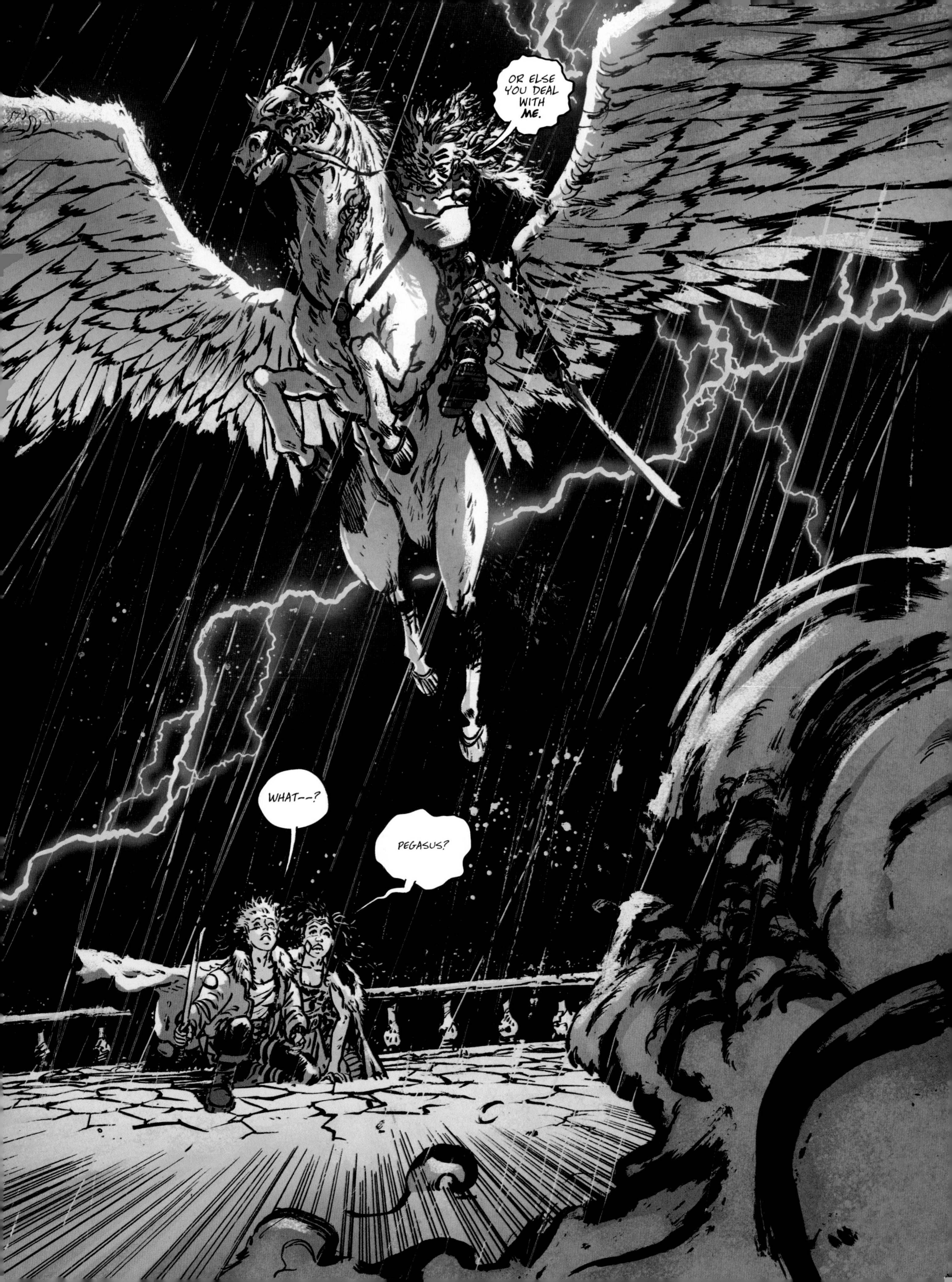
OR ELSE YOU DEAL WITH ME.
WHAT--?
PEGASUS?

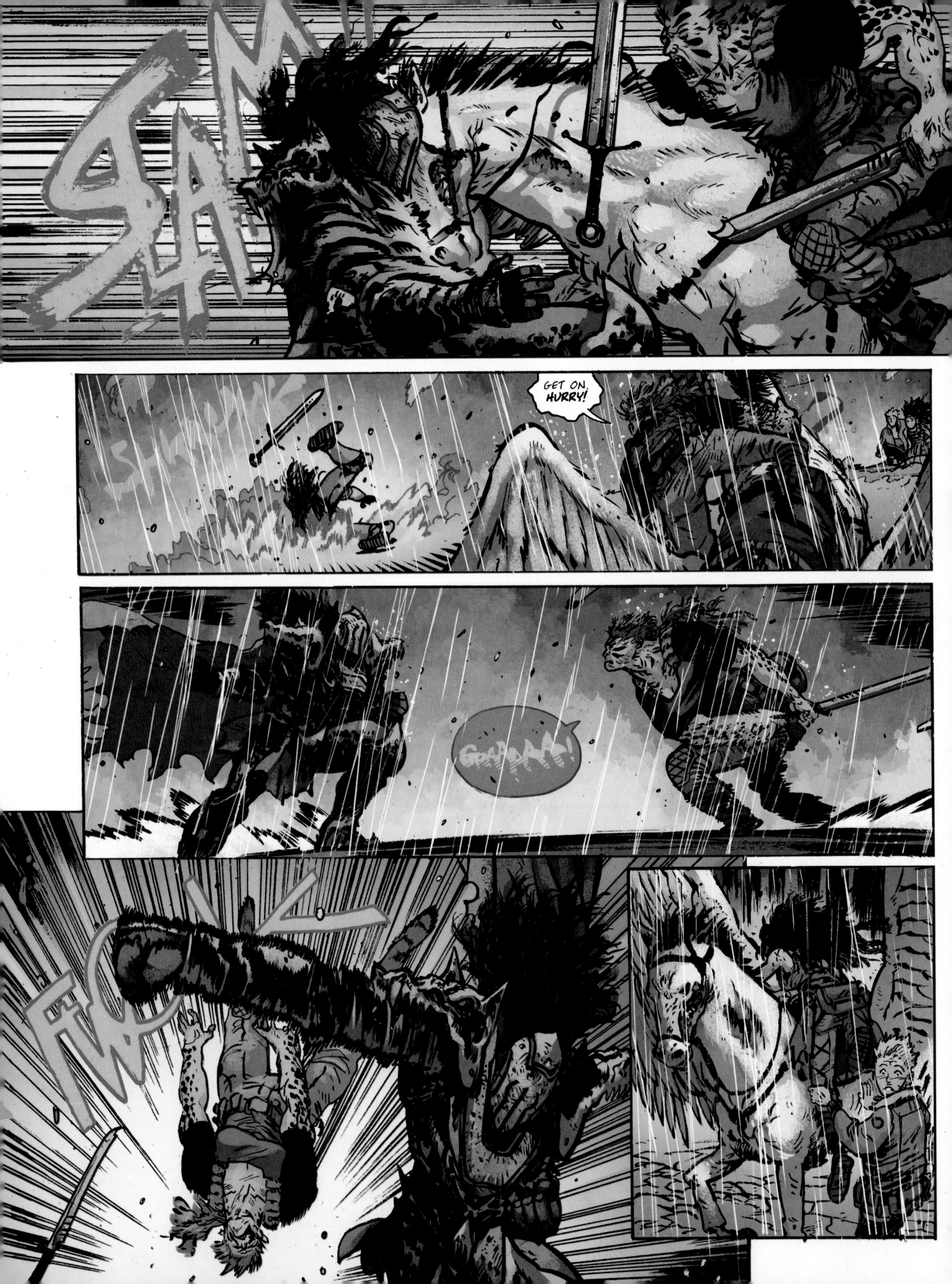
GET ON.
HURRY!

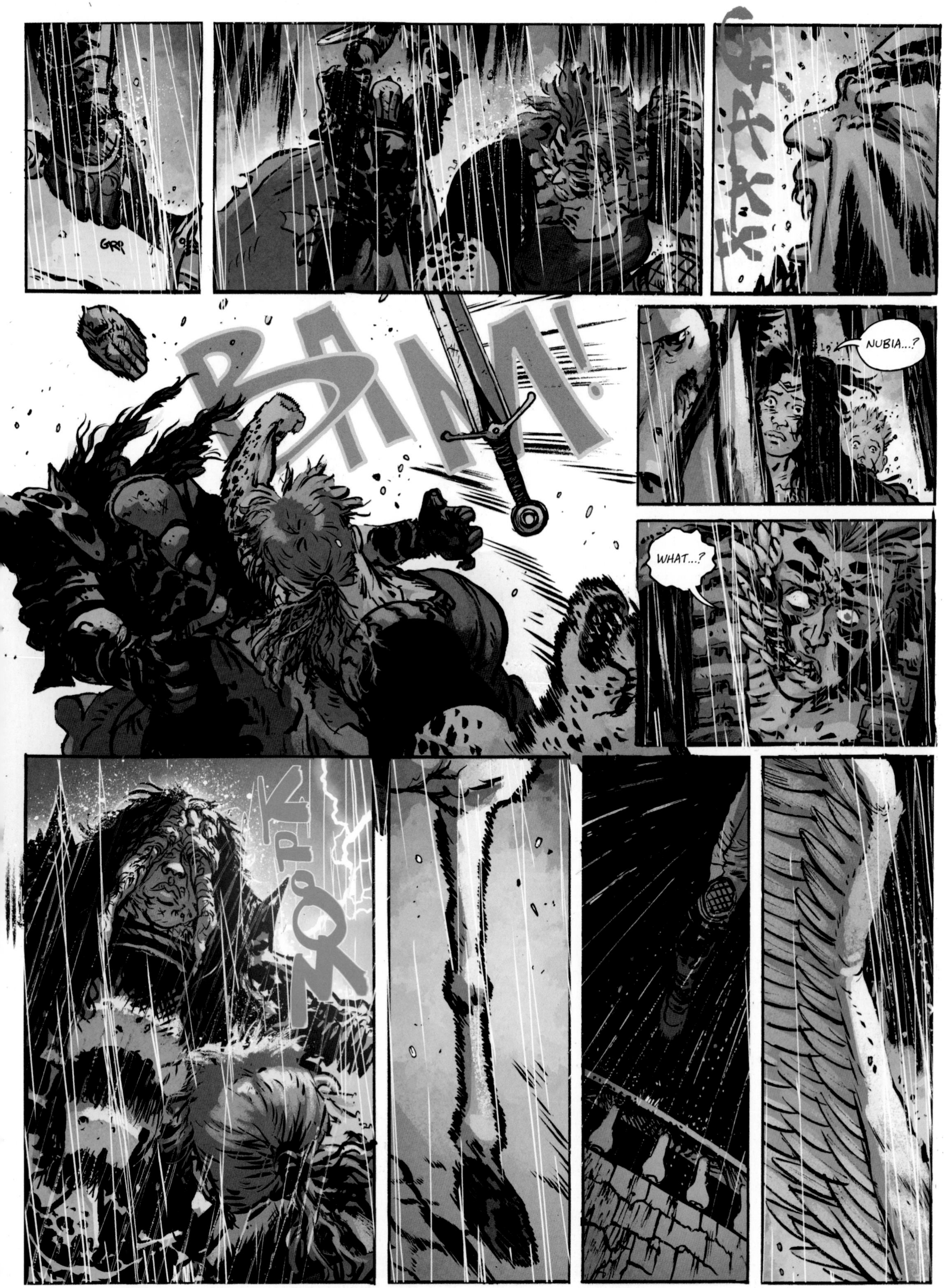
GRR
GAKK
BAM!
NUBIA...?
WHAT...?
KROOM

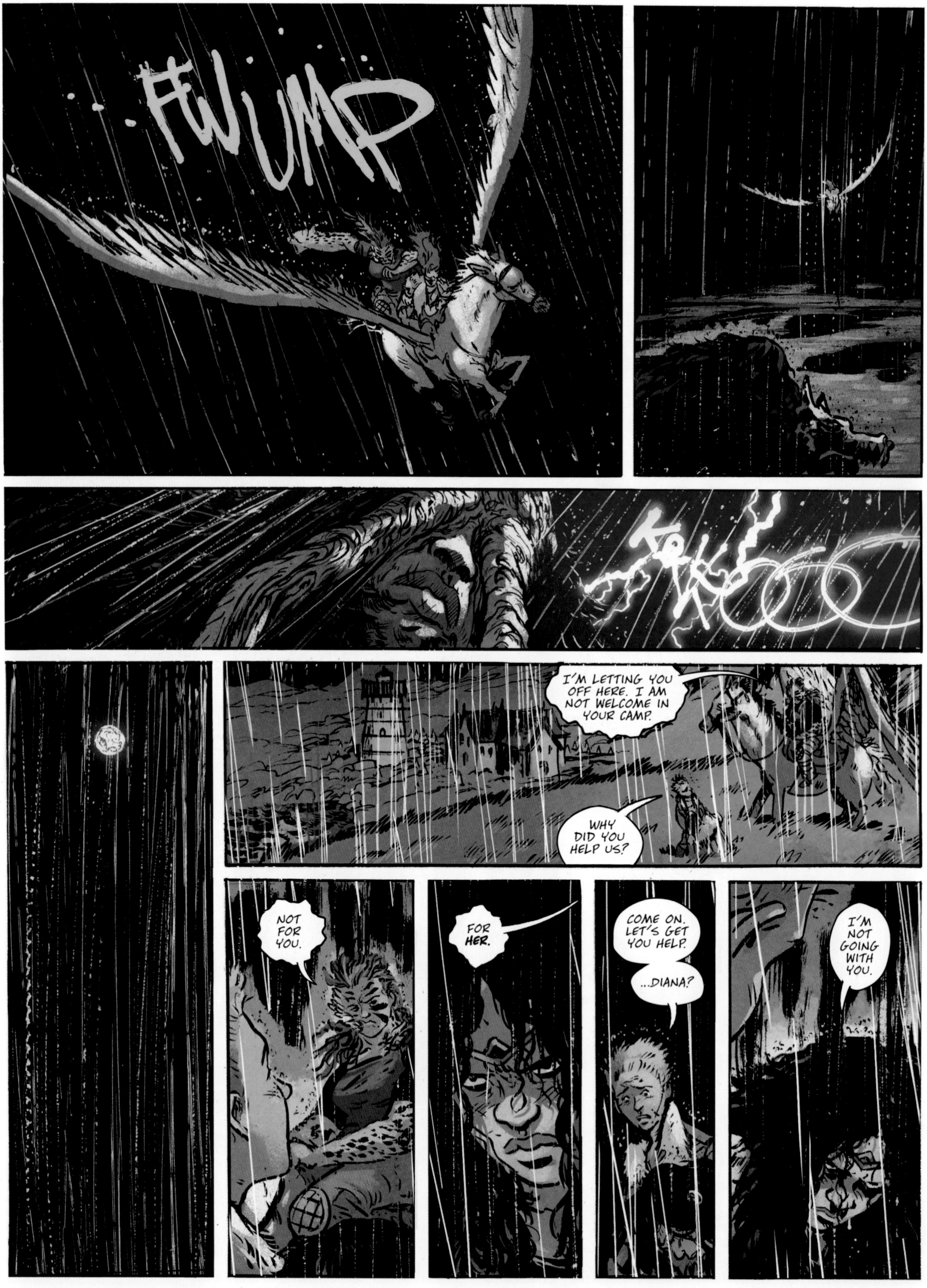
FFWUMP
I'M LETTING YOU OFF HERE. I AM NOT WELCOME IN YOUR CAMP.
WHY DID YOU HELP US?
NOT FOR YOU.
FOR **HER.**
COME ON. LET'S GET YOU HELP.
...DIANA?
I'M NOT GOING WITH YOU.

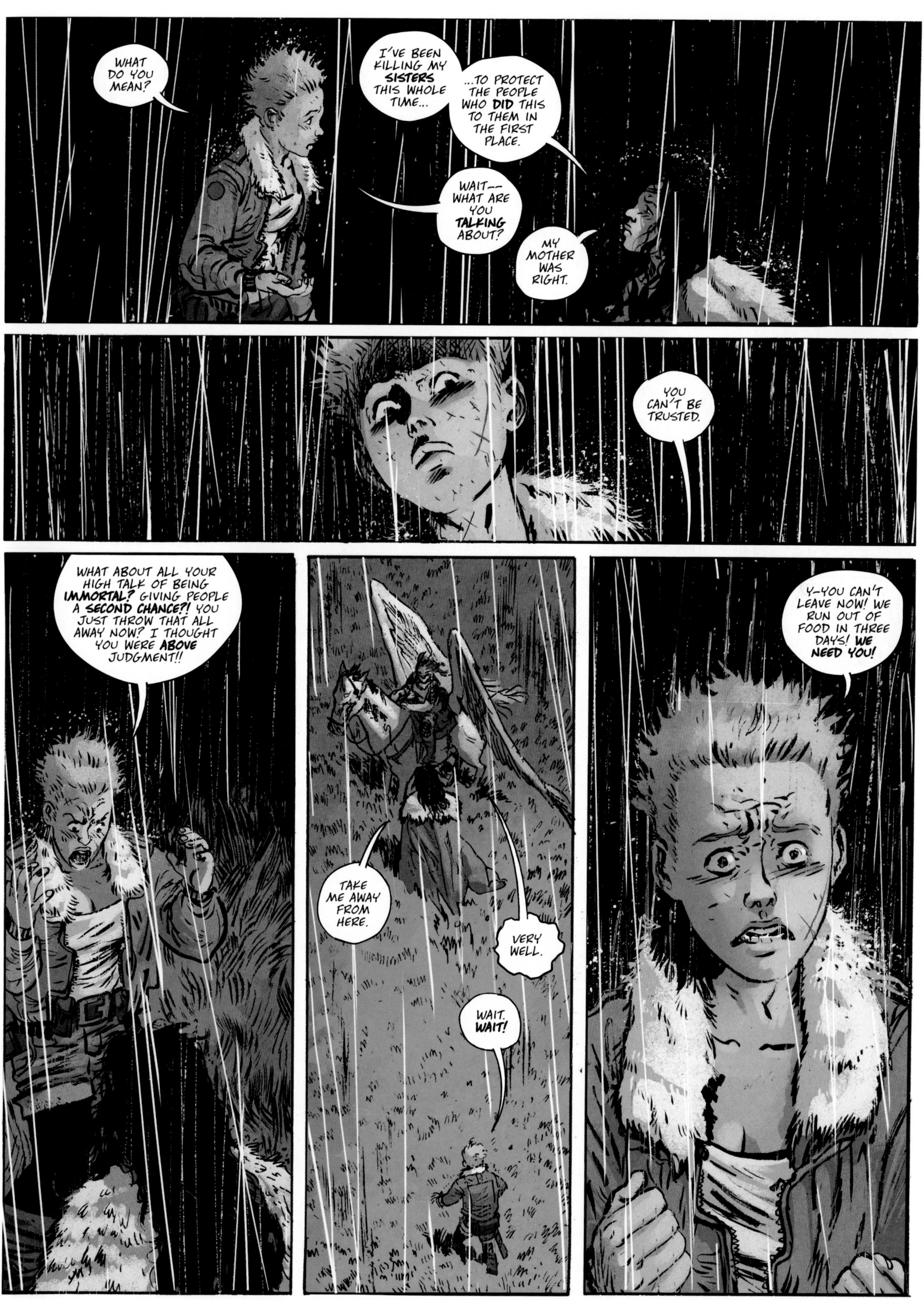
WHAT DO YOU MEAN?
I'VE BEEN KILLING MY **SISTERS** THIS WHOLE TIME...
...TO PROTECT THE PEOPLE WHO **DID** THIS TO THEM IN THE FIRST PLACE.
WAIT-- WHAT ARE YOU **TALKING** ABOUT?
MY MOTHER WAS RIGHT.
YOU CAN'T BE TRUSTED.
WHAT ABOUT ALL YOUR HIGH TALK OF BEING **IMMORTAL?** GIVING PEOPLE A **SECOND CHANCE?!** YOU JUST THROW THAT ALL AWAY NOW? I THOUGHT YOU WERE **ABOVE** JUDGMENT!!
TAKE ME AWAY FROM HERE.
VERY WELL.
WAIT. **WAIT!**
Y-YOU CAN'T LEAVE NOW! WE RUN OUT OF FOOD IN THREE DAYS! **WE NEED YOU!**

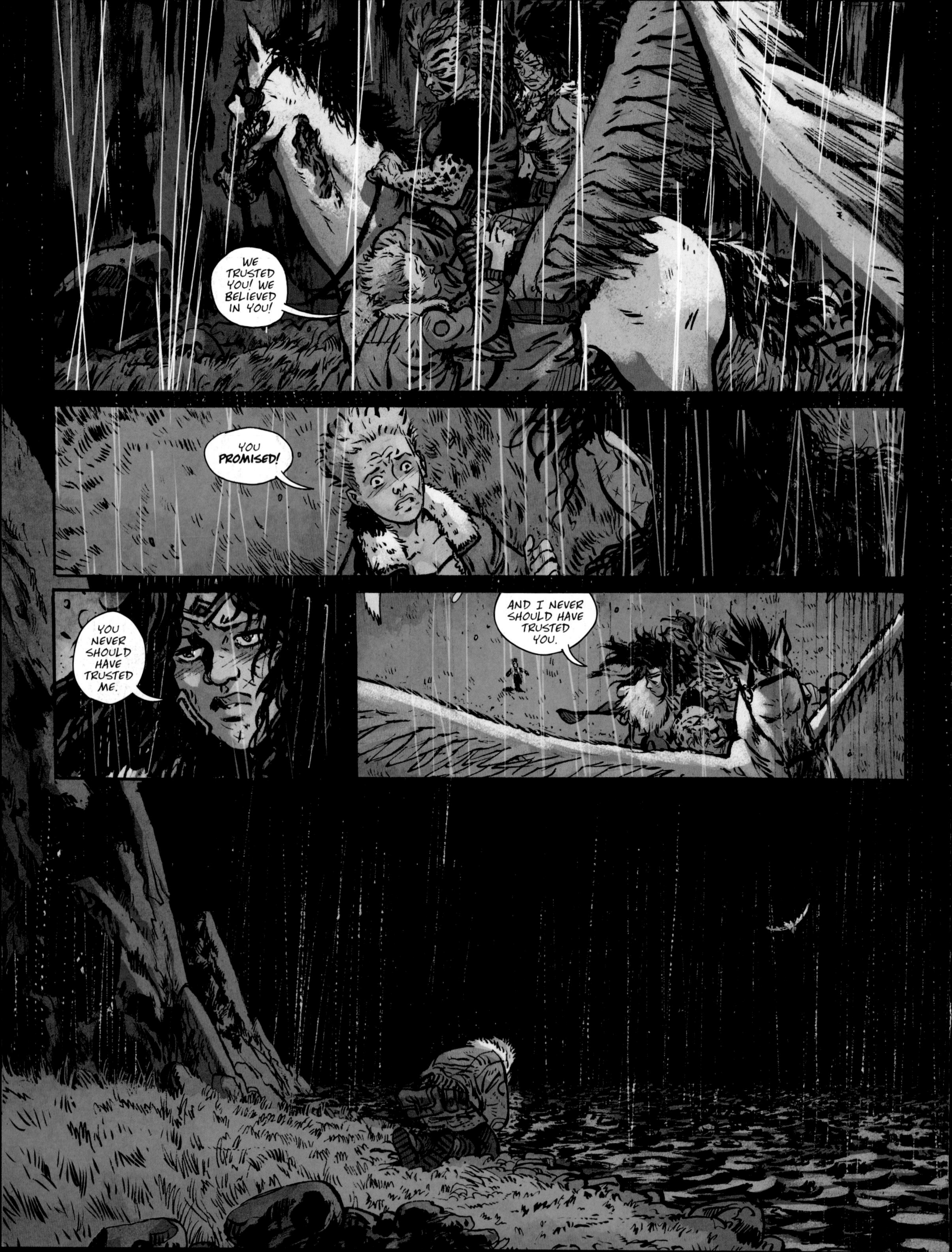
WE TRUSTED YOU! WE BELIEVED IN YOU!
YOU **PROMISED!**
YOU NEVER SHOULD HAVE TRUSTED ME.
AND I NEVER SHOULD HAVE TRUSTED YOU.

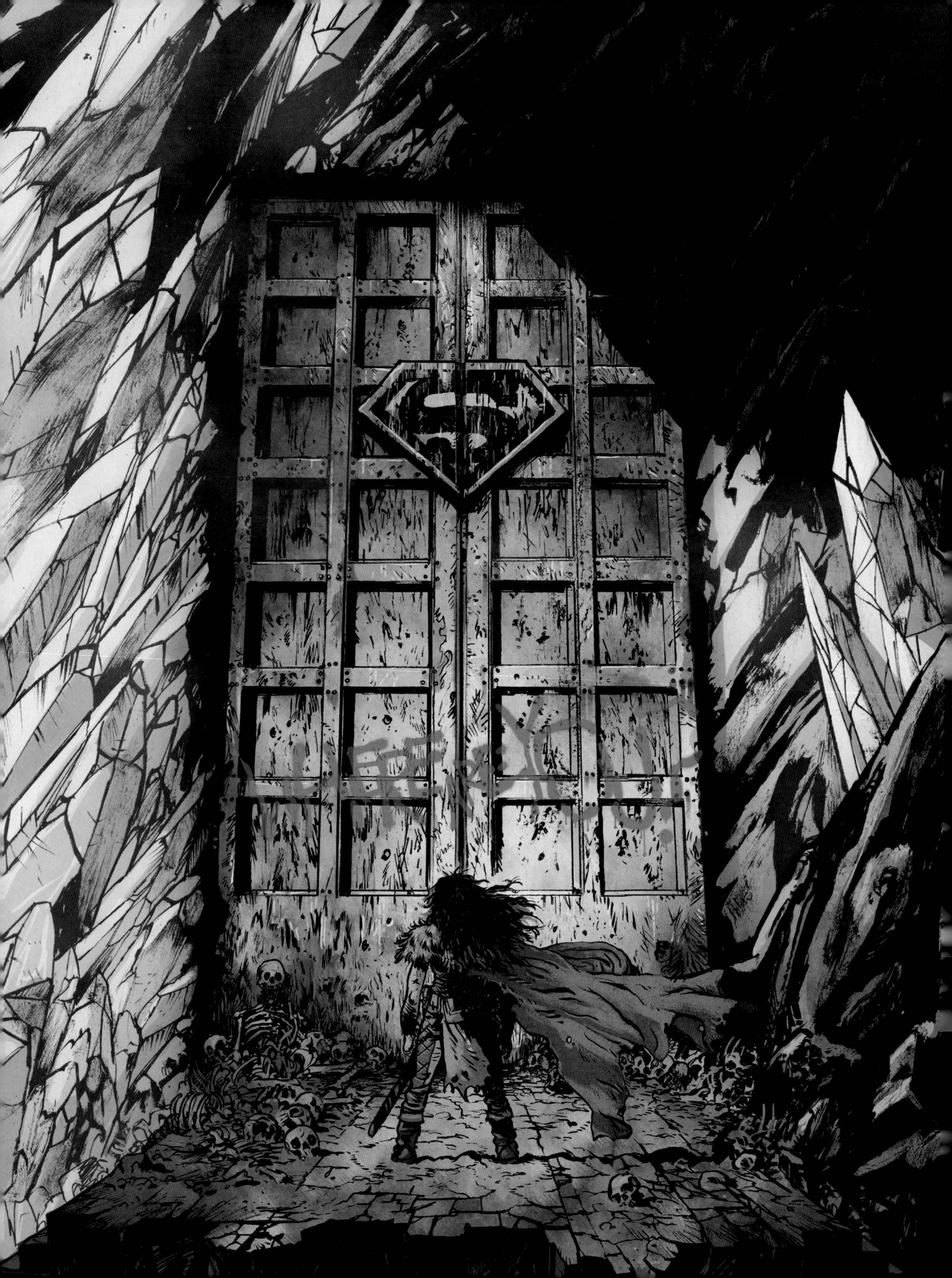

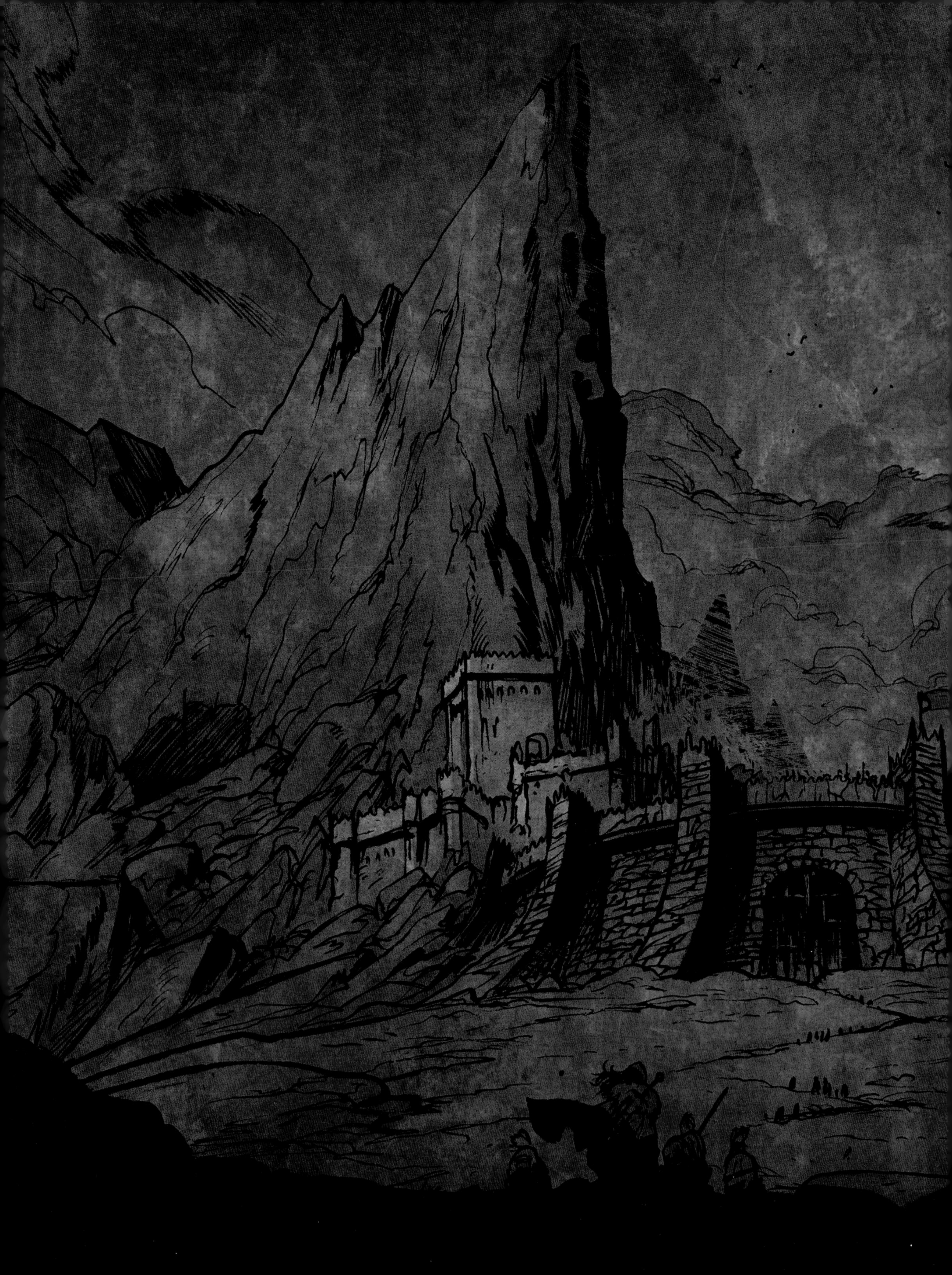

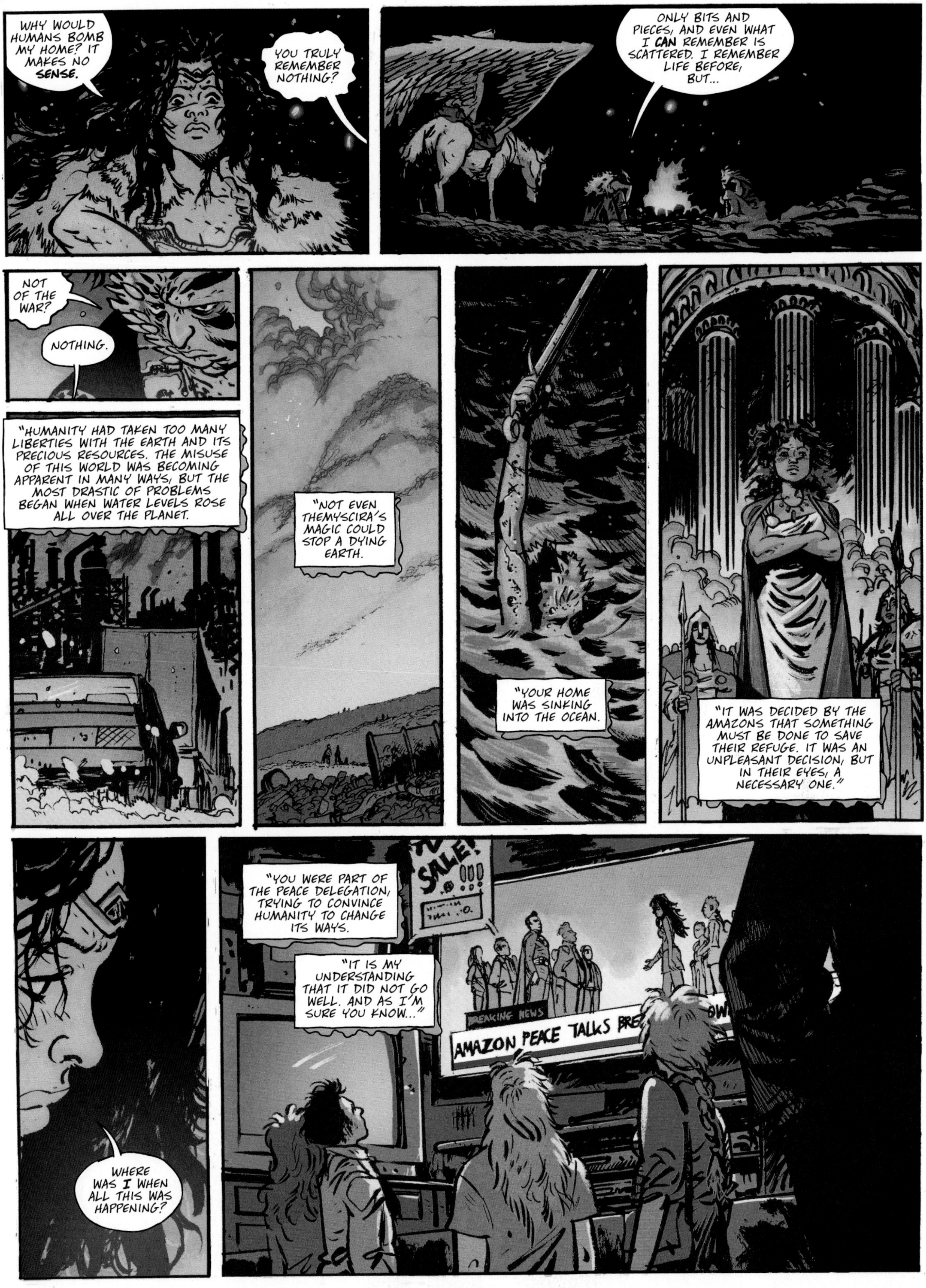
WHY WOULD HUMANS BOMB MY HOME? IT MAKES NO **SENSE.**
YOU TRULY REMEMBER NOTHING?
ONLY BITS AND PIECES, AND EVEN WHAT I **CAN** REMEMBER IS SCATTERED. I REMEMBER LIFE BEFORE, BUT...
NOT OF THE WAR?
NOTHING.
"HUMANITY HAD TAKEN TOO MANY LIBERTIES WITH THE EARTH AND ITS PRECIOUS RESOURCES. THE MISUSE OF THIS WORLD WAS BECOMING APPARENT IN MANY WAYS, BUT THE MOST DRASTIC OF PROBLEMS BEGAN WHEN WATER LEVELS ROSE ALL OVER THE PLANET.
"NOT EVEN THEMYSCIRA'S MAGIC COULD STOP A DYING EARTH.
"YOUR HOME WAS SINKING INTO THE OCEAN.
"IT WAS DECIDED BY THE AMAZONS THAT SOMETHING MUST BE DONE TO SAVE THEIR REFUGE. IT WAS AN UNPLEASANT DECISION, BUT IN THEIR EYES, A NECESSARY ONE."
WHERE WAS **I** WHEN ALL THIS WAS HAPPENING?
"YOU WERE PART OF THE PEACE DELEGATION, TRYING TO CONVINCE HUMANITY TO CHANGE ITS WAYS.
"IT IS MY UNDERSTANDING THAT IT DID NOT GO WELL. AND AS I'M SURE YOU KNOW..."
SALE!
BREAKING NEWS
AMAZON PEACE TALKS BRE

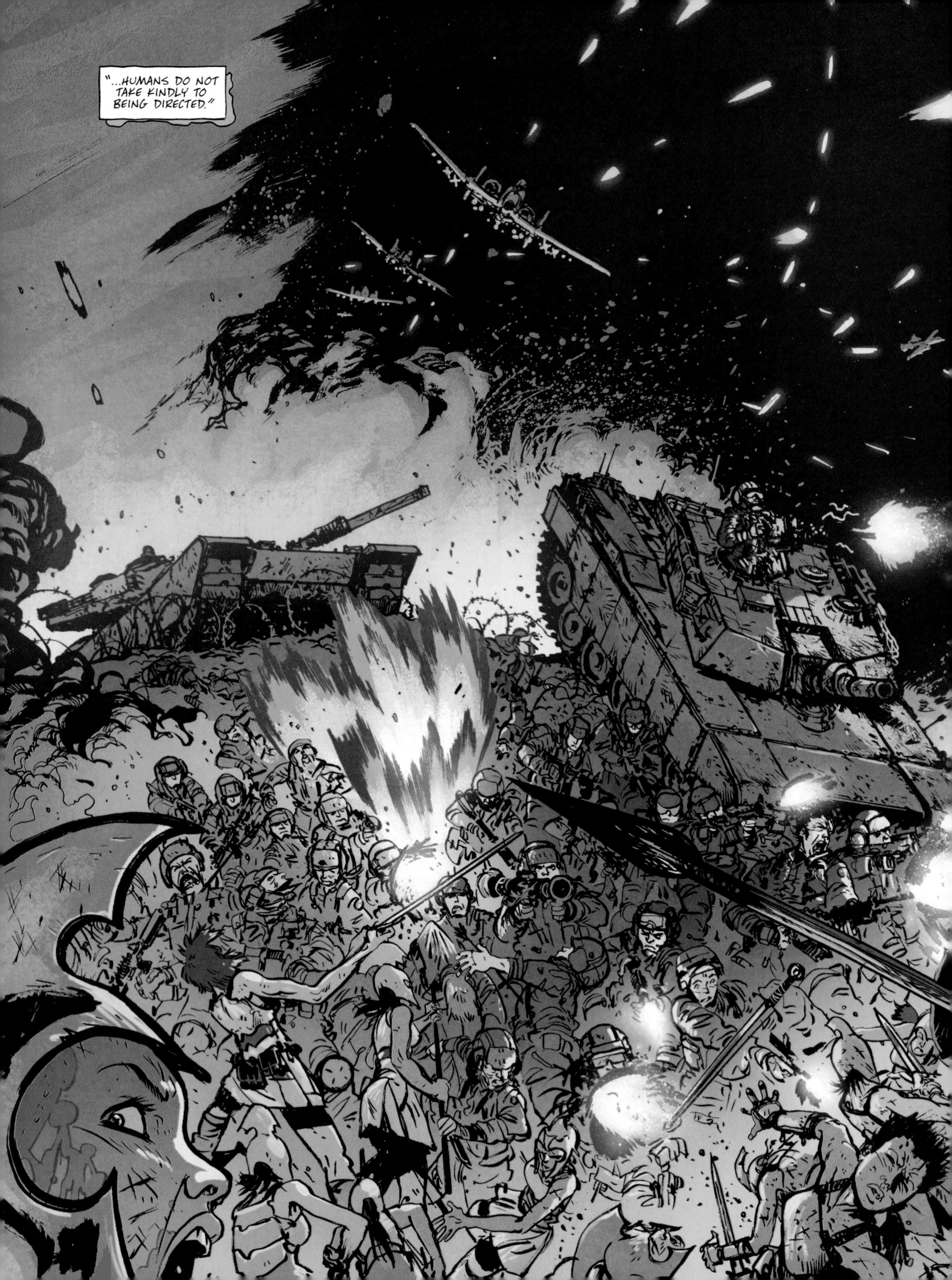
"...HUMANS DO NOT TAKE KINDLY TO BEING DIRECTED."

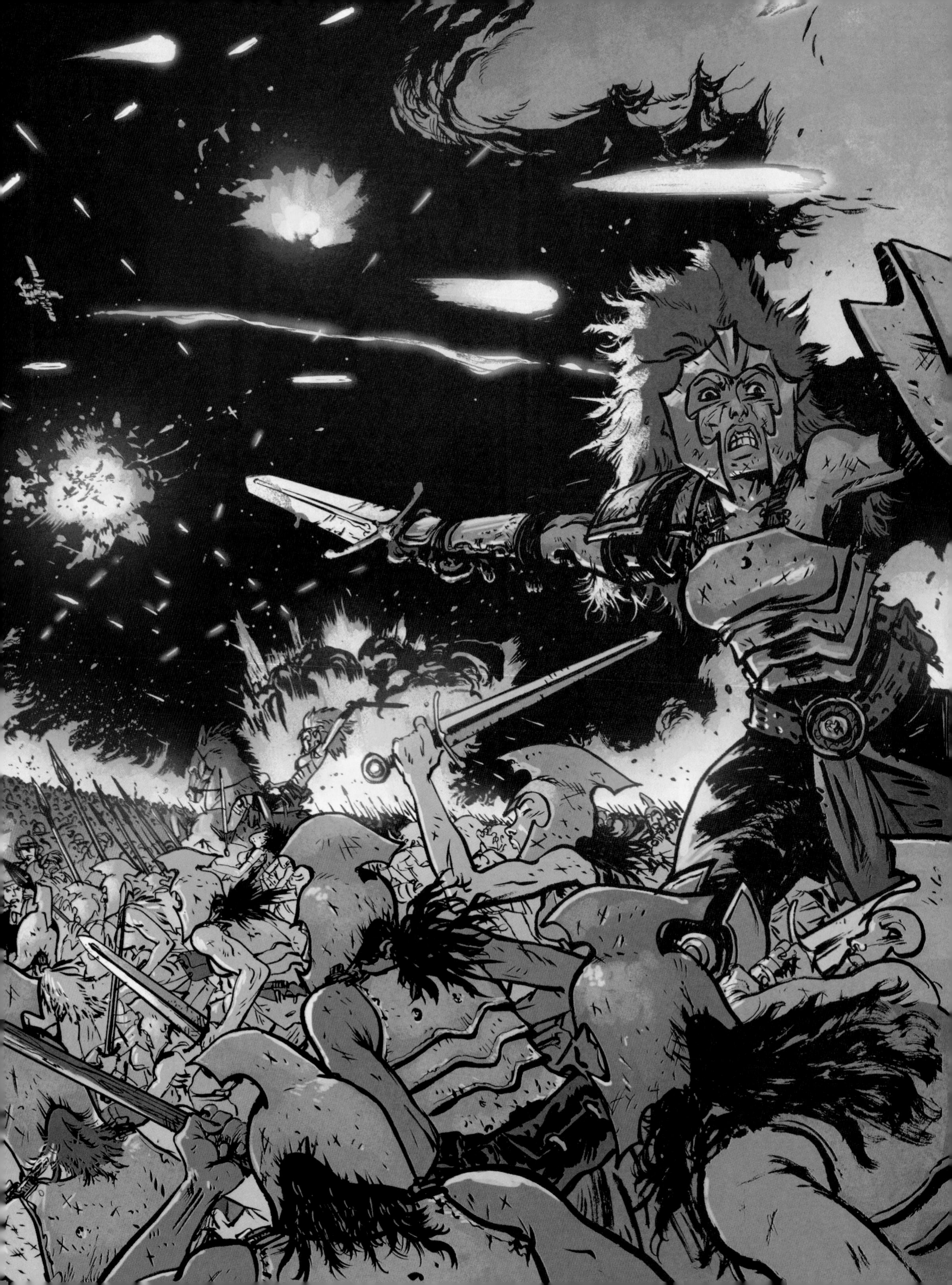

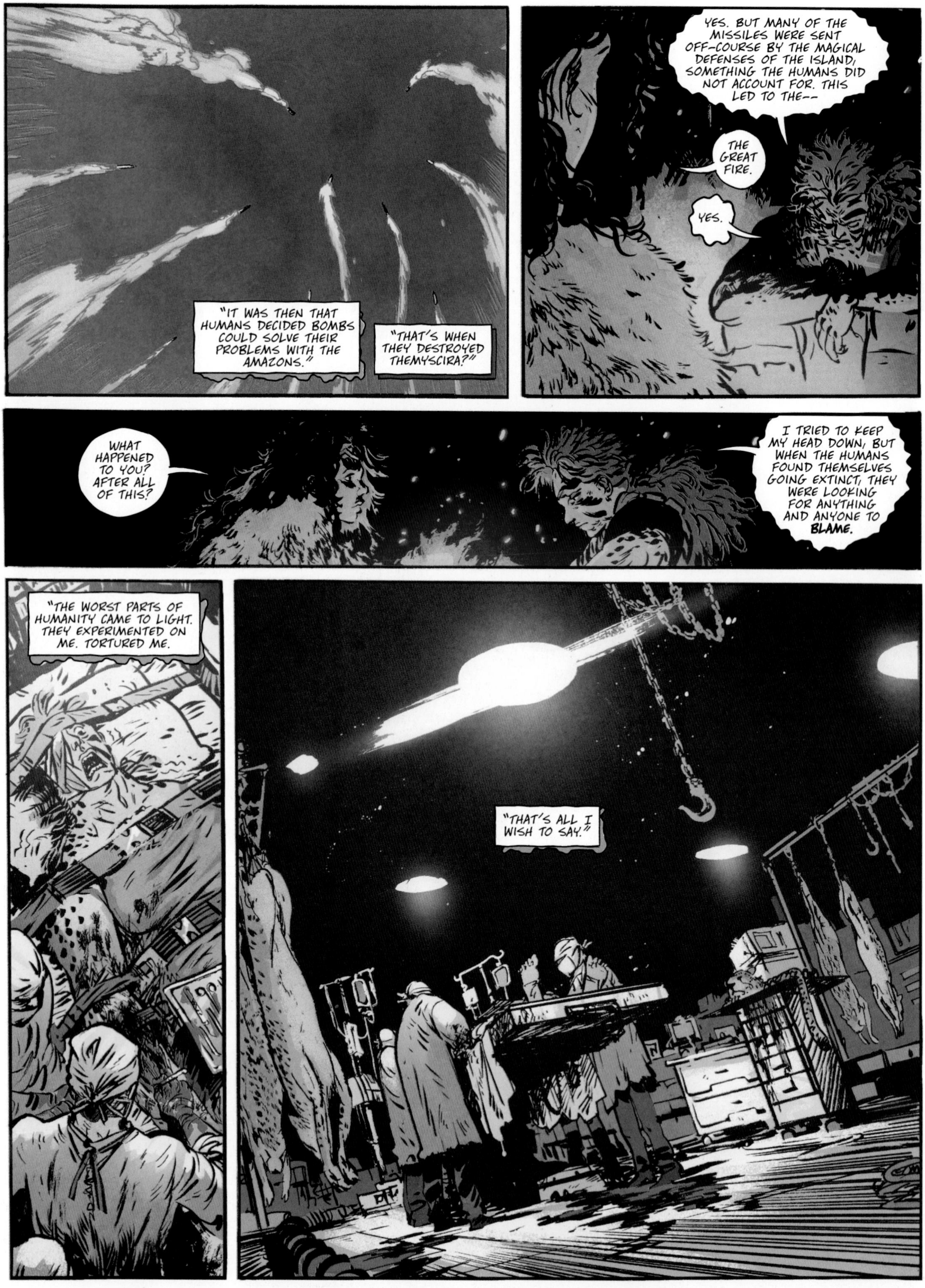
"IT WAS THEN THAT HUMANS DECIDED BOMBS COULD SOLVE THEIR PROBLEMS WITH THE AMAZONS."
"THAT'S WHEN THEY DESTROYED THEMYSCIRA?"
YES. BUT MANY OF THE MISSILES WERE SENT OFF-COURSE BY THE MAGICAL DEFENSES OF THE ISLAND, SOMETHING THE HUMANS DID NOT ACCOUNT FOR. THIS LED TO THE--
THE GREAT FIRE.
YES.
WHAT HAPPENED TO YOU? AFTER ALL OF THIS?
I TRIED TO KEEP MY HEAD DOWN, BUT WHEN THE HUMANS FOUND THEMSELVES GOING EXTINCT, THEY WERE LOOKING FOR ANYTHING AND ANYONE TO BLAME.
"THE WORST PARTS OF HUMANITY CAME TO LIGHT. THEY EXPERIMENTED ON ME. TORTURED ME.
"THAT'S ALL I WISH TO SAY."

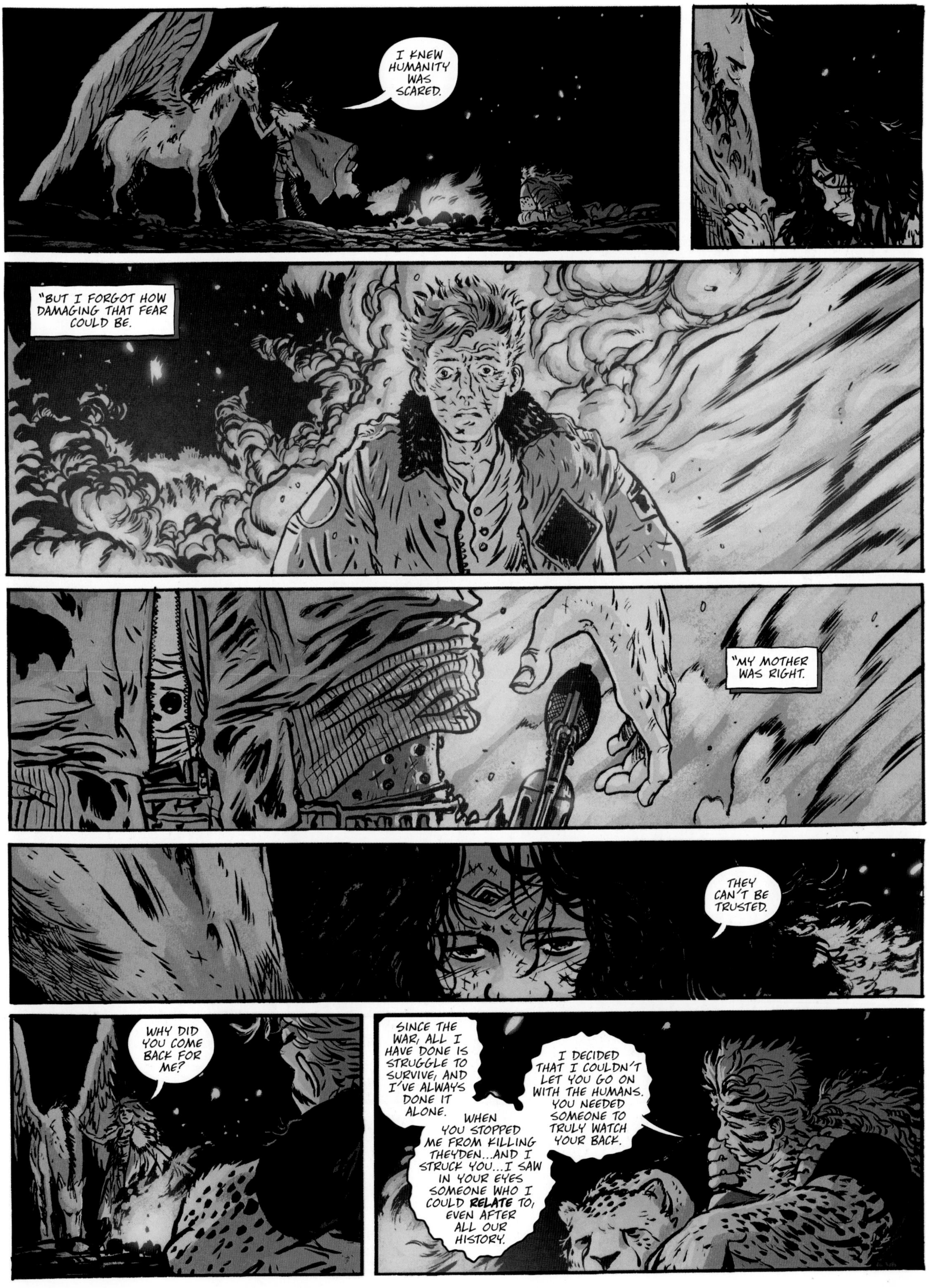
I KNEW HUMANITY WAS SCARED.
"BUT I FORGOT HOW DAMAGING THAT FEAR COULD BE.
"MY MOTHER WAS RIGHT.
THEY CAN'T BE TRUSTED.
WHY DID YOU COME BACK FOR ME?
SINCE THE WAR, ALL I HAVE DONE IS STRUGGLE TO SURVIVE, AND I'VE ALWAYS DONE IT ALONE.
WHEN YOU STOPPED ME FROM KILLING THEYDEN...AND I STRUCK YOU...I SAW IN YOUR EYES SOMEONE WHO I COULD **RELATE** TO, EVEN AFTER ALL OUR HISTORY.
I DECIDED THAT I COULDN'T LET YOU GO ON WITH THE HUMANS. YOU NEEDED SOMEONE TO TRULY WATCH YOUR BACK.

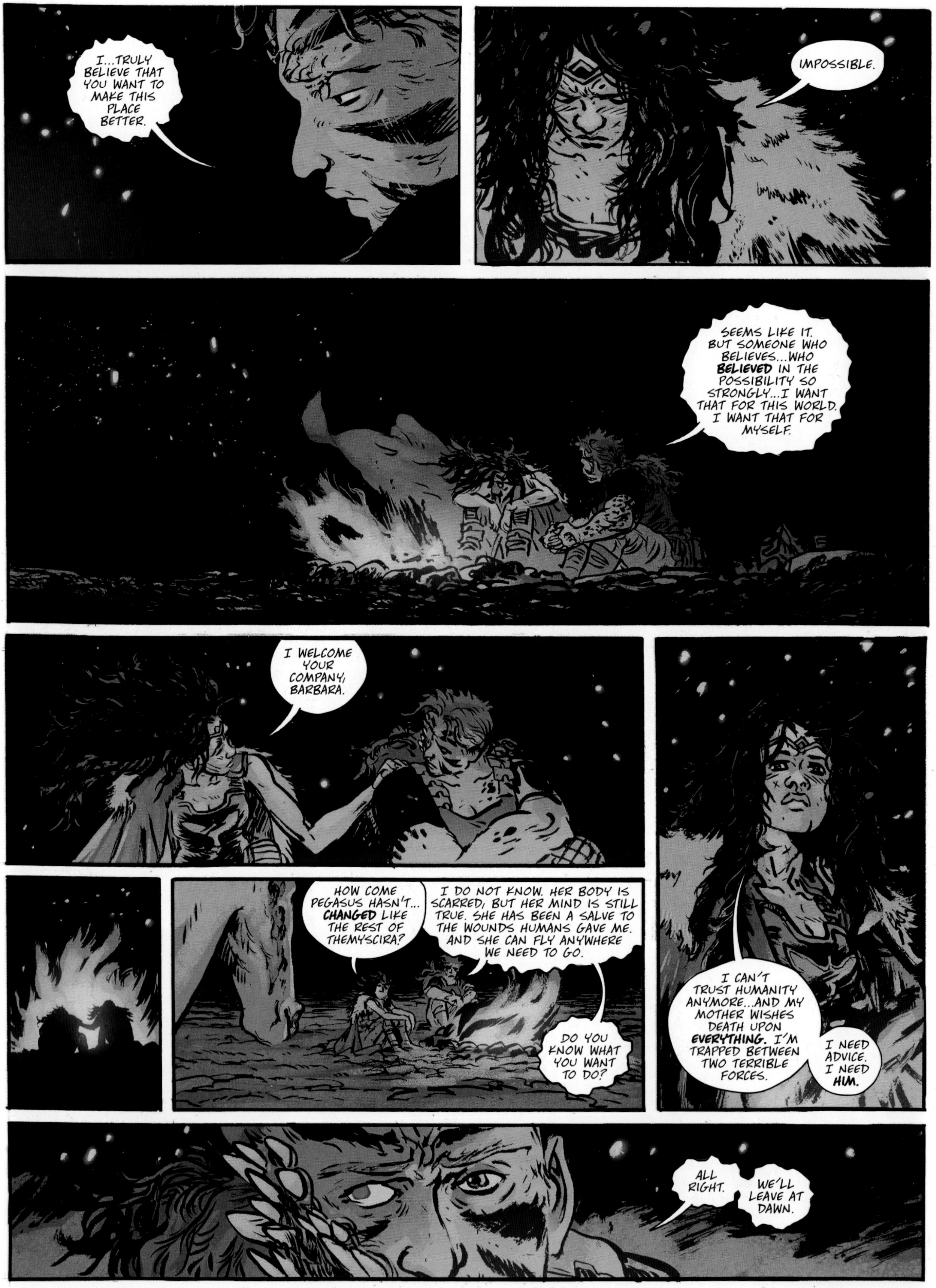
I...TRULY BELIEVE THAT YOU WANT TO MAKE THIS PLACE BETTER.
IMPOSSIBLE.
SEEMS LIKE IT. BUT SOMEONE WHO BELIEVES...WHO **BELIEVED** IN THE POSSIBILITY SO STRONGLY...I WANT THAT FOR THIS WORLD. I WANT THAT FOR MYSELF.
I WELCOME YOUR COMPANY, BARBARA.
HOW COME PEGASUS HASN'T... **CHANGED** LIKE THE REST OF THEMYSCIRA?
I DO NOT KNOW. HER BODY IS SCARRED, BUT HER MIND IS STILL TRUE. SHE HAS BEEN A SALVE TO THE WOUNDS HUMANS GAVE ME. AND SHE CAN FLY ANYWHERE WE NEED TO GO.
DO YOU KNOW WHAT YOU WANT TO DO?
I CAN'T TRUST HUMANITY ANYMORE...AND MY MOTHER WISHES DEATH UPON **EVERYTHING.** I'M TRAPPED BETWEEN TWO TERRIBLE FORCES.
I NEED ADVICE. I NEED **HIM.**
ALL RIGHT.
WE'LL LEAVE AT DAWN.

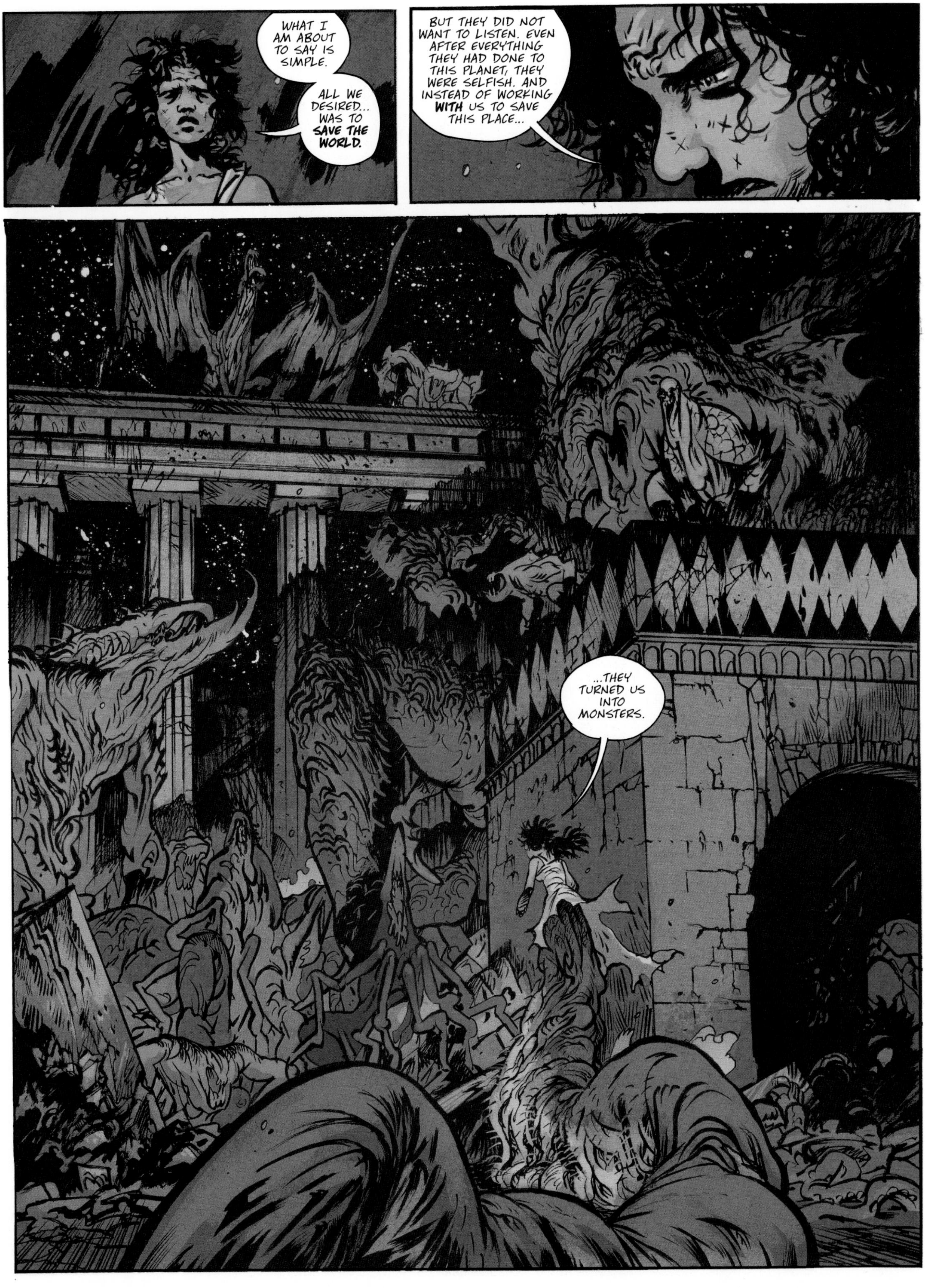
WHAT I AM ABOUT TO SAY IS SIMPLE.
ALL WE DESIRED... WAS TO **SAVE THE WORLD.**
BUT THEY DID NOT WANT TO LISTEN. EVEN AFTER EVERYTHING THEY HAD DONE TO THIS PLANET, THEY WERE SELFISH. AND INSTEAD OF WORKING **WITH** US TO SAVE THIS PLACE...
...THEY TURNED US INTO MONSTERS.

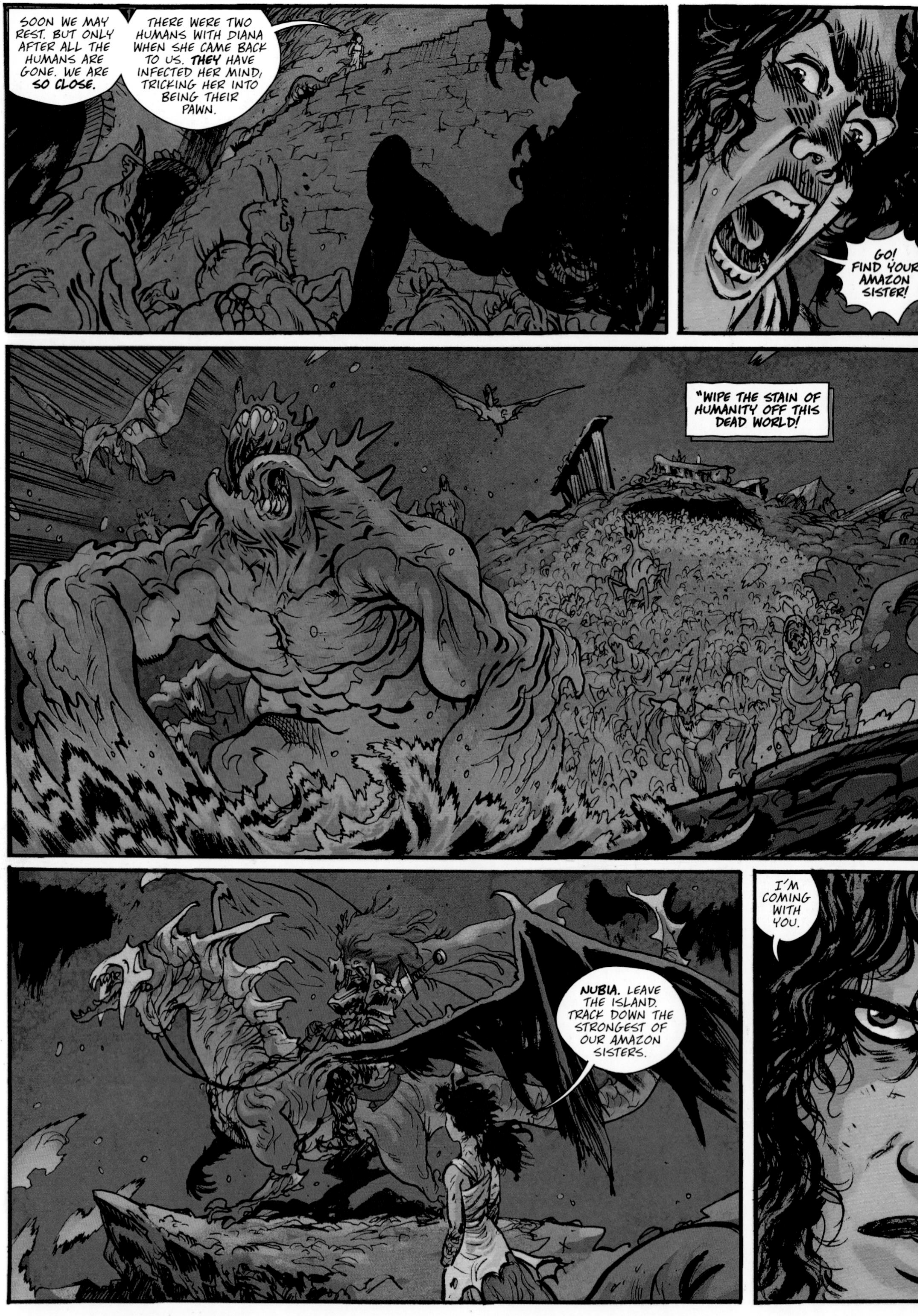
SOON WE MAY REST. BUT ONLY AFTER ALL THE HUMANS ARE GONE. WE ARE **SO CLOSE.**
THERE WERE TWO HUMANS WITH DIANA WHEN SHE CAME BACK TO US. **THEY** HAVE INFECTED HER MIND, TRICKING HER INTO BEING THEIR PAWN.
GO! FIND YOUR AMAZON SISTER!
"WIPE THE STAIN OF HUMANITY OFF THIS DEAD WORLD!
NUBIA. LEAVE THE ISLAND. TRACK DOWN THE STRONGEST OF OUR AMAZON SISTERS.
I'M COMING WITH YOU.

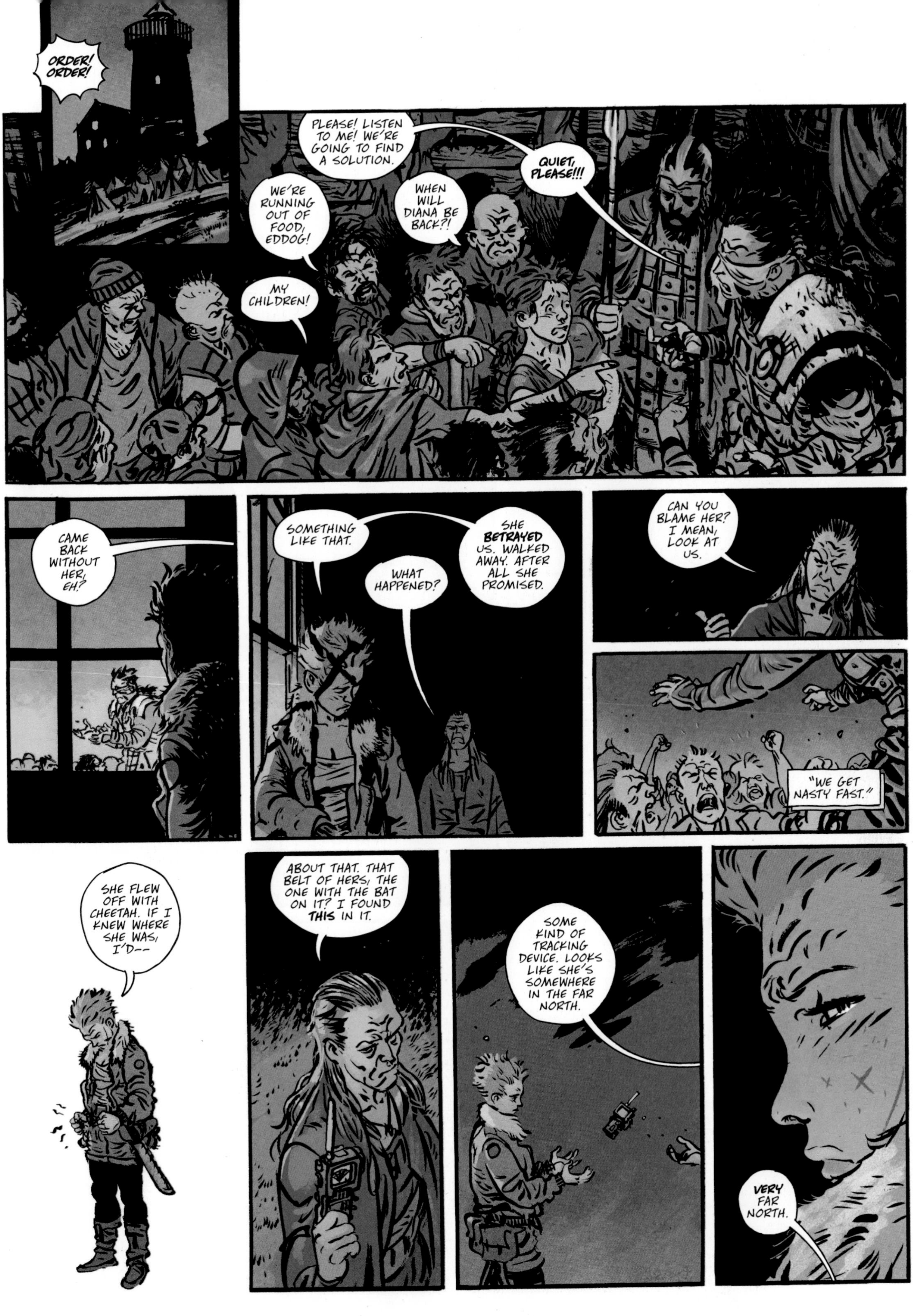

ORDER! ORDER!
PLEASE! LISTEN TO ME! WE'RE GOING TO FIND A SOLUTION.
WE'RE RUNNING OUT OF FOOD, EDDOG!
WHEN WILL DIANA BE BACK?!
QUIET, PLEASE!!!
MY CHILDREN!
CAME BACK WITHOUT HER, EH?
SOMETHING LIKE THAT.
WHAT HAPPENED?
SHE BETRAYED US. WALKED AWAY. AFTER ALL SHE PROMISED.
CAN YOU BLAME HER? I MEAN, LOOK AT US.
"WE GET NASTY FAST."
SHE FLEW OFF WITH CHEETAH. IF I KNEW WHERE SHE WAS, I'D--
ABOUT THAT. THAT BELT OF HERS, THE ONE WITH THE BAT ON IT? I FOUND THIS IN IT.
SOME KIND OF TRACKING DEVICE. LOOKS LIKE SHE'S SOMEWHERE IN THE FAR NORTH.
VERY FAR NORTH.

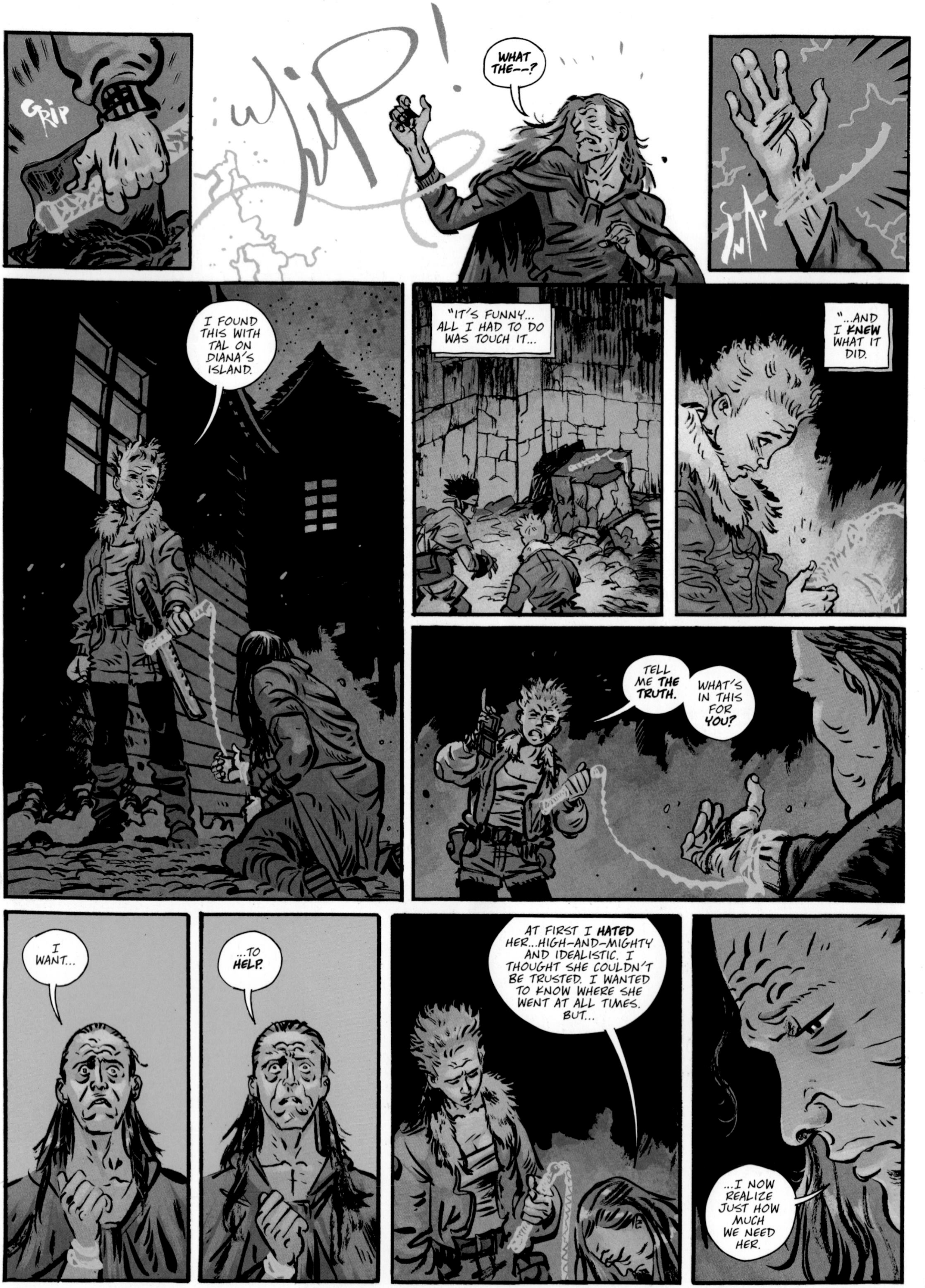
GRIP
WHIP!
WHAT THE--?
SNAP
I FOUND THIS WITH TAL ON DIANA'S ISLAND.
"IT'S FUNNY... ALL I HAD TO DO WAS TOUCH IT...
"...AND I KNEW WHAT IT DID.
TELL ME THE TRUTH.
WHAT'S IN THIS FOR YOU?
I WANT...
...TO HELP.
AT FIRST I HATED HER...HIGH-AND-MIGHTY AND IDEALISTIC. I THOUGHT SHE COULDN'T BE TRUSTED. I WANTED TO KNOW WHERE SHE WENT AT ALL TIMES. BUT...
...I NOW REALIZE JUST HOW MUCH WE NEED HER.

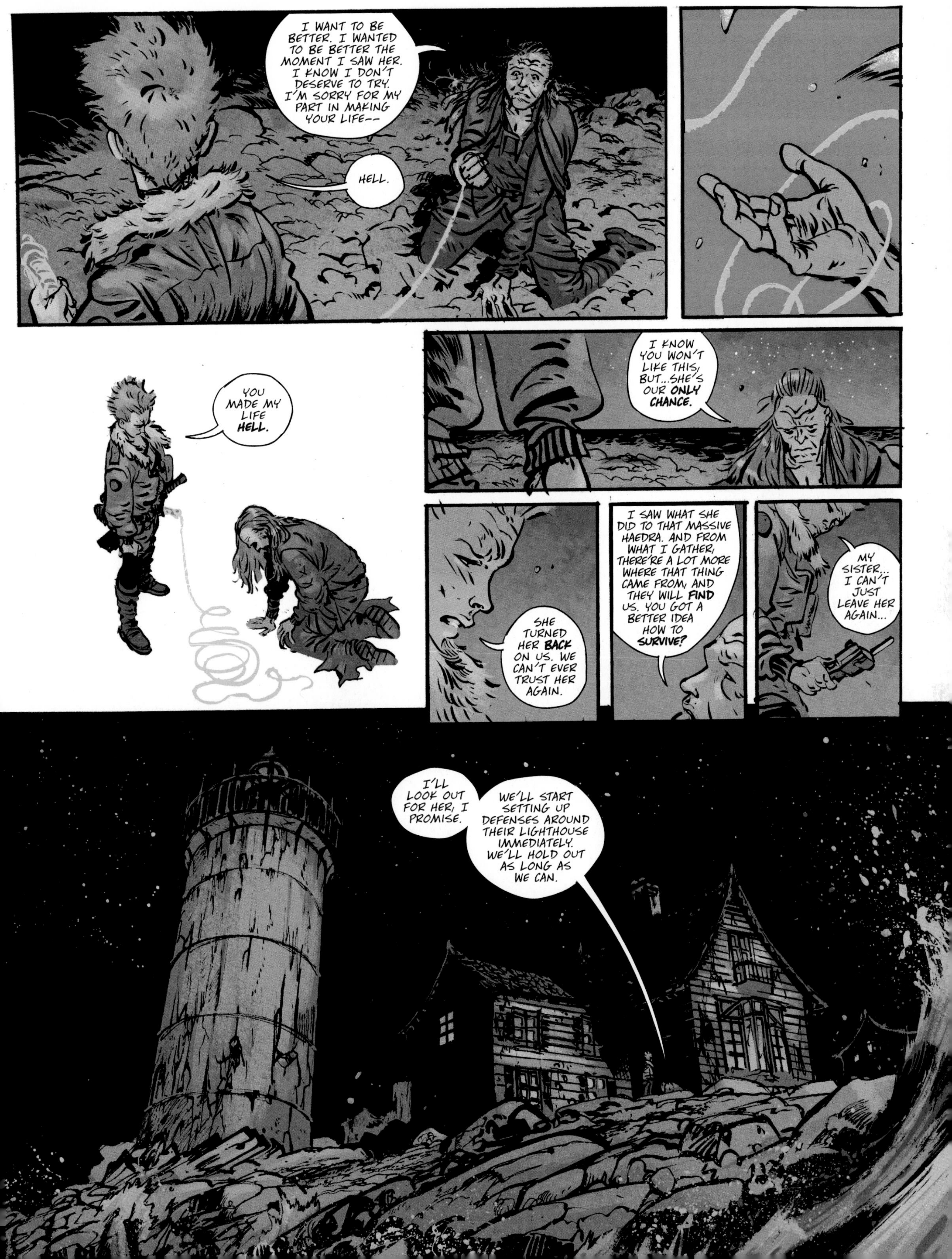
I WANT TO BE BETTER. I WANTED TO BE BETTER THE MOMENT I SAW HER. I KNOW I DON'T DESERVE TO TRY. I'M SORRY FOR MY PART IN MAKING YOUR LIFE--
HELL.
YOU MADE MY LIFE HELL.
I KNOW YOU WON'T LIKE THIS, BUT...SHE'S OUR ONLY CHANCE.
SHE TURNED HER BACK ON US. WE CAN'T EVER TRUST HER AGAIN.
I SAW WHAT SHE DID TO THAT MASSIVE HAEDRA. AND FROM WHAT I GATHER, THERE'RE A LOT MORE WHERE THAT THING CAME FROM, AND THEY WILL FIND US. YOU GOT A BETTER IDEA HOW TO SURVIVE?
MY SISTER... I CAN'T JUST LEAVE HER AGAIN...
I'LL LOOK OUT FOR HER, I PROMISE.
WE'LL START SETTING UP DEFENSES AROUND THEIR LIGHTHOUSE IMMEDIATELY. WE'LL HOLD OUT AS LONG AS WE CAN.

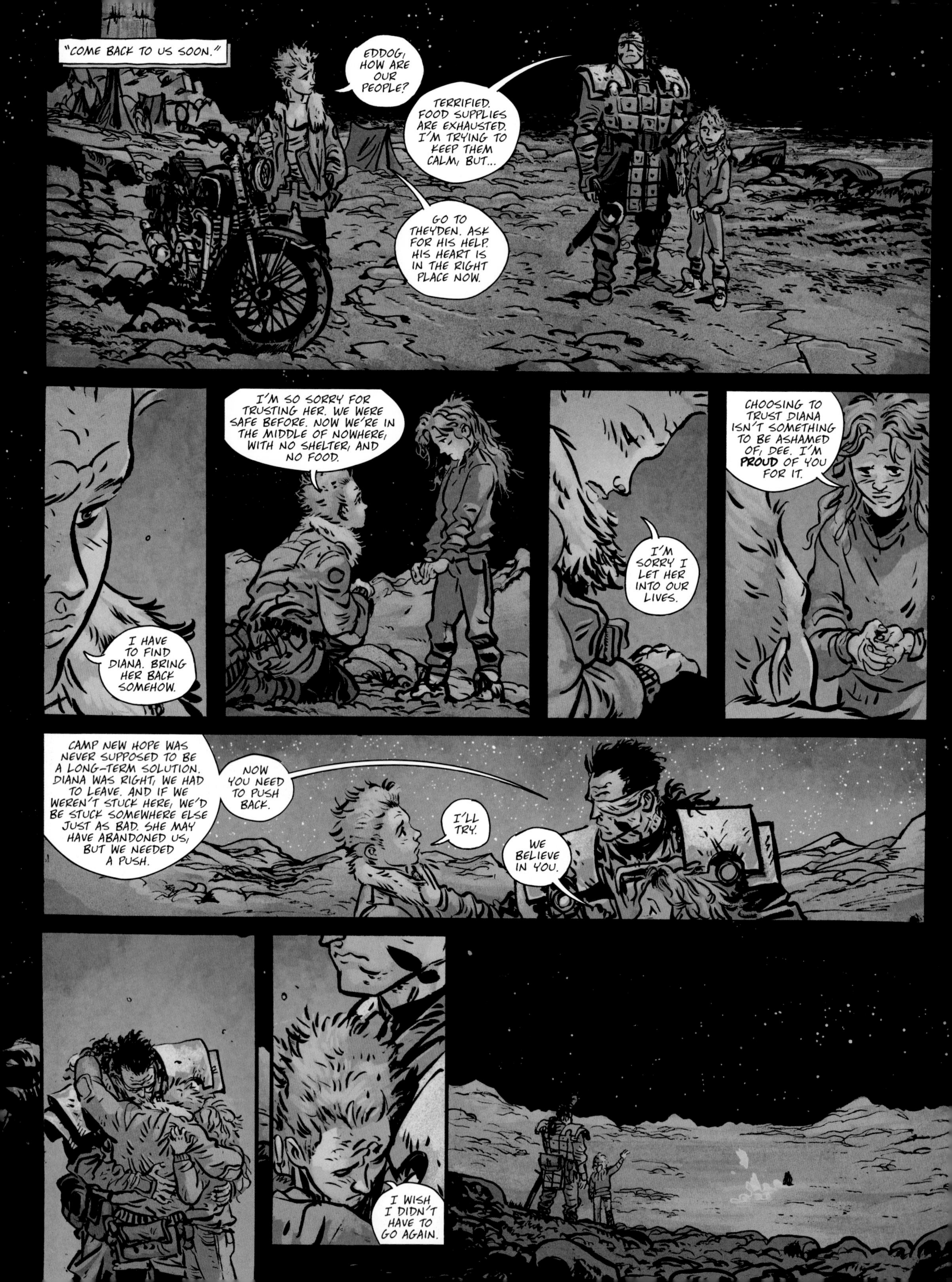
"COME BACK TO US SOON."
EDDOG, HOW ARE OUR PEOPLE?
TERRIFIED. FOOD SUPPLIES ARE EXHAUSTED. I'M TRYING TO KEEP THEM CALM, BUT...
GO TO THEYDEN. ASK FOR HIS HELP. HIS HEART IS IN THE RIGHT PLACE NOW.
I HAVE TO FIND DIANA. BRING HER BACK SOMEHOW.
I'M SO SORRY FOR TRUSTING HER. WE WERE SAFE BEFORE. NOW WE'RE IN THE MIDDLE OF NOWHERE, WITH NO SHELTER, AND NO FOOD.
I'M SORRY I LET HER INTO OUR LIVES.
CHOOSING TO TRUST DIANA ISN'T SOMETHING TO BE ASHAMED OF, DEE. I'M **PROUD** OF YOU FOR IT.
CAMP NEW HOPE WAS NEVER SUPPOSED TO BE A LONG-TERM SOLUTION. DIANA WAS RIGHT, WE HAD TO LEAVE. AND IF WE WEREN'T STUCK HERE, WE'D BE STUCK SOMEWHERE ELSE JUST AS BAD. SHE MAY HAVE ABANDONED US, BUT WE NEEDED A PUSH.
NOW YOU NEED TO PUSH BACK.
I'LL TRY.
WE BELIEVE IN YOU.
I WISH I DIDN'T HAVE TO GO AGAIN.

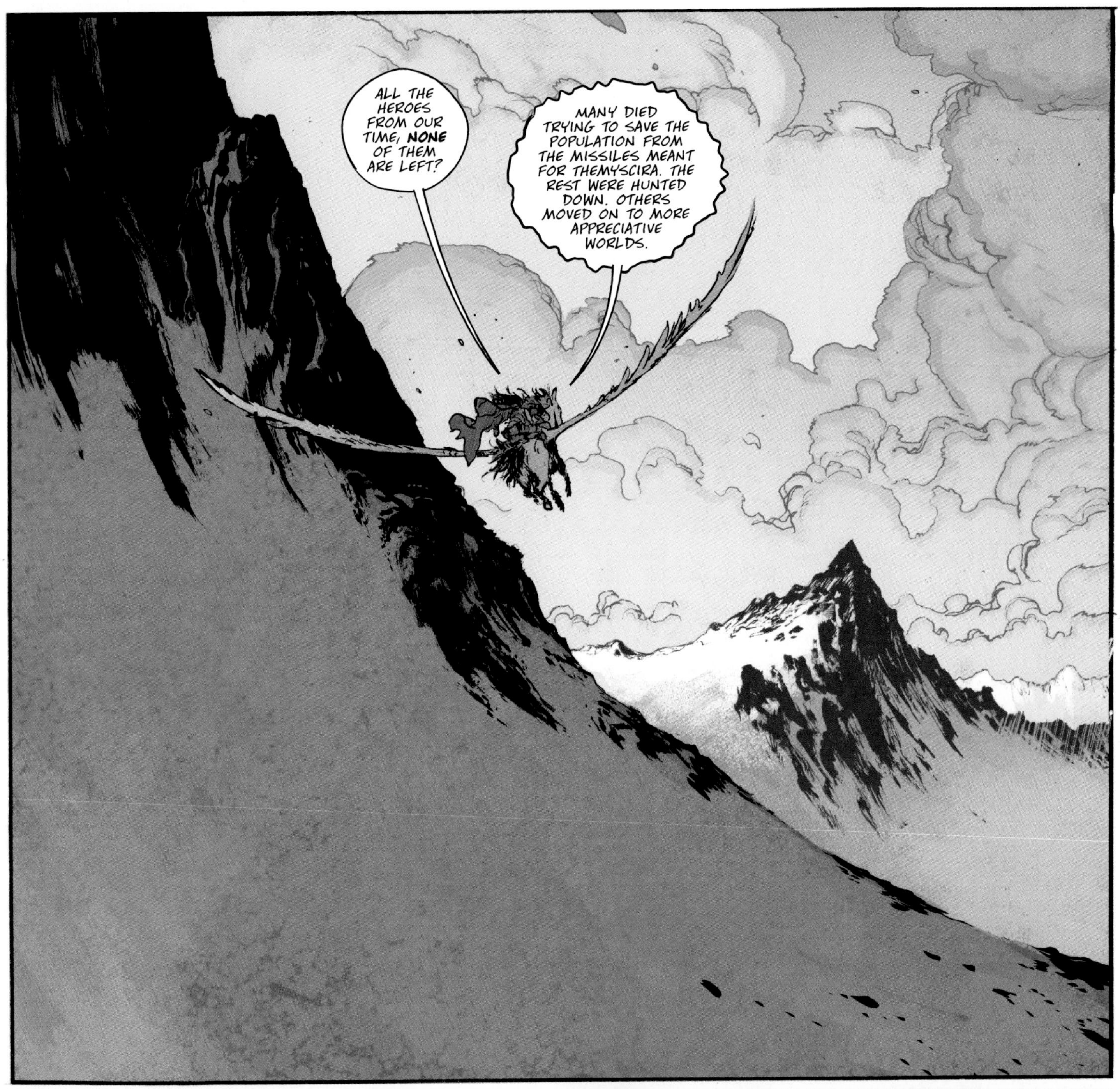
ALL THE HEROES FROM OUR TIME; **NONE** OF THEM ARE LEFT?
MANY DIED TRYING TO SAVE THE POPULATION FROM THE MISSILES MEANT FOR THEMYSCIRA. THE REST WERE HUNTED DOWN. OTHERS MOVED ON TO MORE APPRECIATIVE WORLDS.

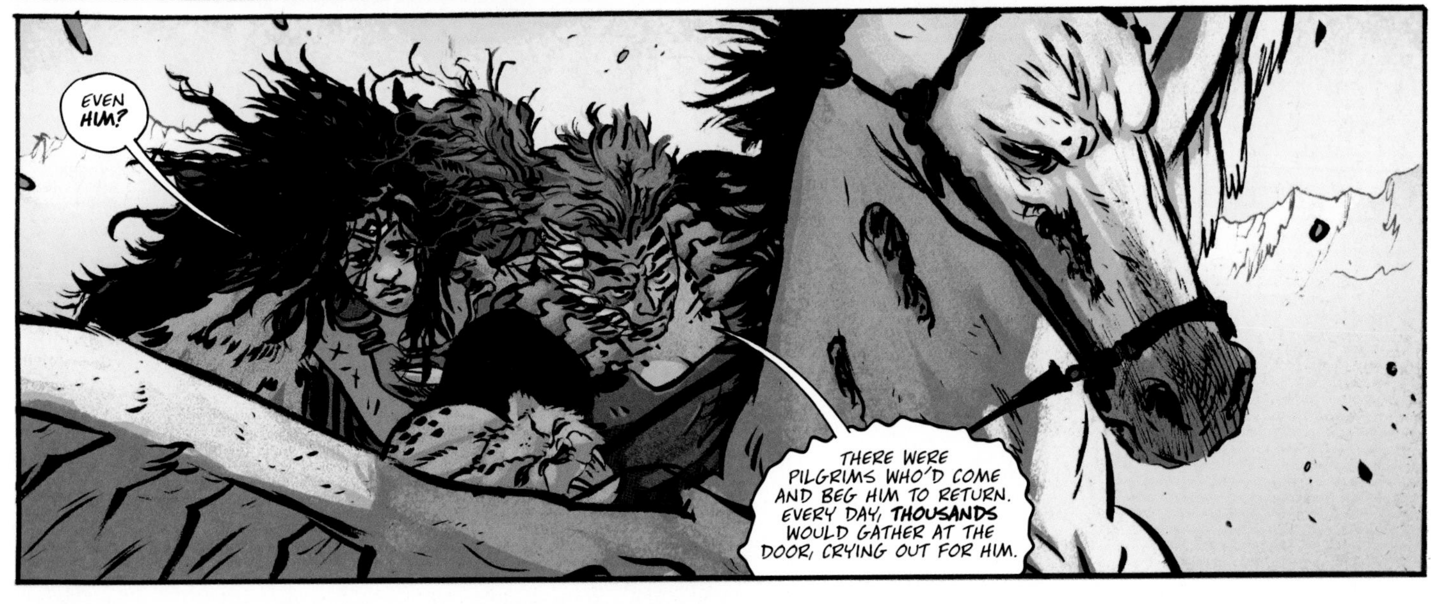
EVEN **HIM?**
THERE WERE PILGRIMS WHO'D COME AND BEG HIM TO RETURN. EVERY DAY, **THOUSANDS** WOULD GATHER AT THE DOOR, CRYING OUT FOR HIM.

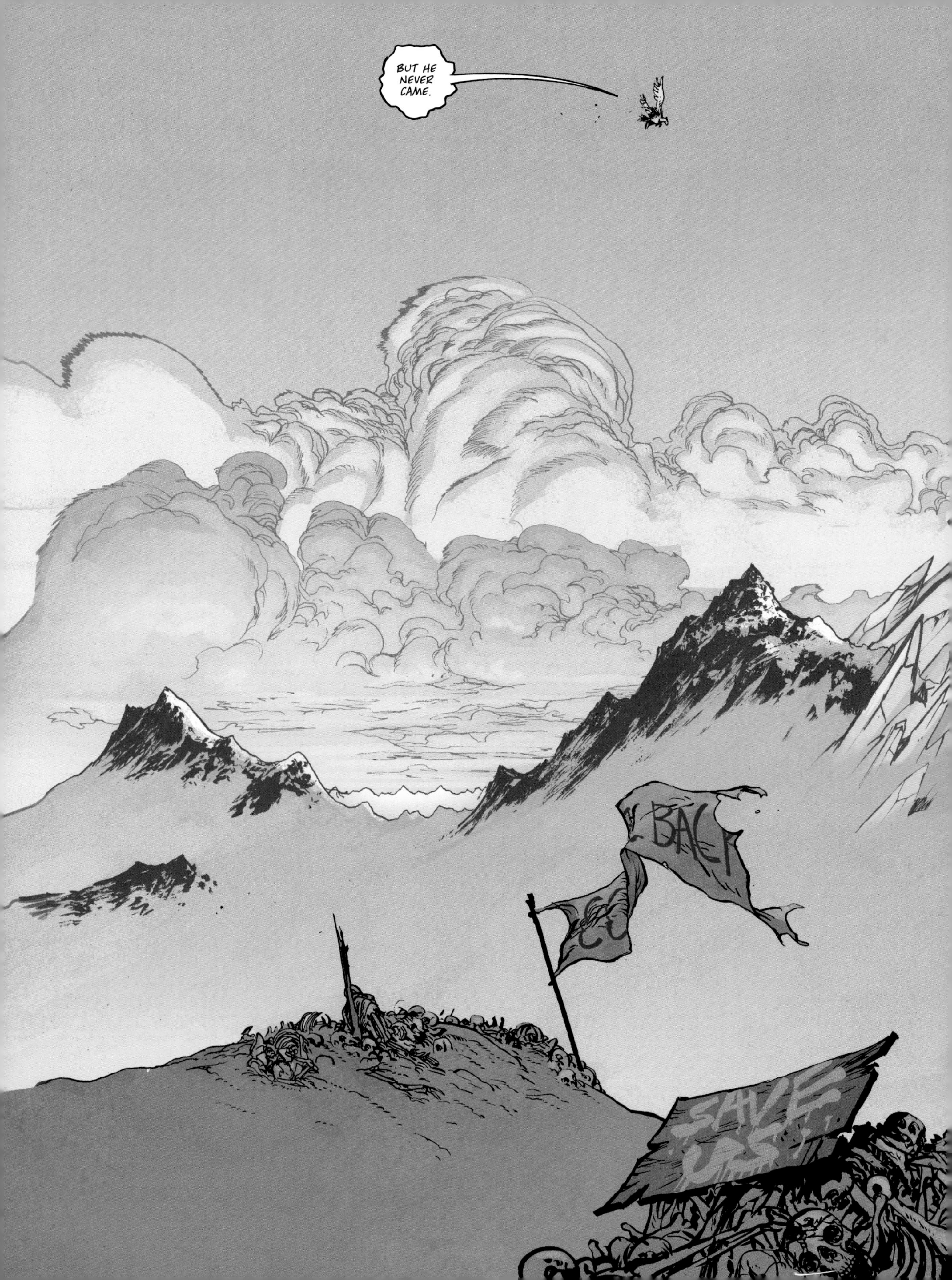
BUT HE NEVER CAME.
SAVE US

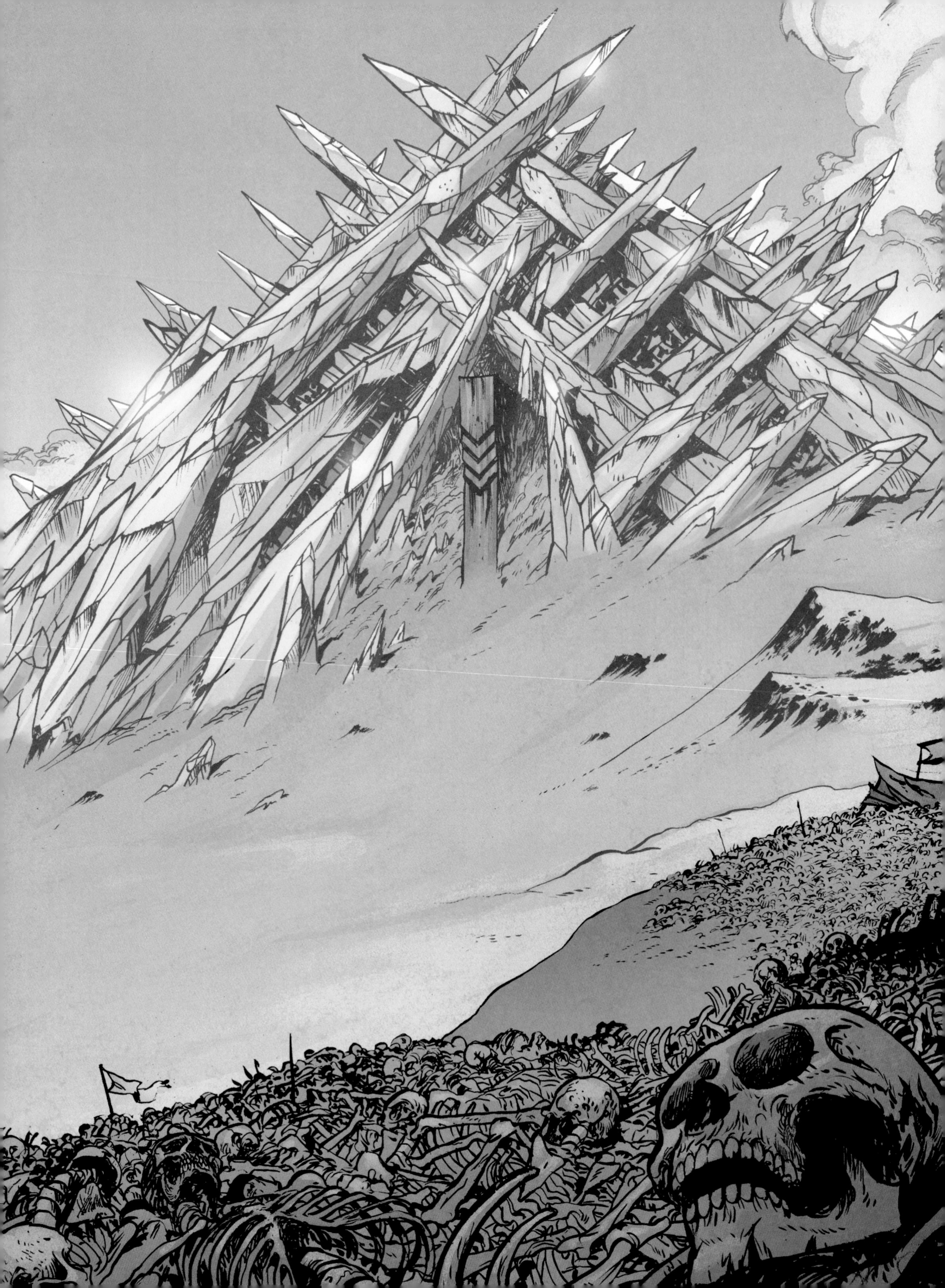

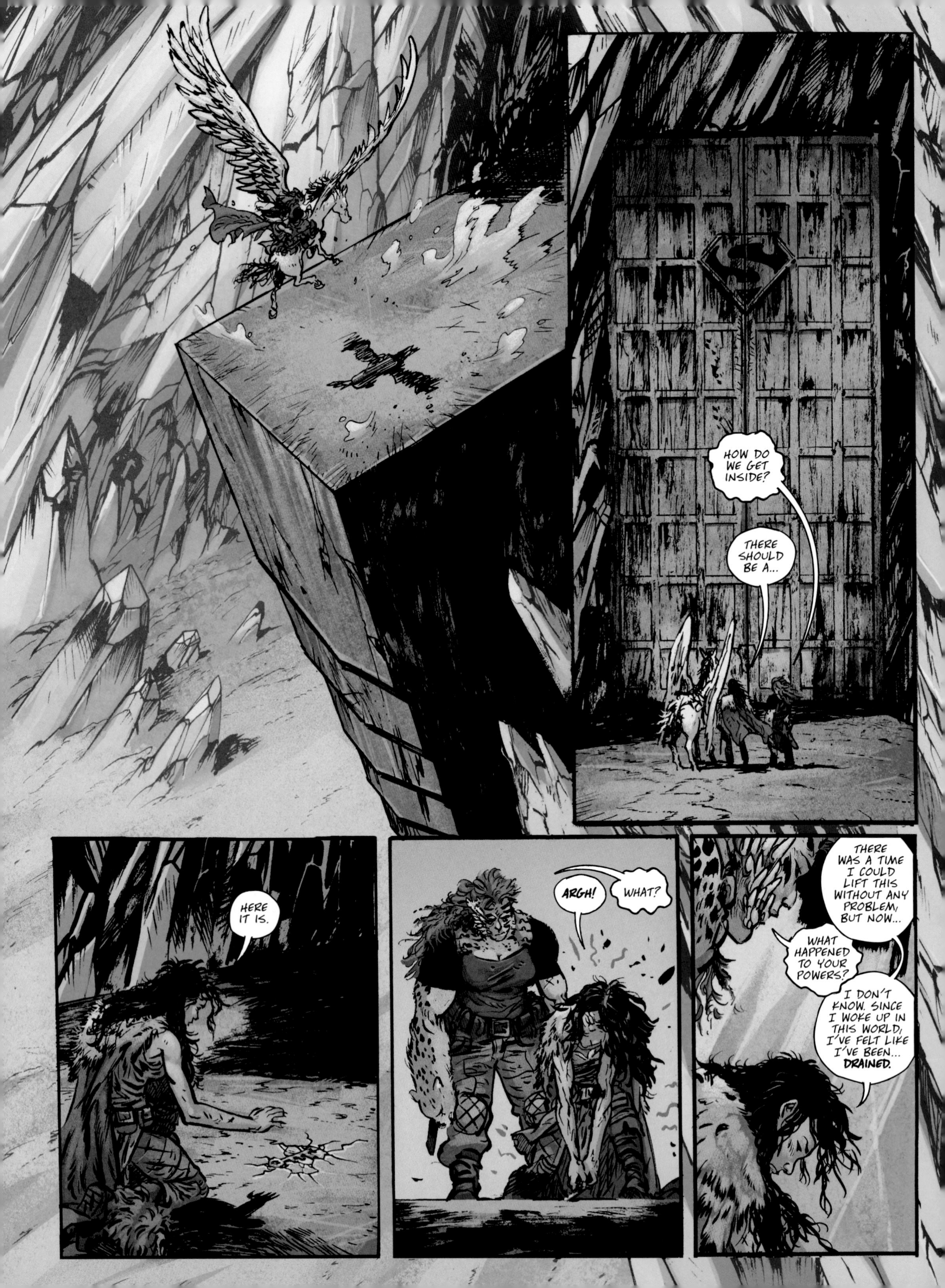
HOW DO WE GET INSIDE?
THERE SHOULD BE A...
HERE IT IS.
ARGH!
WHAT?
THERE WAS A TIME I COULD LIFT THIS WITHOUT ANY PROBLEM, BUT NOW...
WHAT HAPPENED TO YOUR POWERS?
I DON'T KNOW. SINCE I WOKE UP IN THIS WORLD, I'VE FELT LIKE I'VE BEEN... **DRAINED.**

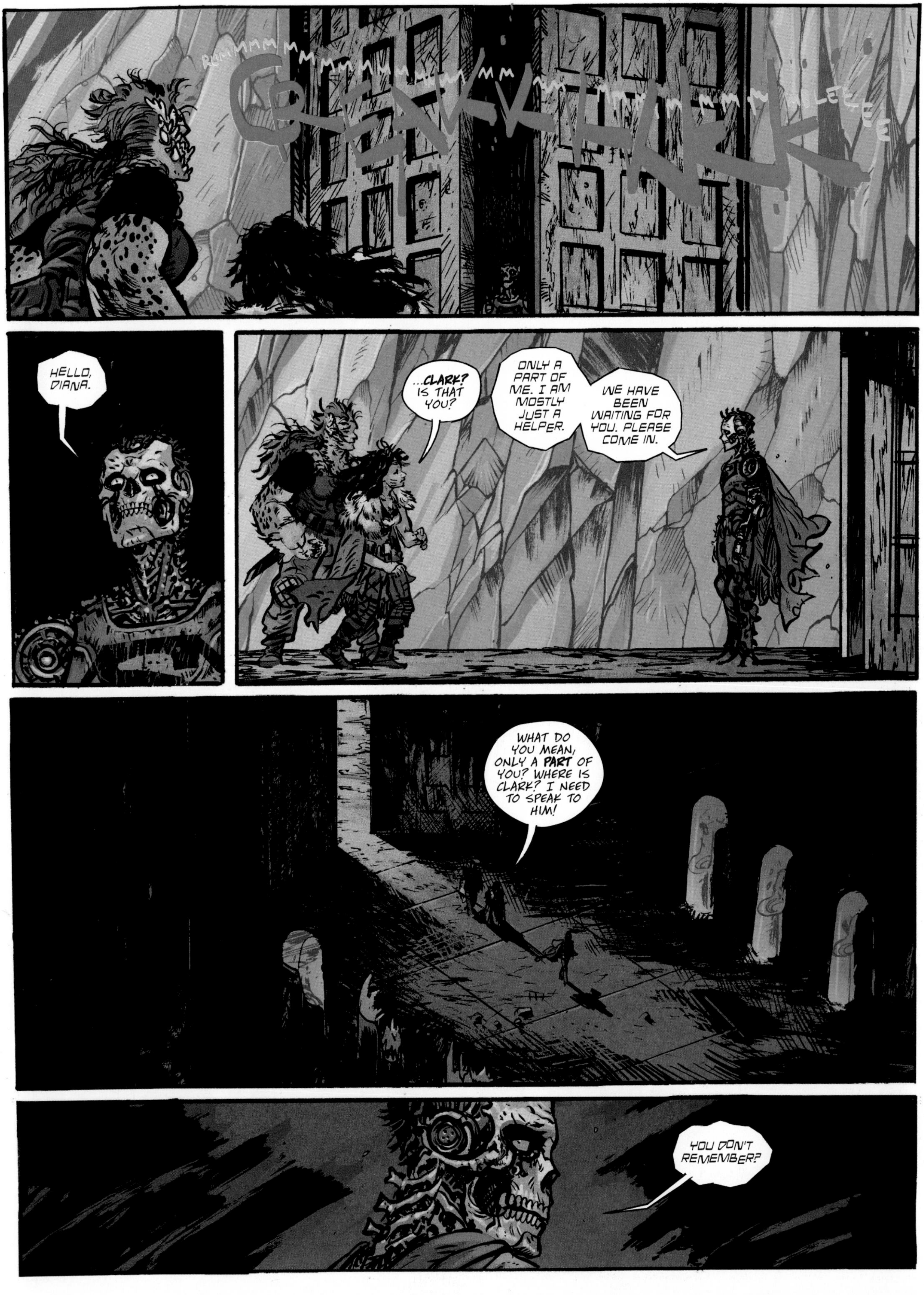

HELLO, DIANA.
...CLARK? IS THAT YOU?
ONLY A PART OF ME. I AM MOSTLY JUST A HELPER.
WE HAVE BEEN WAITING FOR YOU. PLEASE COME IN.
WHAT DO YOU MEAN, ONLY A PART OF YOU? WHERE IS CLARK? I NEED TO SPEAK TO HIM!
YOU DON'T REMEMBER?

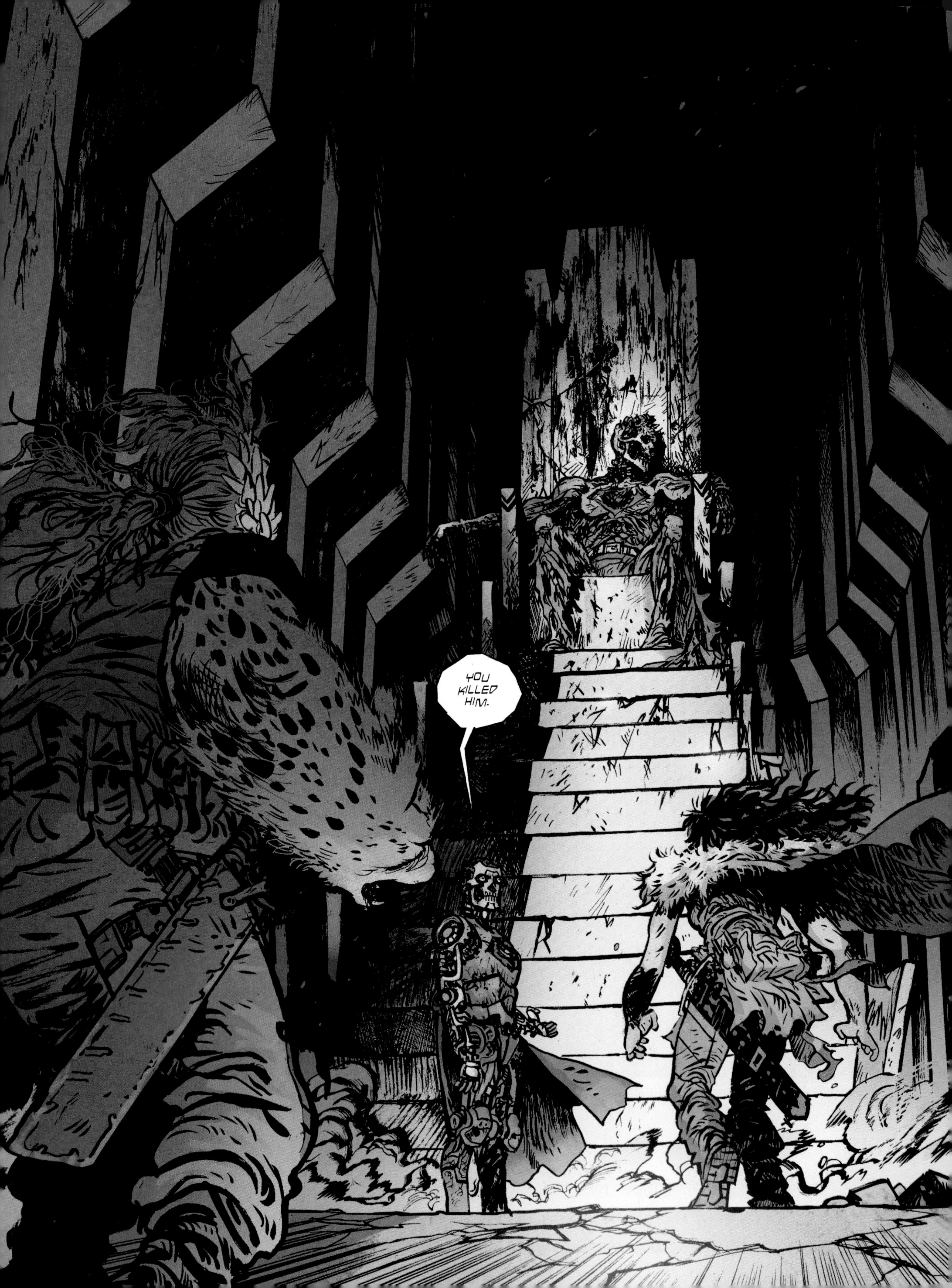
YOU KILLED HIM.

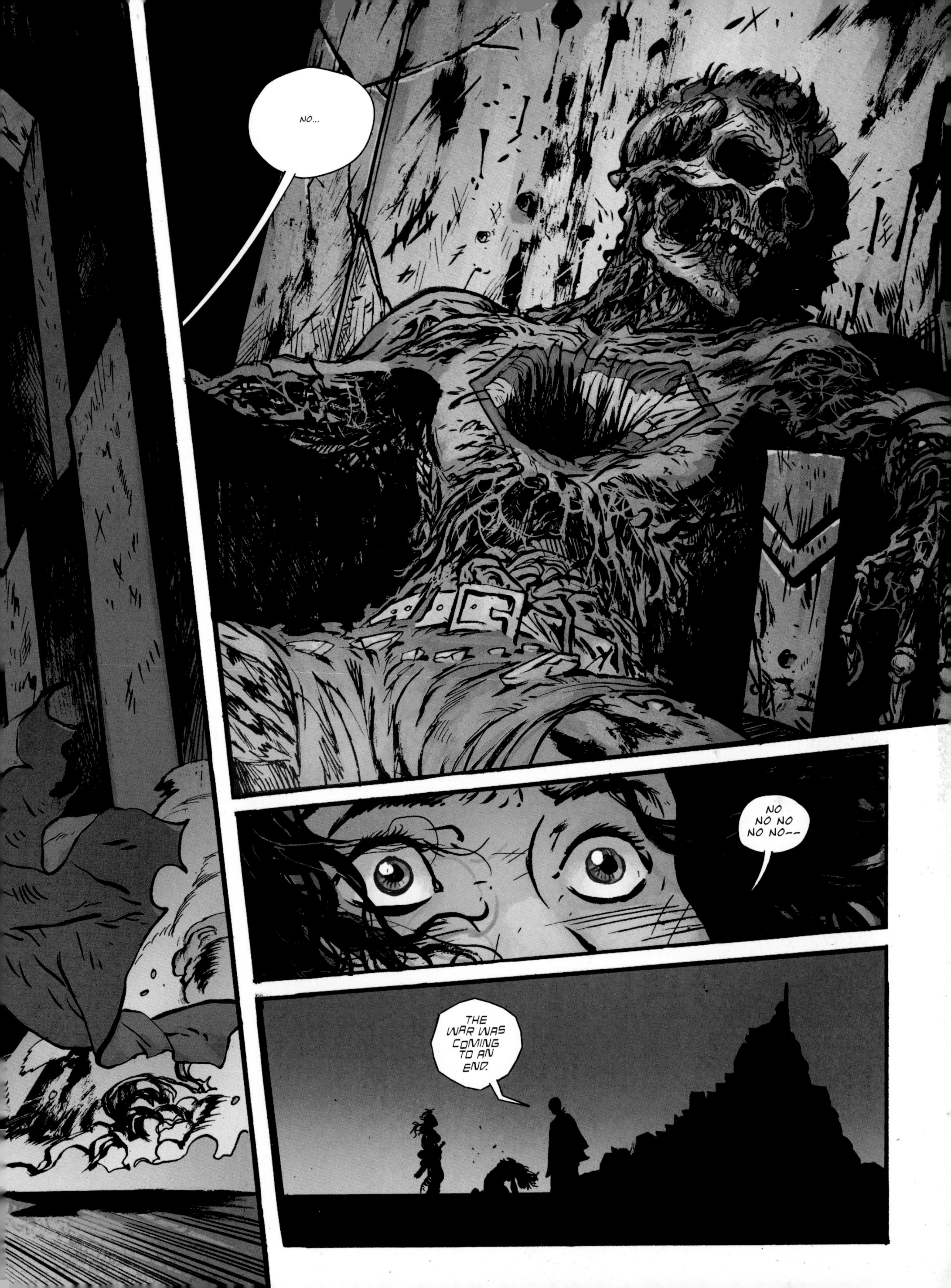
NO...
NO NO NO NO NO--
THE WAR WAS COMING TO AN END.

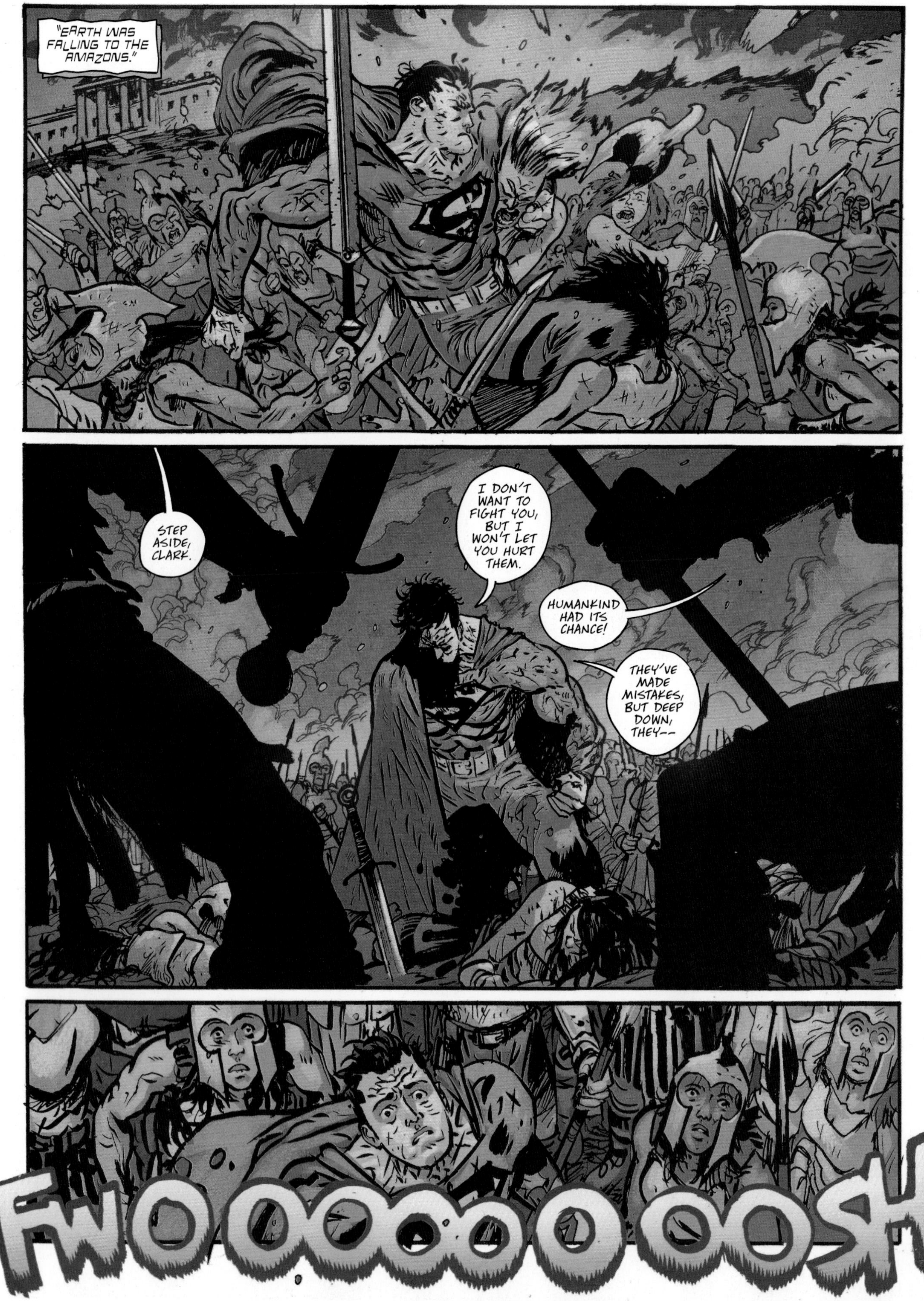
"EARTH WAS FALLING TO THE AMAZONS."
STEP ASIDE, CLARK.
I DON'T WANT TO FIGHT YOU, BUT I WON'T LET YOU HURT THEM.
HUMANKIND HAD ITS CHANCE!
THEY'VE MADE MISTAKES, BUT DEEP DOWN, THEY--
FWOOOOOOOSH

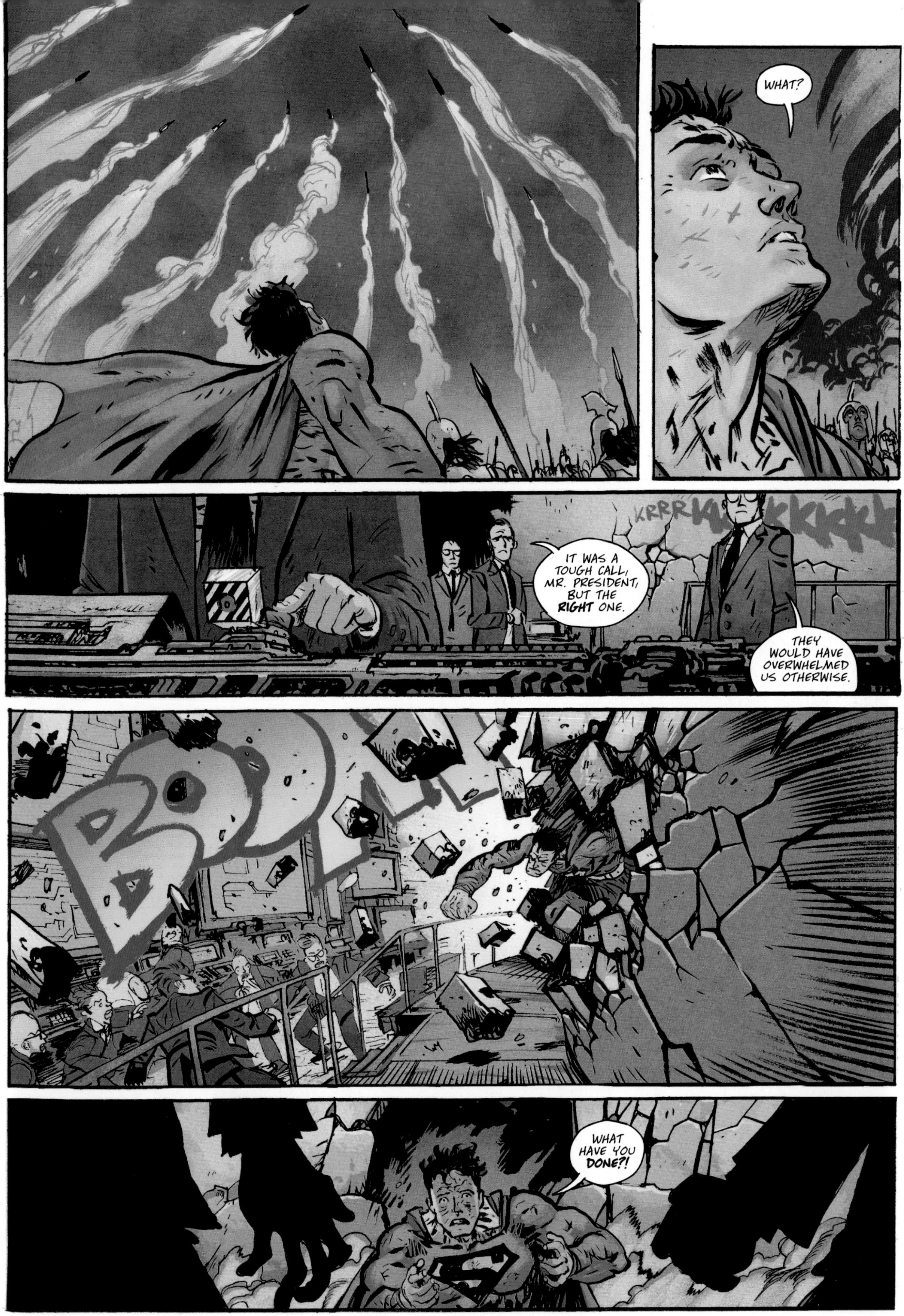
WHAT?
KRRRKKKKKK
IT WAS A TOUGH CALL, MR. PRESIDENT, BUT THE **RIGHT** ONE.
THEY WOULD HAVE OVERWHELMED US OTHERWISE.
WHAT HAVE YOU **DONE?!**

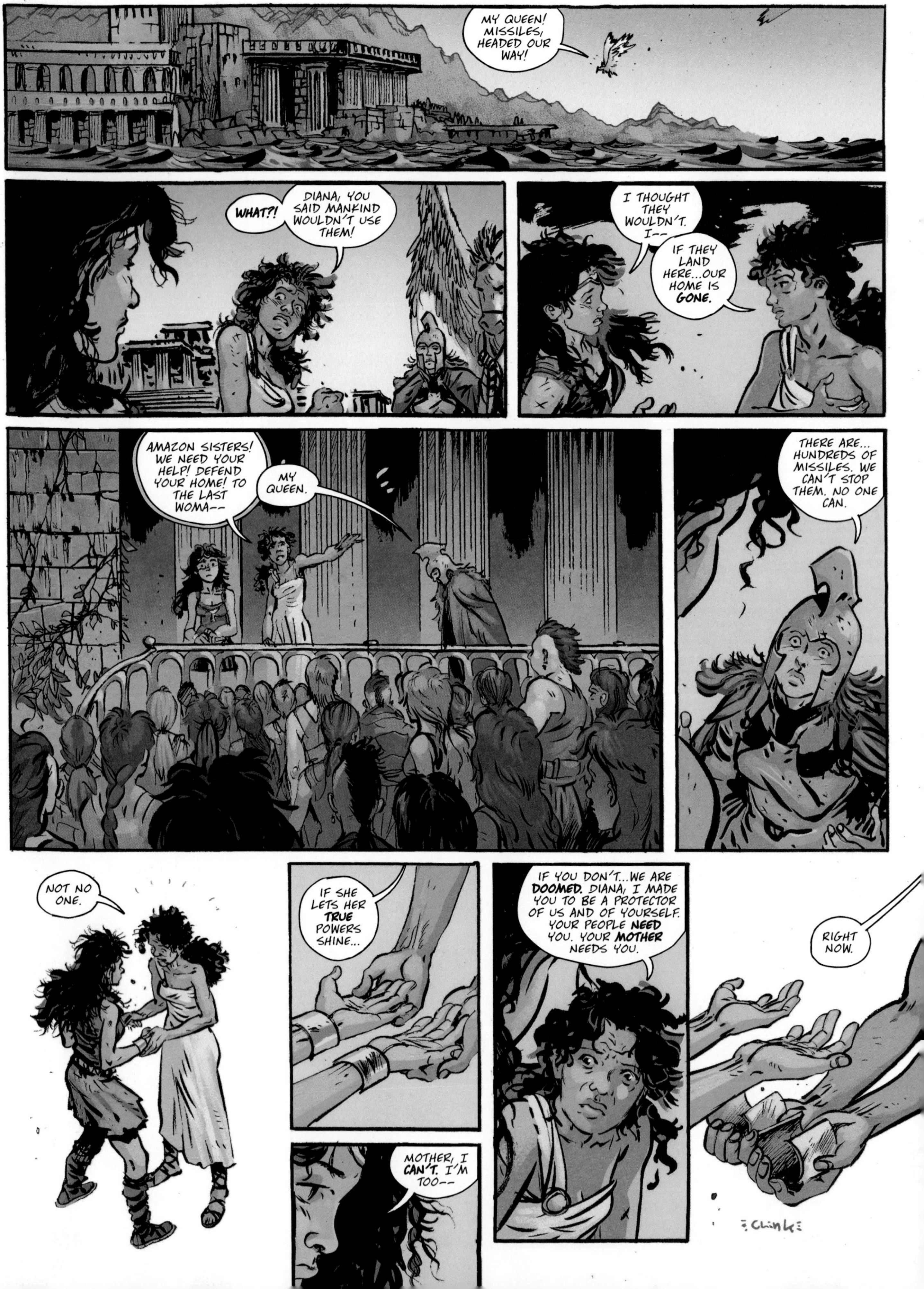
MY QUEEN! MISSILES, HEADED OUR WAY!
WHAT?!
DIANA, YOU SAID MANKIND WOULDN'T USE THEM!
I THOUGHT THEY WOULDN'T. I--
IF THEY LAND HERE...OUR HOME IS **GONE.**
AMAZON SISTERS! WE NEED YOUR HELP! DEFEND YOUR HOME! TO THE LAST WOMA--
MY QUEEN.
THERE ARE... HUNDREDS OF MISSILES. WE CAN'T STOP THEM. NO ONE CAN.
NOT NO ONE.
IF SHE LETS HER **TRUE** POWERS SHINE...
MOTHER, I **CAN'T.** I'M TOO--
IF YOU DON'T...WE ARE **DOOMED.** DIANA, I MADE YOU TO BE A PROTECTOR OF US AND OF YOURSELF. YOUR PEOPLE **NEED** YOU. YOUR **MOTHER** NEEDS YOU.
RIGHT NOW.
CLINK

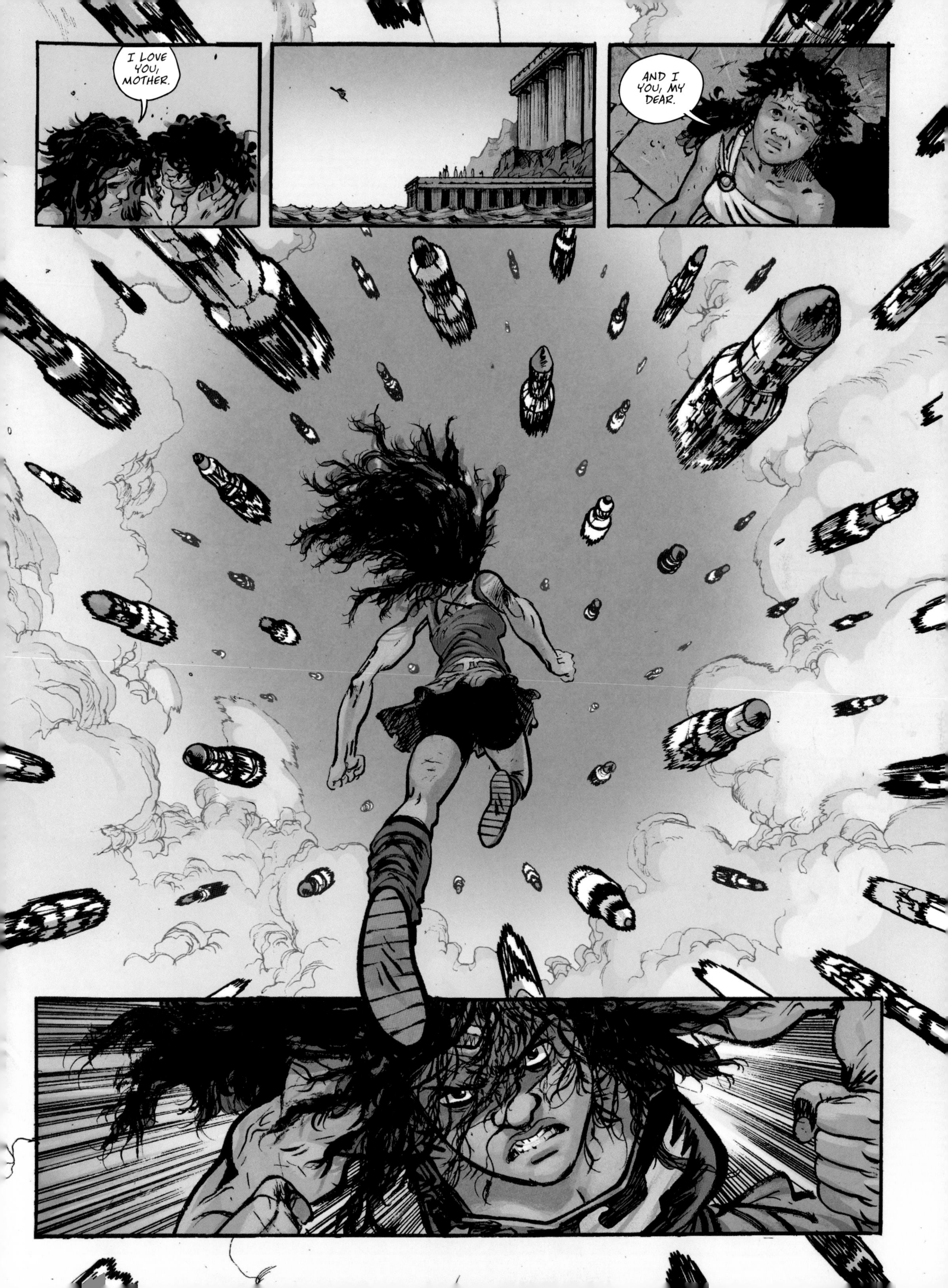
I LOVE YOU, MOTHER.
AND I YOU, MY DEAR.

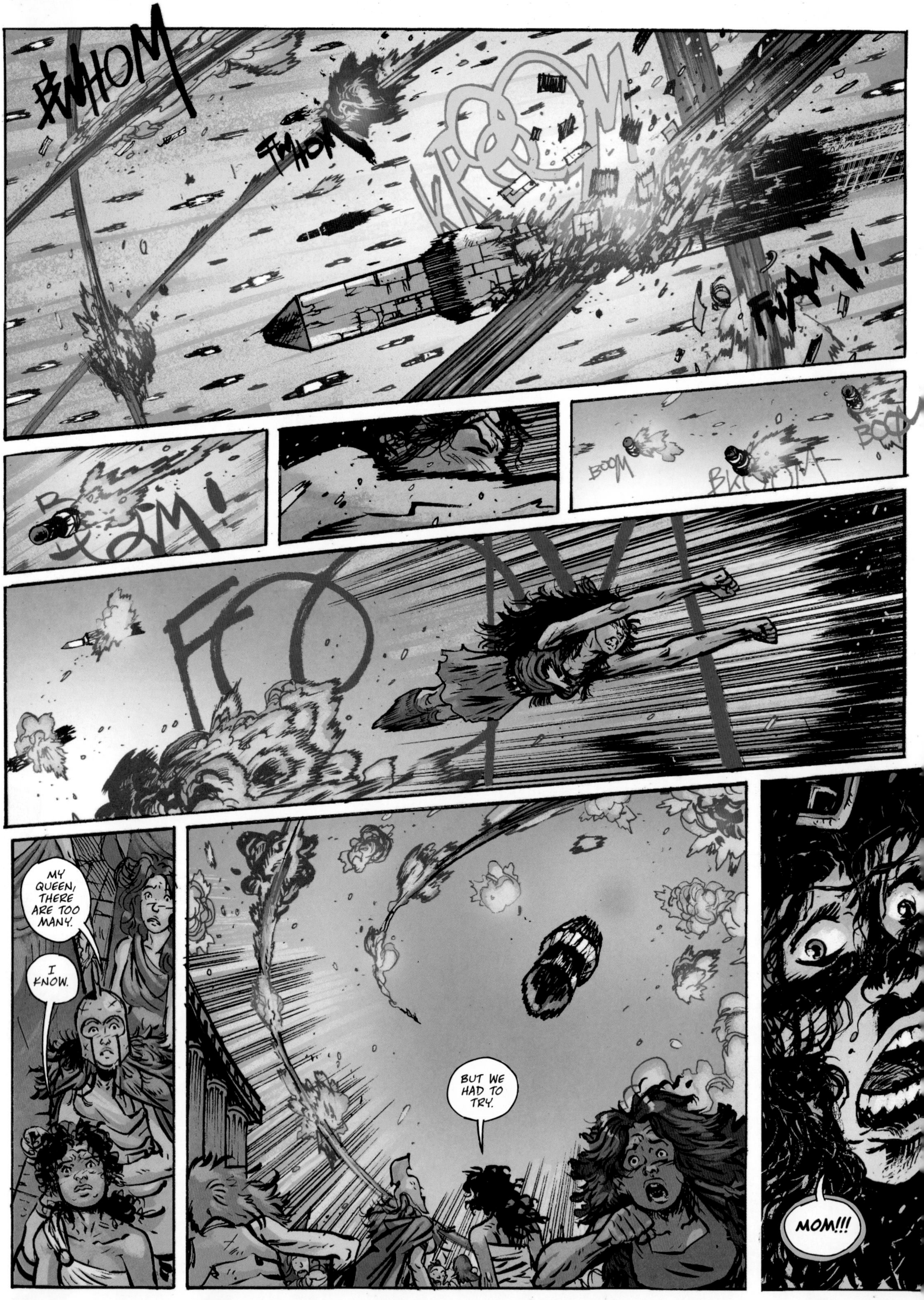

KROOM
FWAM!
BOOM
MY QUEEN, THERE ARE TOO MANY.
I KNOW.
BUT WE HAD TO TRY.
MOM!!!

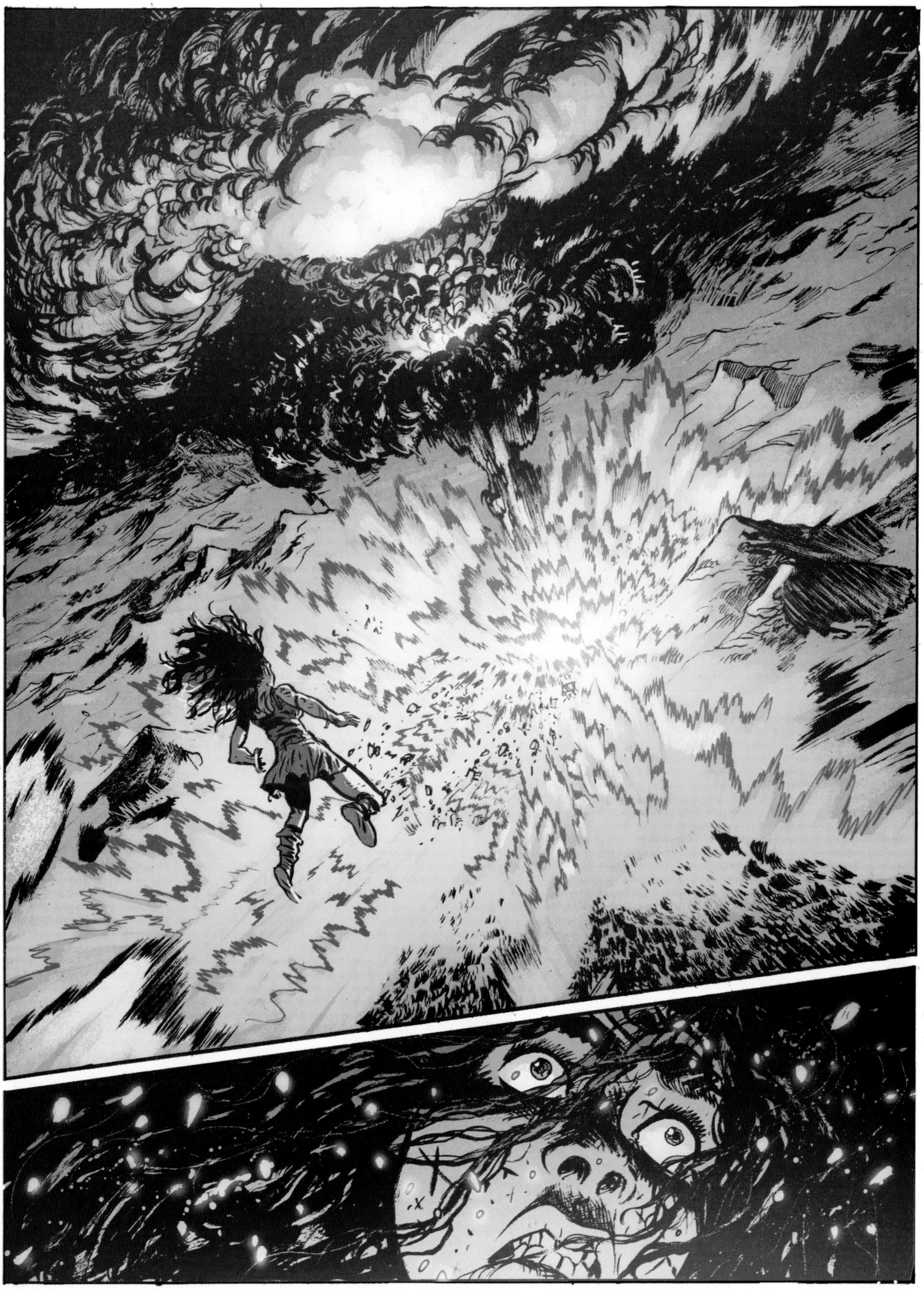

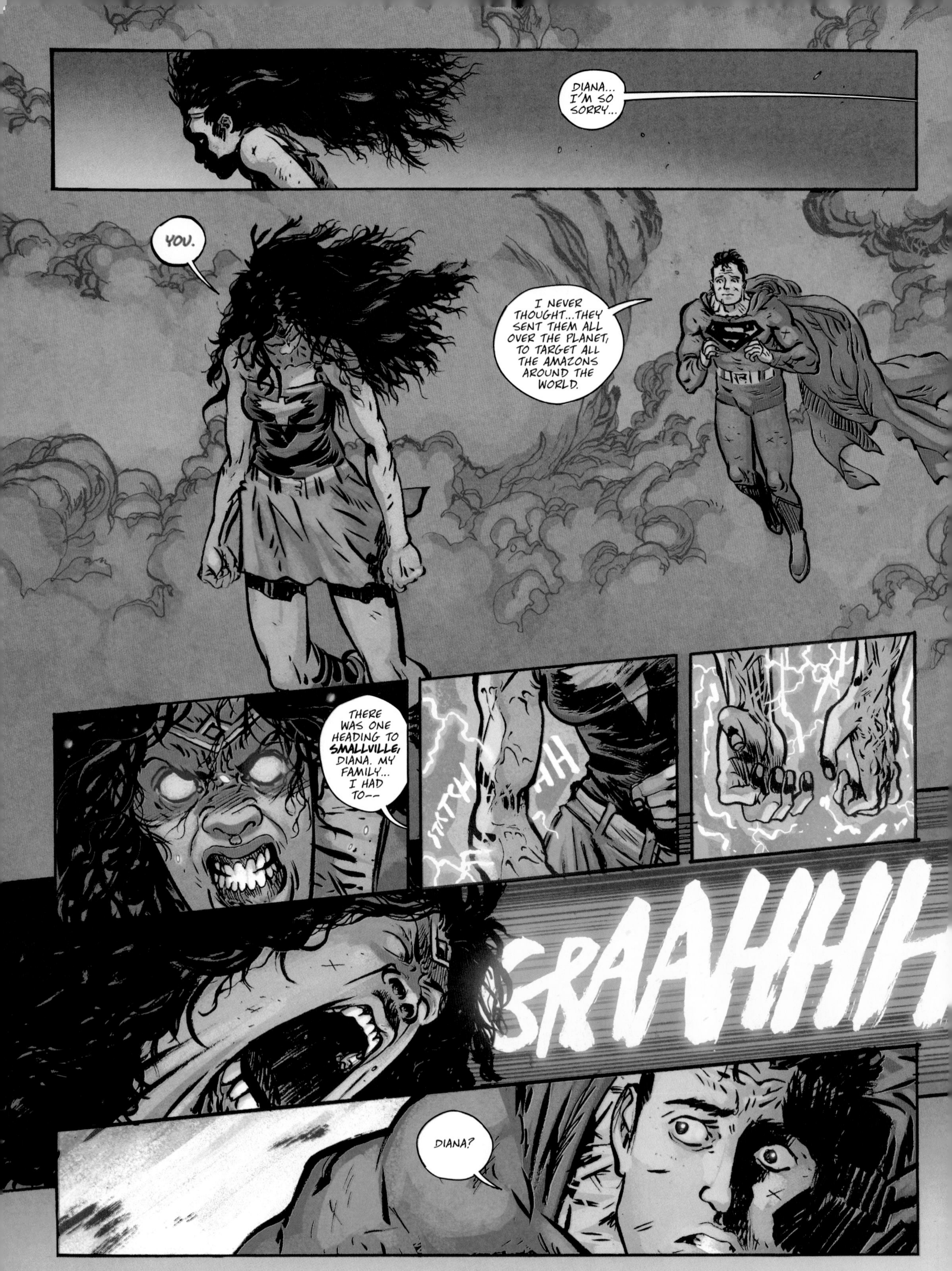
DIANA... I'M SO SORRY...
YOU.
I NEVER THOUGHT...THEY SENT THEM ALL OVER THE PLANET, TO TARGET ALL THE AMAZONS AROUND THE WORLD.
THERE WAS ONE HEADING TO SMALLVILLE, DIANA. MY FAMILY... I HAD TO--
GRAAHHHH
DIANA?

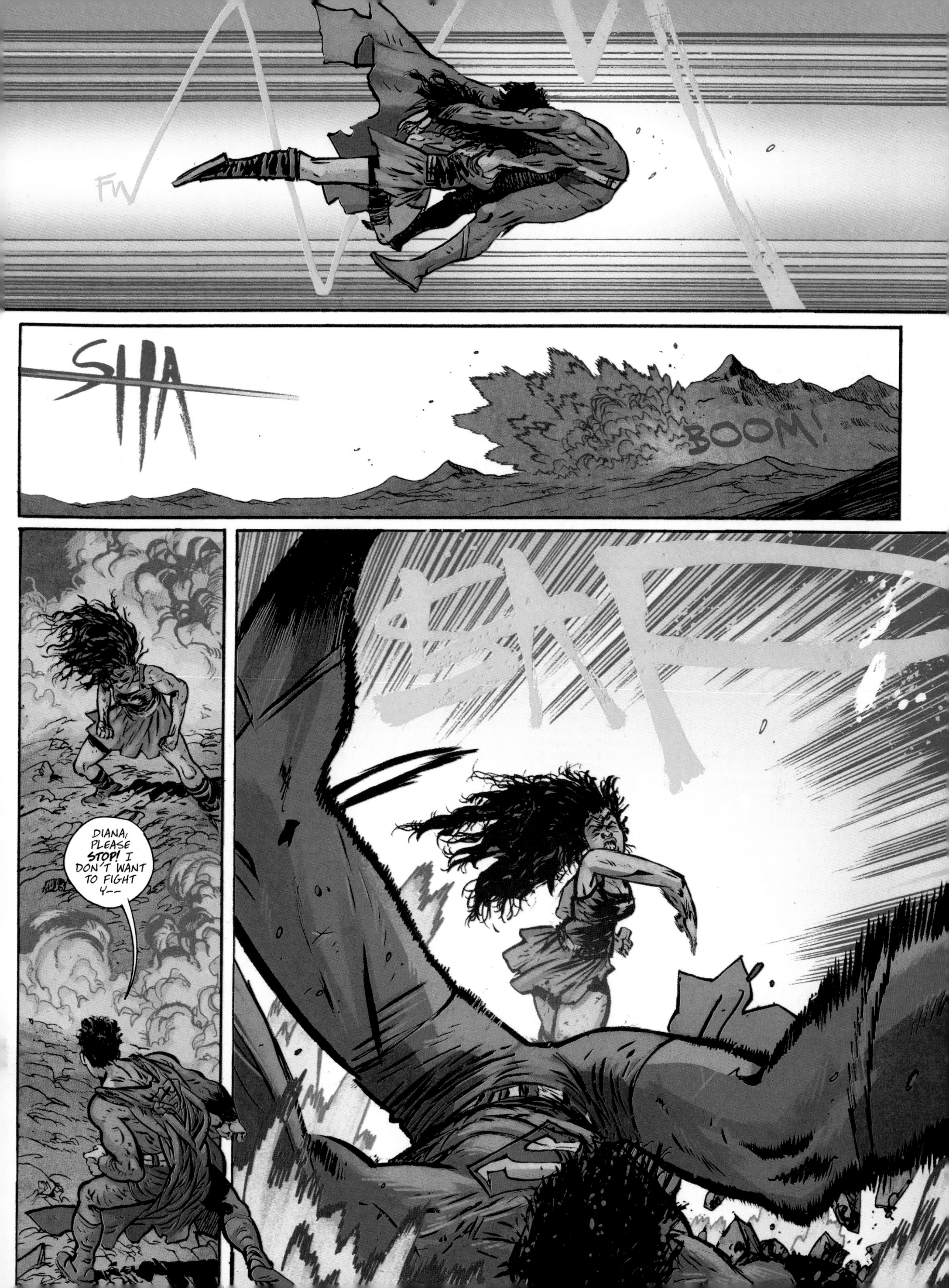
FWV
SHA
BOOM!
DIANA, PLEASE STOP! I DON'T WANT TO FIGHT Y--
SHF

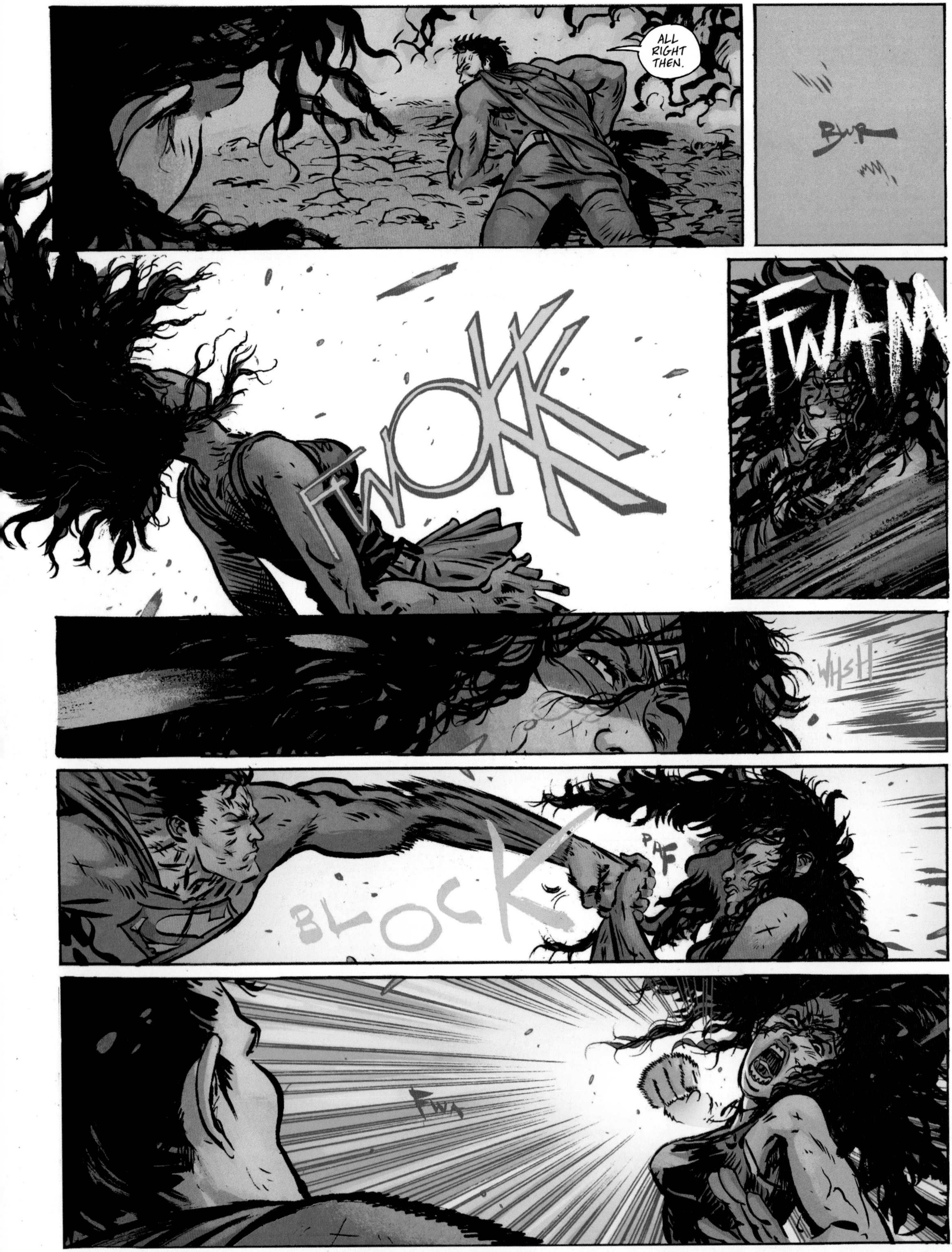
ALL RIGHT THEN.
BLUR
FWOKK
FWAM
WHSH
PAF
BLOCK
FWA

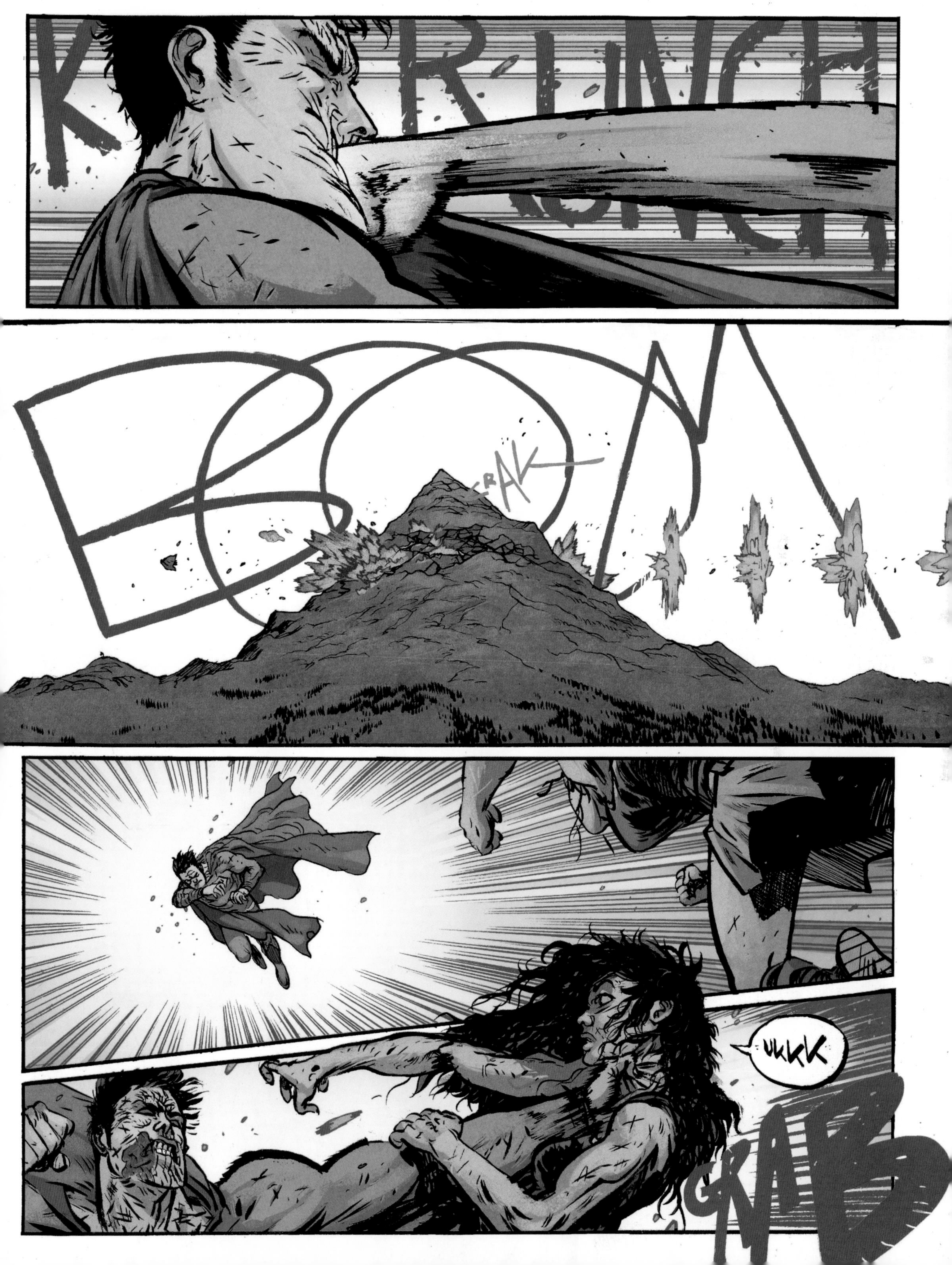
KRUNCH
BOOM
KRAK
UKKK
GRAB

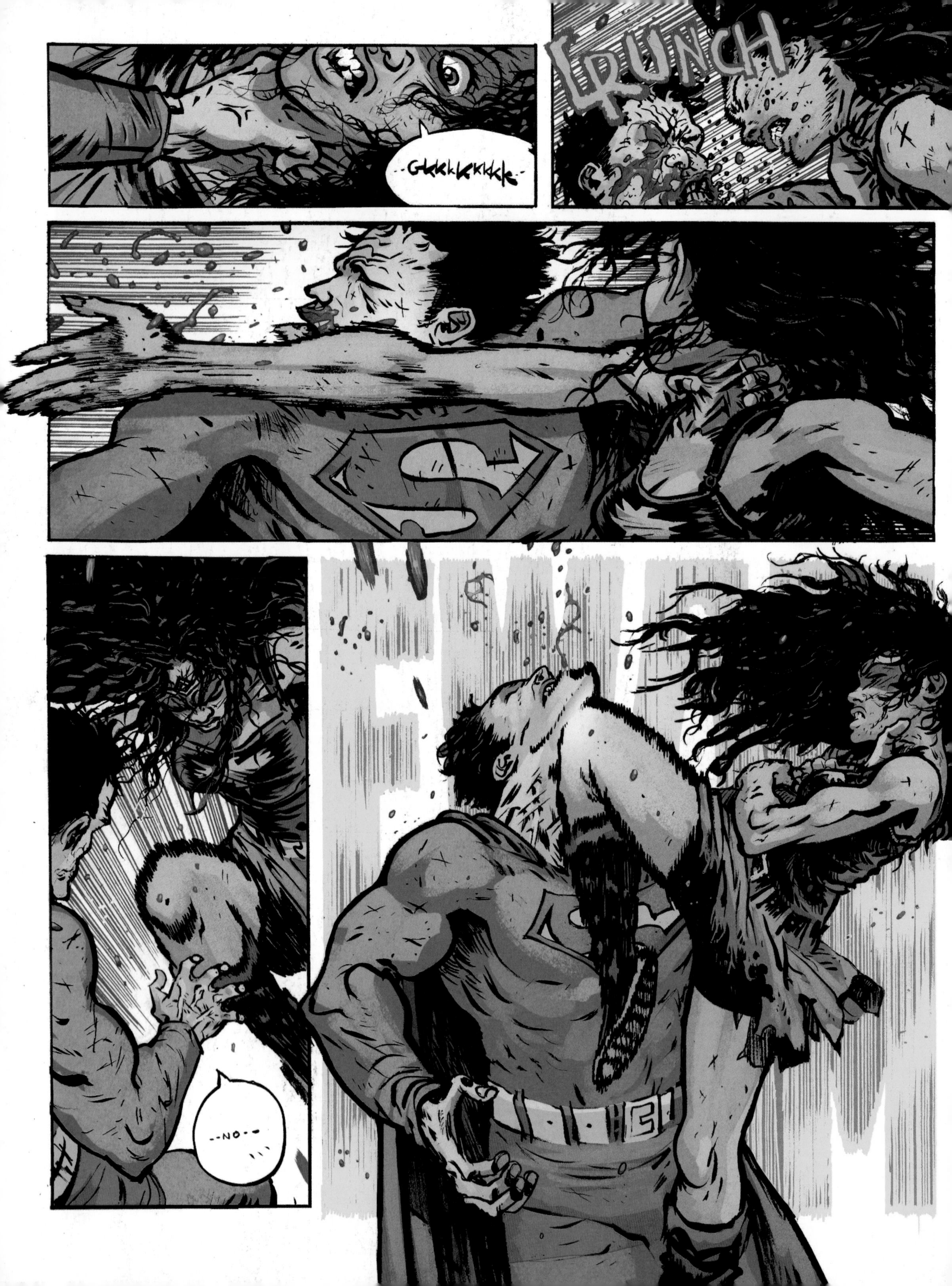
--Gkkkkkkkkk--
CRUNCH
--NO--

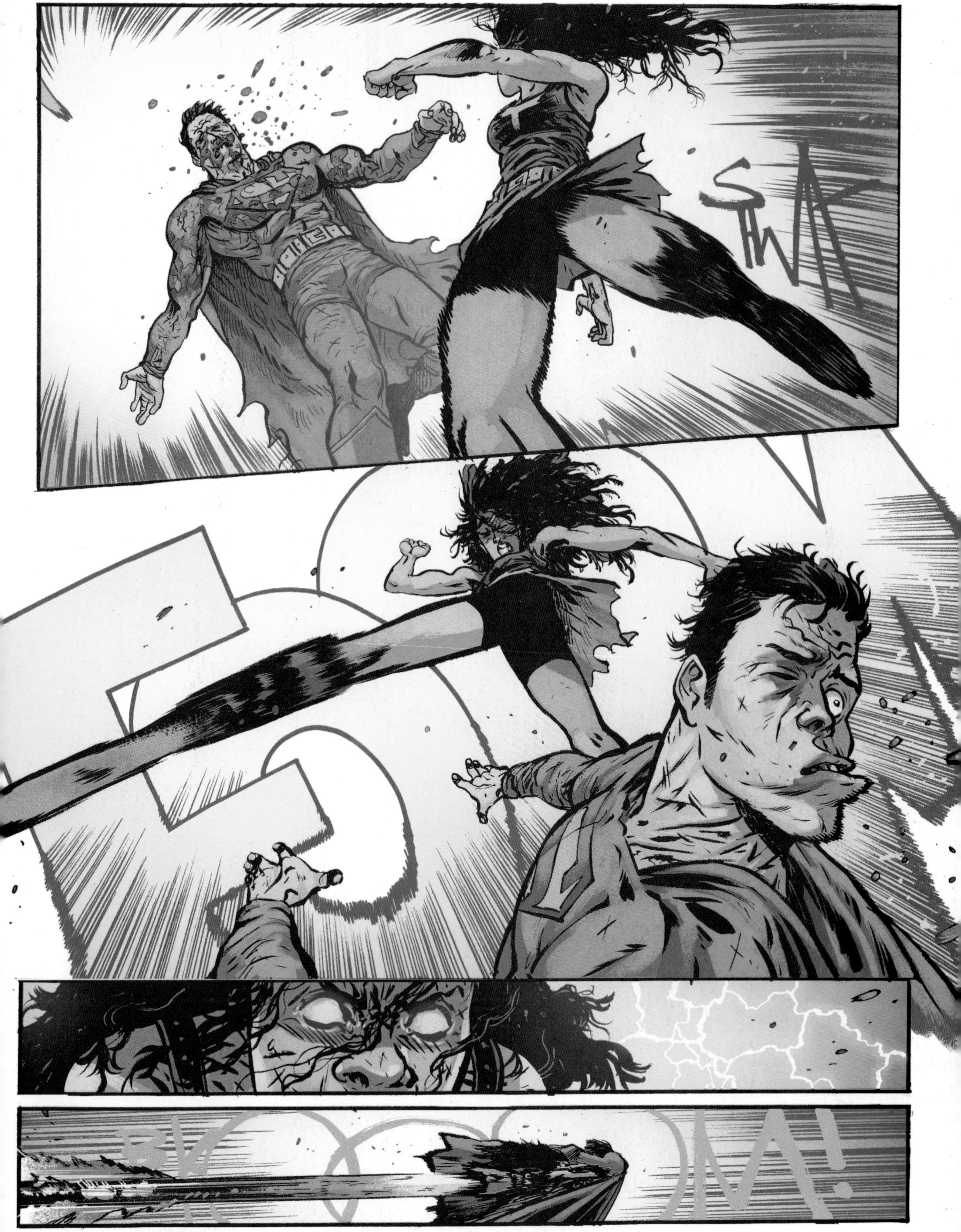
SHWAK

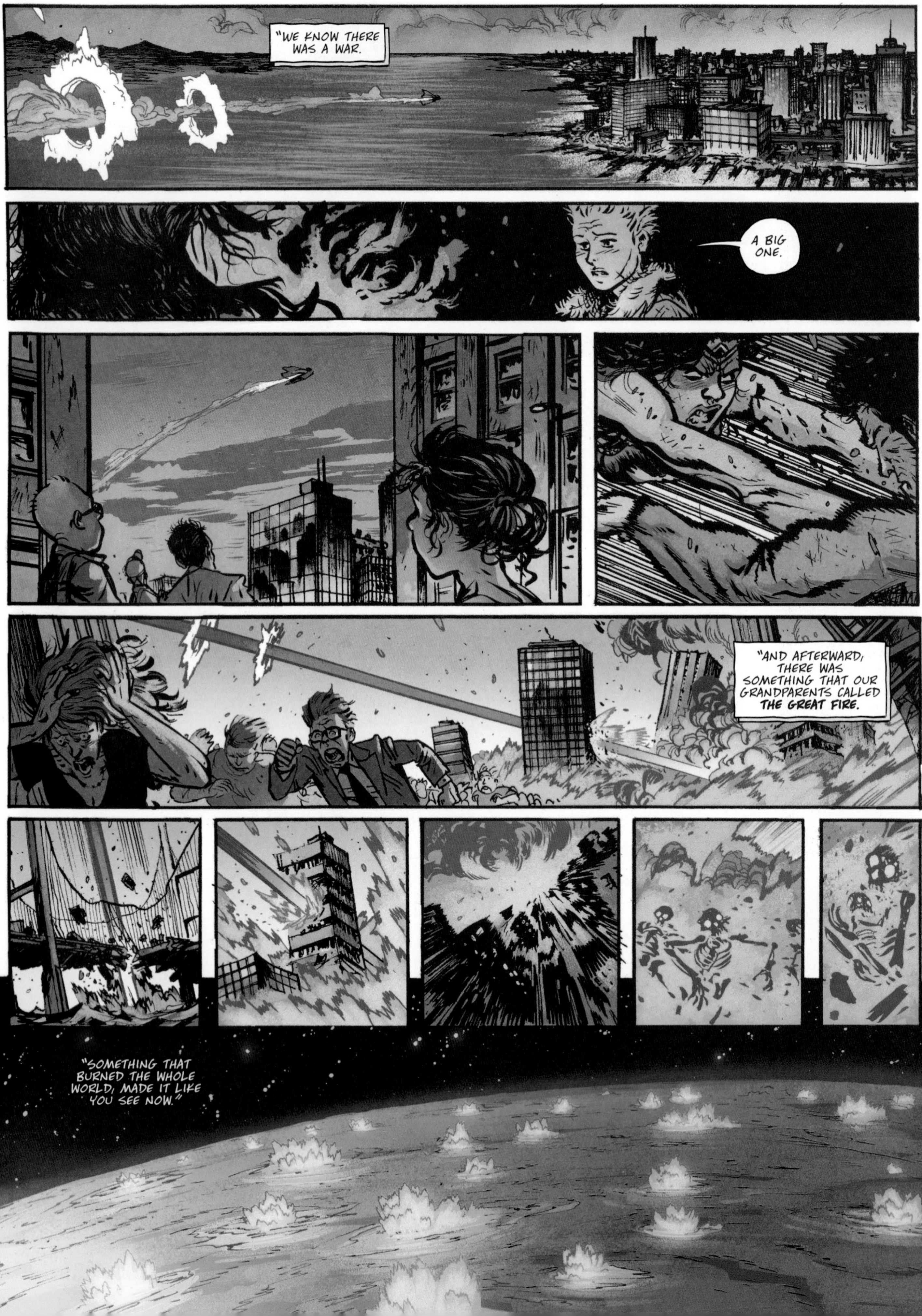
"WE KNOW THERE WAS A WAR.
A BIG ONE.
"AND AFTERWARD, THERE WAS SOMETHING THAT OUR GRANDPARENTS CALLED **THE GREAT FIRE.**
"SOMETHING THAT BURNED THE WHOLE WORLD, MADE IT LIKE YOU SEE NOW."

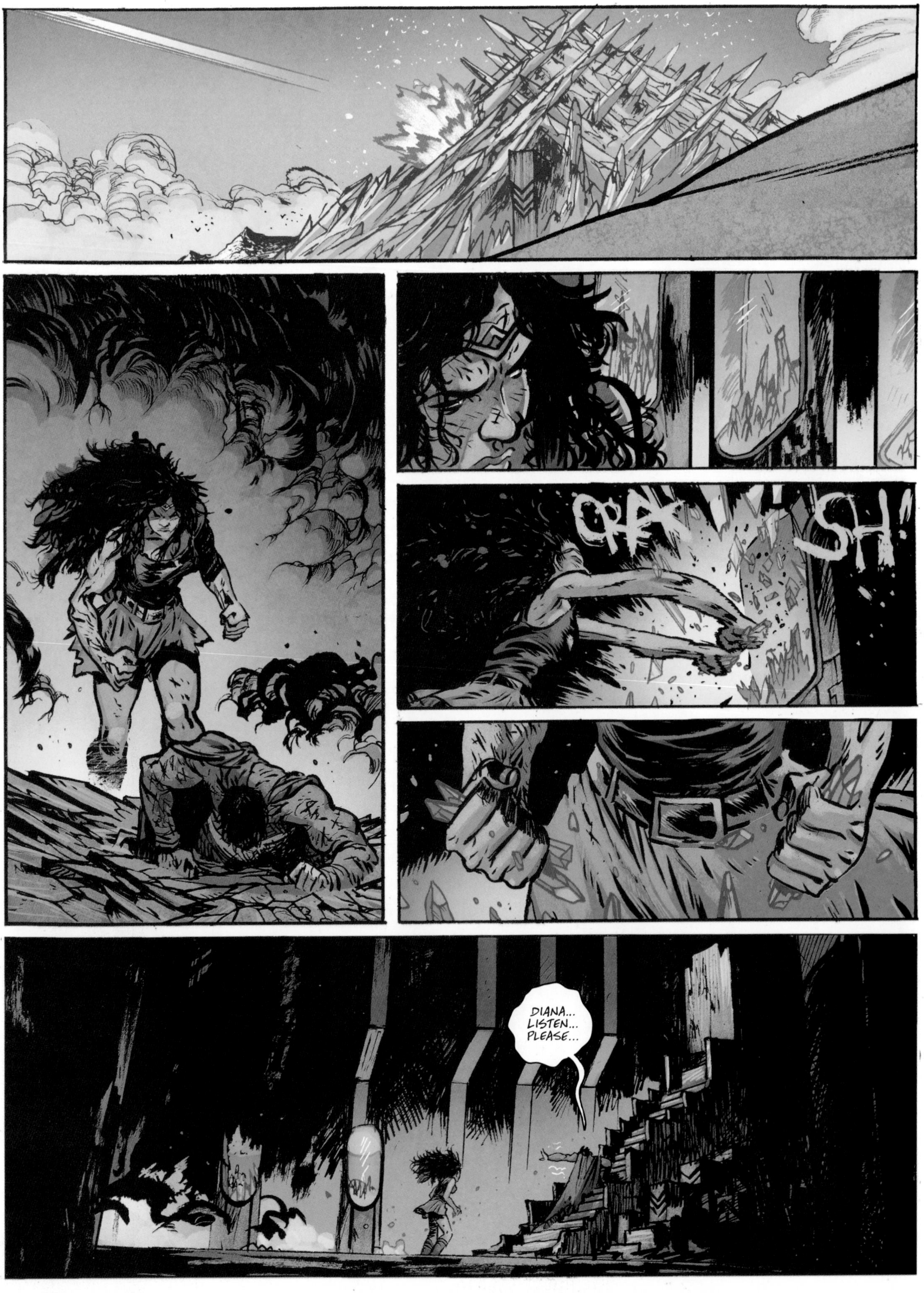
CRASH!
DIANA... LISTEN... PLEASE...

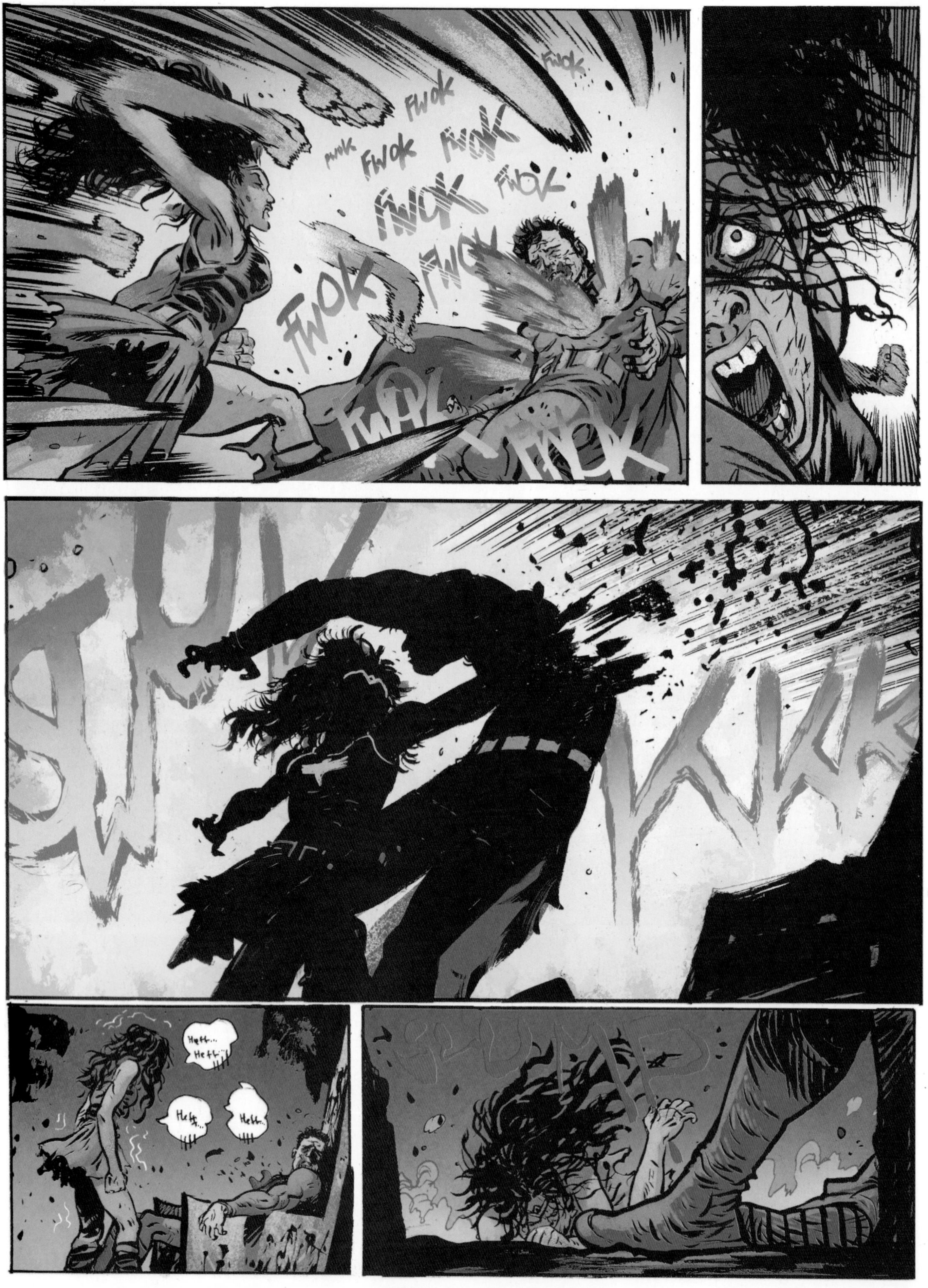
FWOK
FWOK
FWOK
FWOK
FWOK
FWOK
FWOK
FWOK
Heff... Heff...
Heff...
Hehh...
SLUMP

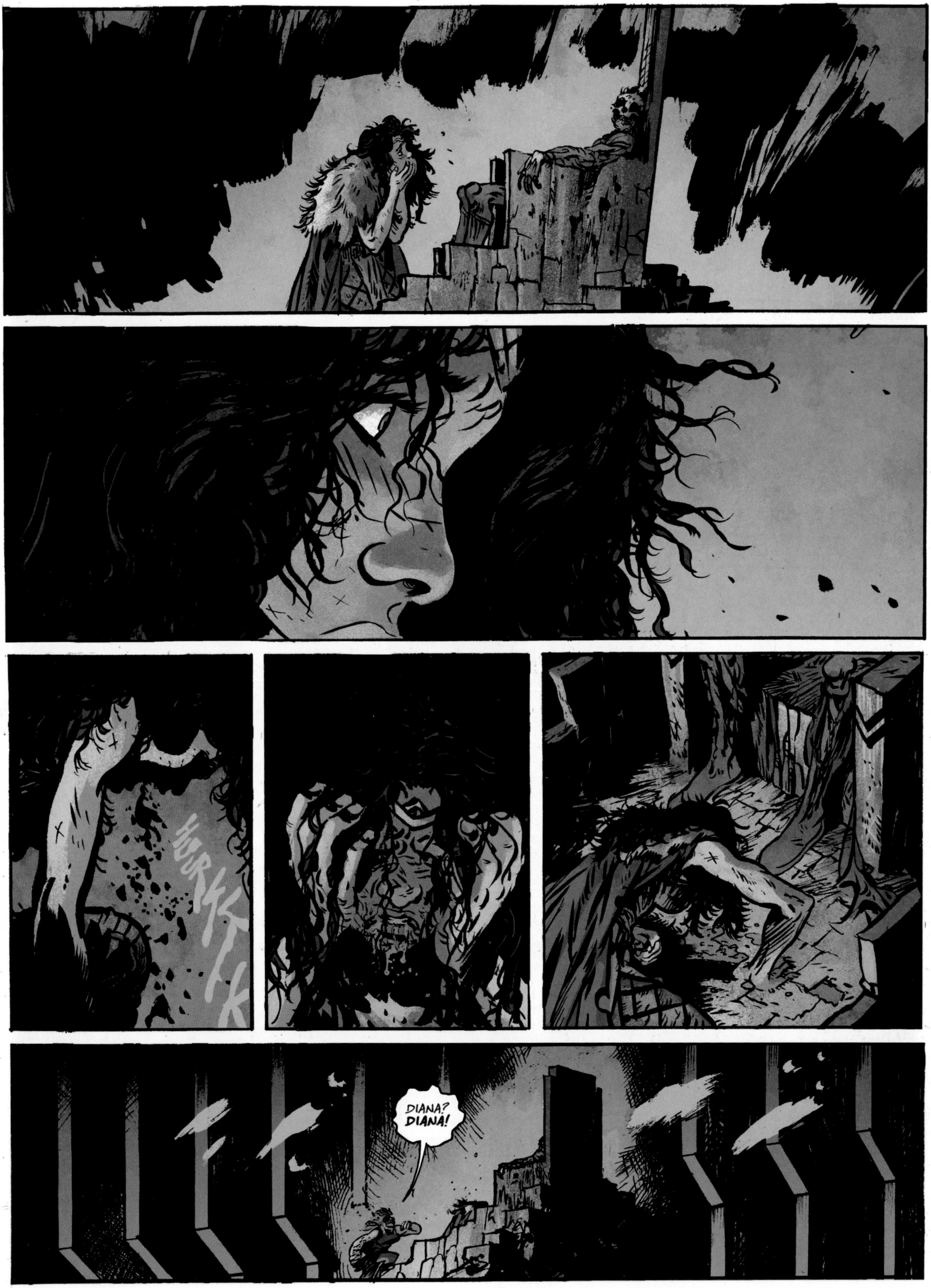

HURKKK
DIANA? DIANA!

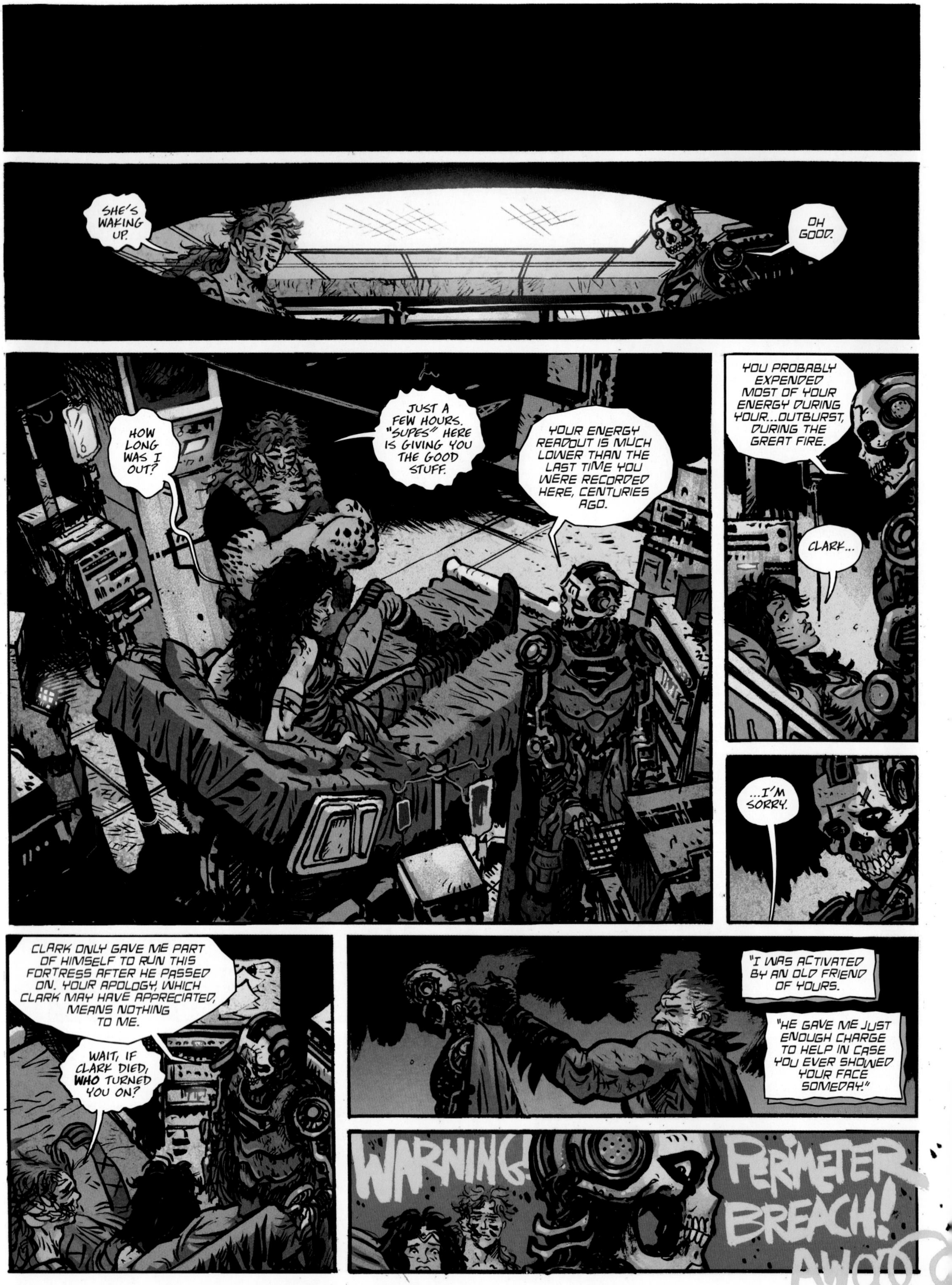
SHE'S WAKING UP.
OH GOOD.
HOW LONG WAS I OUT?
JUST A FEW HOURS. "SUPES" HERE IS GIVING YOU THE GOOD STUFF.
YOUR ENERGY READOUT IS MUCH LOWER THAN THE LAST TIME YOU WERE RECORDED HERE, CENTURIES AGO.
YOU PROBABLY EXPENDED MOST OF YOUR ENERGY DURING YOUR...OUTBURST, DURING THE GREAT FIRE.
CLARK...
...I'M SORRY.
CLARK ONLY GAVE ME PART OF HIMSELF TO RUN THIS FORTRESS AFTER HE PASSED ON. YOUR APOLOGY, WHICH CLARK MAY HAVE APPRECIATED, MEANS NOTHING TO ME.
WAIT, IF CLARK DIED, **WHO** TURNED YOU ON?
"I WAS ACTIVATED BY AN OLD FRIEND OF YOURS.
"HE GAVE ME JUST ENOUGH CHARGE TO HELP IN CASE YOU EVER SHOWED YOUR FACE SOMEDAY."
WARNING!
PERIMETER BREACH!
AWOOO

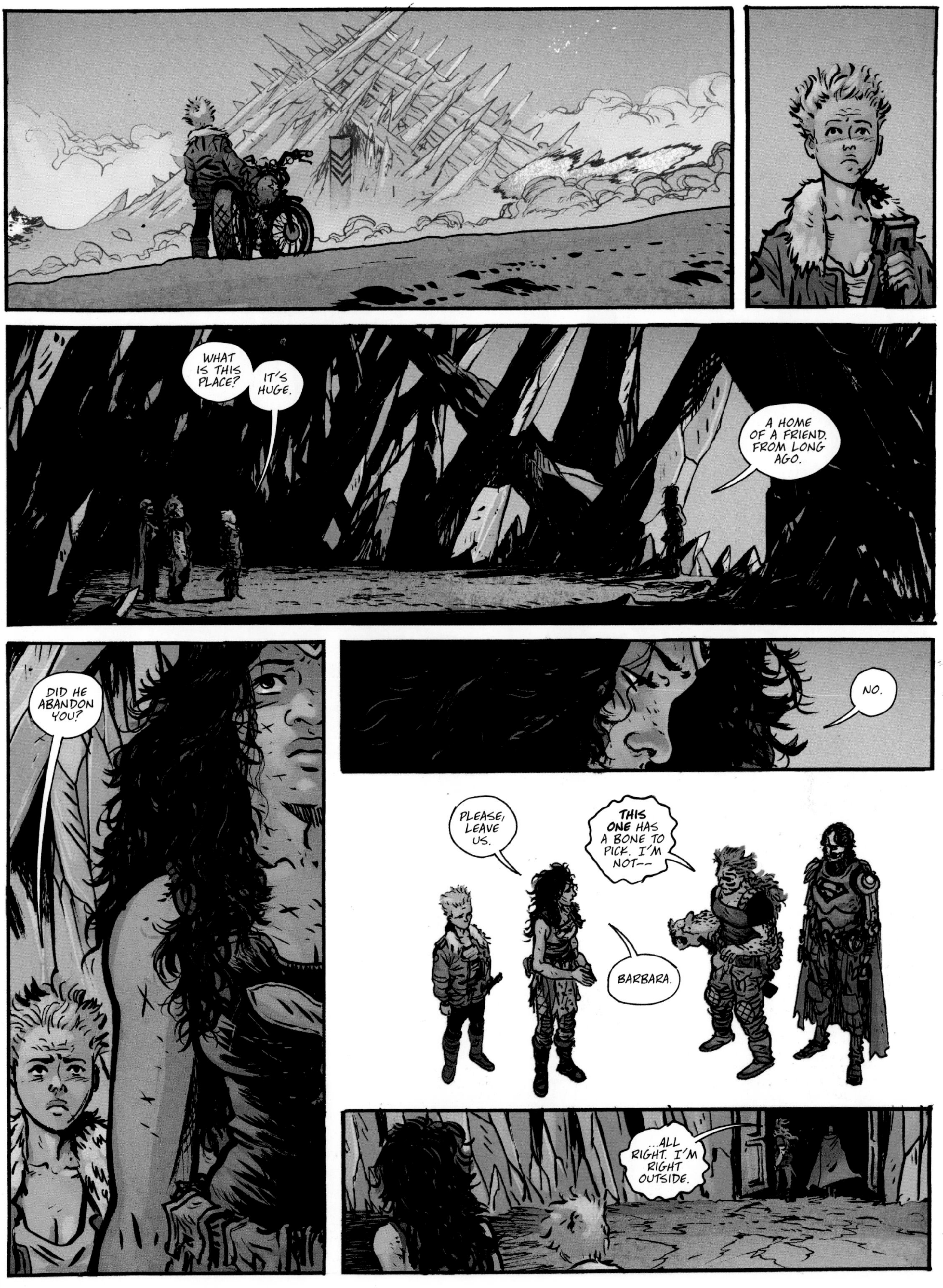
WHAT IS THIS PLACE?
IT'S HUGE.
A HOME OF A FRIEND. FROM LONG AGO.
DID HE ABANDON YOU?
NO.
PLEASE, LEAVE US.
THIS ONE HAS A BONE TO PICK. I'M NOT--
BARBARA.
...ALL RIGHT. I'M RIGHT OUTSIDE.

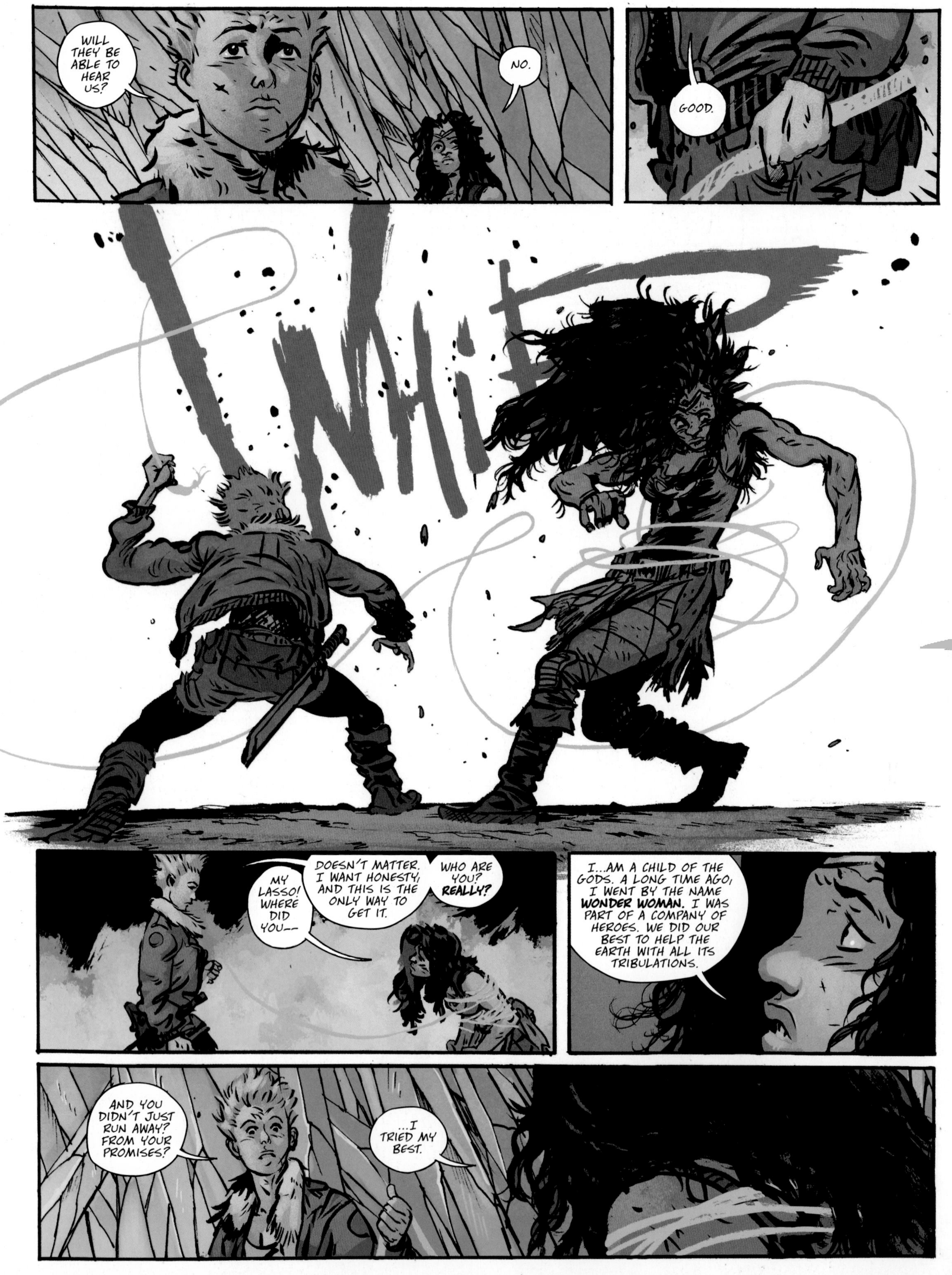
WILL THEY BE ABLE TO HEAR US?
NO.
GOOD.
WHIP
MY LASSO! WHERE DID YOU--
DOESN'T MATTER. I WANT HONESTY, AND THIS IS THE ONLY WAY TO GET IT.
WHO ARE YOU? **REALLY?**
I...AM A CHILD OF THE GODS. A LONG TIME AGO, I WENT BY THE NAME **WONDER WOMAN.** I WAS PART OF A COMPANY OF HEROES. WE DID OUR BEST TO HELP THE EARTH WITH ALL ITS TRIBULATIONS.
AND YOU DIDN'T JUST RUN AWAY? FROM YOUR PROMISES?
...I TRIED MY BEST.

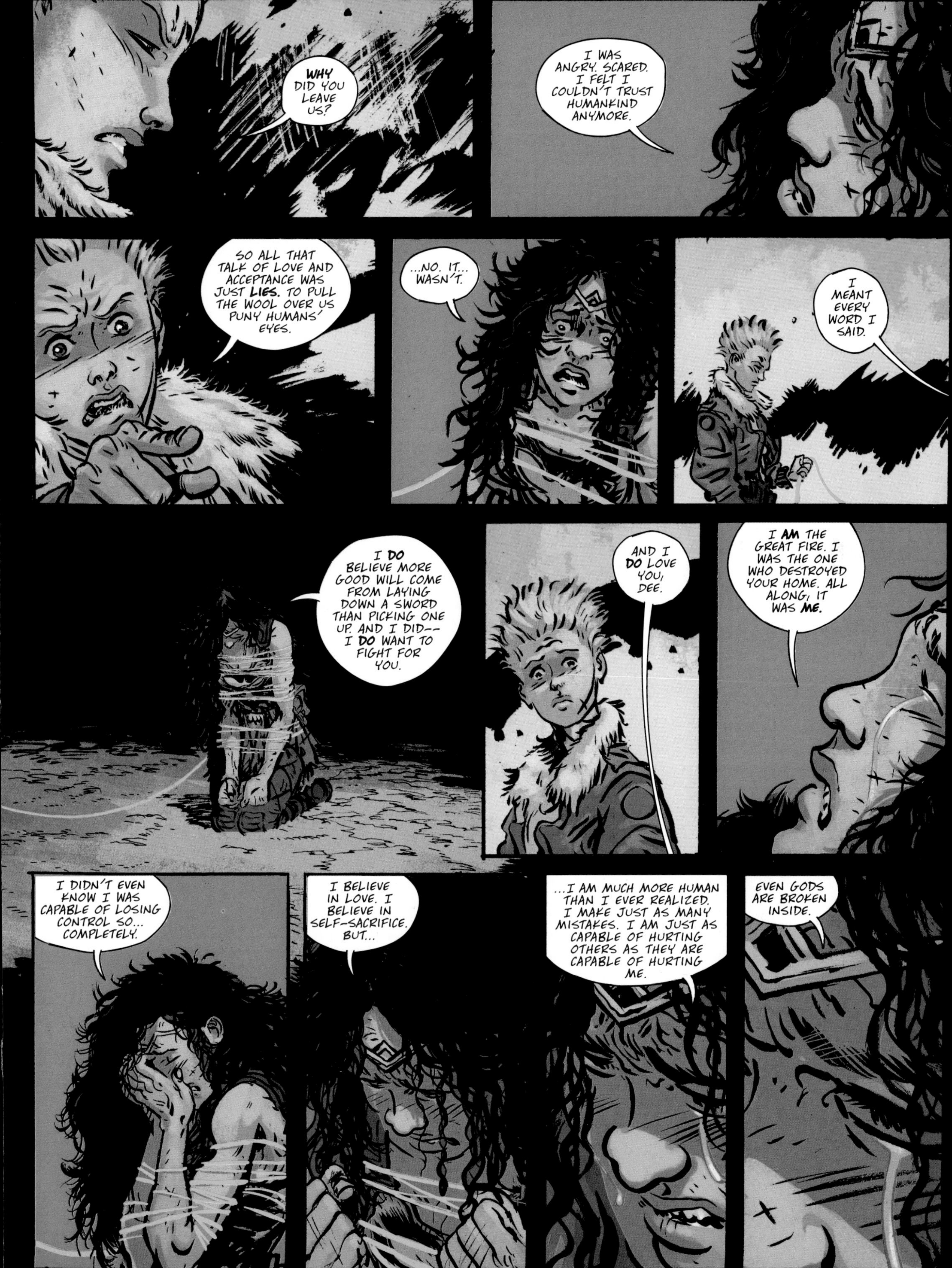
WHY DID YOU LEAVE US?
I WAS ANGRY. SCARED. I FELT I COULDN'T TRUST HUMANKIND ANYMORE.
SO ALL THAT TALK OF LOVE AND ACCEPTANCE WAS JUST LIES. TO PULL THE WOOL OVER US PUNY HUMANS' EYES.
...NO. IT... WASN'T.
I MEANT EVERY WORD I SAID.
I DO BELIEVE MORE GOOD WILL COME FROM LAYING DOWN A SWORD THAN PICKING ONE UP. AND I DID-- I DO WANT TO FIGHT FOR YOU.
AND I DO LOVE YOU, DEE.
I AM THE GREAT FIRE. I WAS THE ONE WHO DESTROYED YOUR HOME. ALL ALONG, IT WAS ME.
I DIDN'T EVEN KNOW I WAS CAPABLE OF LOSING CONTROL SO... COMPLETELY.
I BELIEVE IN LOVE. I BELIEVE IN SELF-SACRIFICE. BUT...
...I AM MUCH MORE HUMAN THAN I EVER REALIZED. I MAKE JUST AS MANY MISTAKES. I AM JUST AS CAPABLE OF HURTING OTHERS AS THEY ARE CAPABLE OF HURTING ME.
EVEN GODS ARE BROKEN INSIDE.

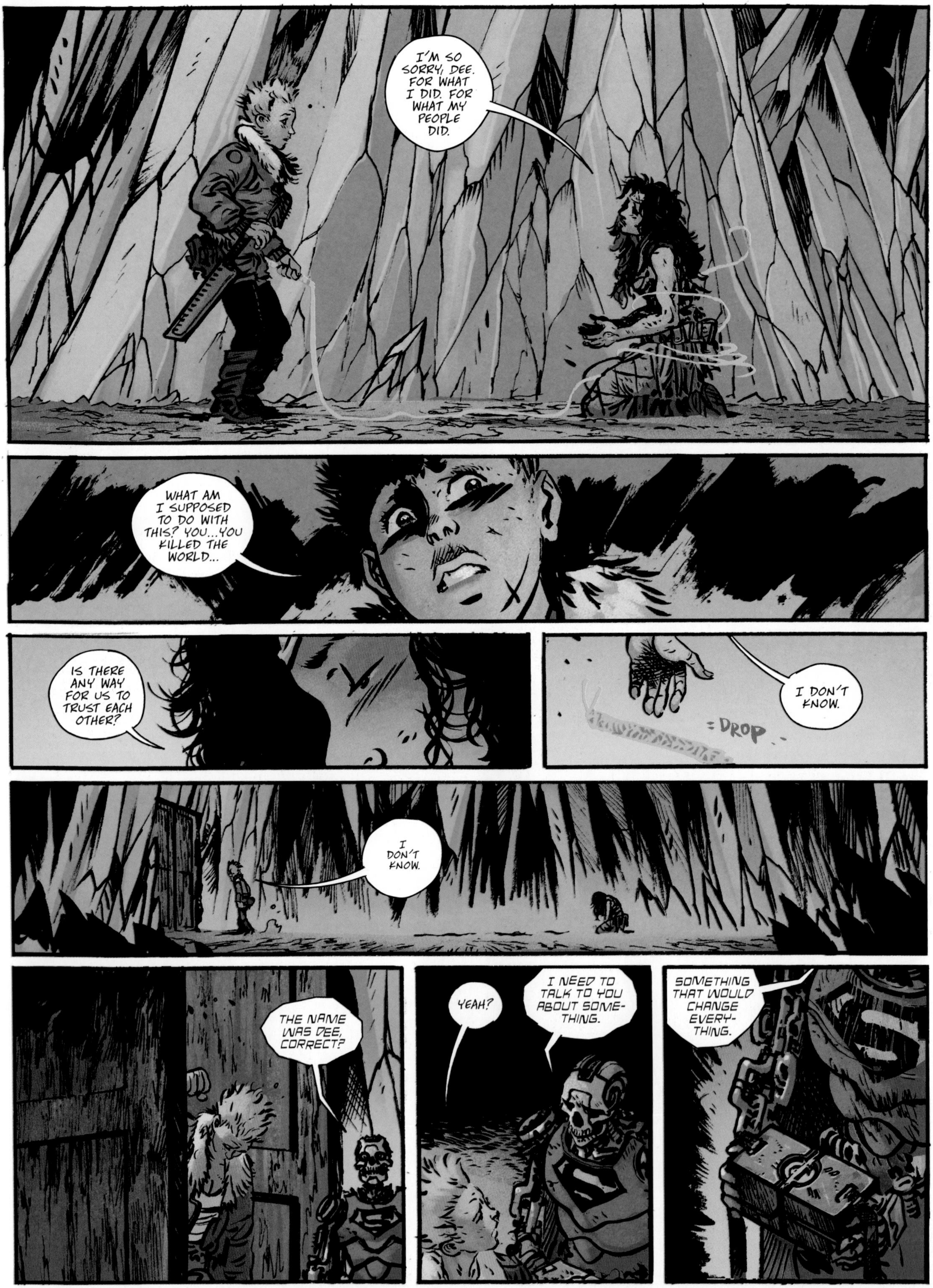
I'M SO SORRY, DEE. FOR WHAT I DID. FOR WHAT MY PEOPLE DID.
WHAT AM I SUPPOSED TO DO WITH THIS? YOU...YOU KILLED THE WORLD...
IS THERE ANY WAY FOR US TO TRUST EACH OTHER?
I DON'T KNOW.
DROP
I DON'T KNOW.
THE NAME WAS DEE, CORRECT?
YEAH?
I NEED TO TALK TO YOU ABOUT SOME-THING.
SOMETHING THAT WOULD CHANGE EVERY-THING.

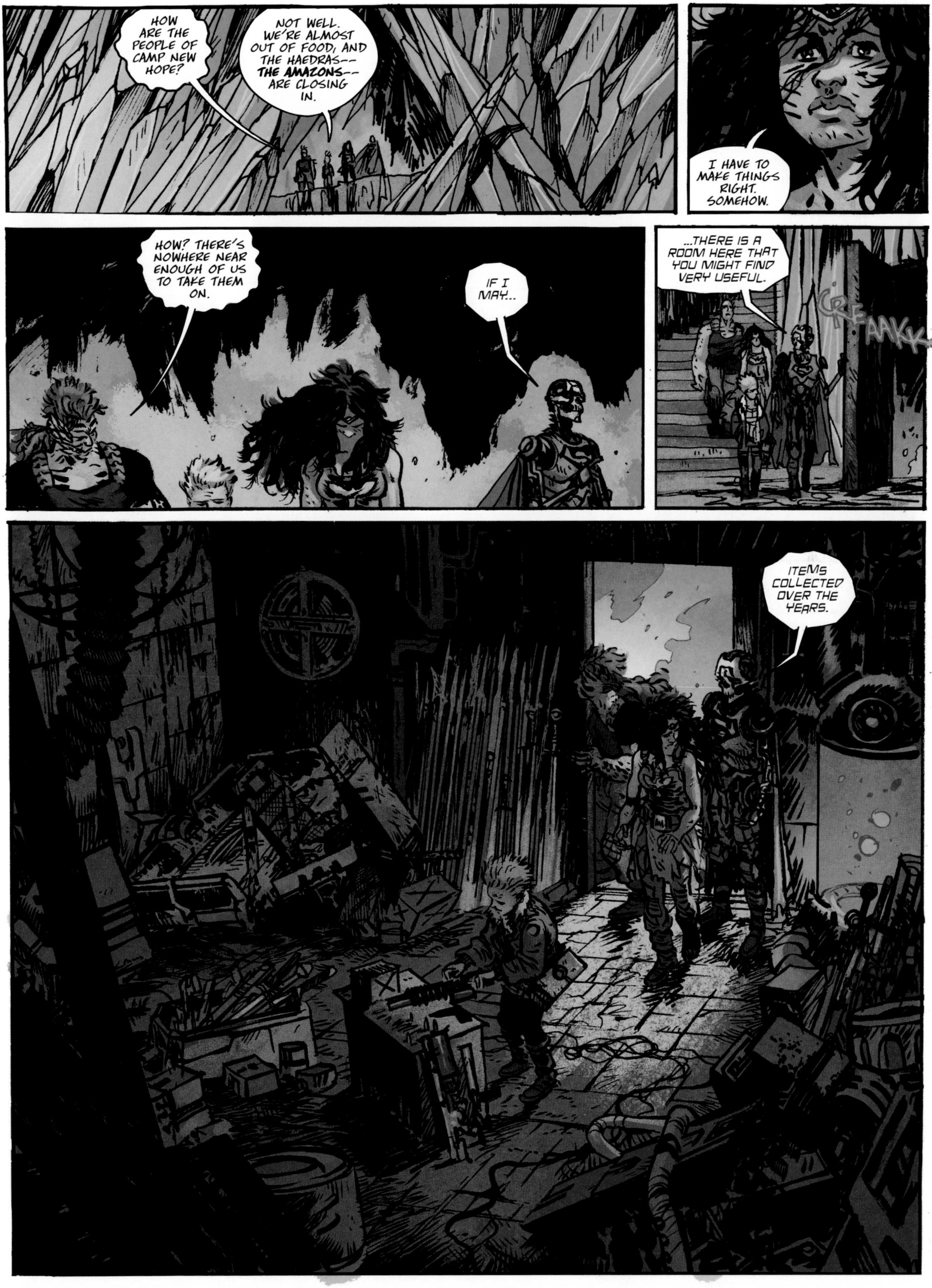
HOW ARE THE PEOPLE OF CAMP NEW HOPE?
NOT WELL. WE'RE ALMOST OUT OF FOOD, AND THE HAEDRAS-- **THE AMAZONS**-- ARE CLOSING IN.
I HAVE TO MAKE THINGS RIGHT. SOMEHOW.
HOW? THERE'S NOWHERE NEAR ENOUGH OF US TO TAKE THEM ON.
IF I MAY...
...THERE IS A ROOM HERE THAT YOU MIGHT FIND VERY USEFUL.
CREAAKK
ITEMS COLLECTED OVER THE YEARS.

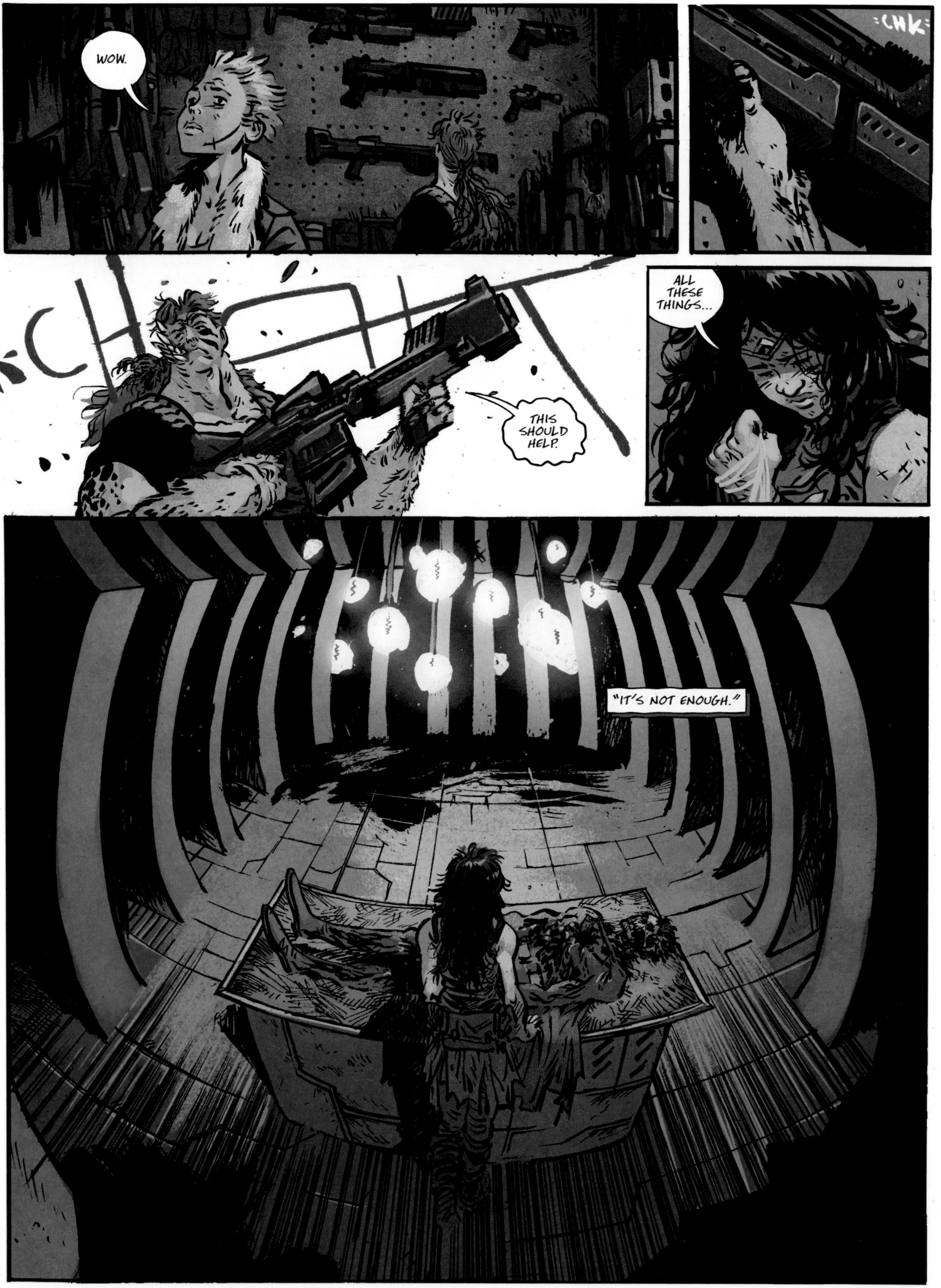

WOW.
CHK
K-CHAK
THIS SHOULD HELP.
ALL THESE THINGS...
"IT'S NOT ENOUGH."

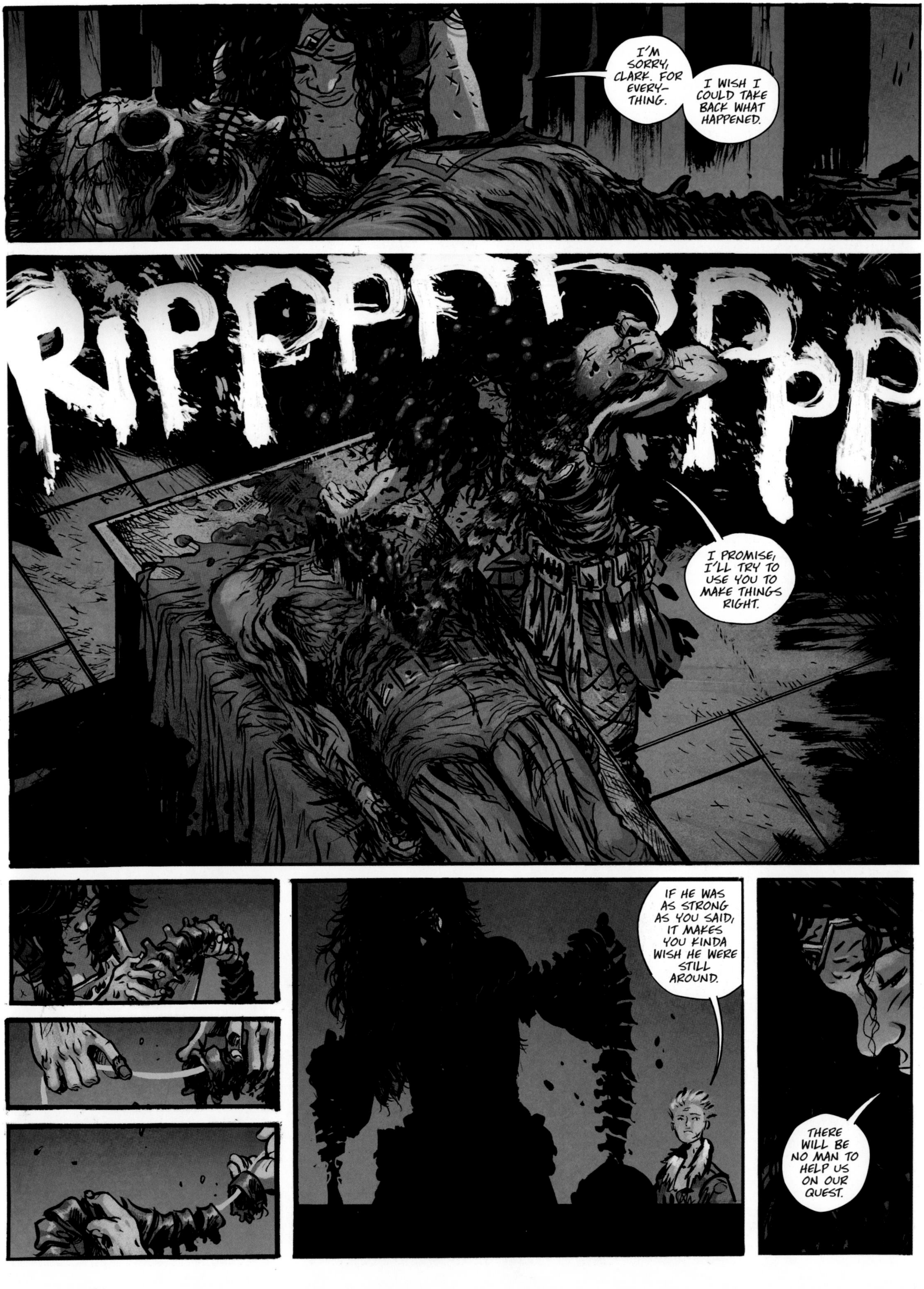
I'M SORRY, CLARK. FOR EVERY-THING.
I WISH I COULD TAKE BACK WHAT HAPPENED.
RIPPPPPPPP
I PROMISE, I'LL TRY TO USE YOU TO MAKE THINGS RIGHT.
IF HE WAS AS STRONG AS YOU SAID, IT MAKES YOU KINDA WISH HE WERE STILL AROUND.
THERE WILL BE NO MAN TO HELP US ON OUR QUEST.

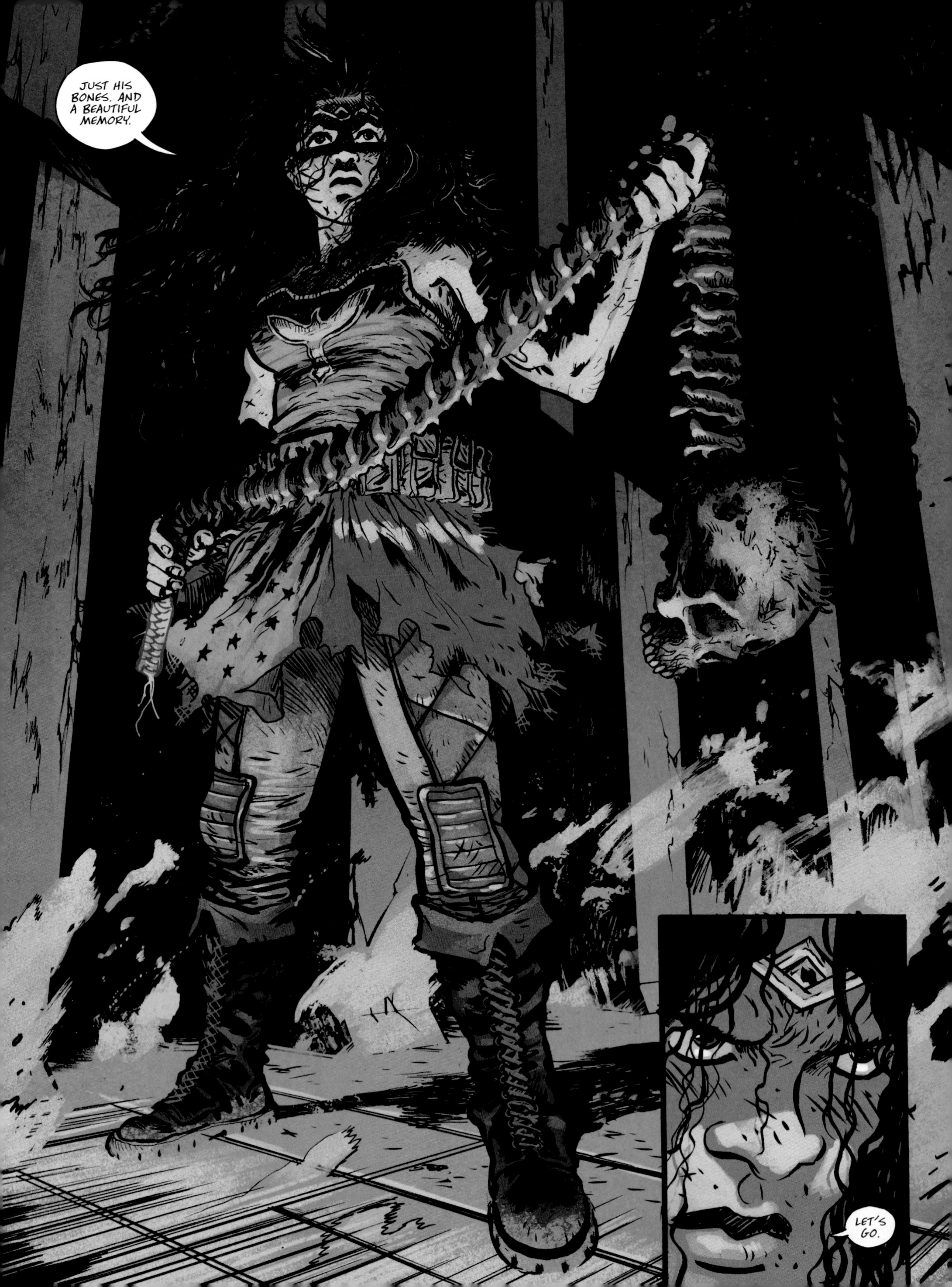
JUST HIS BONES. AND A BEAUTIFUL MEMORY.
LET'S GO.

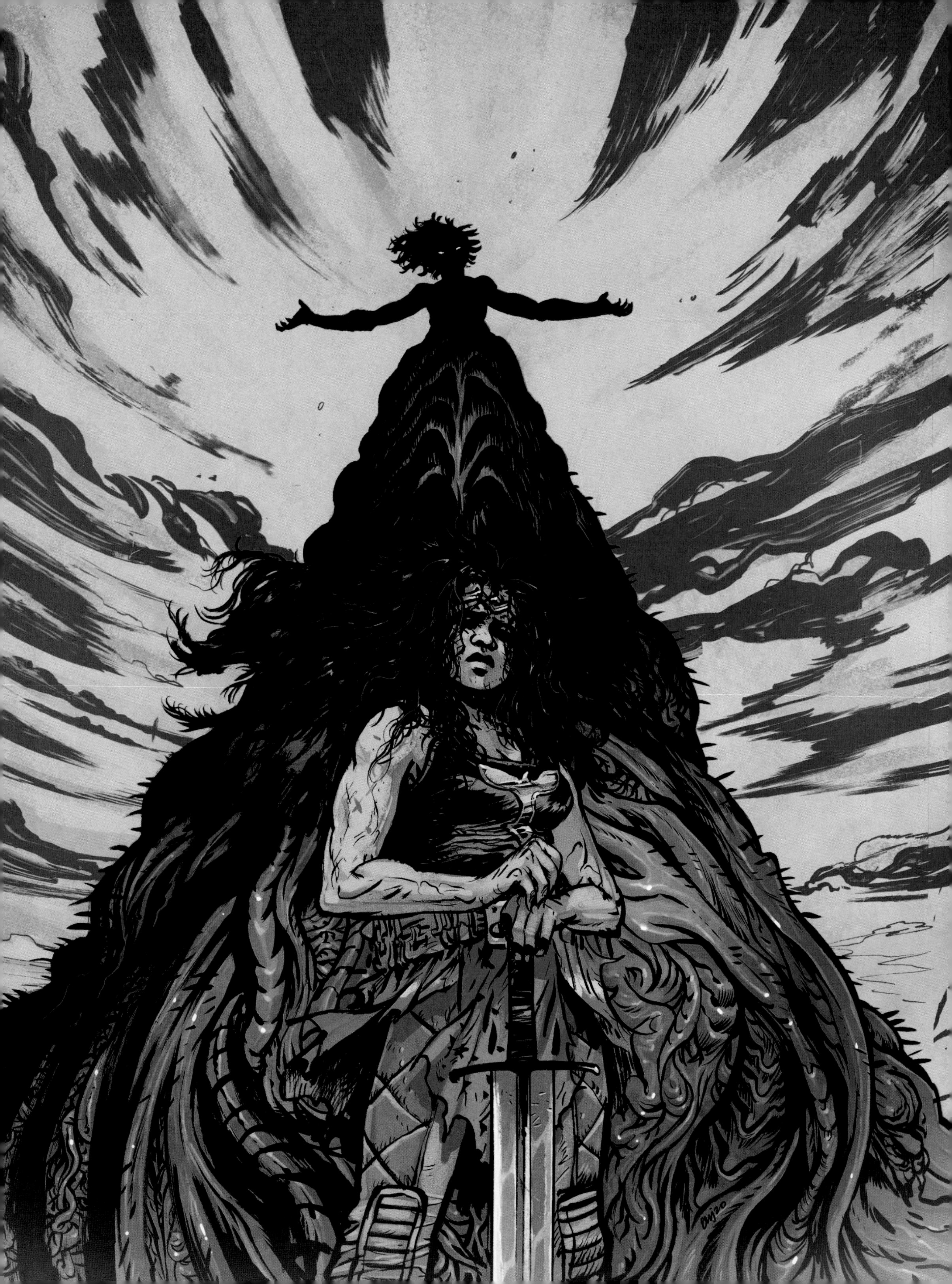

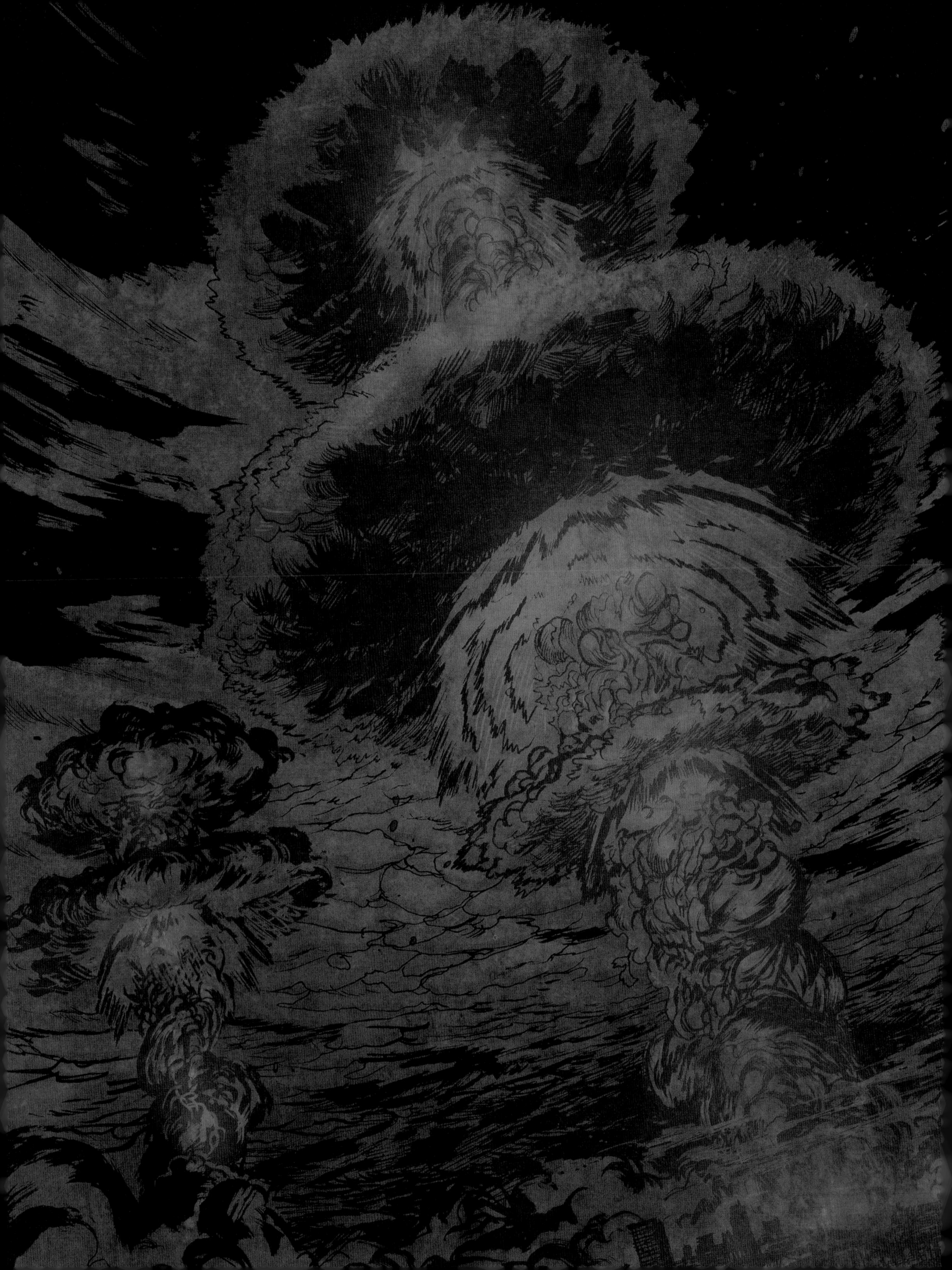

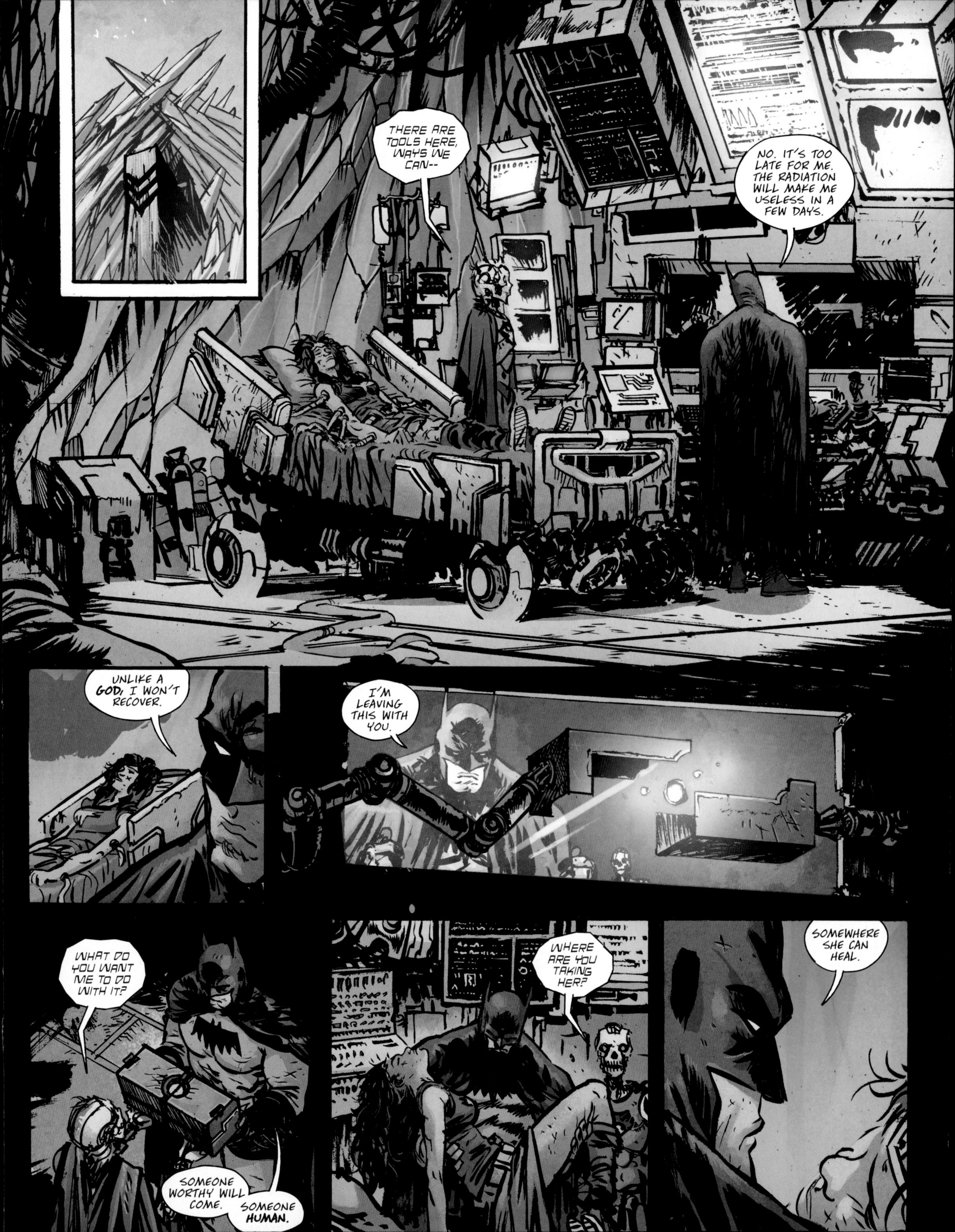
THERE ARE TOOLS HERE, WAYS WE CAN--
NO. IT'S TOO LATE FOR ME. THE RADIATION WILL MAKE ME USELESS IN A FEW DAYS.
UNLIKE A GOD, I WON'T RECOVER.
I'M LEAVING THIS WITH YOU.
WHAT DO YOU WANT ME TO DO WITH IT?
SOMEONE WORTHY WILL COME.
SOMEONE HUMAN.
WHERE ARE YOU TAKING HER?
SOMEWHERE SHE CAN HEAL.

"I HATE DOING THIS."

I WISH I COULD **END YOU**, RIGHT NOW, FOR WHAT YOU'VE DONE.

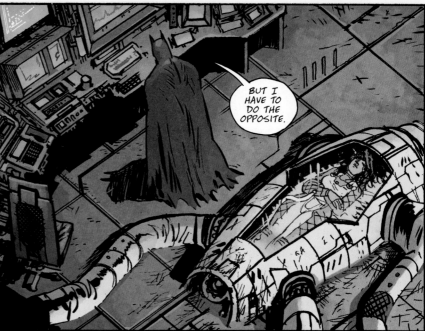

BUT I HAVE TO DO THE OPPOSITE.

BEGIN RECONSTRUCTION?

YOU MAY HAVE BROKEN THE WORLD...

...BUT I KNOW YOU'RE THE ONLY ONE WHO CAN FIX IT.

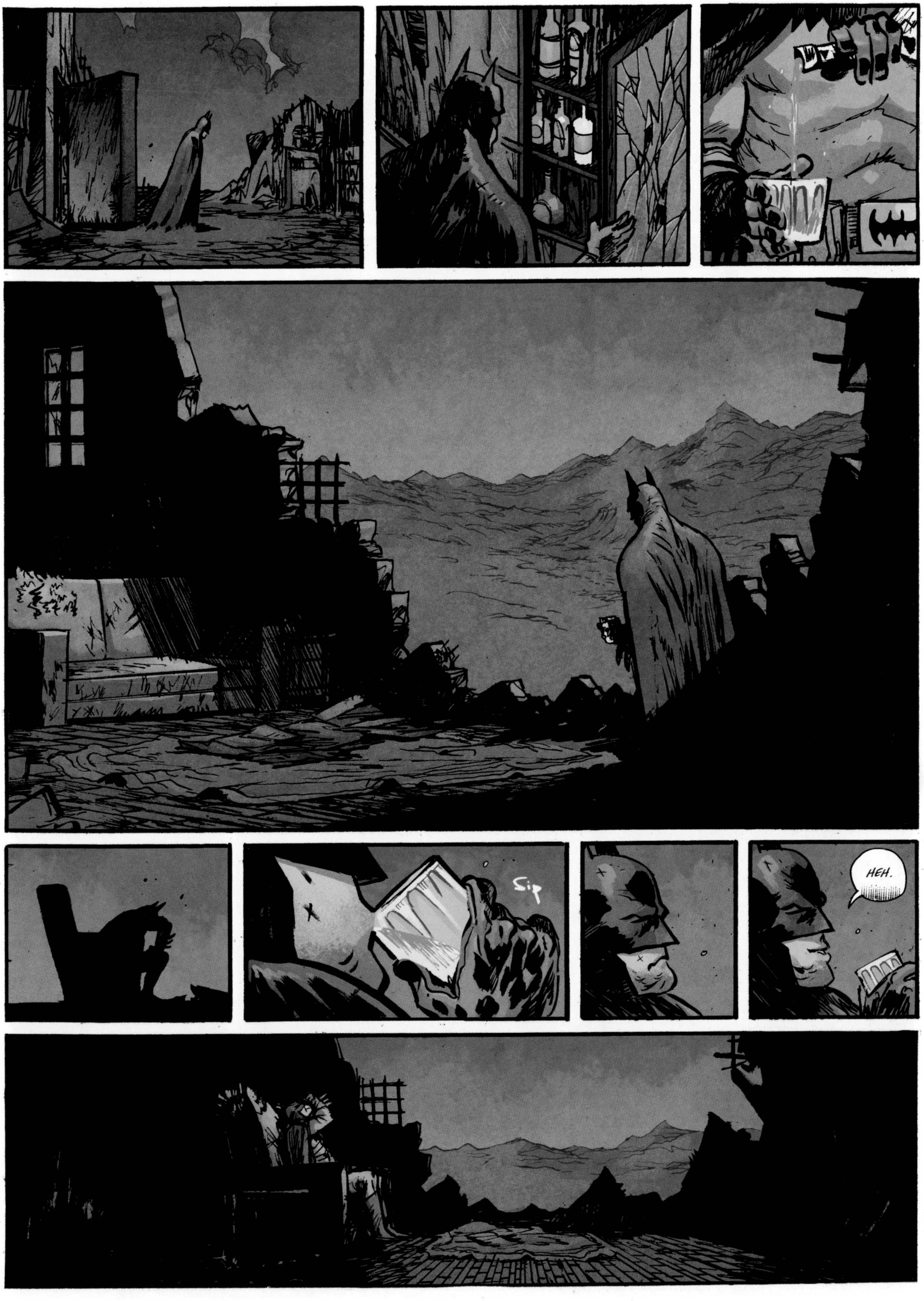
Sip
HEH.

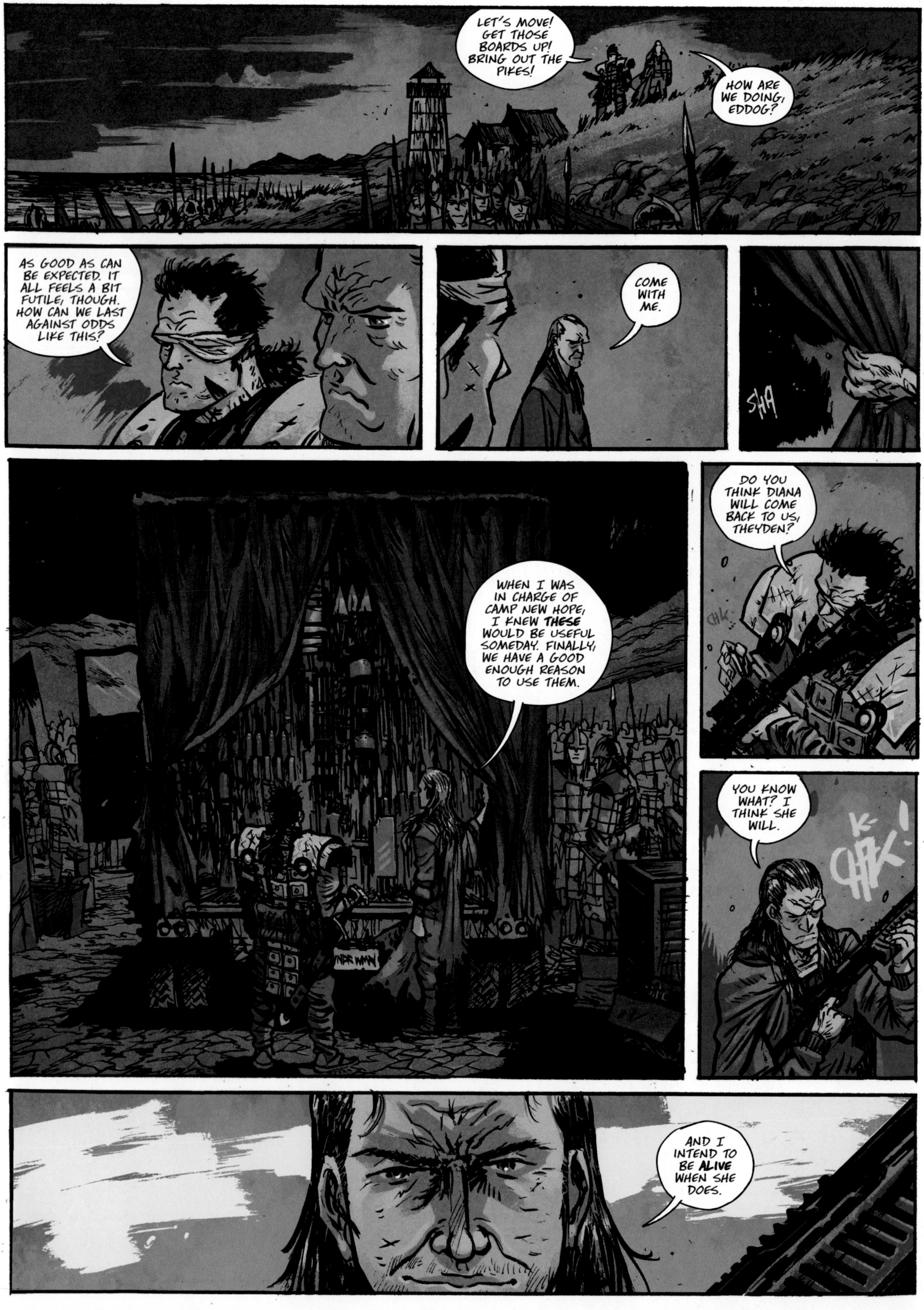

LET'S MOVE! GET THOSE BOARDS UP! BRING OUT THE PIKES!
HOW ARE WE DOING, EDDOG?
AS GOOD AS CAN BE EXPECTED. IT ALL FEELS A BIT FUTILE, THOUGH. HOW CAN WE LAST AGAINST ODDS LIKE THIS?
COME WITH ME.
SHA
WHEN I WAS IN CHARGE OF CAMP NEW HOPE, I KNEW **THESE** WOULD BE USEFUL SOMEDAY. FINALLY, WE HAVE A GOOD ENOUGH REASON TO USE THEM.
DO YOU THINK DIANA WILL COME BACK TO US, THEYDEN?
CHK
YOU KNOW WHAT? I THINK SHE WILL.
K-CHAK!
AND I INTEND TO BE **ALIVE** WHEN SHE DOES.

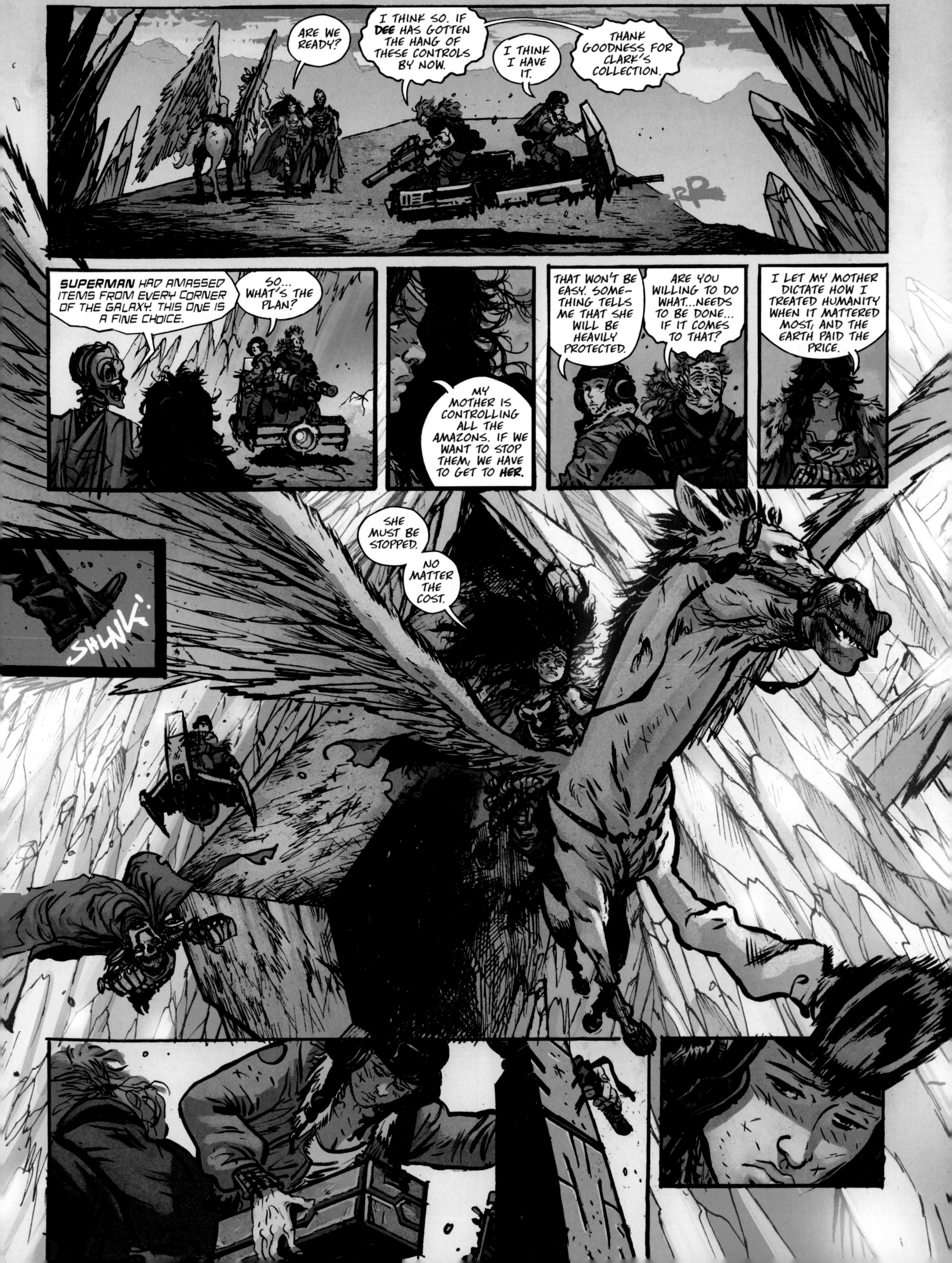
ARE WE READY?
I THINK SO. IF DEE HAS GOTTEN THE HANG OF THESE CONTROLS BY NOW.
I THINK I HAVE IT.
THANK GOODNESS FOR CLARK'S COLLECTION.
RRR
SUPERMAN HAD AMASSED ITEMS FROM EVERY CORNER OF THE GALAXY. THIS ONE IS A FINE CHOICE.
SO... WHAT'S THE PLAN?
MY MOTHER IS CONTROLLING ALL THE AMAZONS. IF WE WANT TO STOP THEM, WE HAVE TO GET TO HER.
THAT WON'T BE EASY. SOME-THING TELLS ME THAT SHE WILL BE HEAVILY PROTECTED.
ARE YOU WILLING TO DO WHAT...NEEDS TO BE DONE... IF IT COMES TO THAT?
I LET MY MOTHER DICTATE HOW I TREATED HUMANITY WHEN IT MATTERED MOST, AND THE EARTH PAID THE PRICE.
SHLNK!
SHE MUST BE STOPPED.
NO MATTER THE COST.

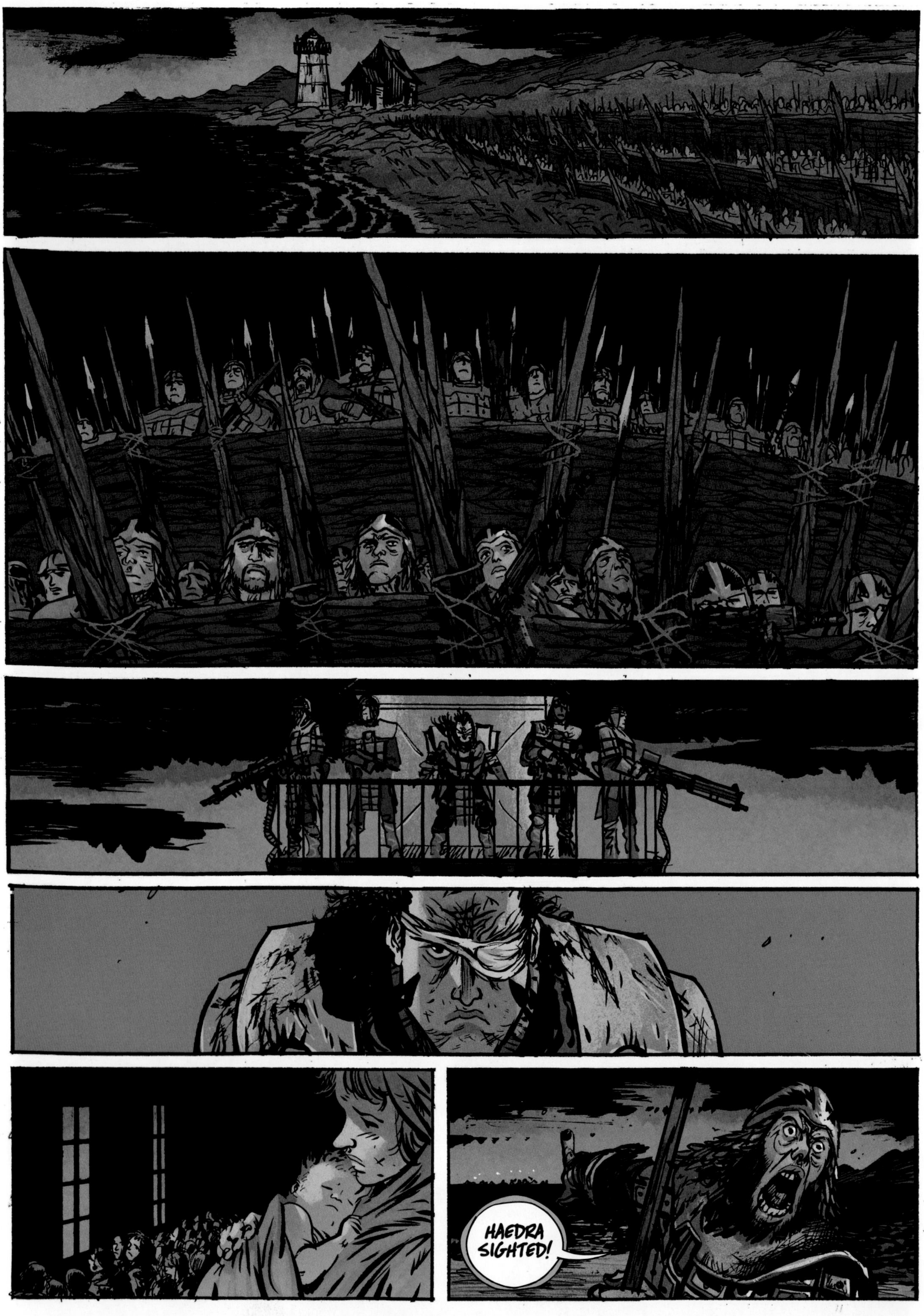
HAEDRA SIGHTED!

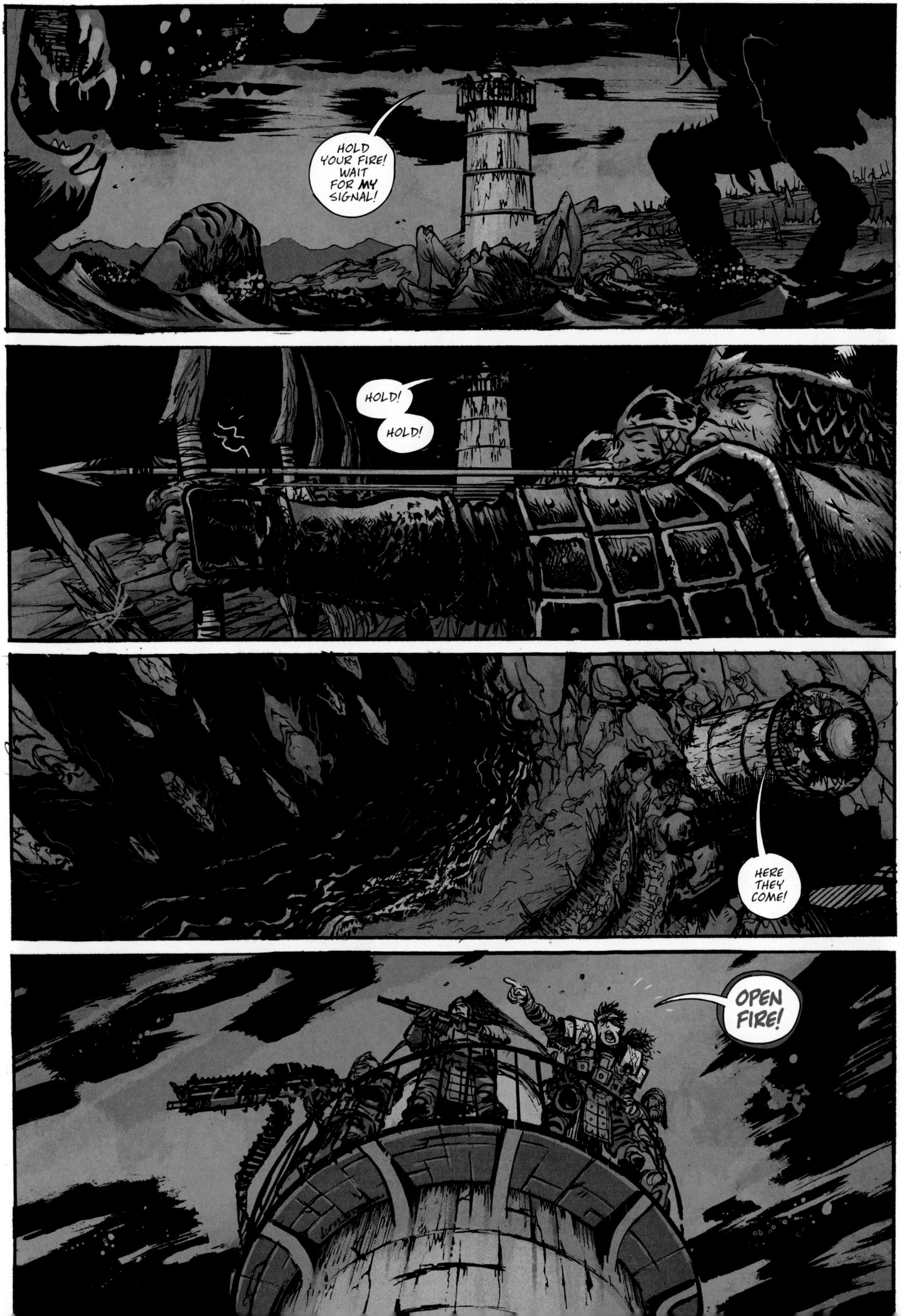
HOLD YOUR FIRE! WAIT FOR MY SIGNAL!
HOLD!
HOLD!
HERE THEY COME!
OPEN FIRE!

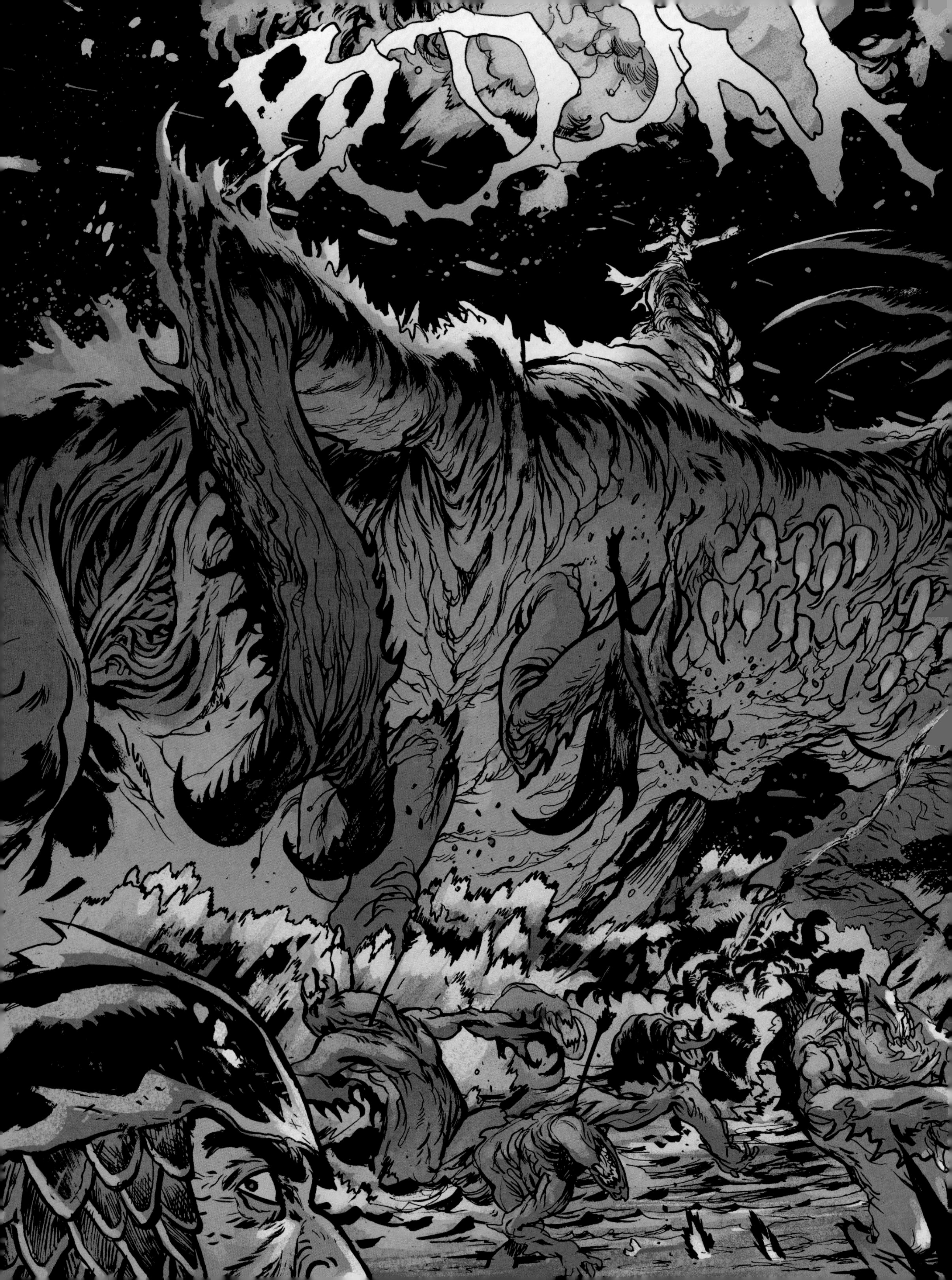

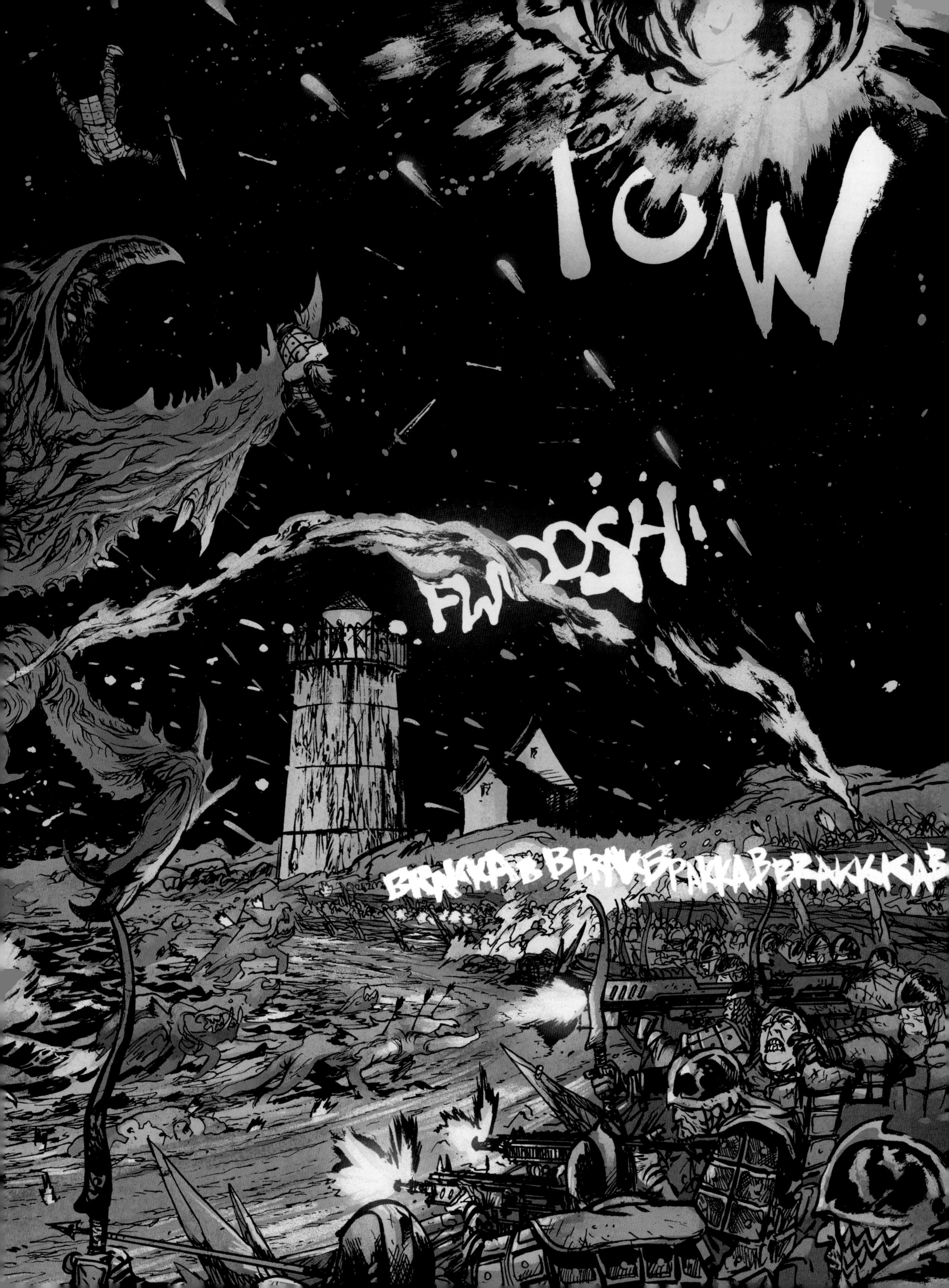
IOW
FWOOSH!
BRAKKAB

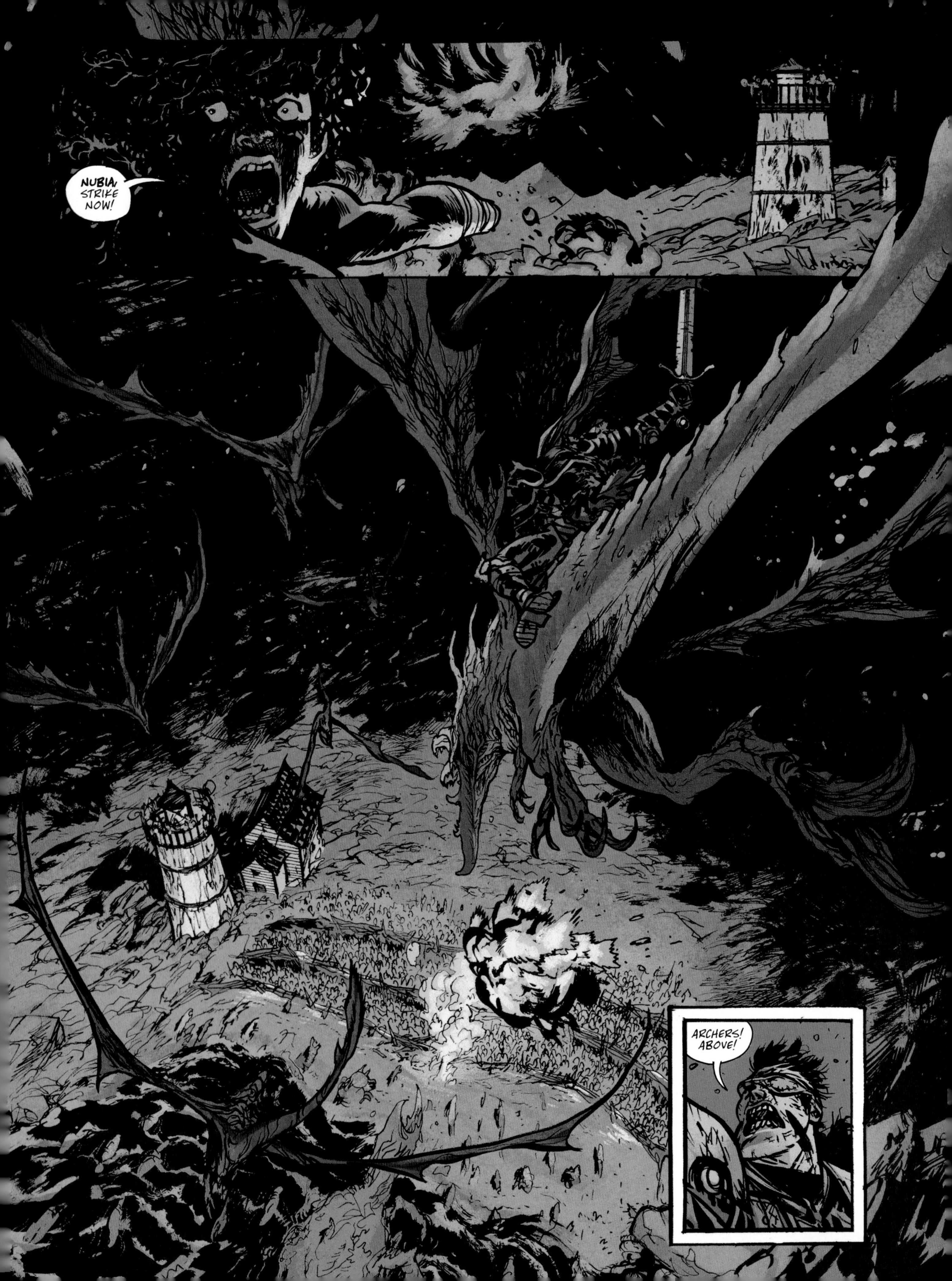
NUBIA, STRIKE NOW!
ARCHERS! ABOVE!

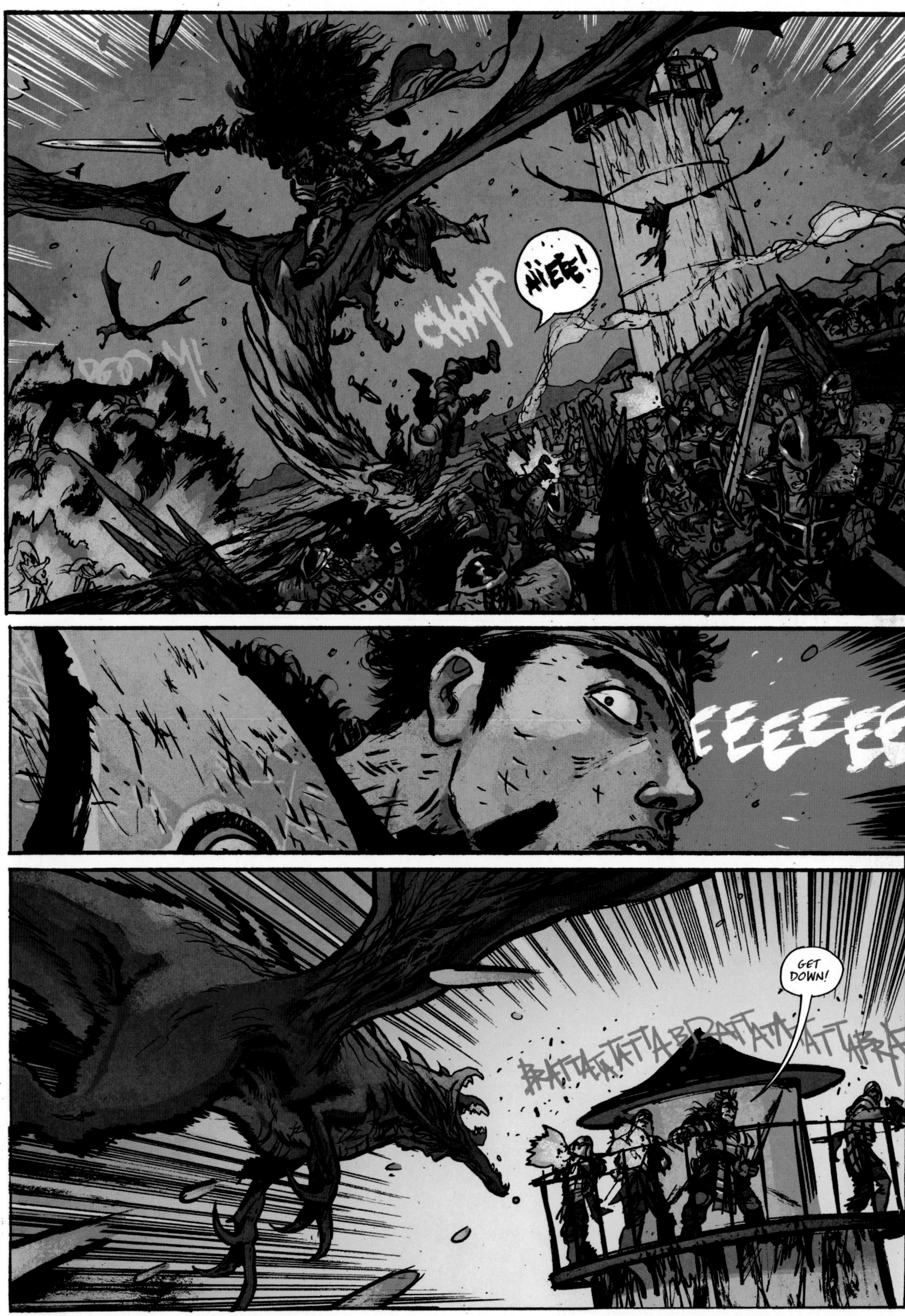
CHOMP
AIEEE!
GET DOWN!

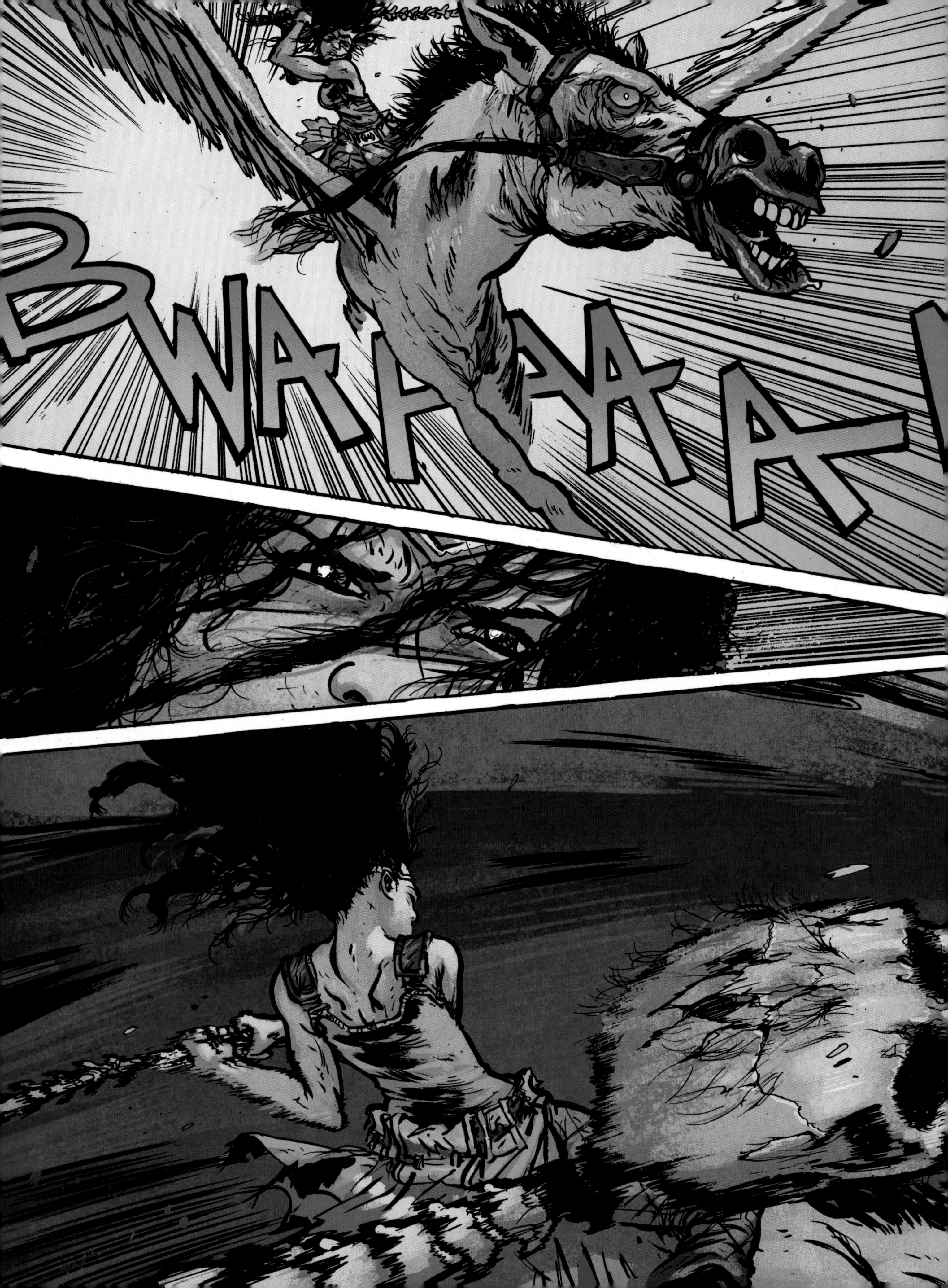
BWAAAAA

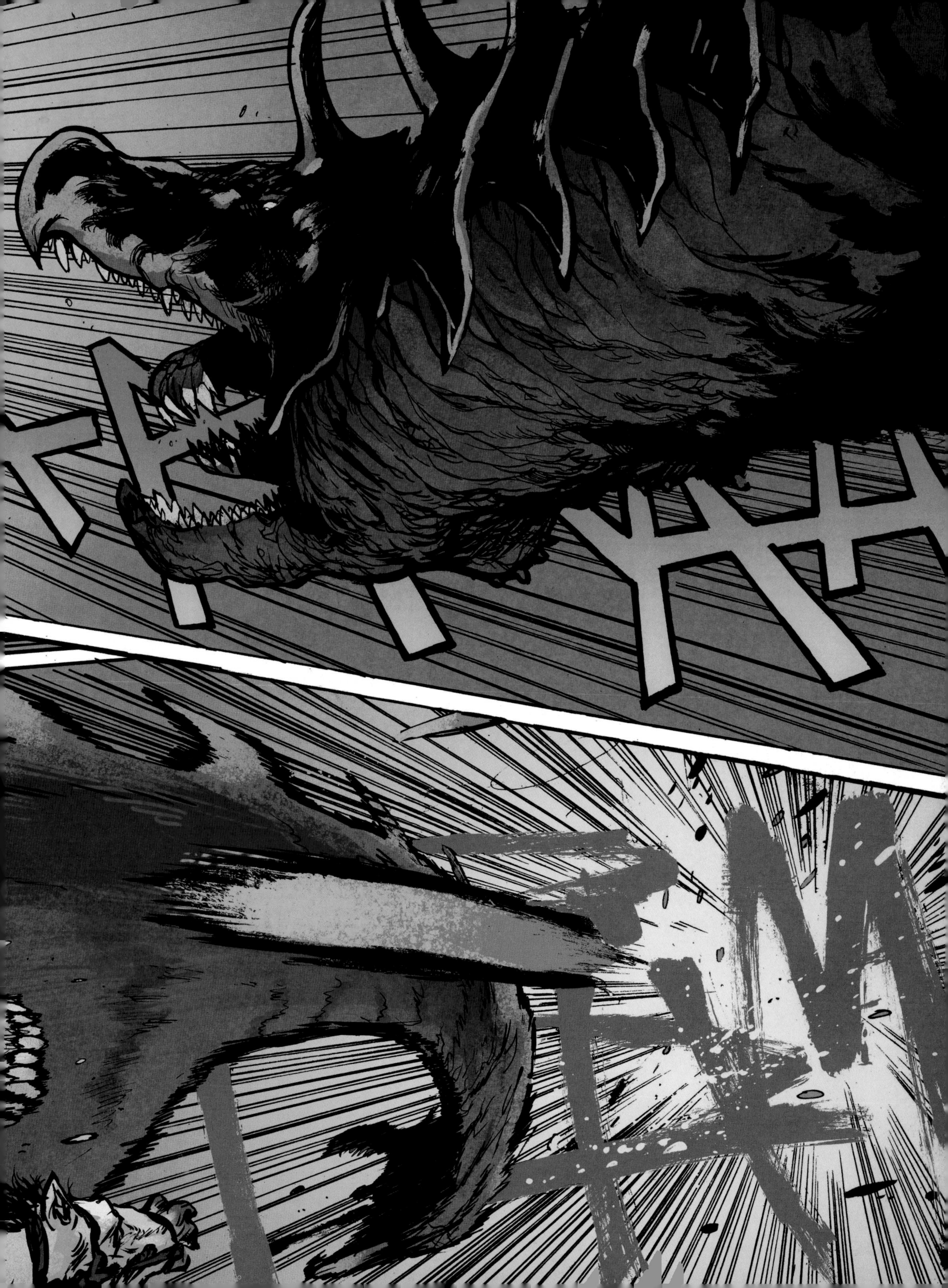

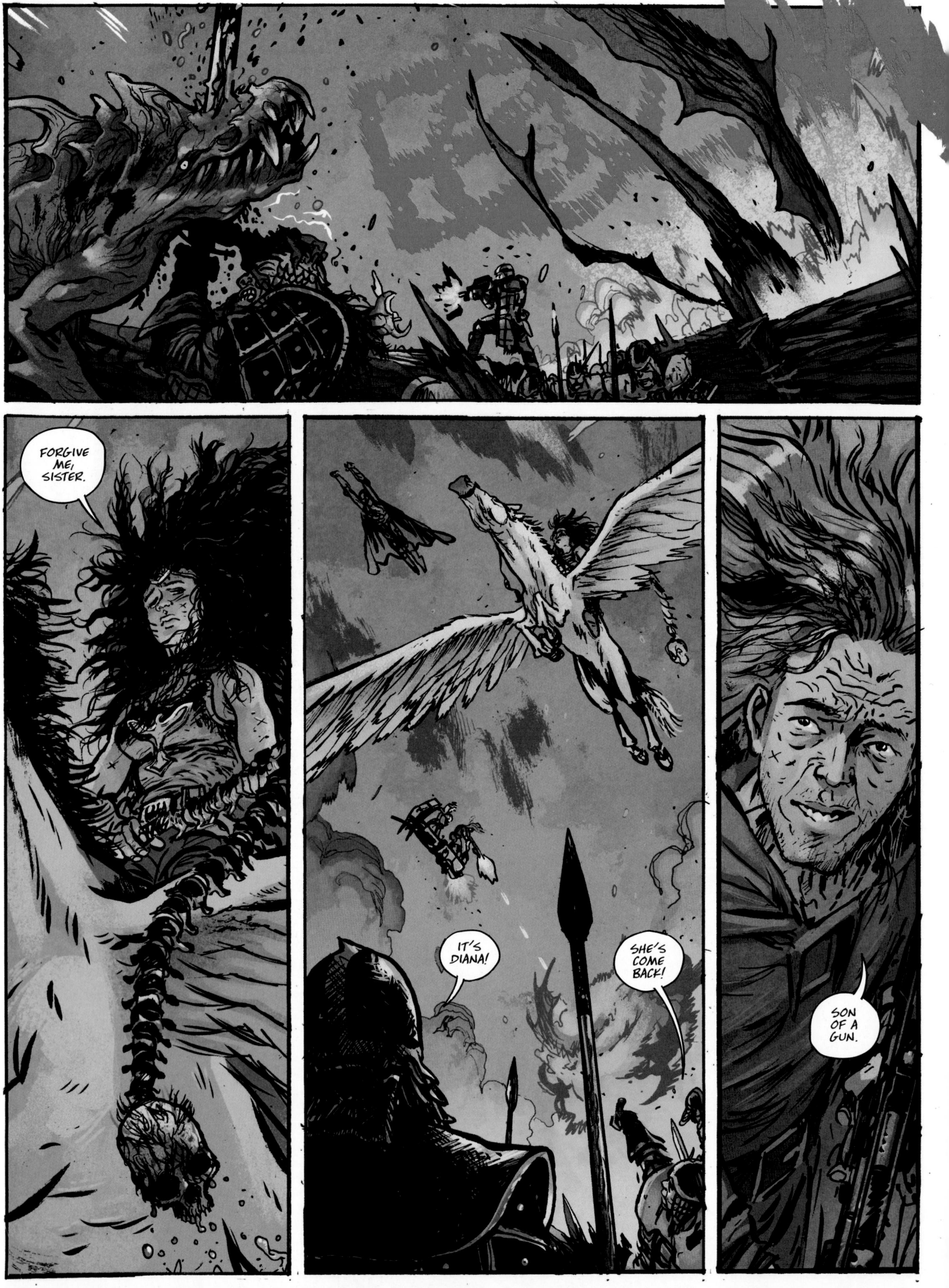
FORGIVE ME, SISTER.
IT'S DIANA!
SHE'S COME BACK!
SON OF A GUN.

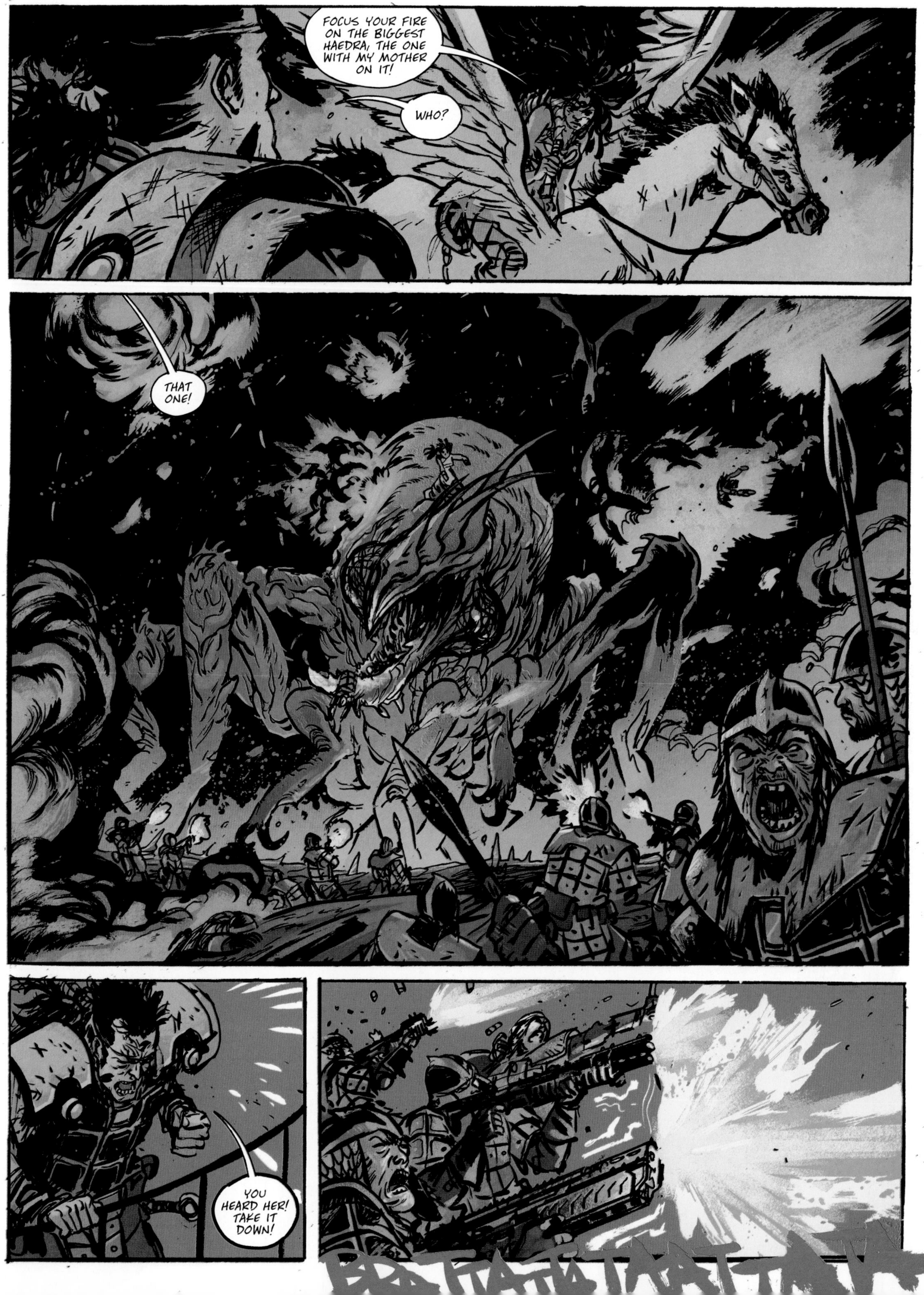
FOCUS YOUR FIRE ON THE BIGGEST HAEDRA, THE ONE WITH MY MOTHER ON IT!
WHO?
THAT ONE!
YOU HEARD HER! TAKE IT DOWN!

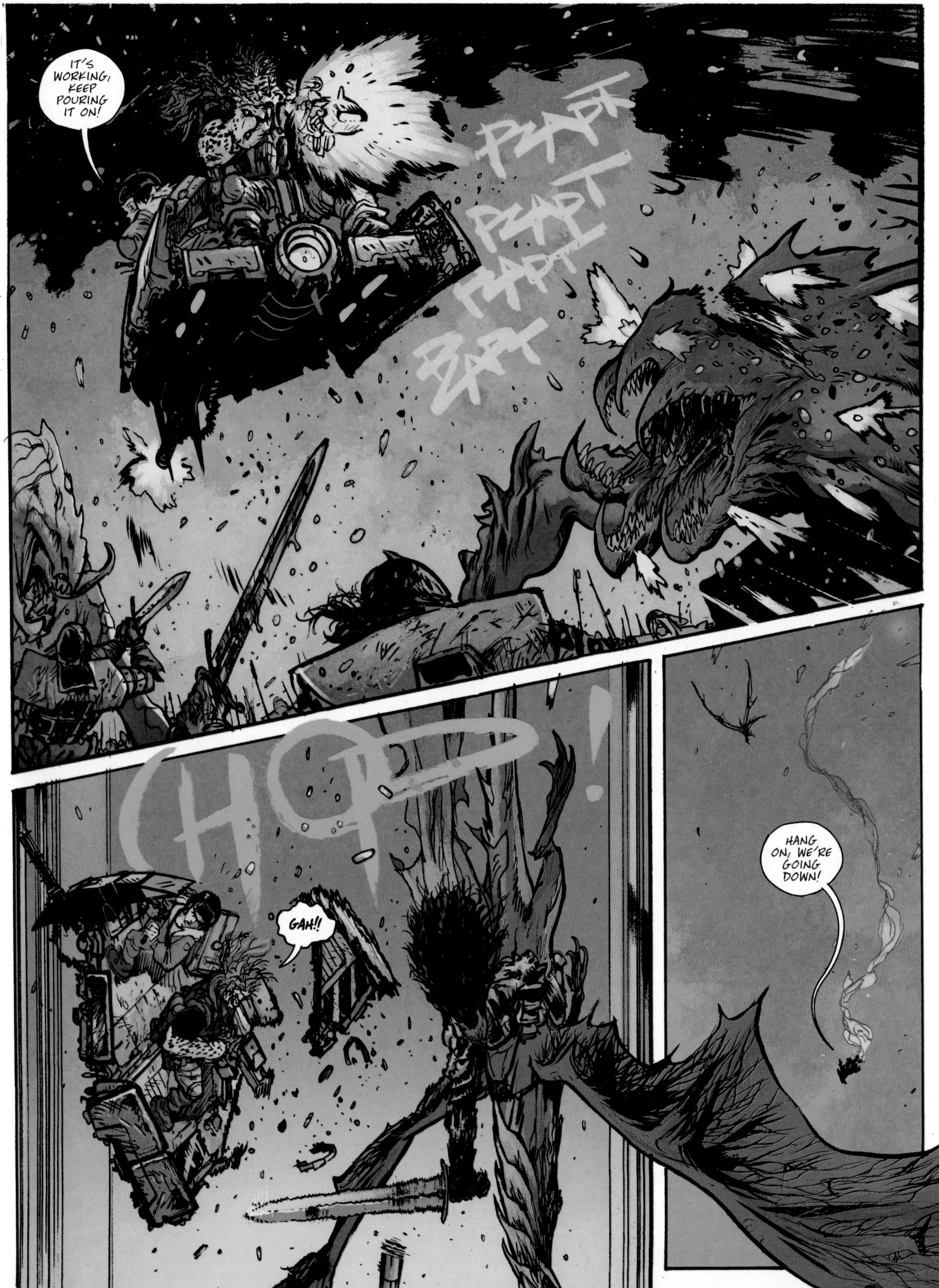
IT'S WORKING, KEEP POURING IT ON!
GAH!!
HANG ON, WE'RE GOING DOWN!

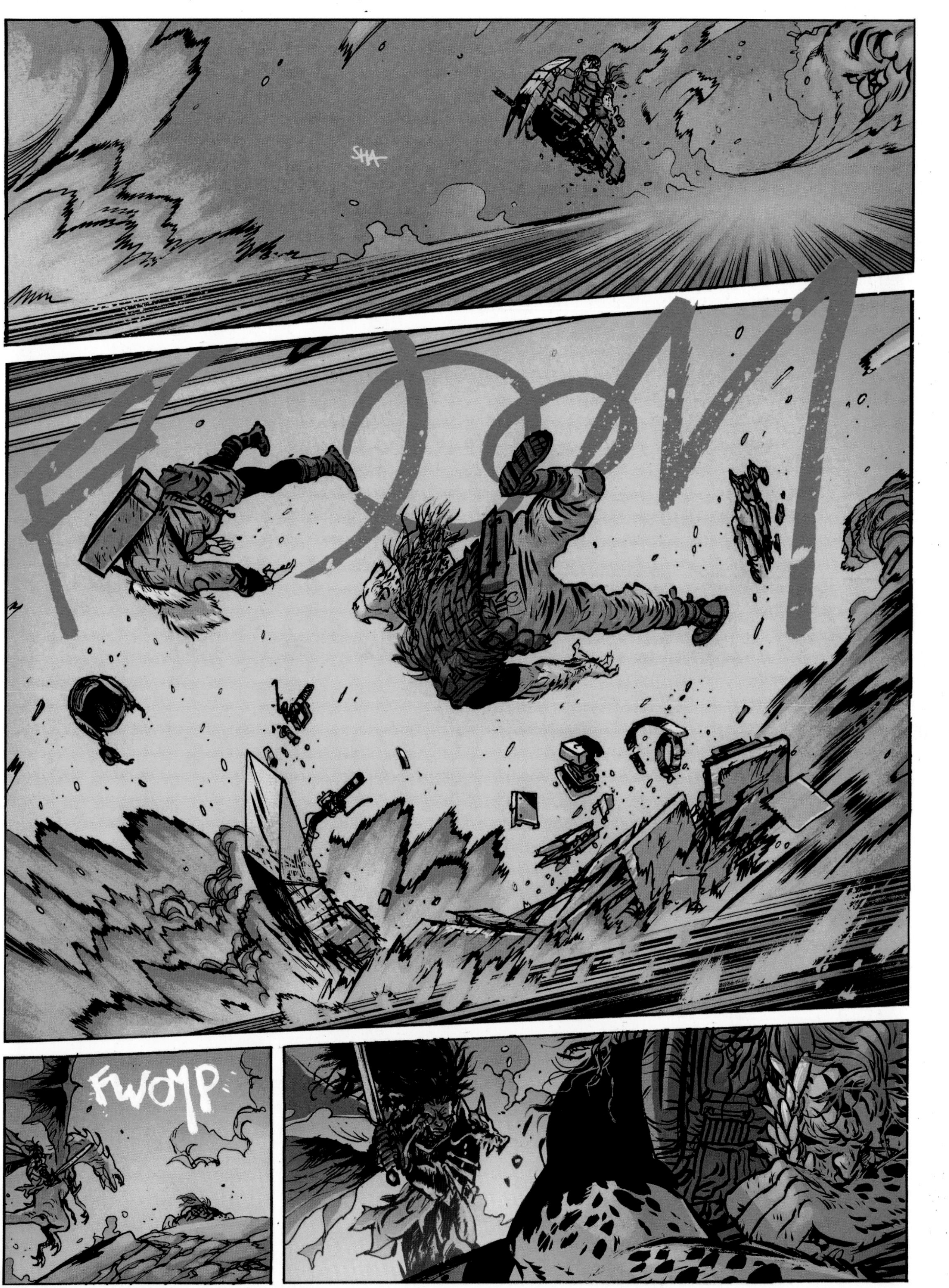
SHA
FOOM
FWOMP

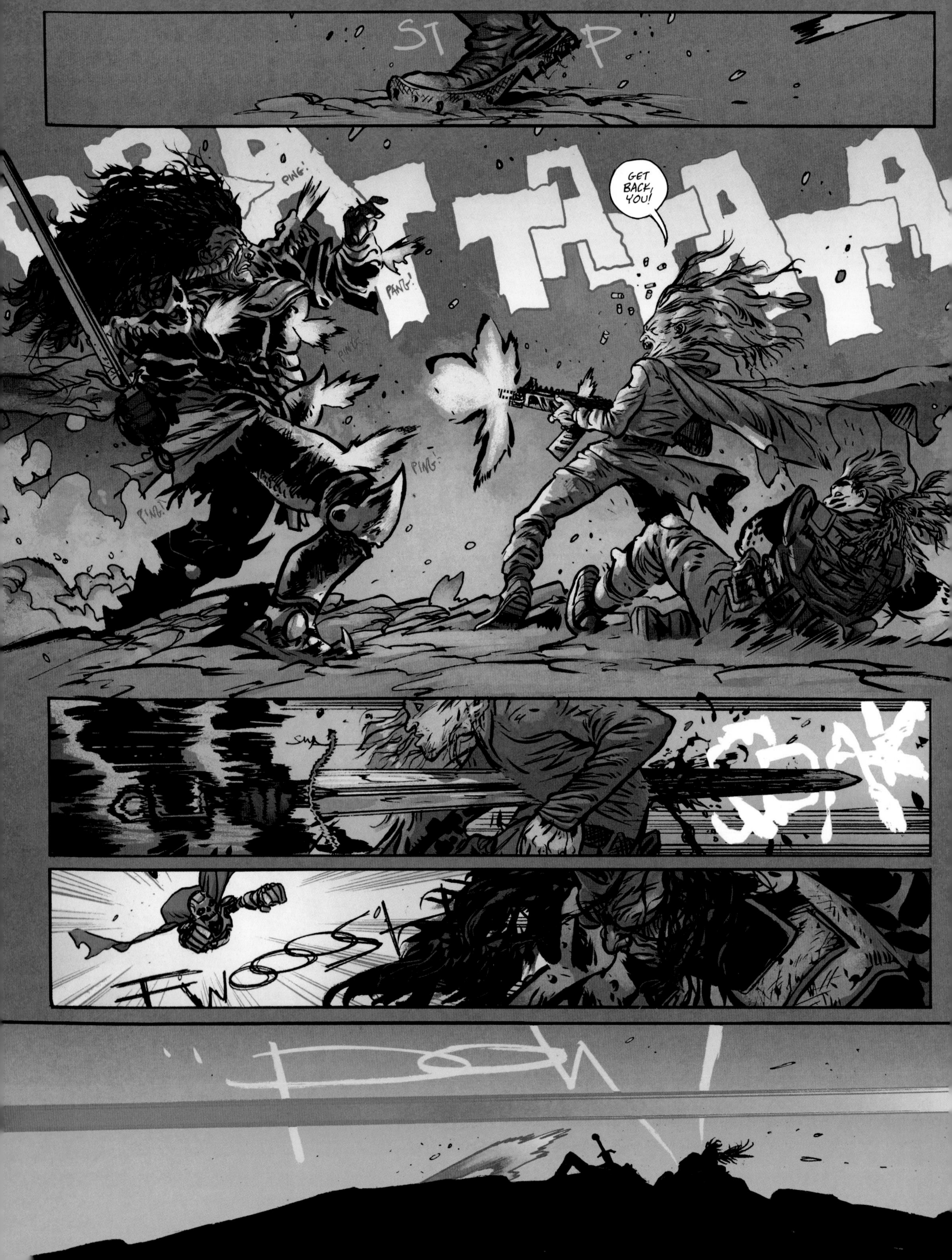
PING!
PANG!
PING!
PING!
PING!
GET BACK, YOU!
FWOOOSH!

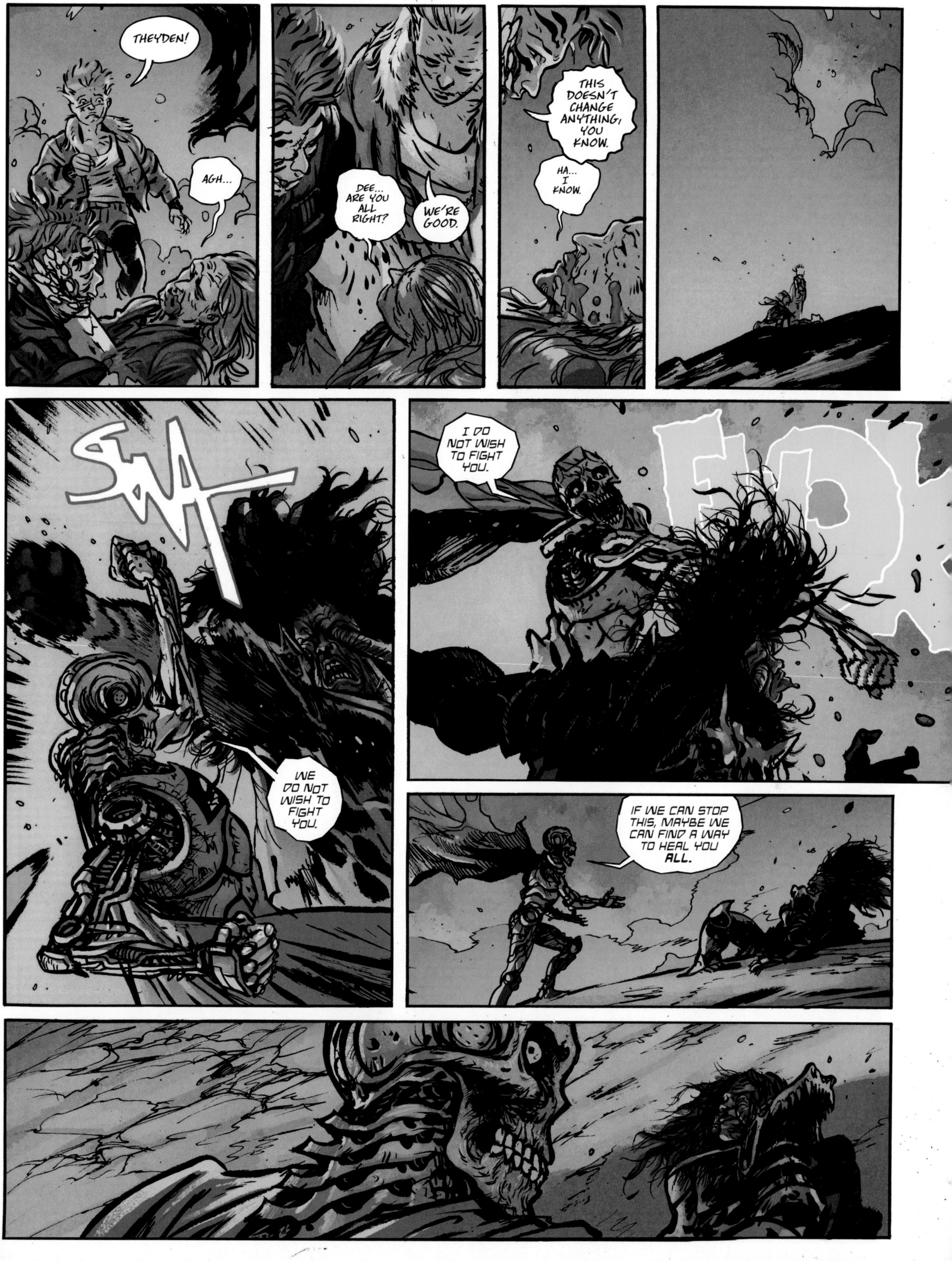
THEYDEN!
AGH...
DEE... ARE YOU ALL RIGHT?
WE'RE GOOD.
THIS DOESN'T CHANGE ANYTHING, YOU KNOW.
HA... I KNOW.
WE DO NOT WISH TO FIGHT YOU.
I DO NOT WISH TO FIGHT YOU.
IF WE CAN STOP THIS, MAYBE WE CAN FIND A WAY TO HEAL YOU ALL.

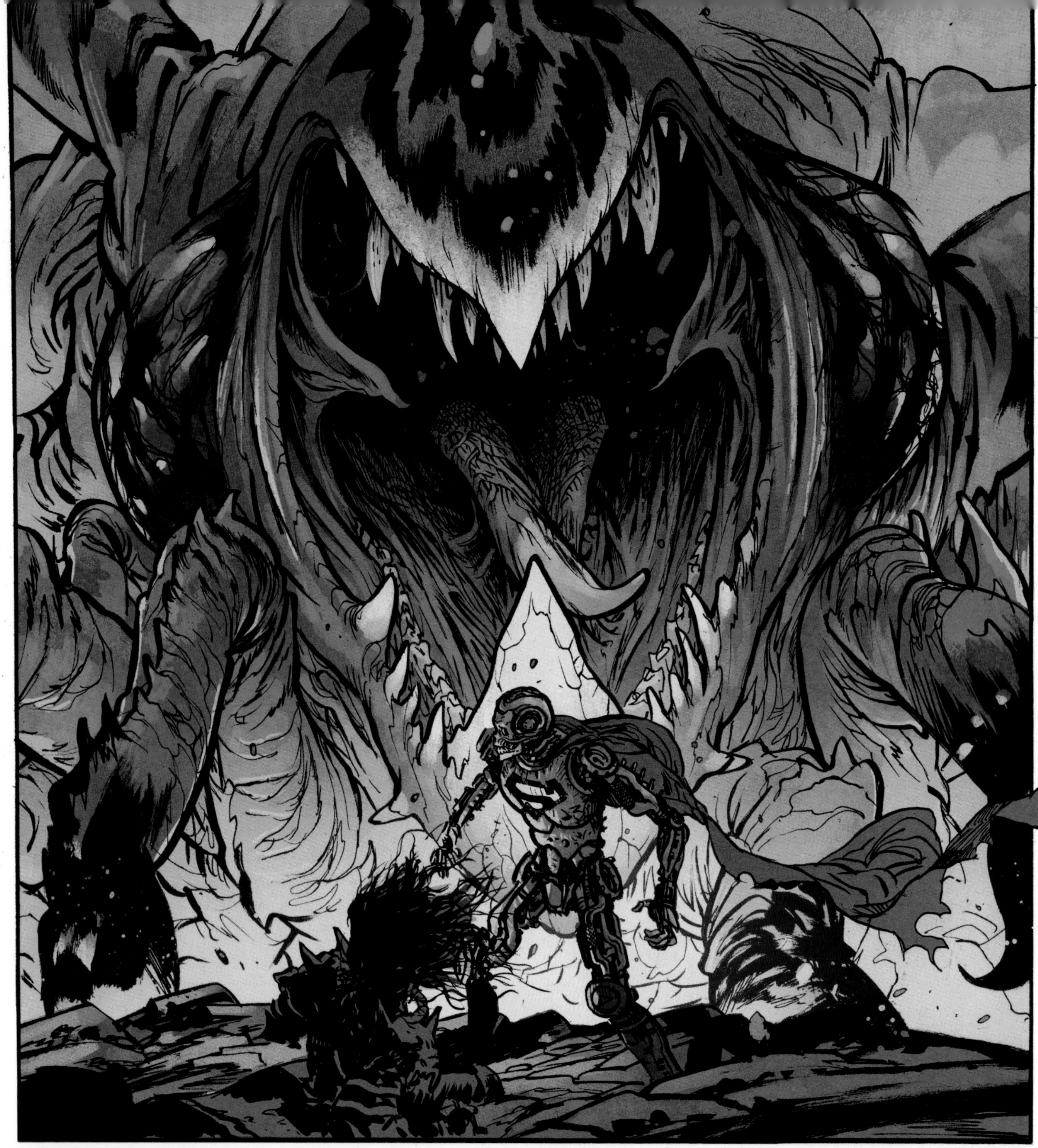

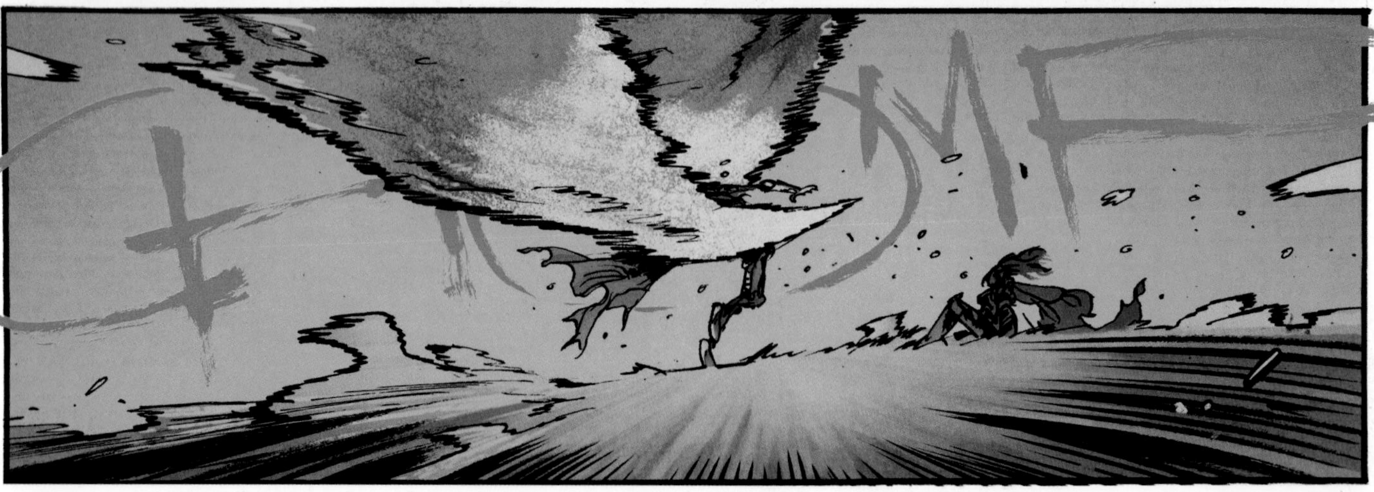

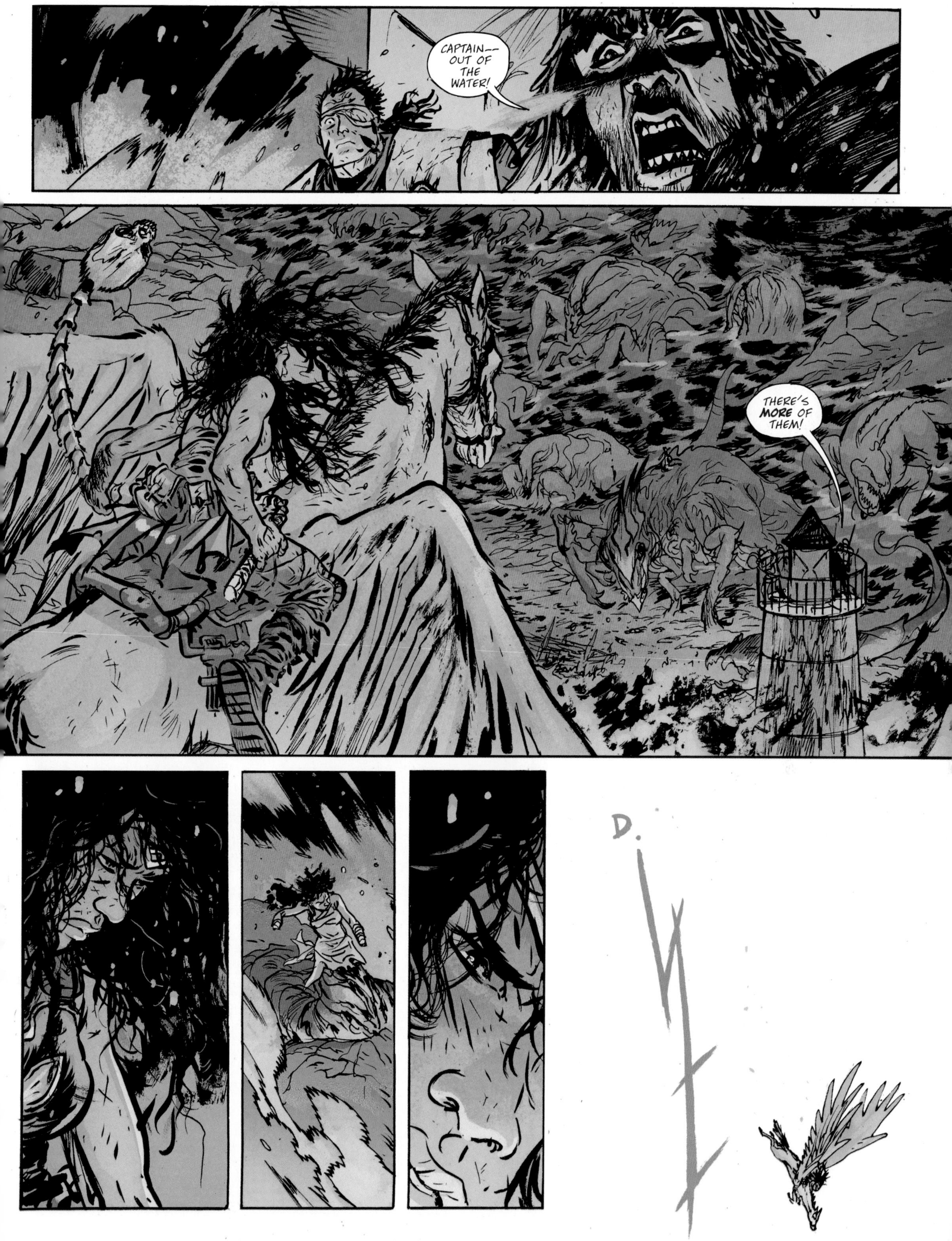
CAPTAIN-- OUT OF THE WATER!
THERE'S **MORE** OF THEM!

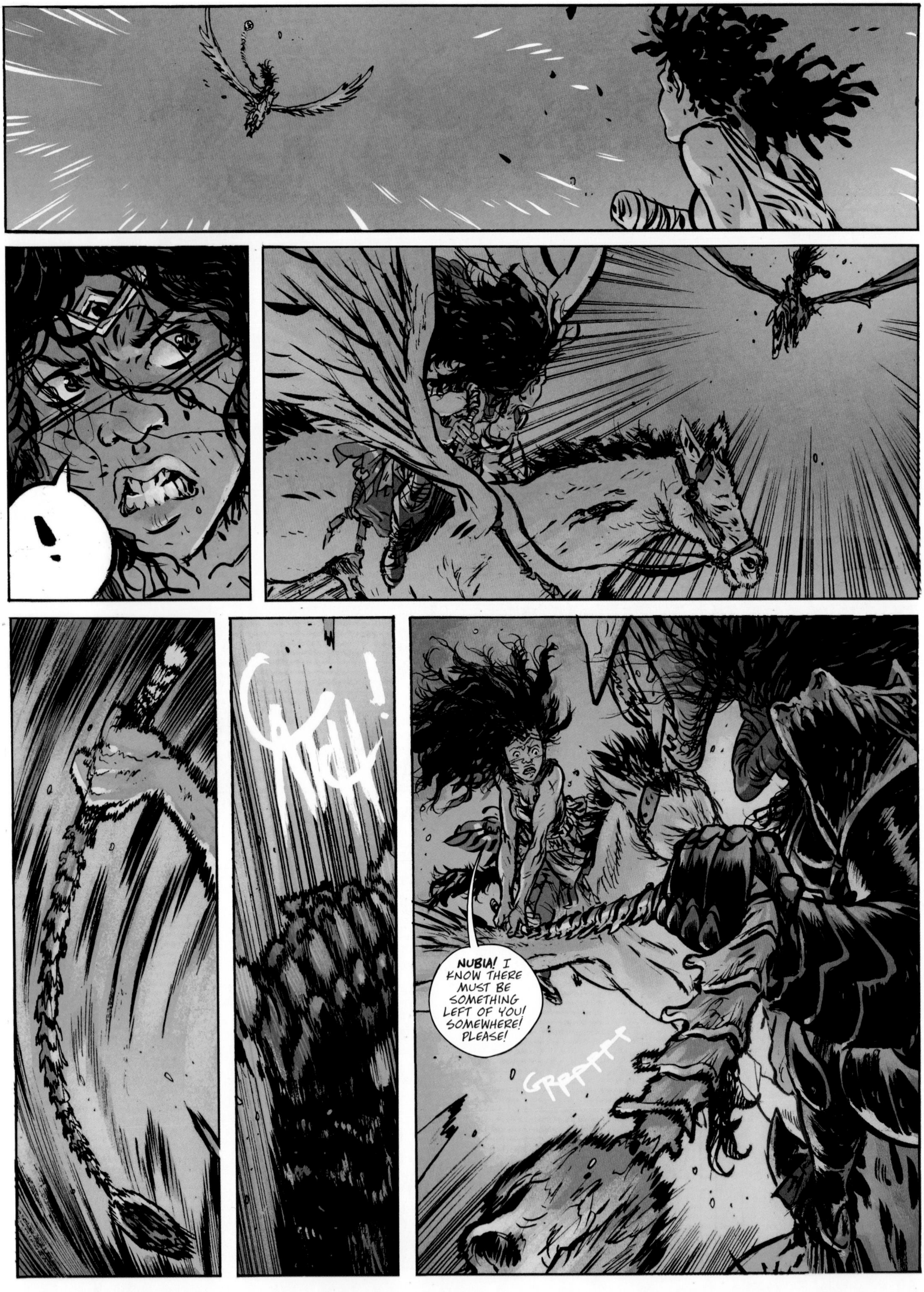
!
CATCH!
NUBIA! I KNOW THERE MUST BE SOMETHING LEFT OF YOU! SOMEWHERE! PLEASE!
GRRRRRR

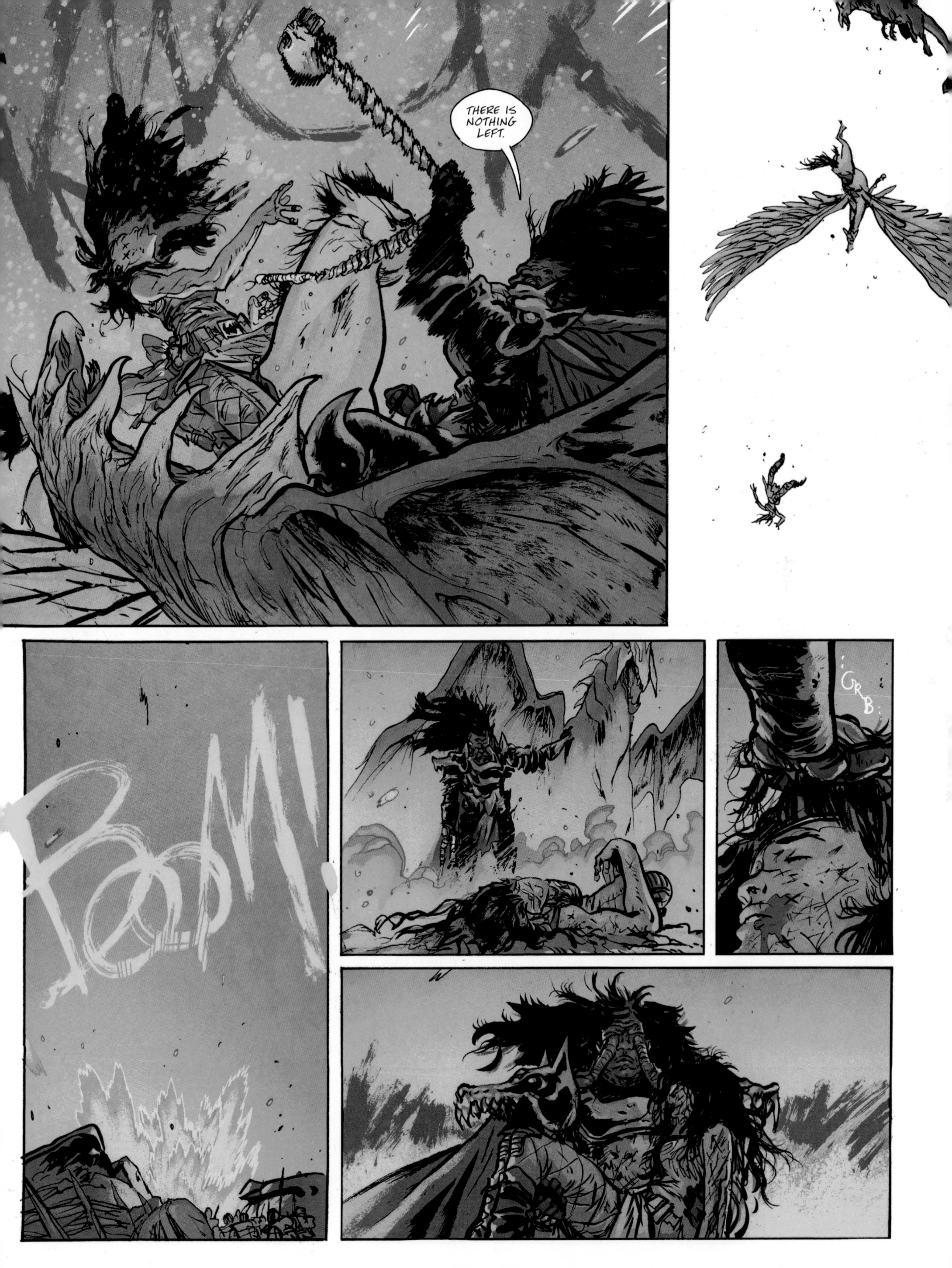
THERE IS NOTHING LEFT.
BOOM!
GRB

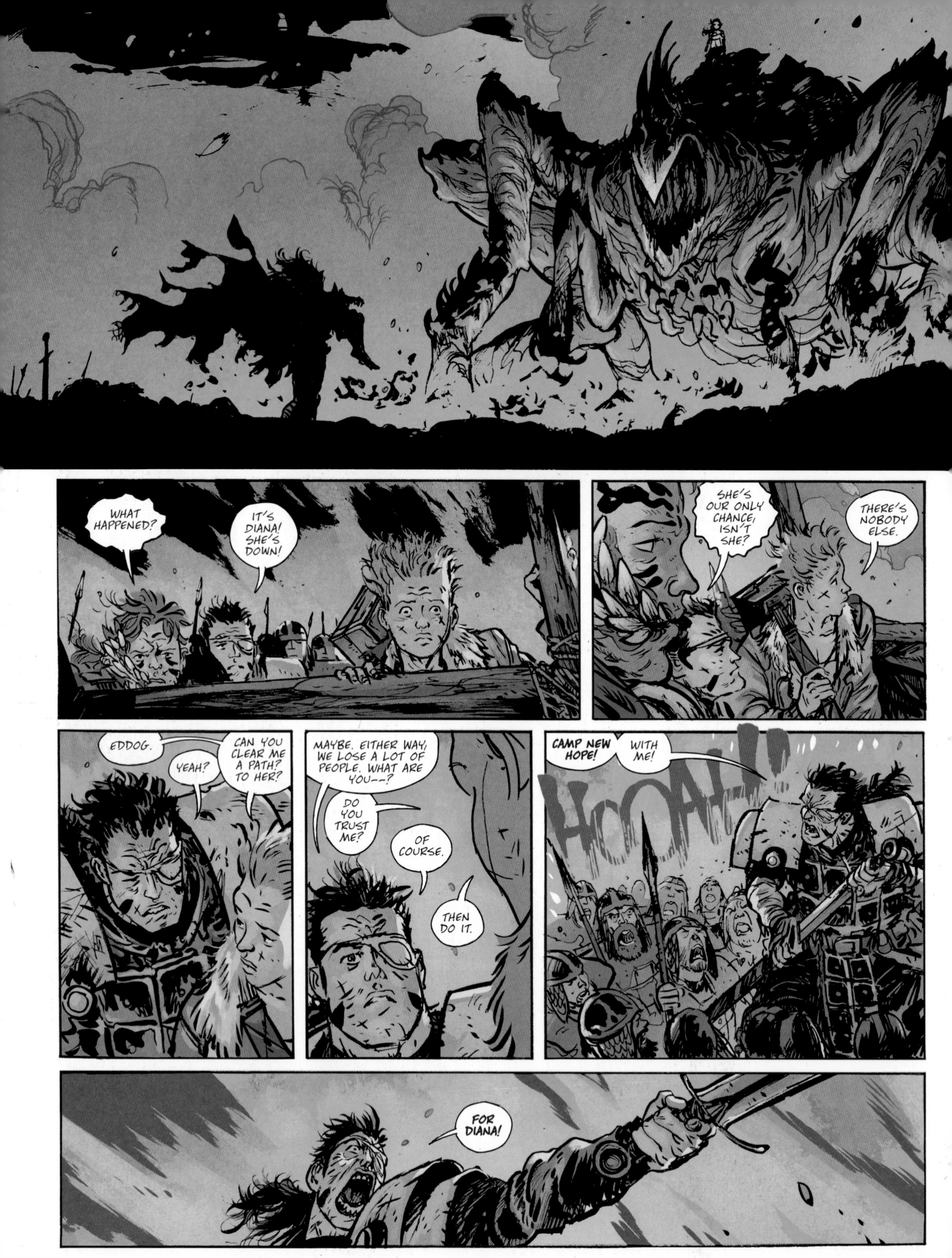
WHAT HAPPENED?
IT'S DIANA! SHE'S DOWN!
SHE'S OUR ONLY CHANCE, ISN'T SHE?
THERE'S NOBODY ELSE.
EDDOG.
YEAH?
CAN YOU CLEAR ME A PATH? TO HER?
MAYBE. EITHER WAY, WE LOSE A LOT OF PEOPLE. WHAT ARE YOU--?
DO YOU TRUST ME?
OF COURSE.
THEN DO IT.
CAMP NEW HOPE!
WITH ME!
HOOAH!!
FOR DIANA!

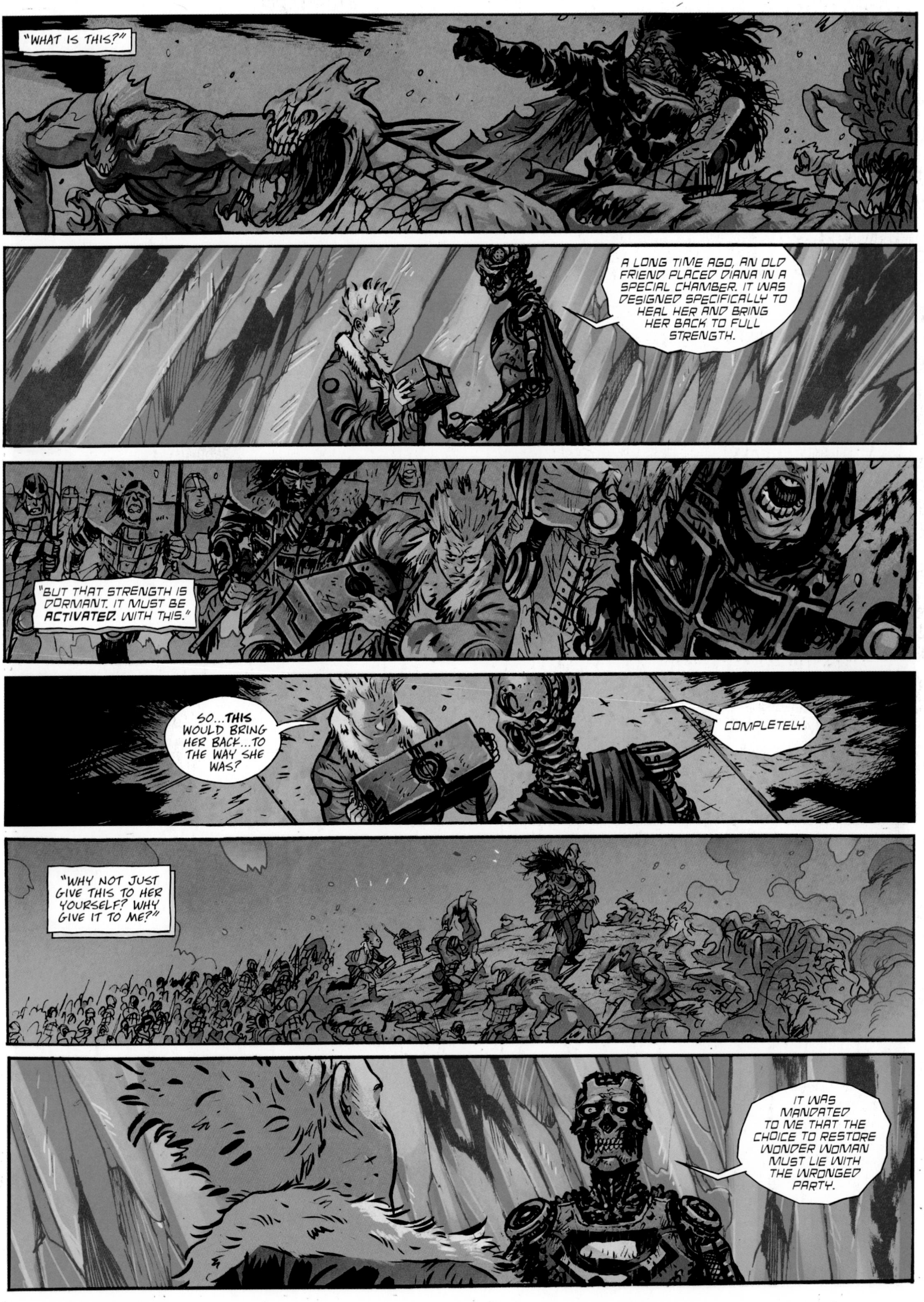
"WHAT IS THIS?"
A LONG TIME AGO, AN OLD FRIEND PLACED DIANA IN A SPECIAL CHAMBER. IT WAS DESIGNED SPECIFICALLY TO HEAL HER AND BRING HER BACK TO FULL STRENGTH.
"BUT THAT STRENGTH IS DORMANT. IT MUST BE ACTIVATED. WITH THIS."
SO...THIS WOULD BRING HER BACK...TO THE WAY SHE WAS?
COMPLETELY.
"WHY NOT JUST GIVE THIS TO HER YOURSELF? WHY GIVE IT TO ME?"
IT WAS MANDATED TO ME THAT THE CHOICE TO RESTORE WONDER WOMAN MUST LIE WITH THE WRONGED PARTY.

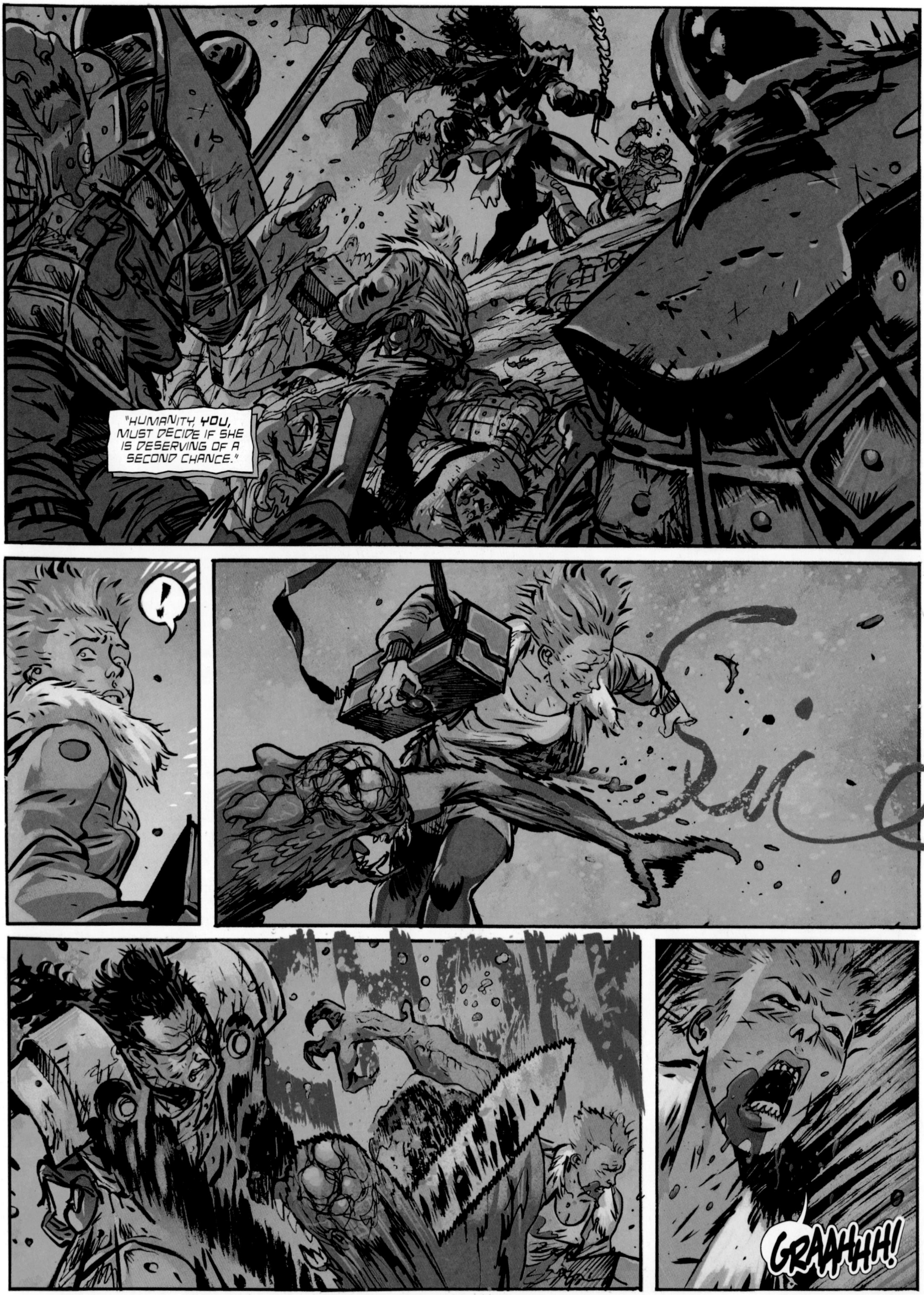
"HUMANITY, YOU, MUST DECIDE IF SHE IS DESERVING OF A SECOND CHANCE."
!
GRAAHHH!

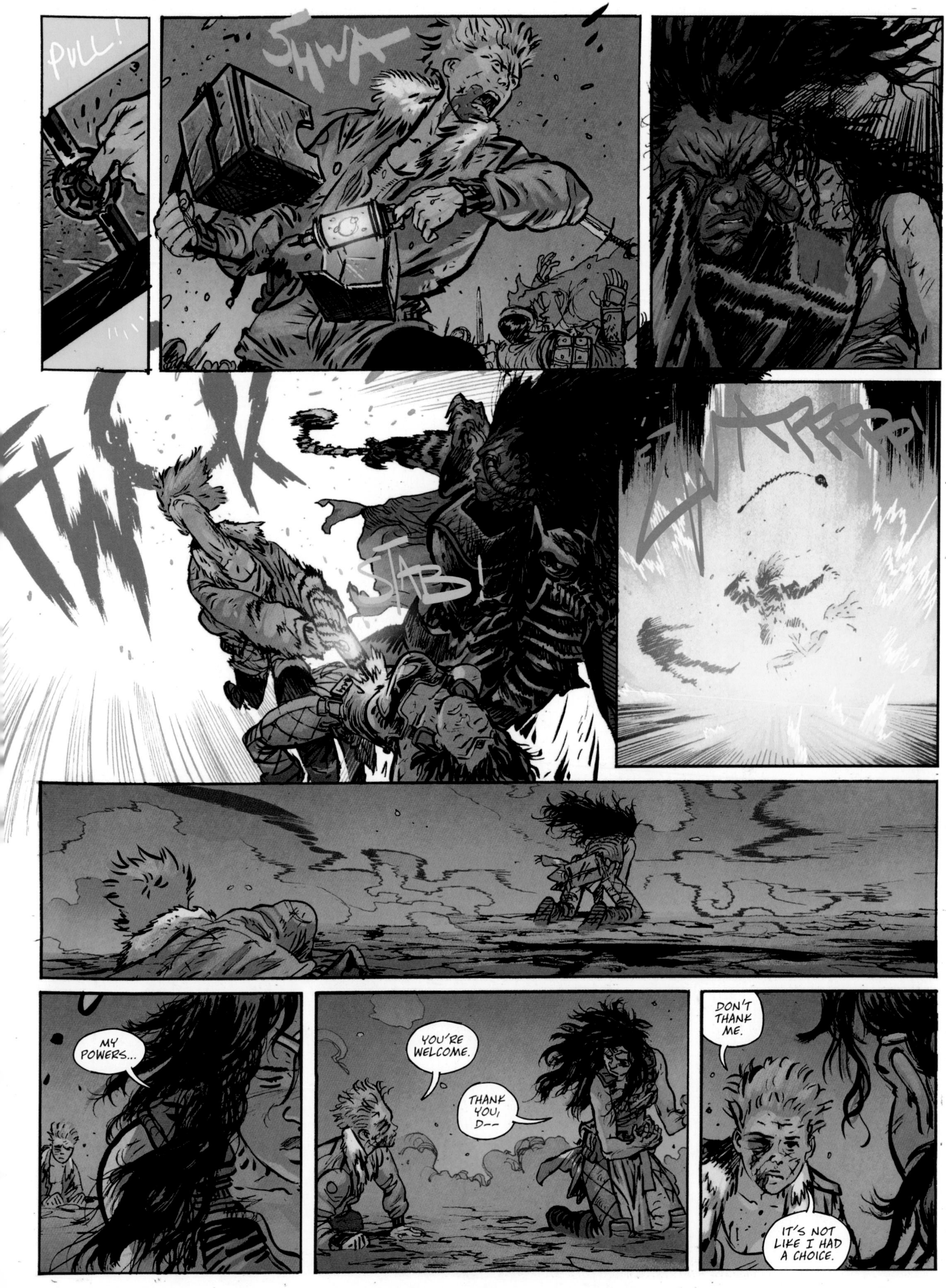
PULL!
SHWA
STAB!
MY POWERS...
YOU'RE WELCOME.
THANK YOU, D--
DON'T THANK ME.
IT'S NOT LIKE I HAD A CHOICE.

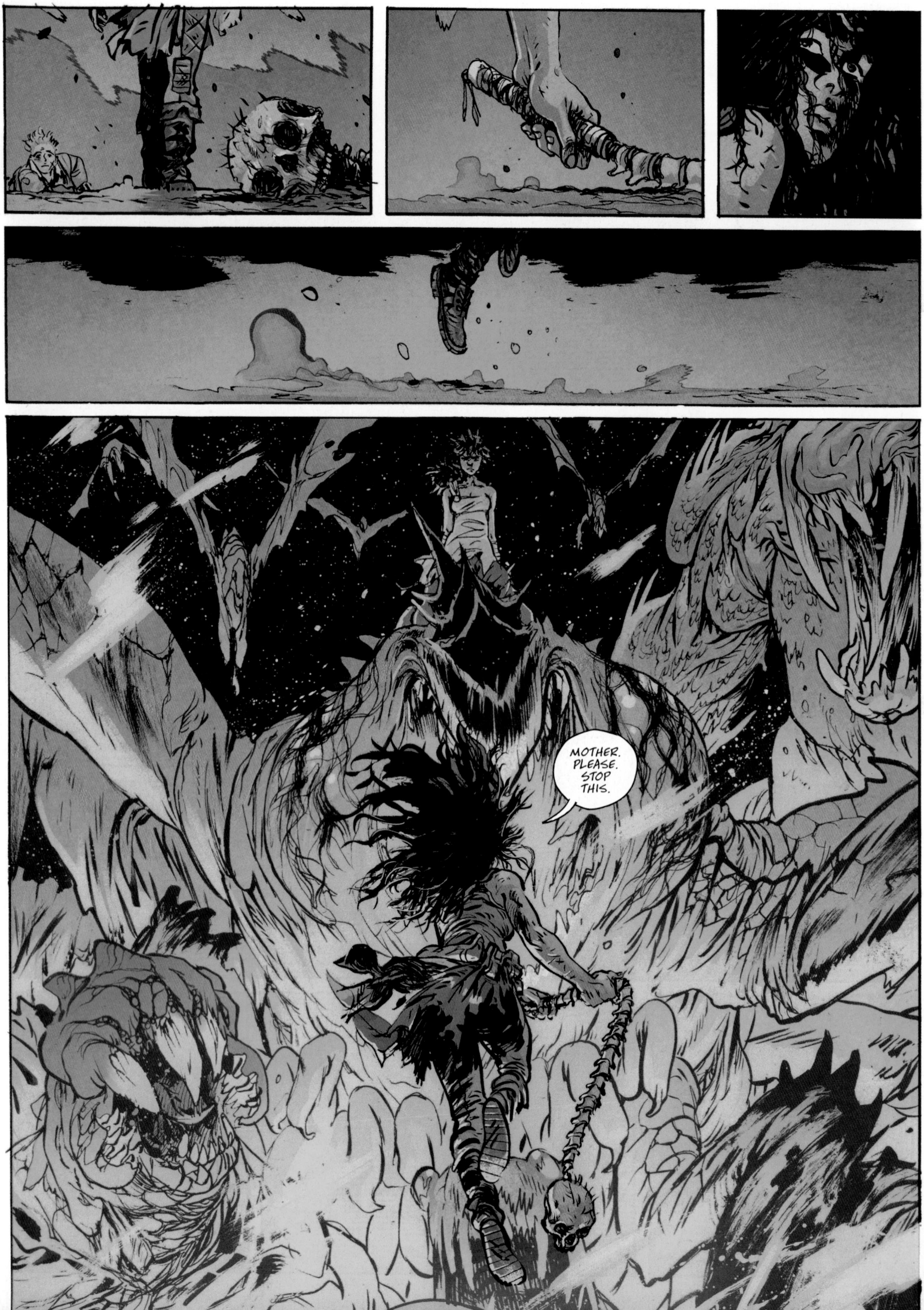
MOTHER. PLEASE. STOP THIS.

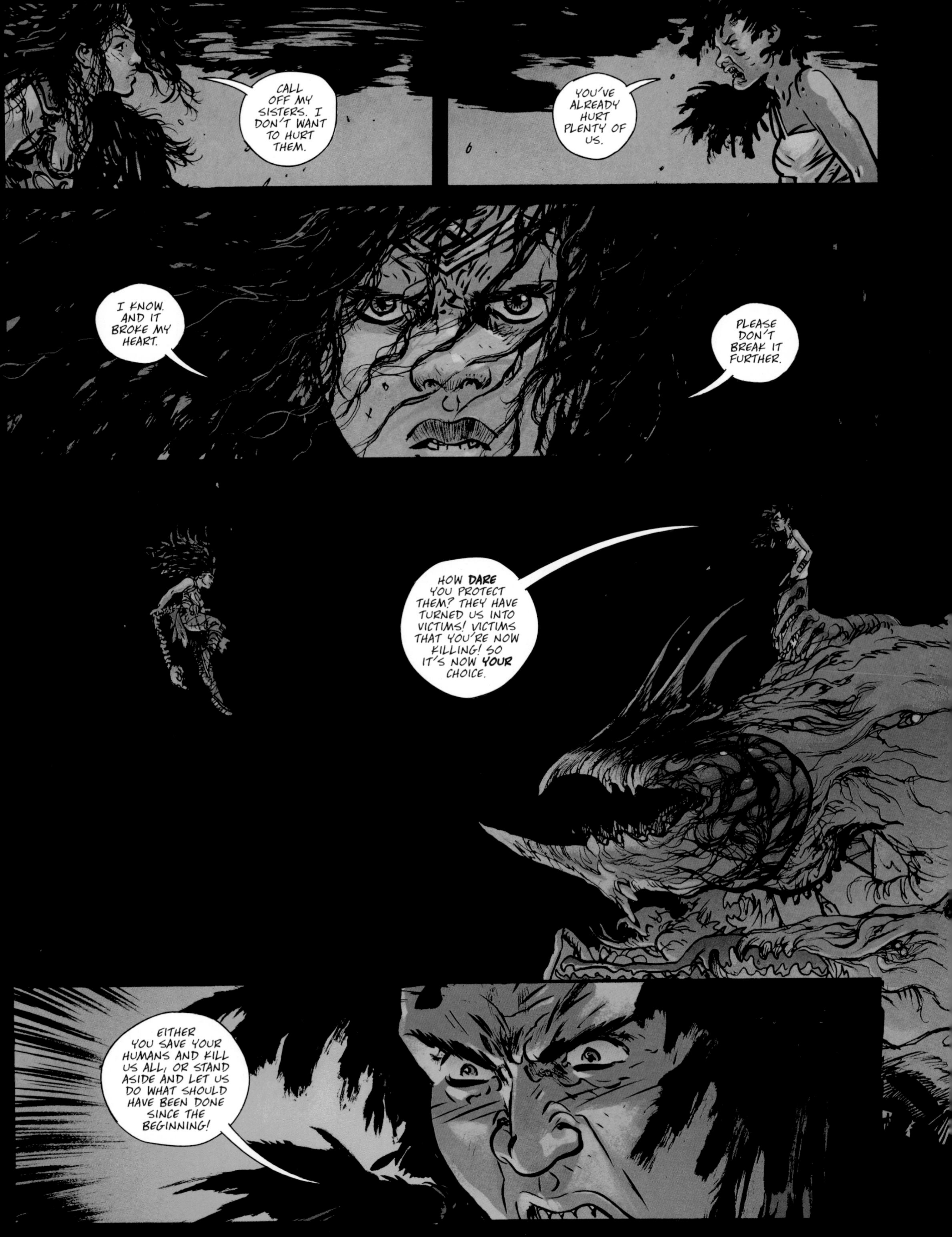
CALL OFF MY SISTERS. I DON'T WANT TO HURT THEM.
YOU'VE ALREADY HURT PLENTY OF US.
I KNOW. AND IT BROKE MY HEART.
PLEASE DON'T BREAK IT FURTHER.
HOW DARE YOU PROTECT THEM? THEY HAVE TURNED US INTO VICTIMS! VICTIMS THAT YOU'RE NOW KILLING! SO IT'S NOW YOUR CHOICE.
EITHER YOU SAVE YOUR HUMANS AND KILL US ALL, OR STAND ASIDE AND LET US DO WHAT SHOULD HAVE BEEN DONE SINCE THE BEGINNING!

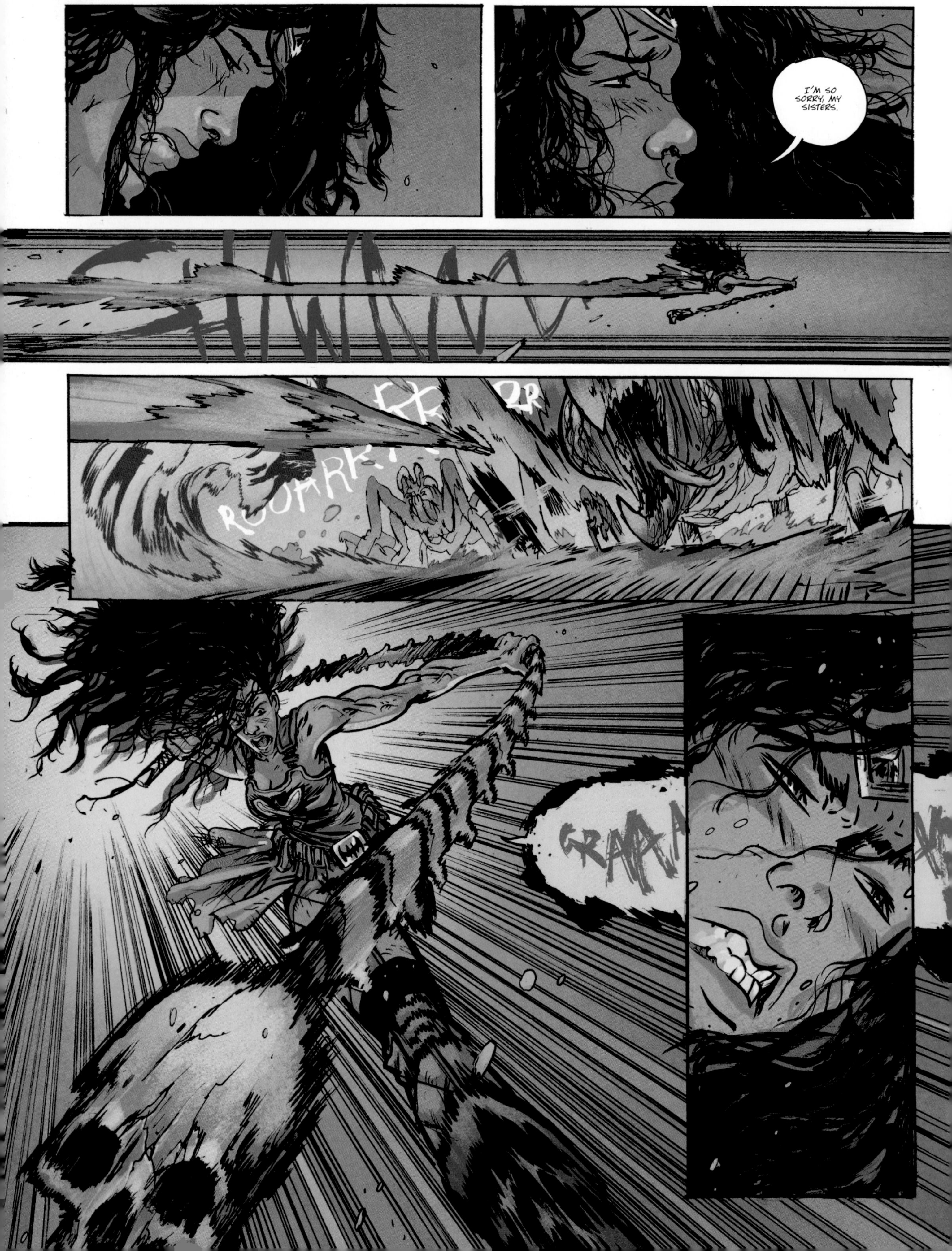
I'M SO SORRY, MY SISTERS.

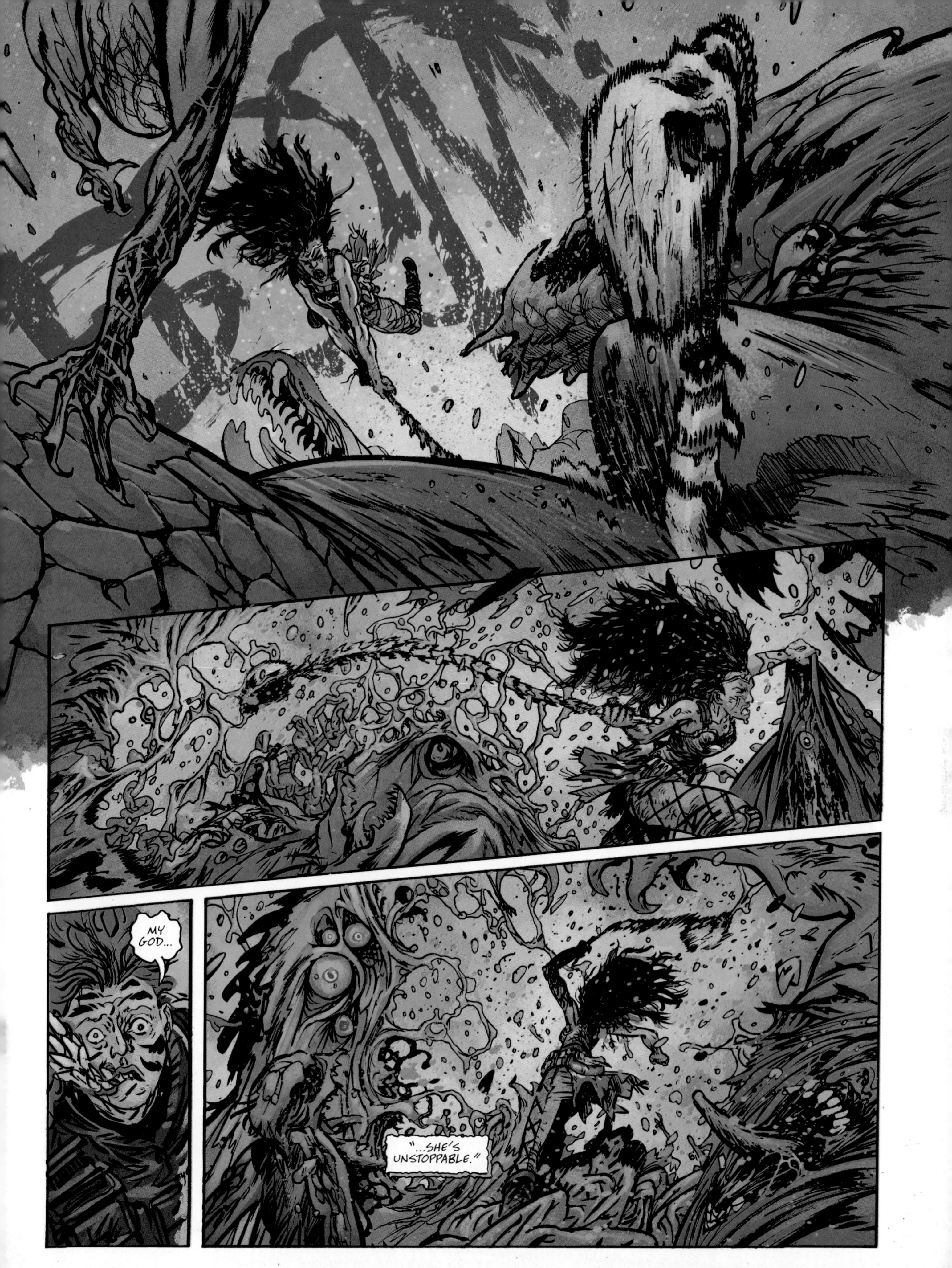
MY GOD...
"...SHE'S UNSTOPPABLE."

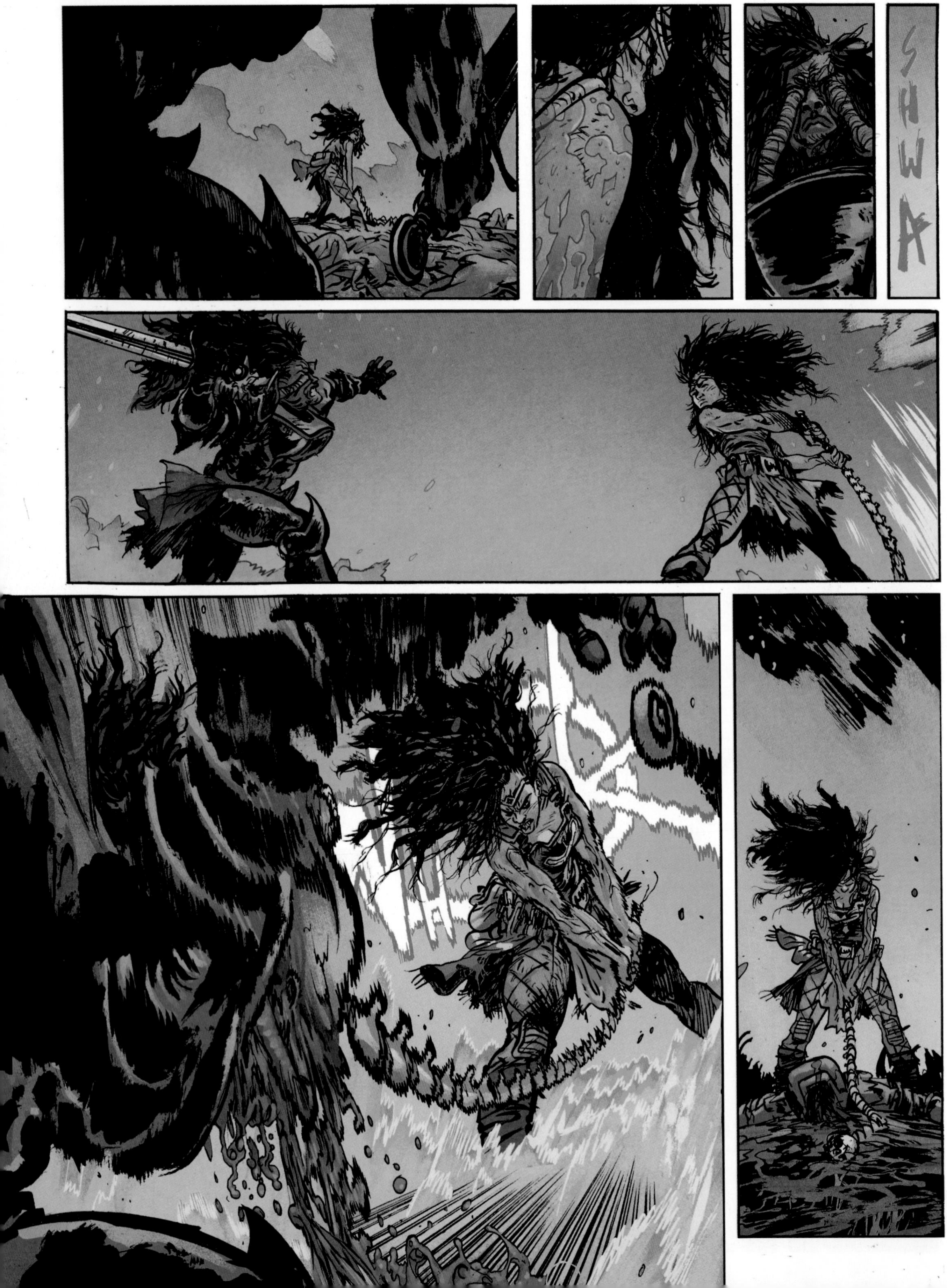
SHWA

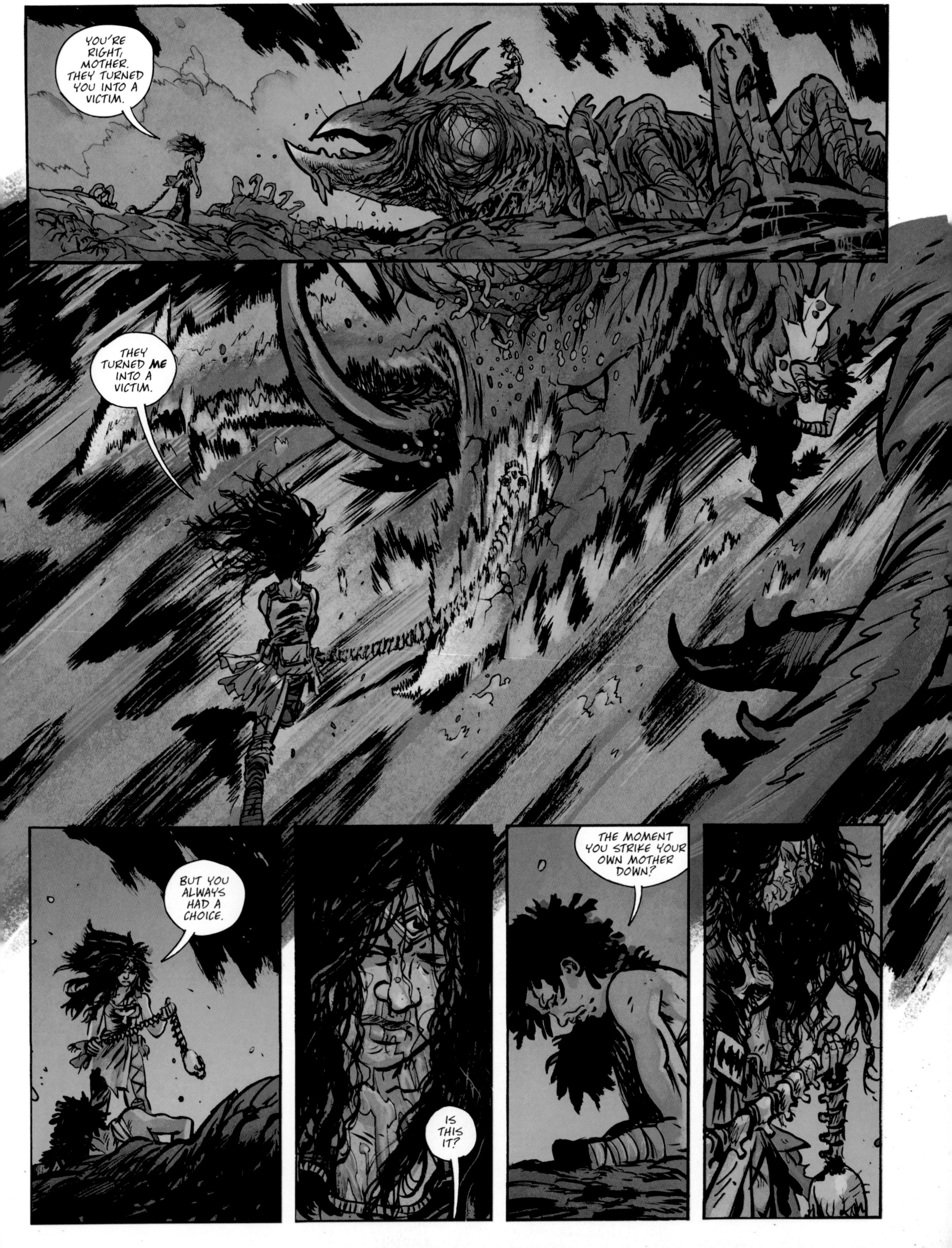
YOU'RE RIGHT, MOTHER. THEY TURNED YOU INTO A VICTIM.
THEY TURNED ME INTO A VICTIM.
BUT YOU ALWAYS HAD A CHOICE.
IS THIS IT?
THE MOMENT YOU STRIKE YOUR OWN MOTHER DOWN?

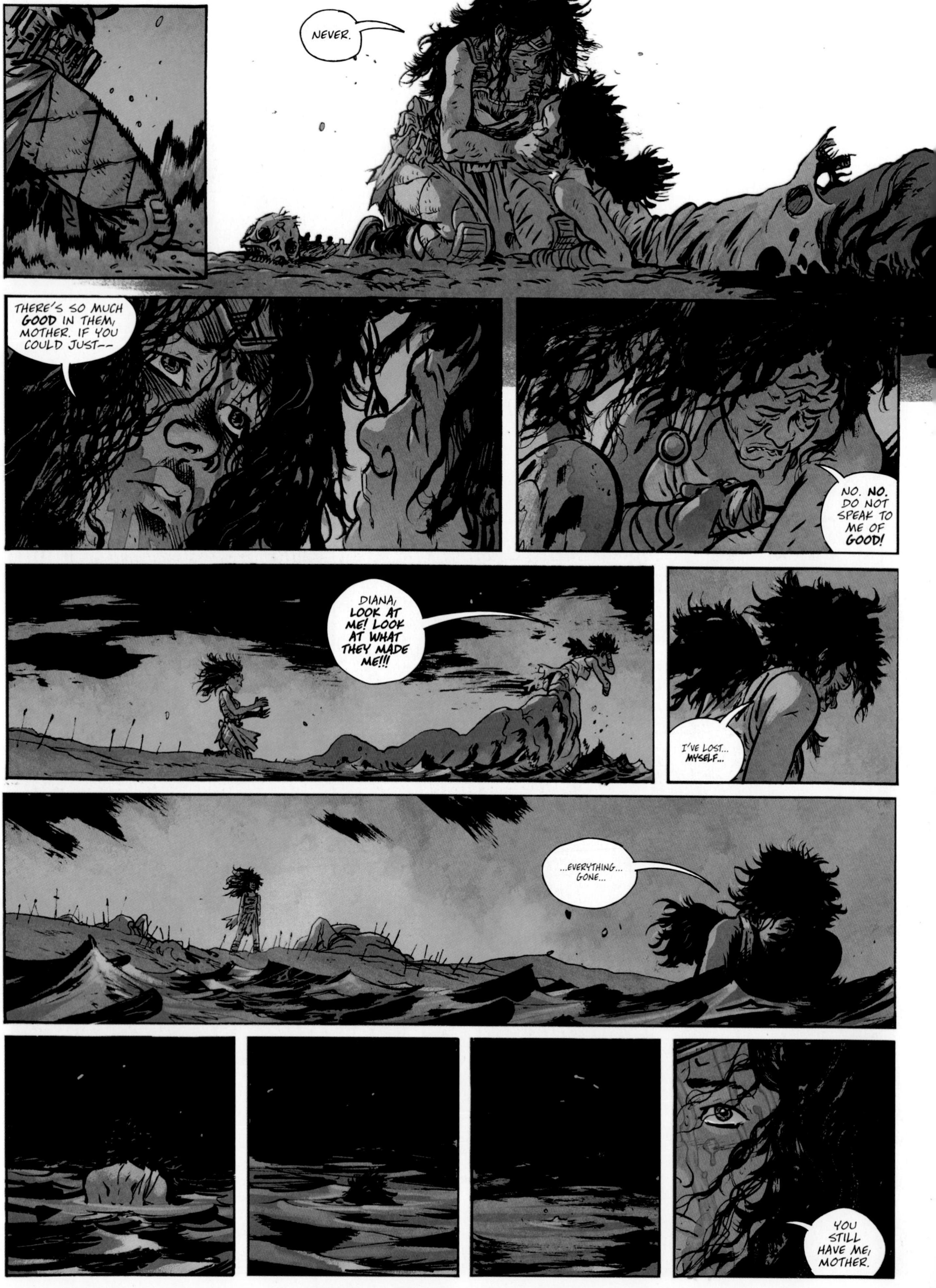
NEVER.
THERE'S SO MUCH GOOD IN THEM, MOTHER. IF YOU COULD JUST--
NO. NO. DO NOT SPEAK TO ME OF GOOD!
DIANA, LOOK AT ME! LOOK AT WHAT THEY MADE ME!!!
I'VE LOST... MYSELF...
...EVERYTHING... GONE...
YOU STILL HAVE ME, MOTHER.

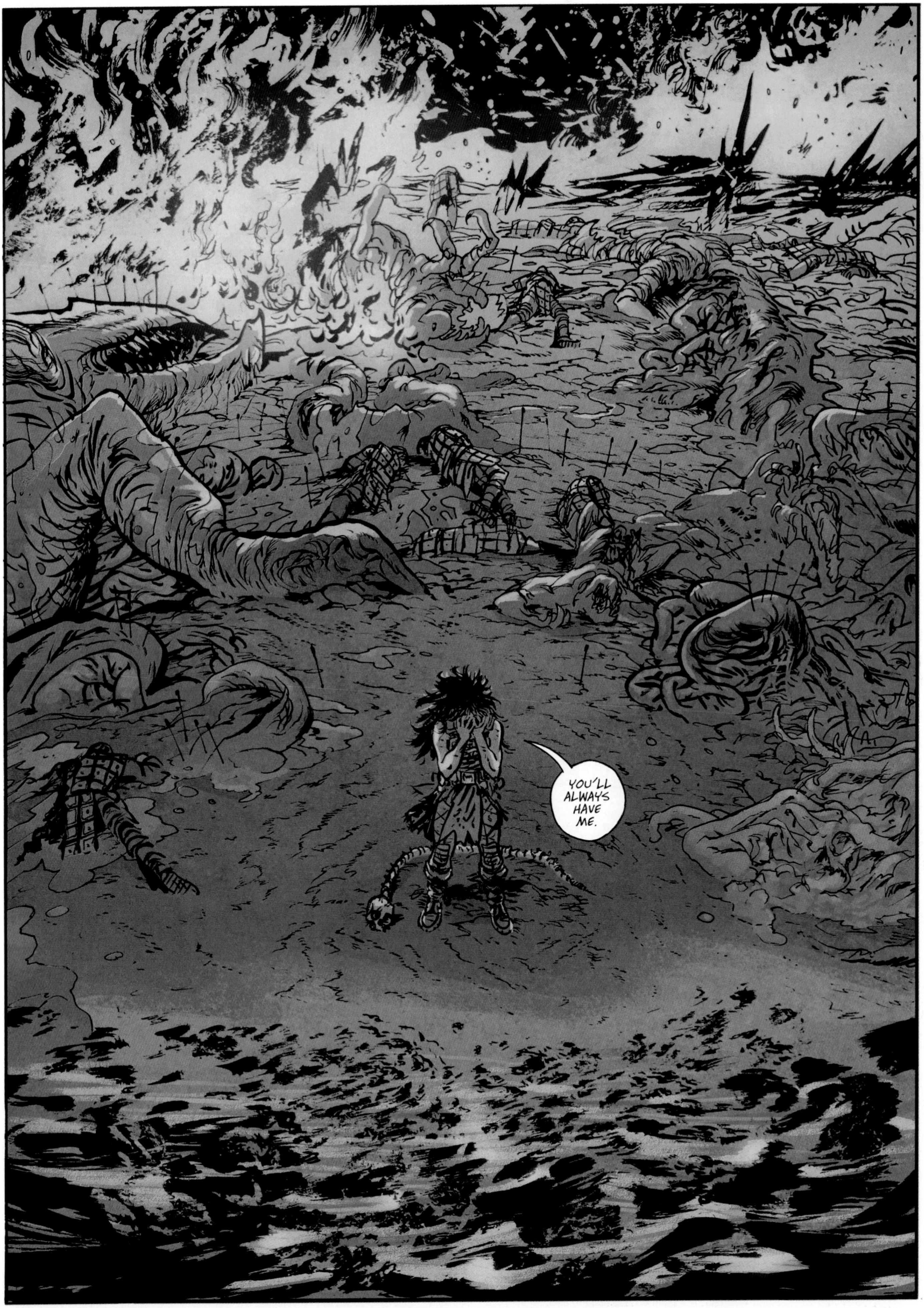
YOU'LL ALWAYS HAVE ME.

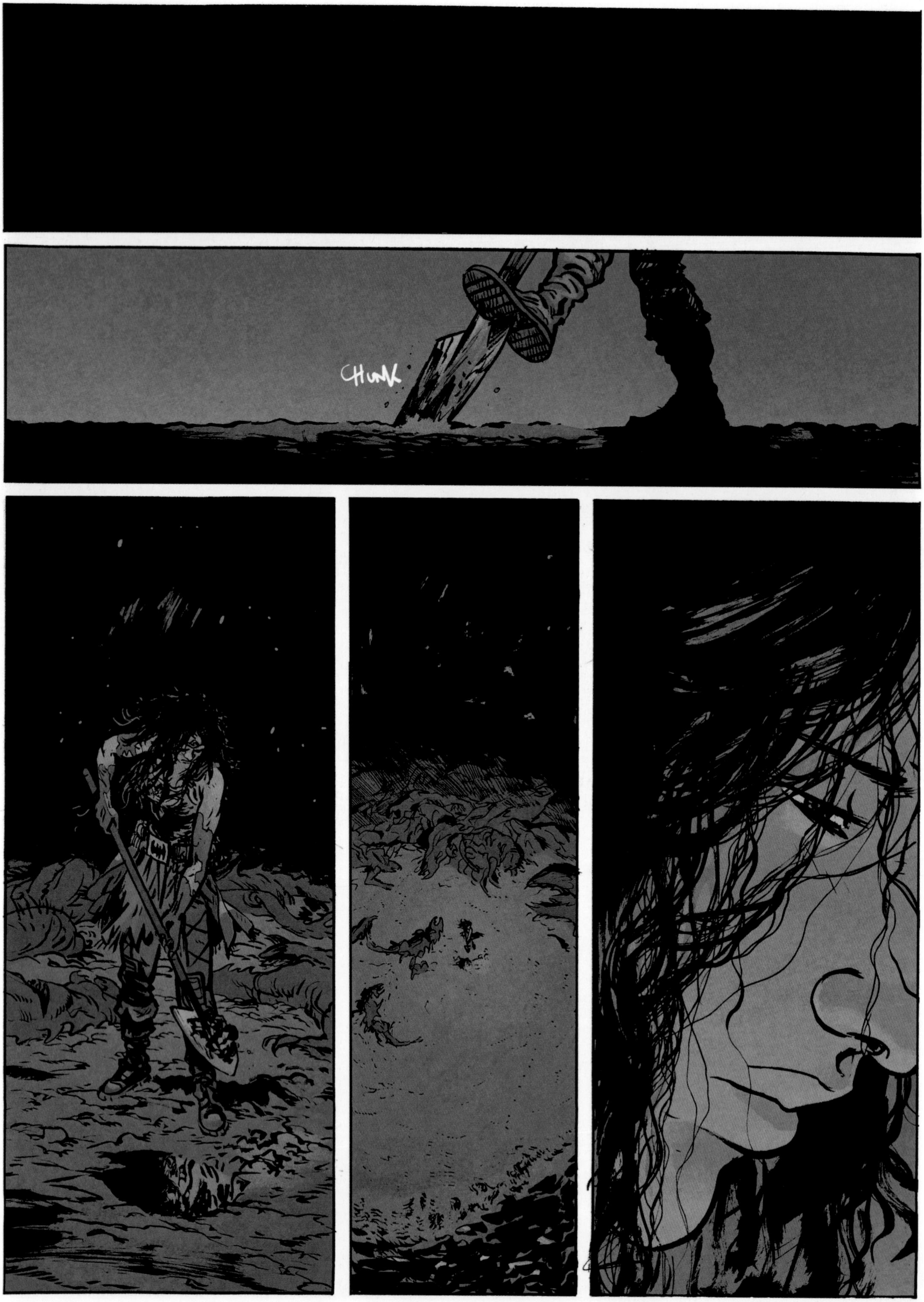
CHUNK

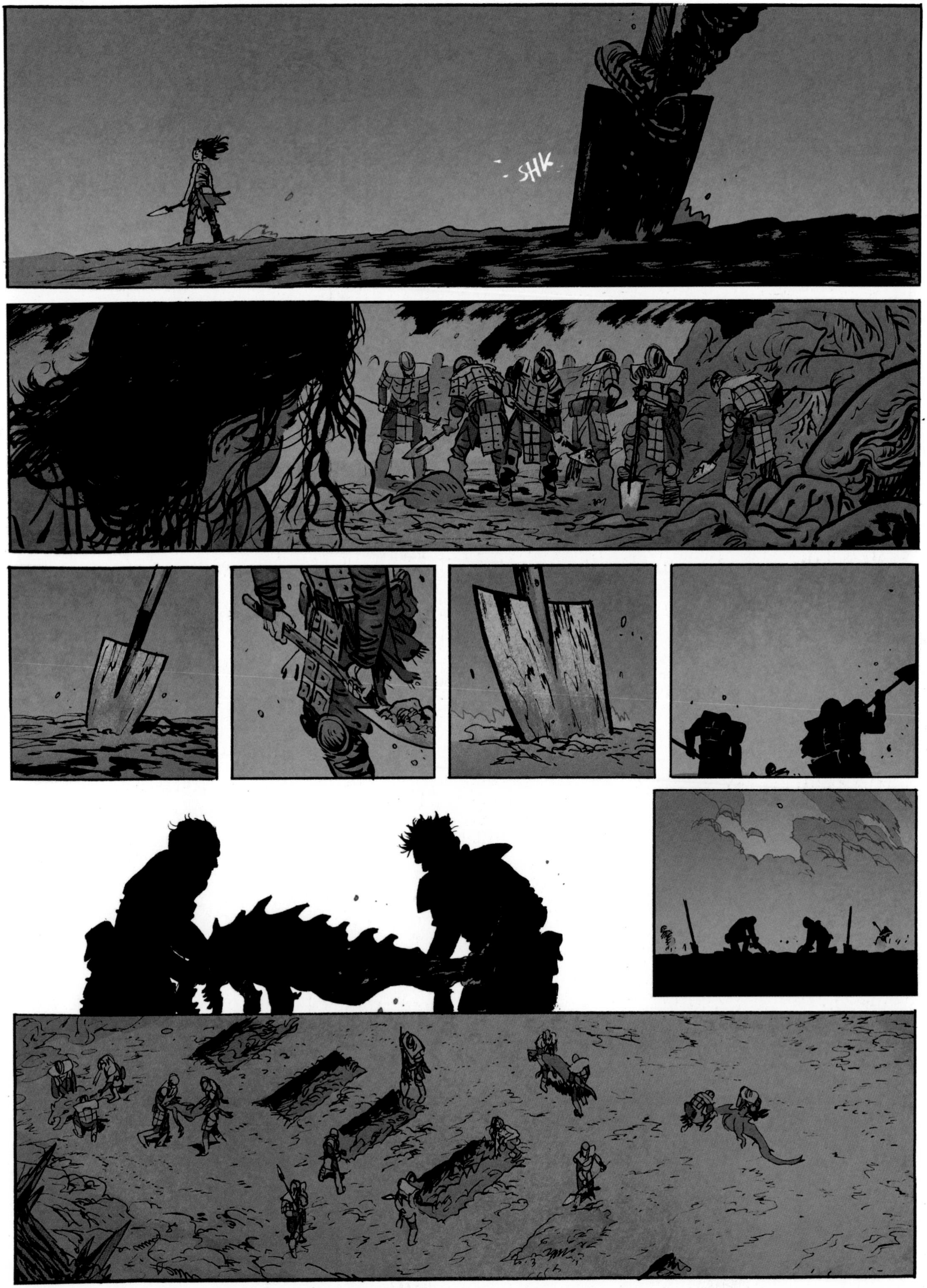
SHK

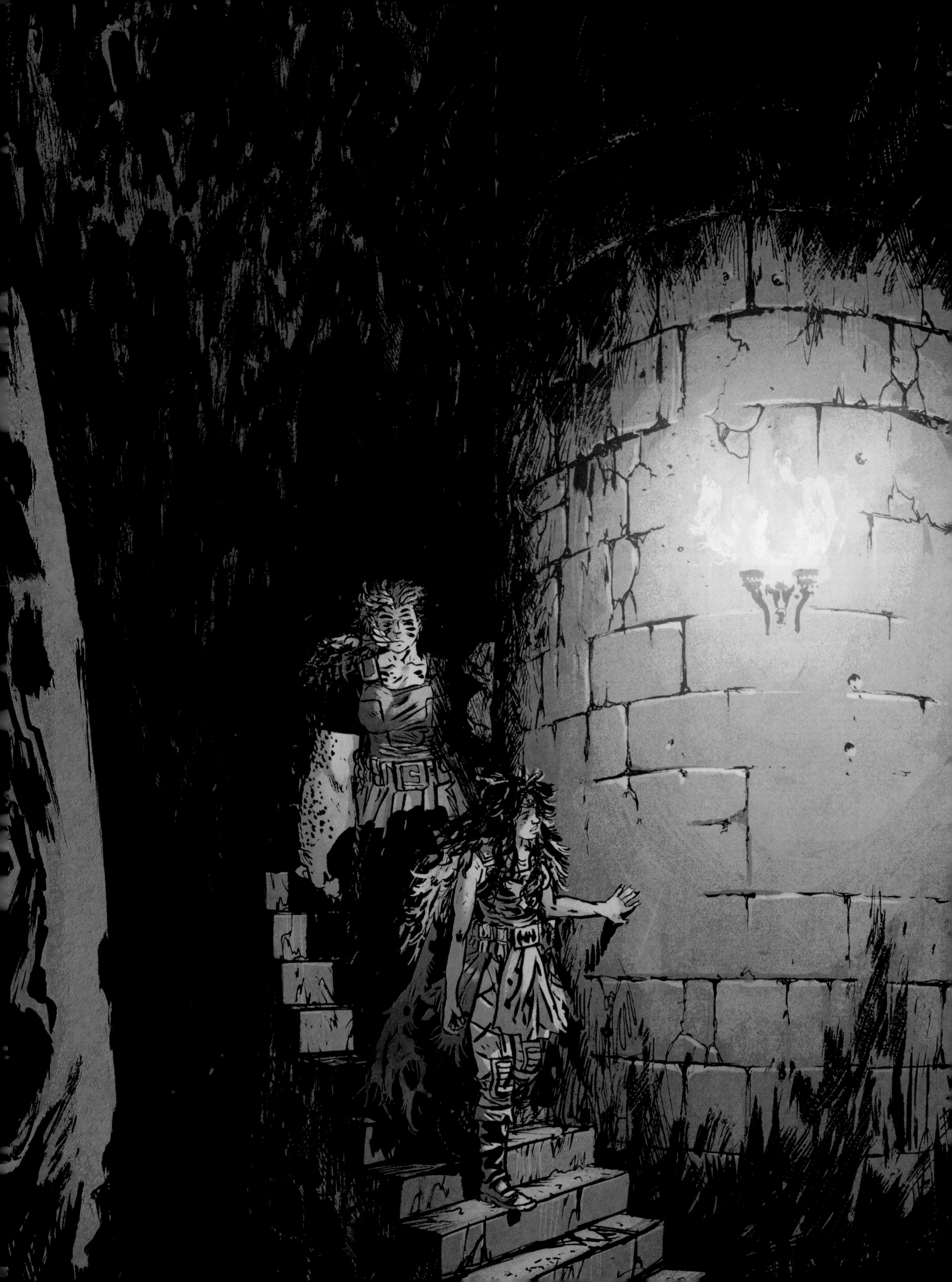

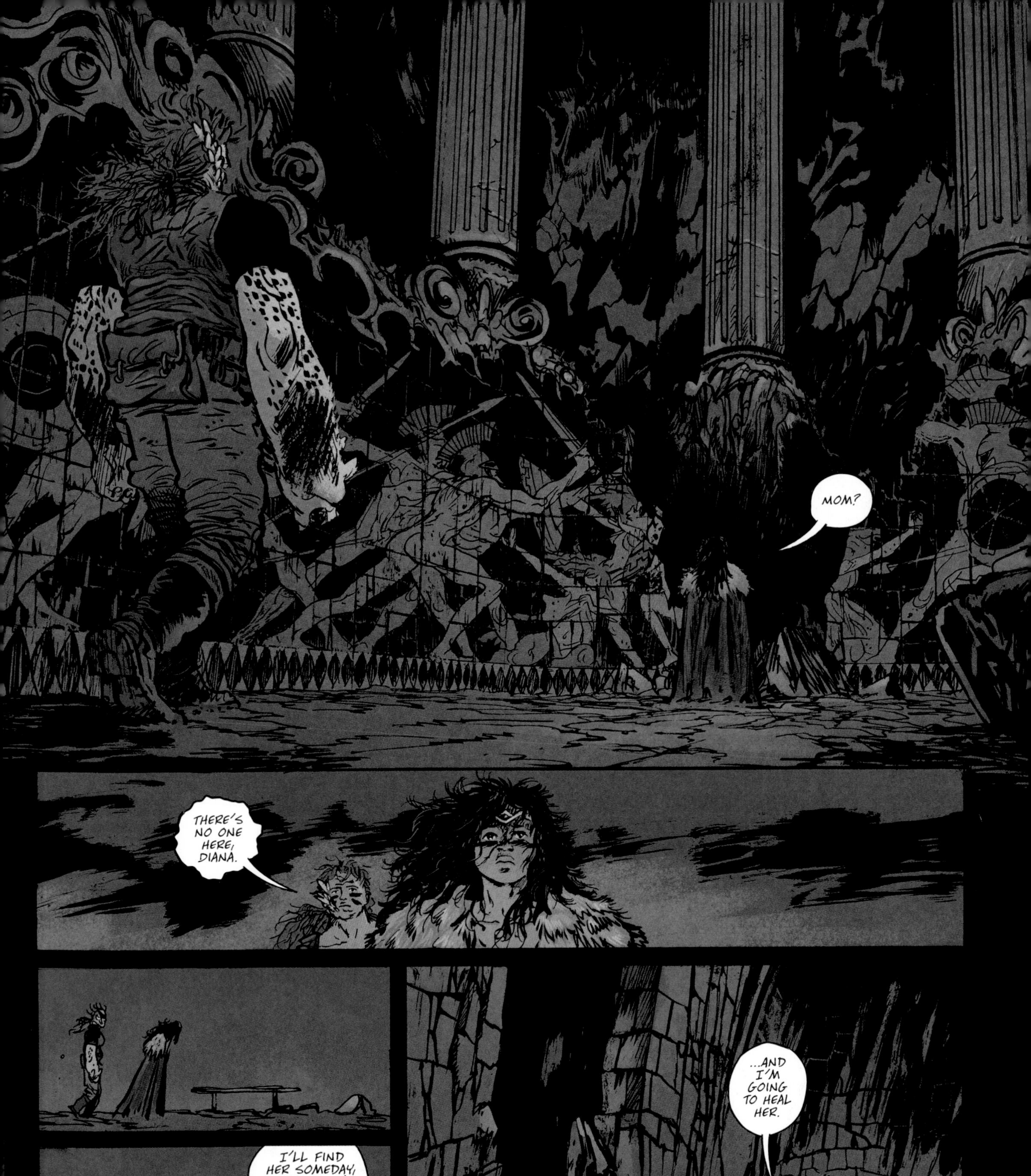
MOM?
THERE'S NO ONE HERE, DIANA.
I'LL FIND HER SOMEDAY, BARBARA. I'M GOING TO FIND HER...
...AND I'M GOING TO HEAL HER.

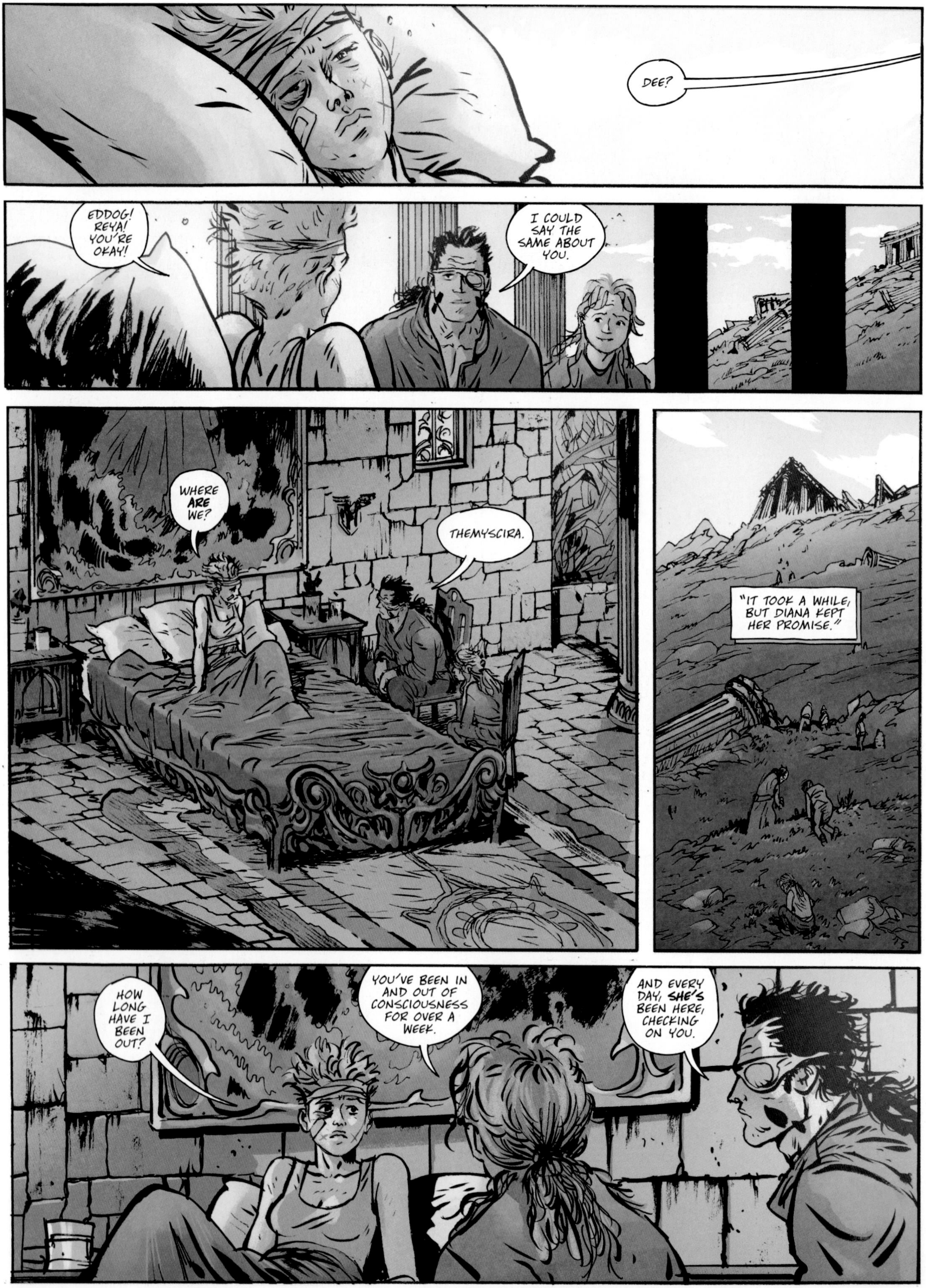
DEE?
EDDOG! REYA! YOU'RE OKAY!
I COULD SAY THE SAME ABOUT YOU.
WHERE ARE WE?
THEMYSCIRA.
"IT TOOK A WHILE, BUT DIANA KEPT HER PROMISE."
HOW LONG HAVE I BEEN OUT?
YOU'VE BEEN IN AND OUT OF CONSCIOUSNESS FOR OVER A WEEK.
AND EVERY DAY, SHE'S BEEN HERE, CHECKING ON YOU.

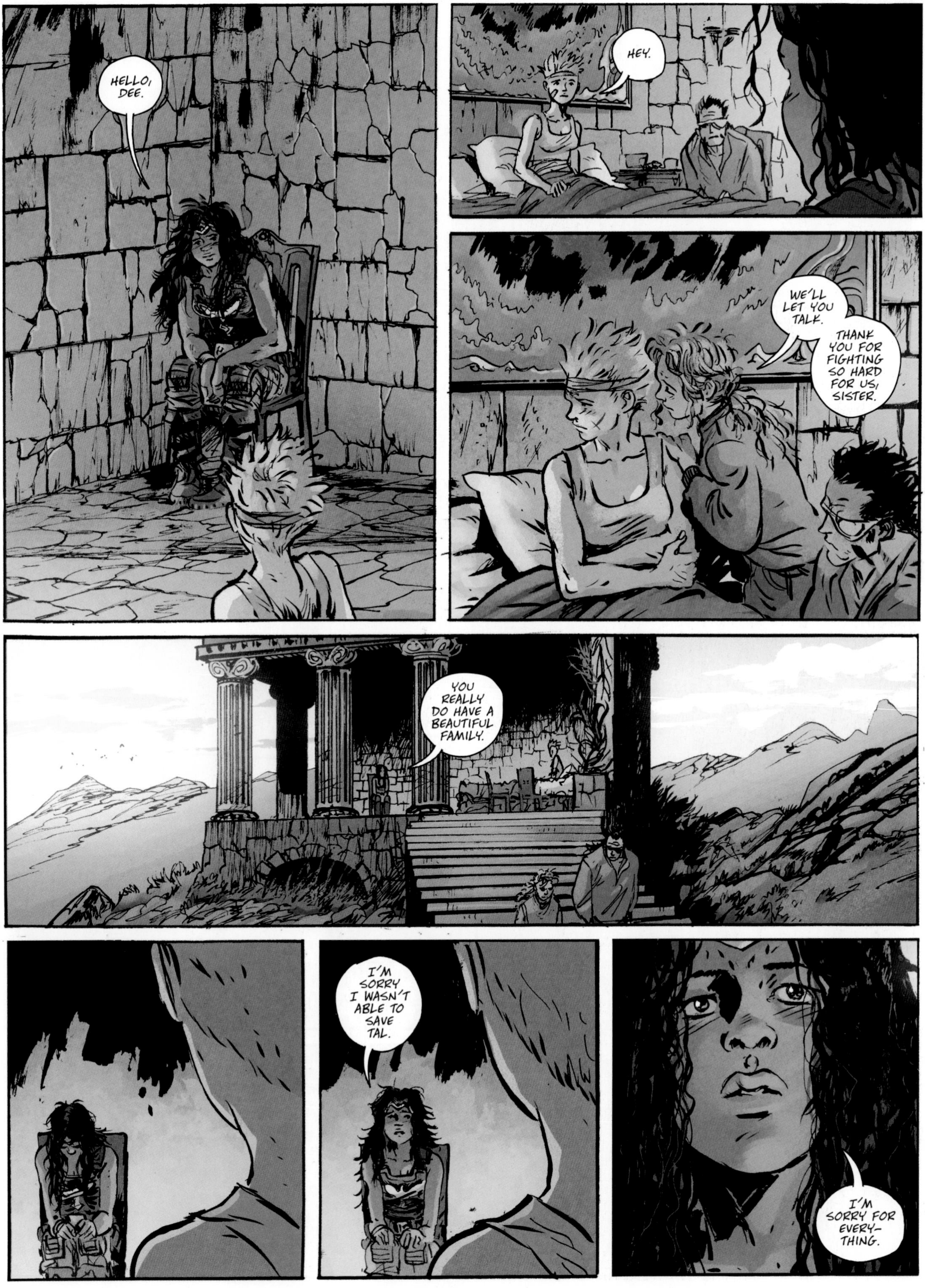
HELLO, DEE.
HEY.
WE'LL LET YOU TALK.
THANK YOU FOR FIGHTING SO HARD FOR US, SISTER.
YOU REALLY DO HAVE A BEAUTIFUL FAMILY.
I'M SORRY I WASN'T ABLE TO SAVE TAL.
I'M SORRY FOR EVERY-THING.

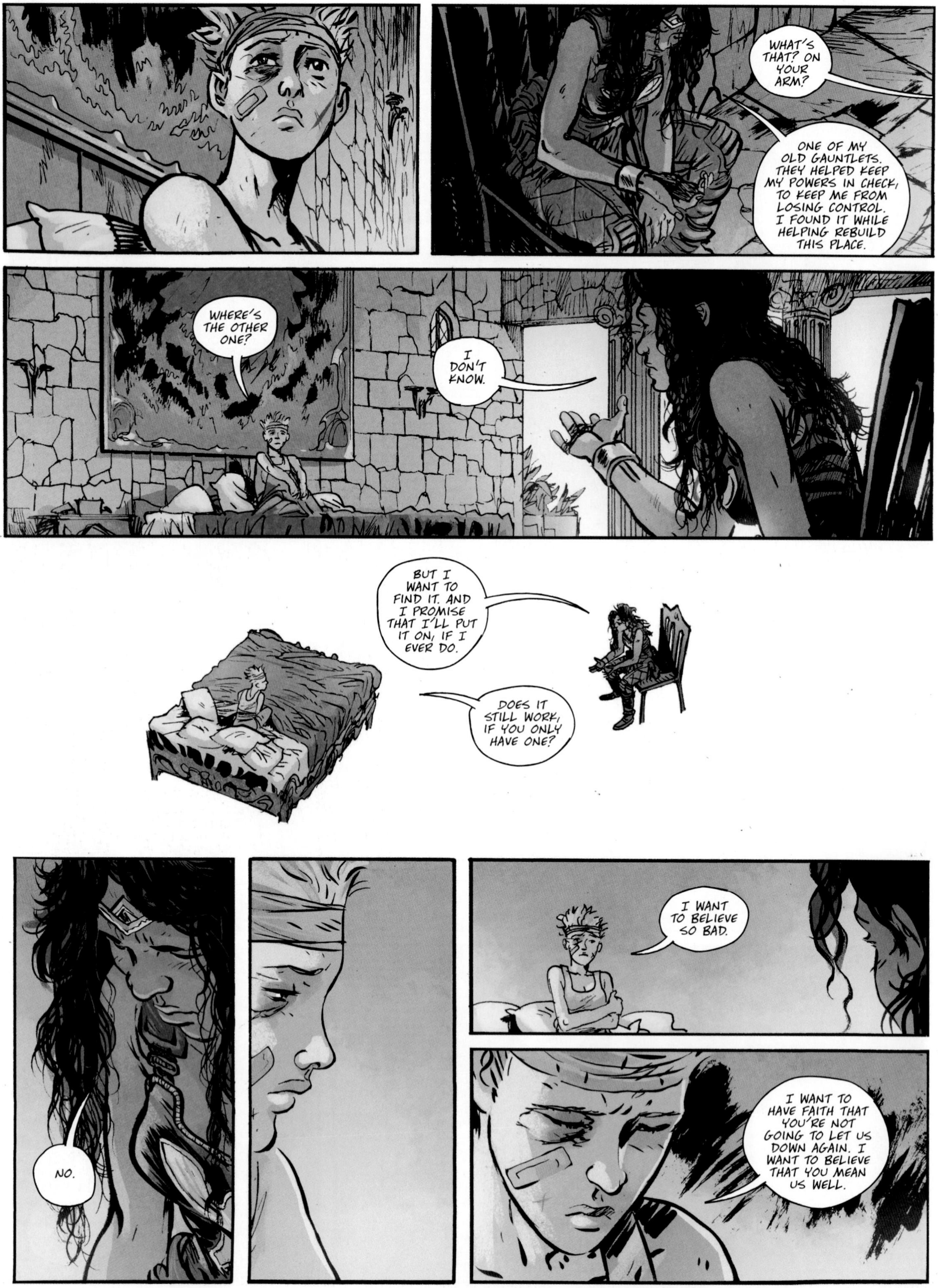
WHAT'S THAT? ON YOUR ARM?
ONE OF MY OLD GAUNTLETS. THEY HELPED KEEP MY POWERS IN CHECK, TO KEEP ME FROM LOSING CONTROL. I FOUND IT WHILE HELPING REBUILD THIS PLACE.
WHERE'S THE OTHER ONE?
I DON'T KNOW.
BUT I WANT TO FIND IT. AND I PROMISE THAT I'LL PUT IT ON, IF I EVER DO.
DOES IT STILL WORK, IF YOU ONLY HAVE ONE?
NO.
I WANT TO BELIEVE SO BAD.
I WANT TO HAVE FAITH THAT YOU'RE NOT GOING TO LET US DOWN AGAIN. I WANT TO BELIEVE THAT YOU MEAN US WELL.

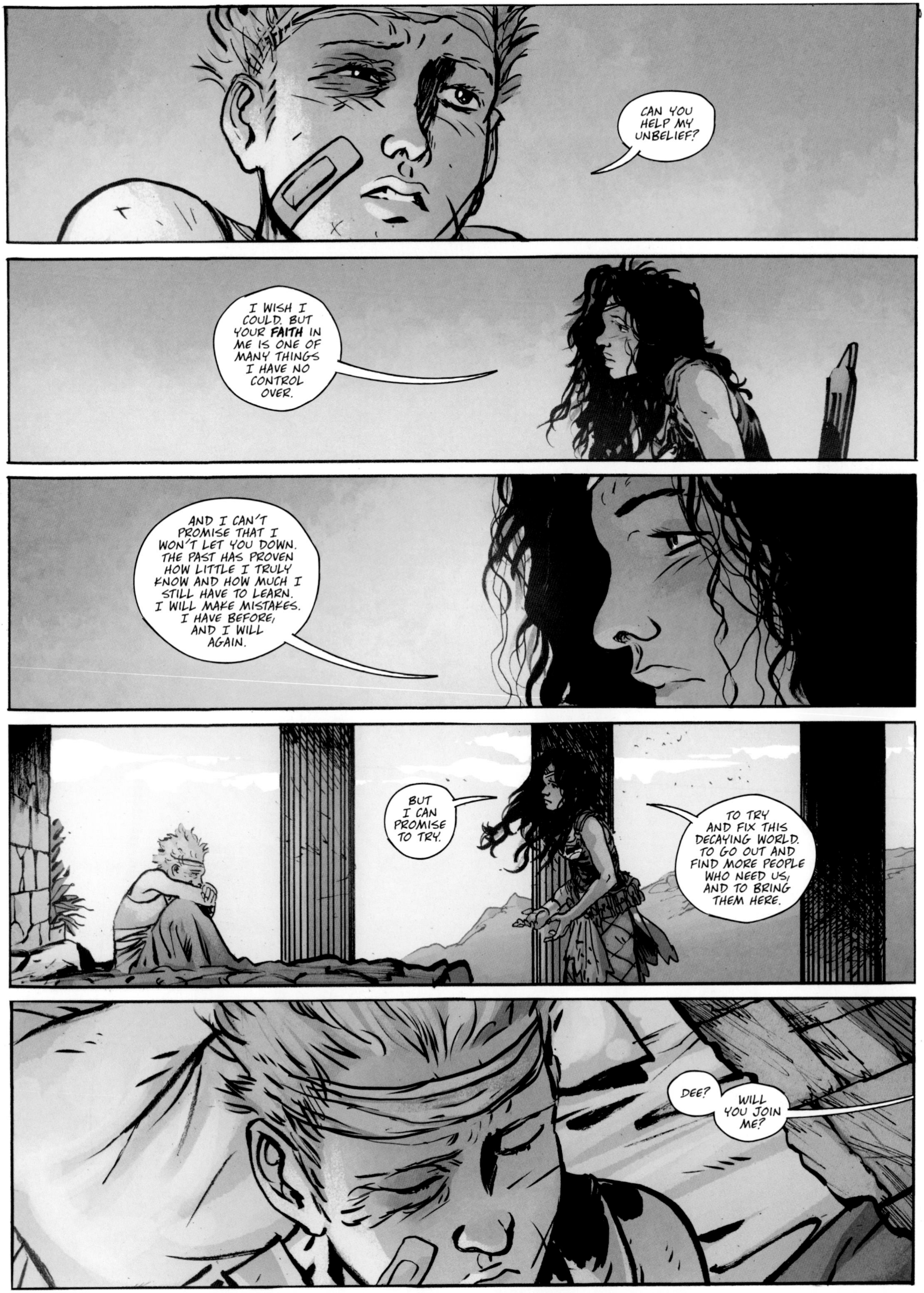
CAN YOU HELP MY UNBELIEF?
I WISH I COULD. BUT YOUR FAITH IN ME IS ONE OF MANY THINGS I HAVE NO CONTROL OVER.
AND I CAN'T PROMISE THAT I WON'T LET YOU DOWN. THE PAST HAS PROVEN HOW LITTLE I TRULY KNOW AND HOW MUCH I STILL HAVE TO LEARN. I WILL MAKE MISTAKES. I HAVE BEFORE, AND I WILL AGAIN.
BUT I CAN PROMISE TO TRY.
TO TRY AND FIX THIS DECAYING WORLD. TO GO OUT AND FIND MORE PEOPLE WHO NEED US, AND TO BRING THEM HERE.
DEE?
WILL YOU JOIN ME?

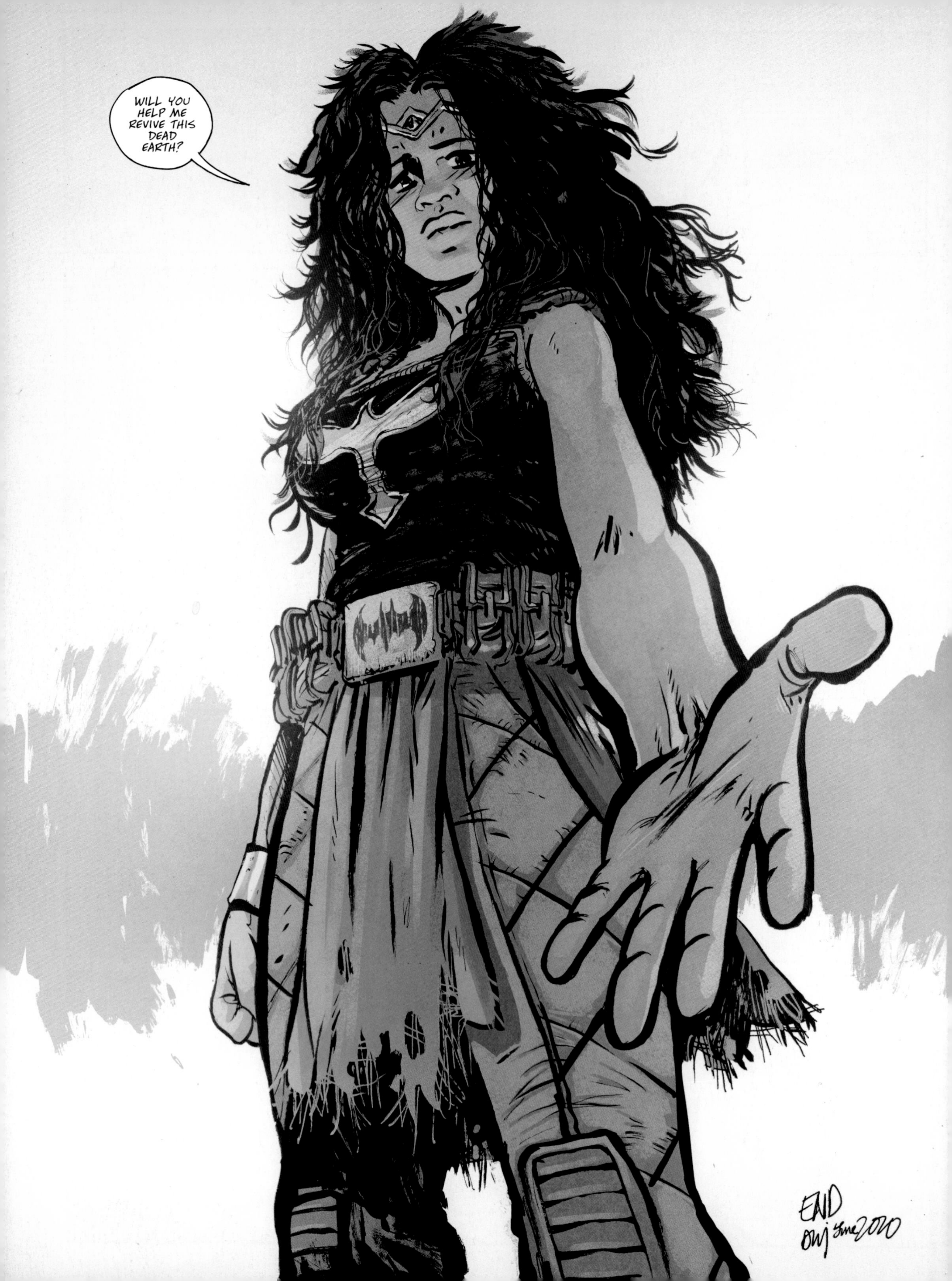
WILL YOU HELP ME REVIVE THIS DEAD EARTH?
END
OWJ June 2020

COVER GALLERY

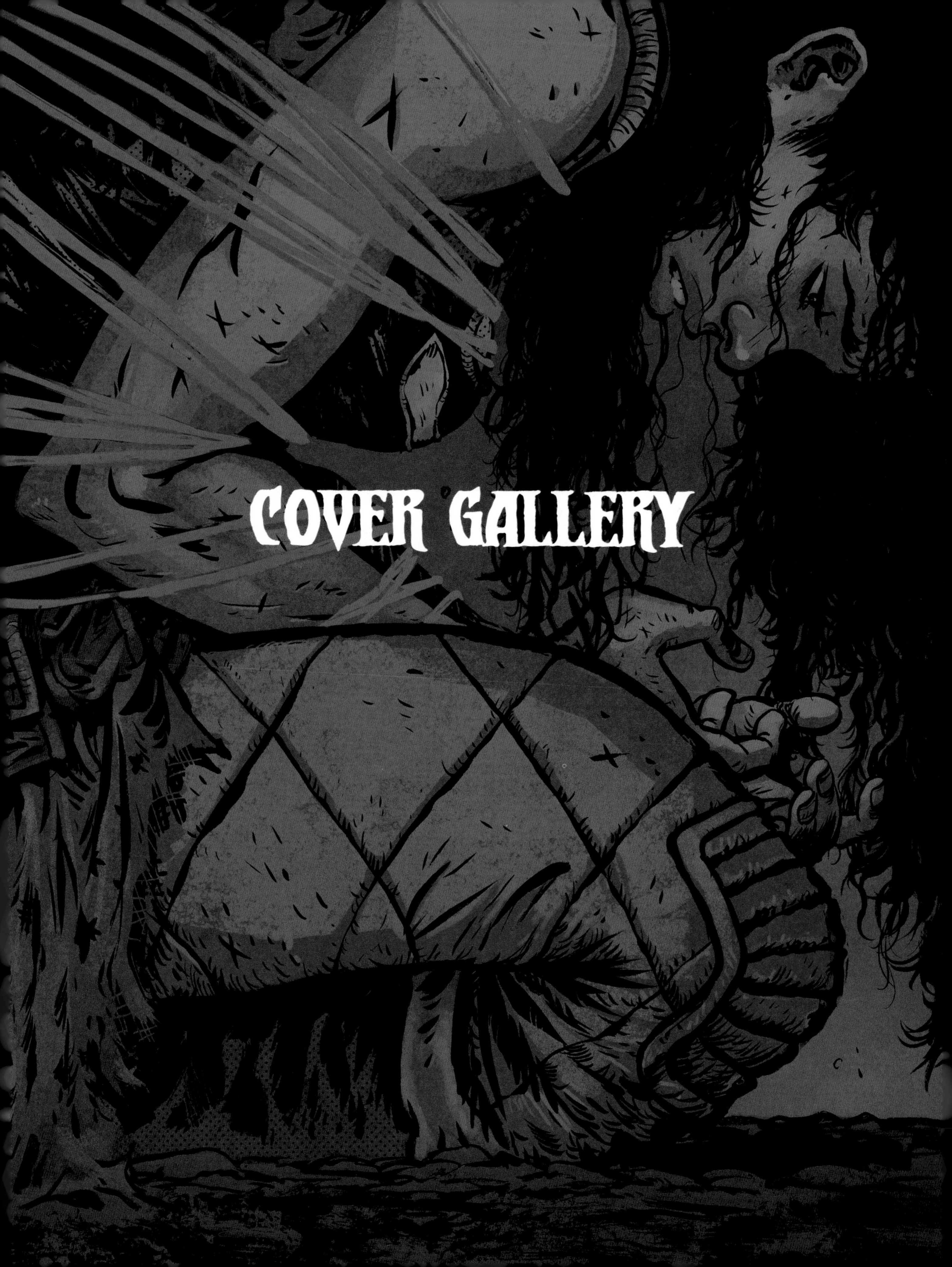

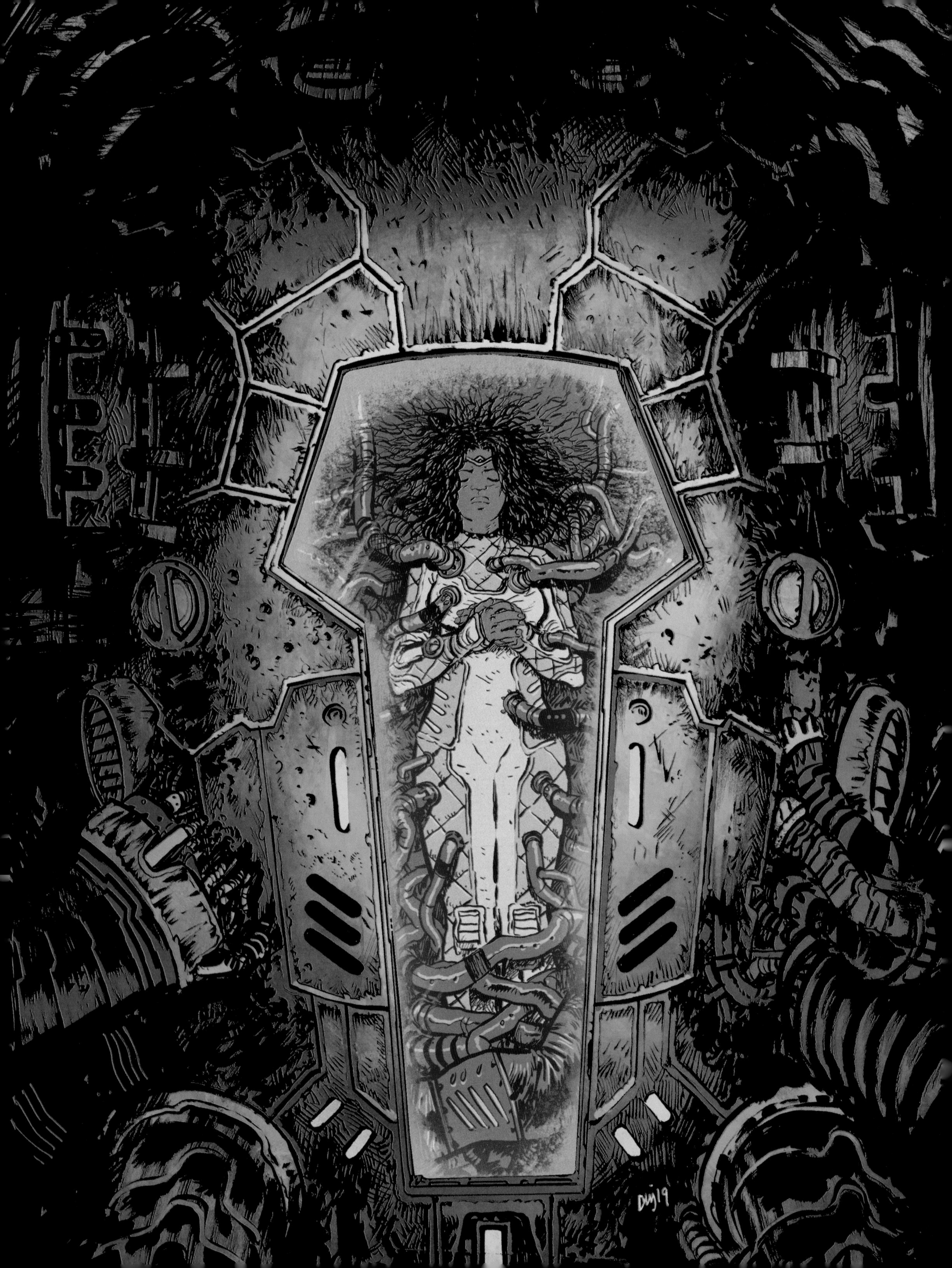

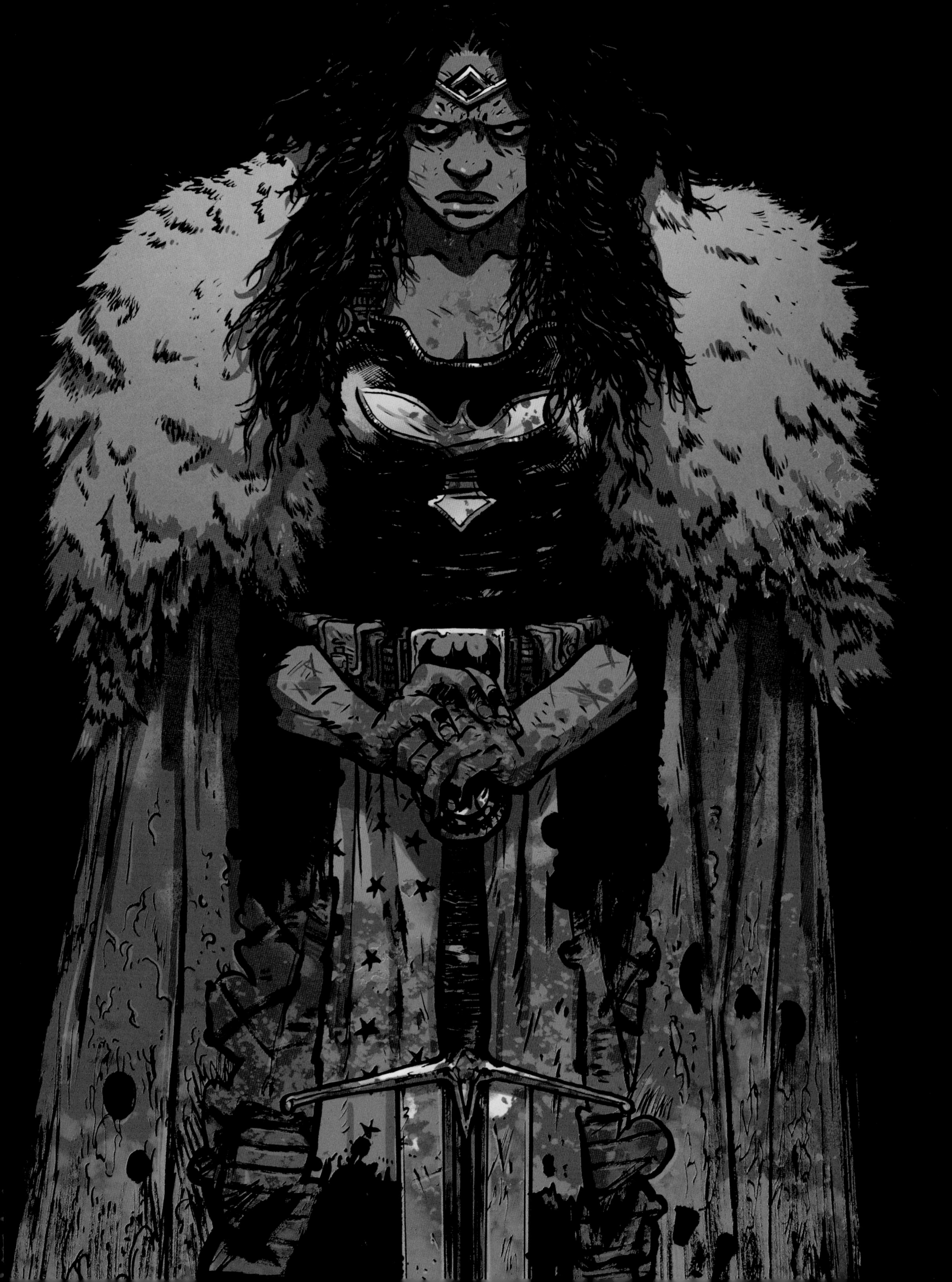

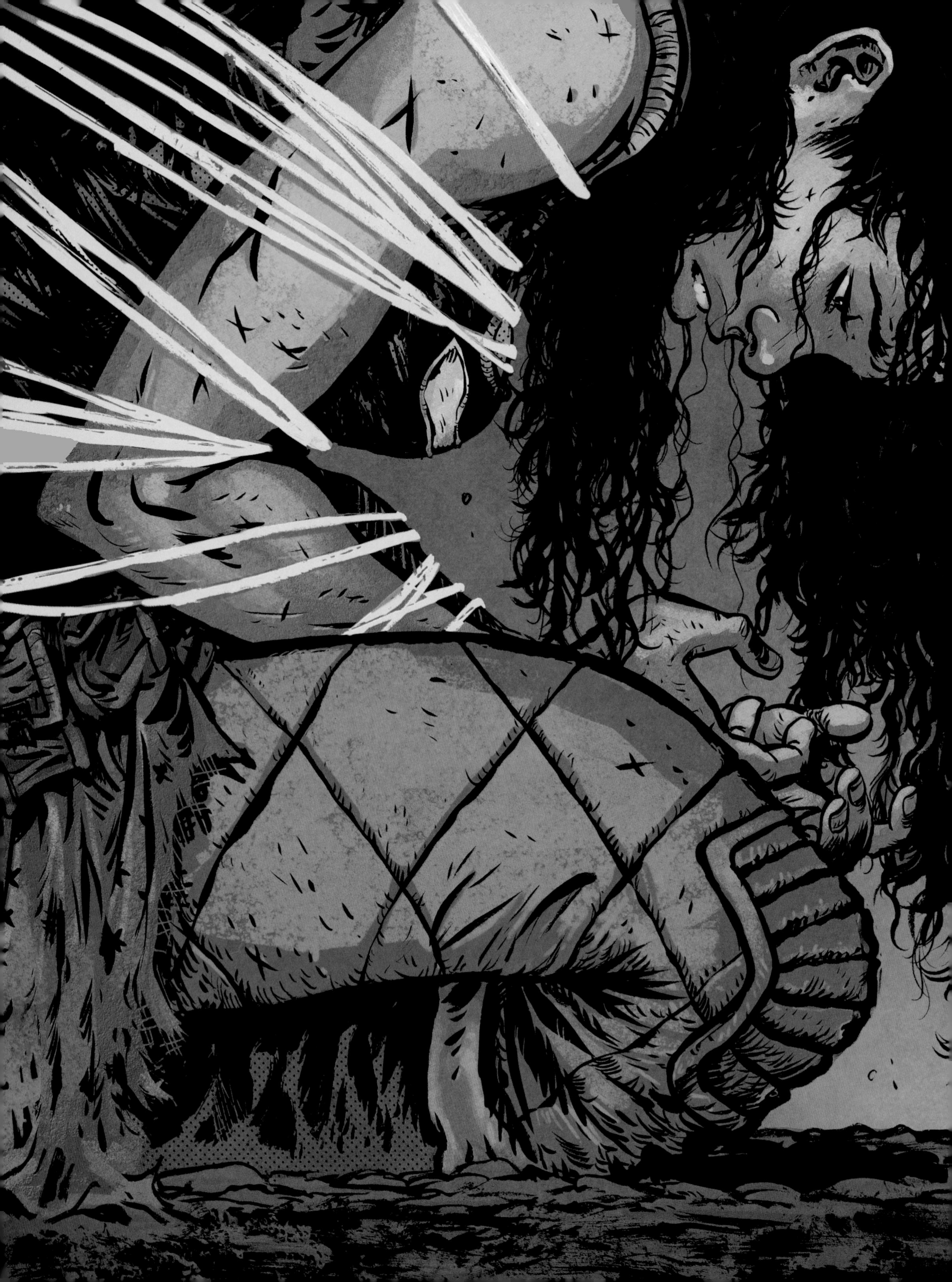

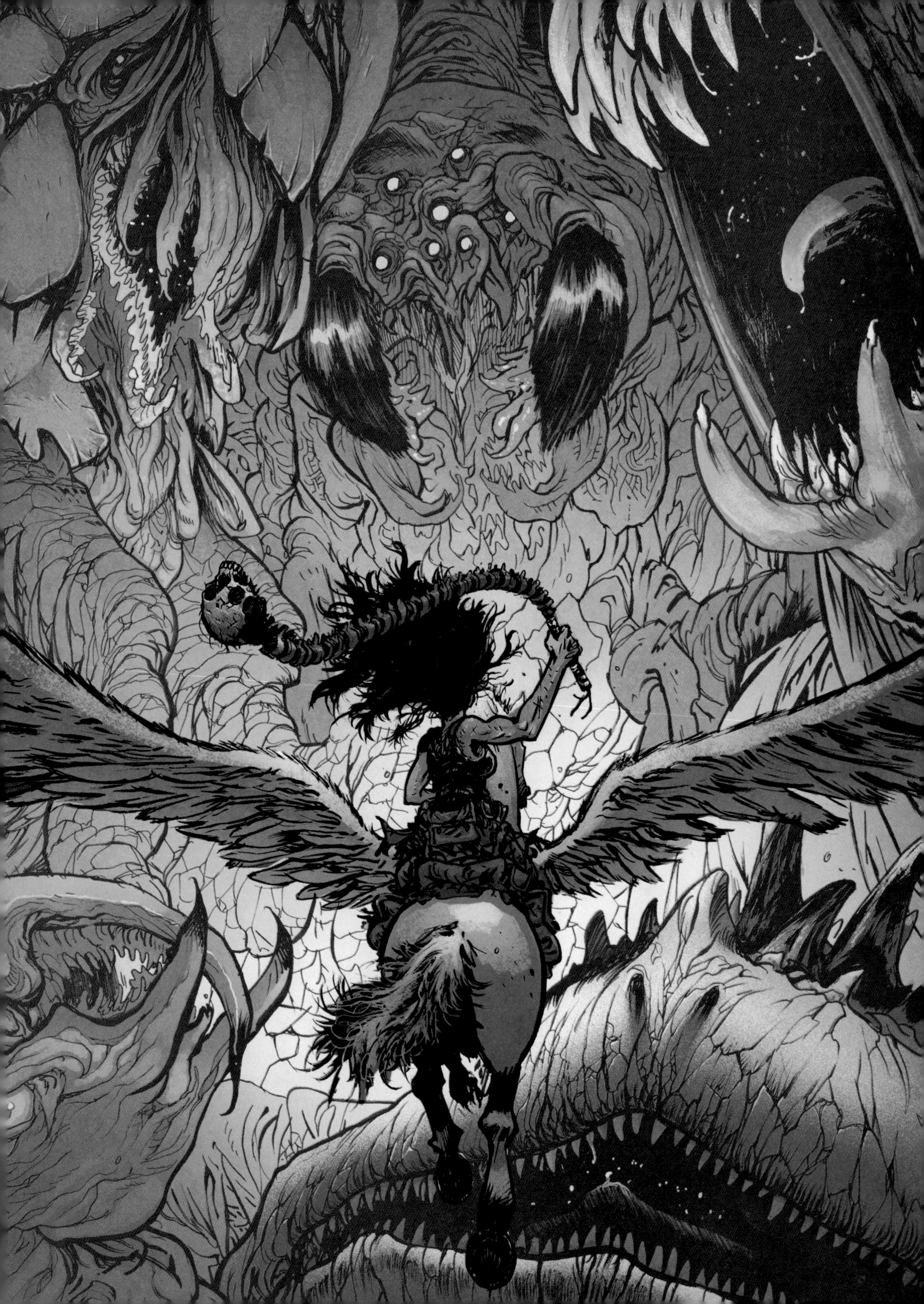

WONDER WOMAN: DEAD EARTH

Sketchbook by Daniel Warren Johnson

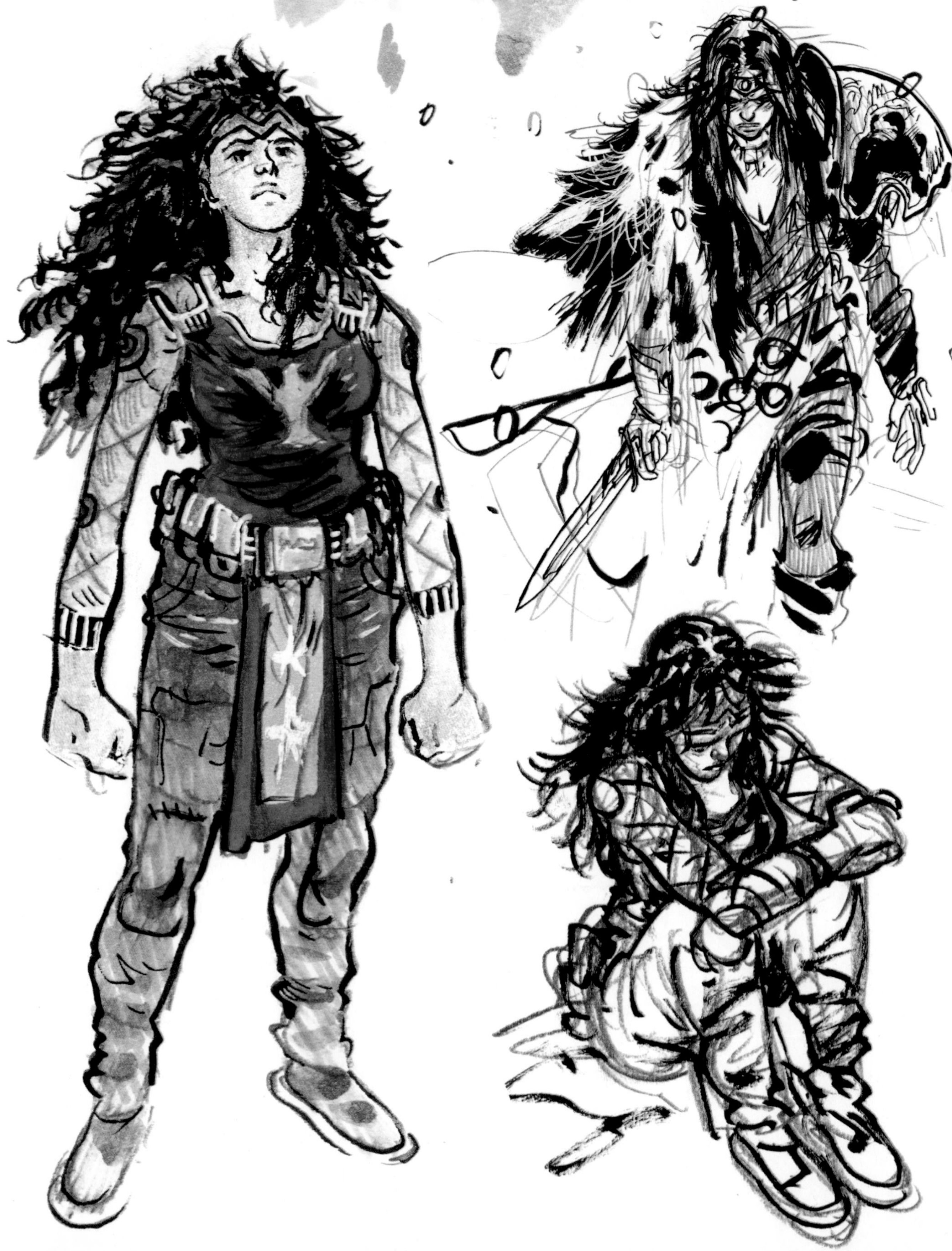

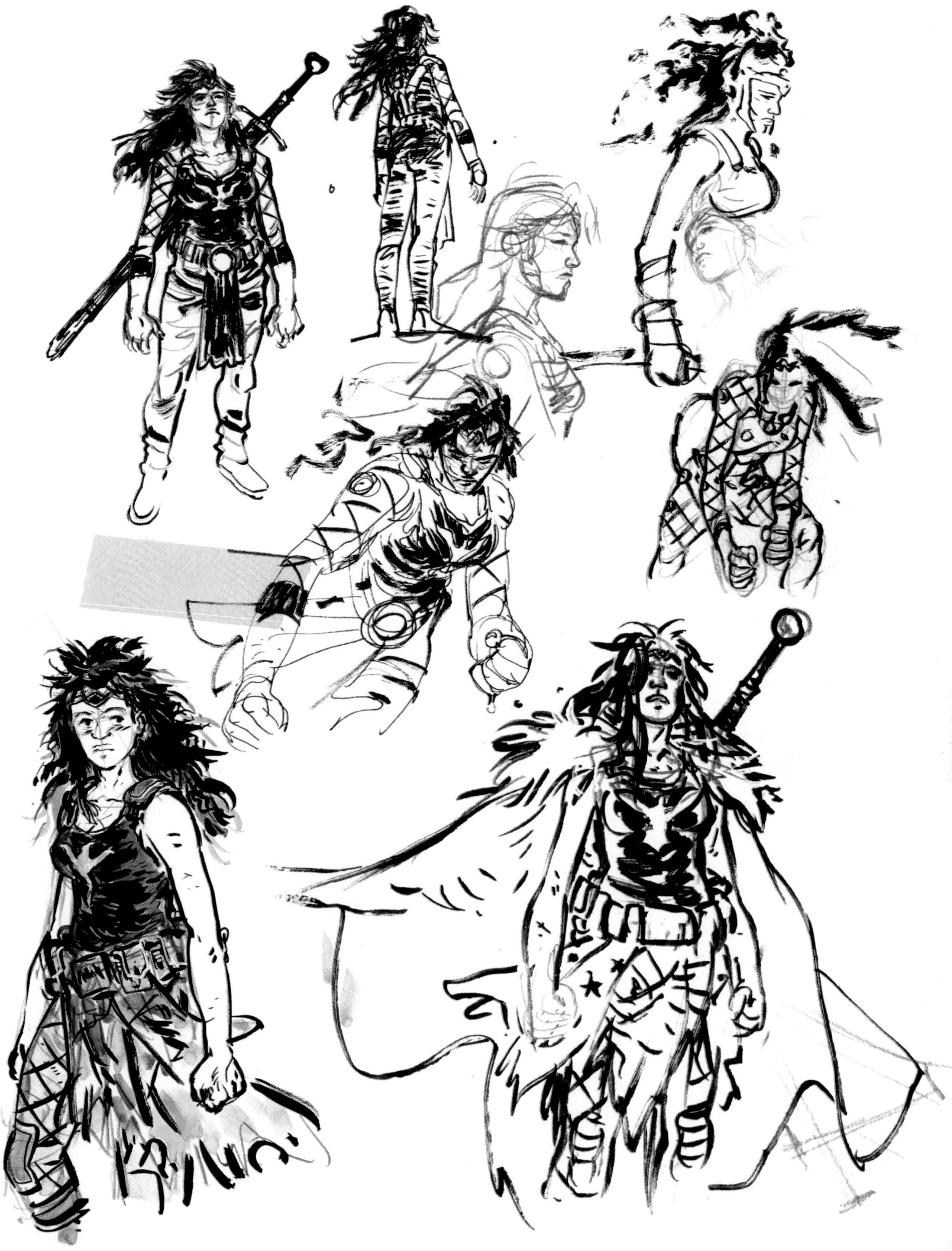

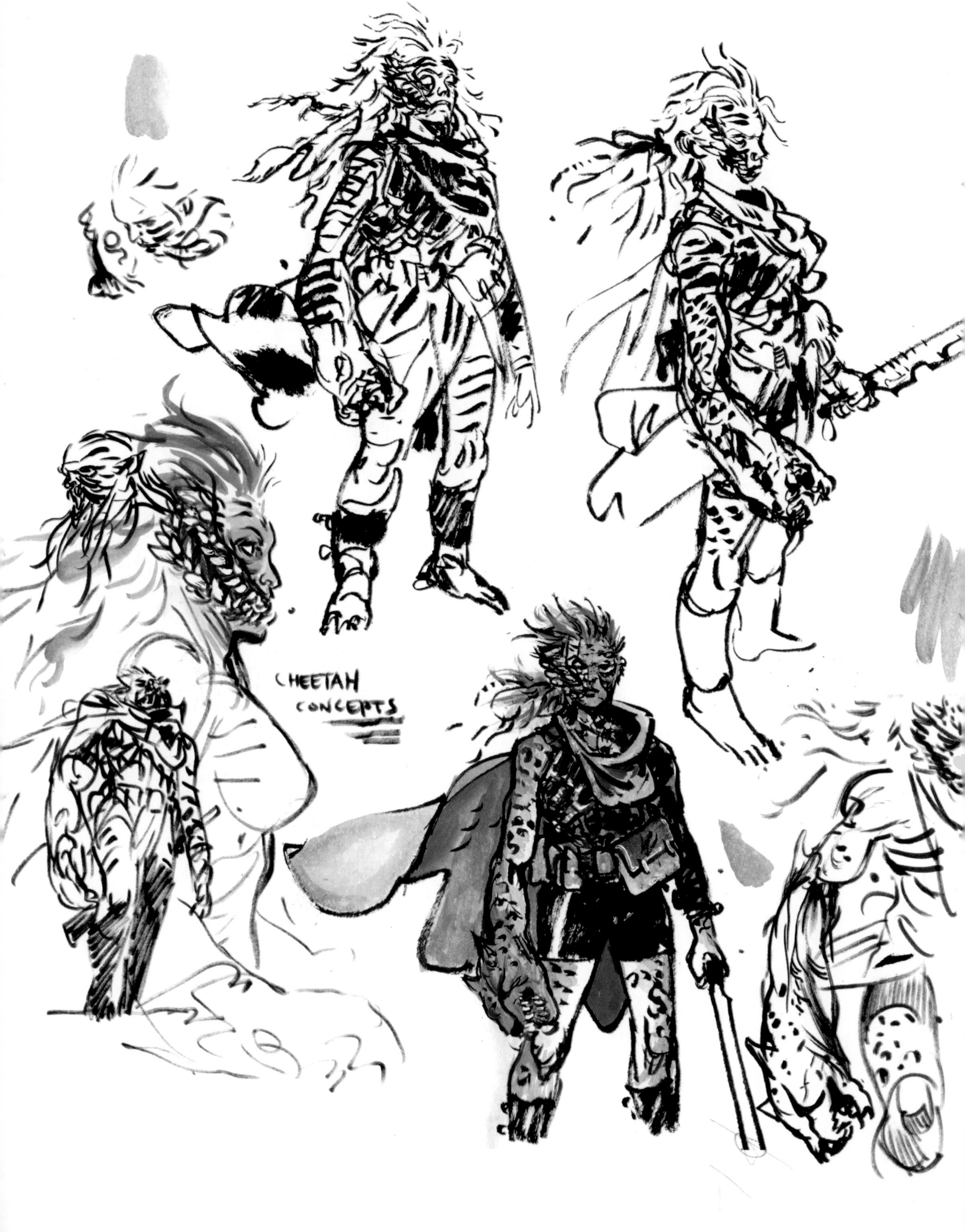
CHEETAH
CONCEPTS

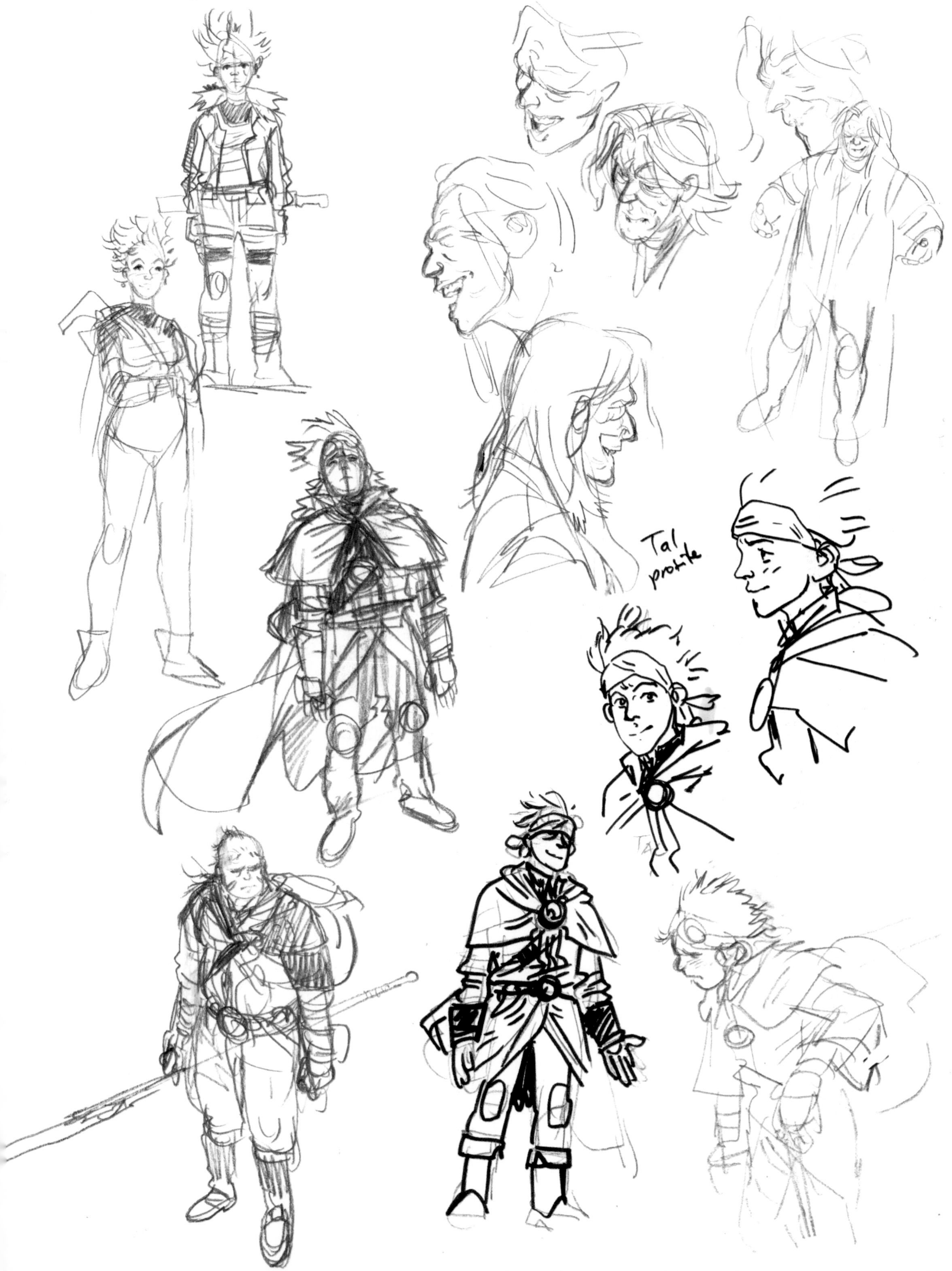
Tal profile

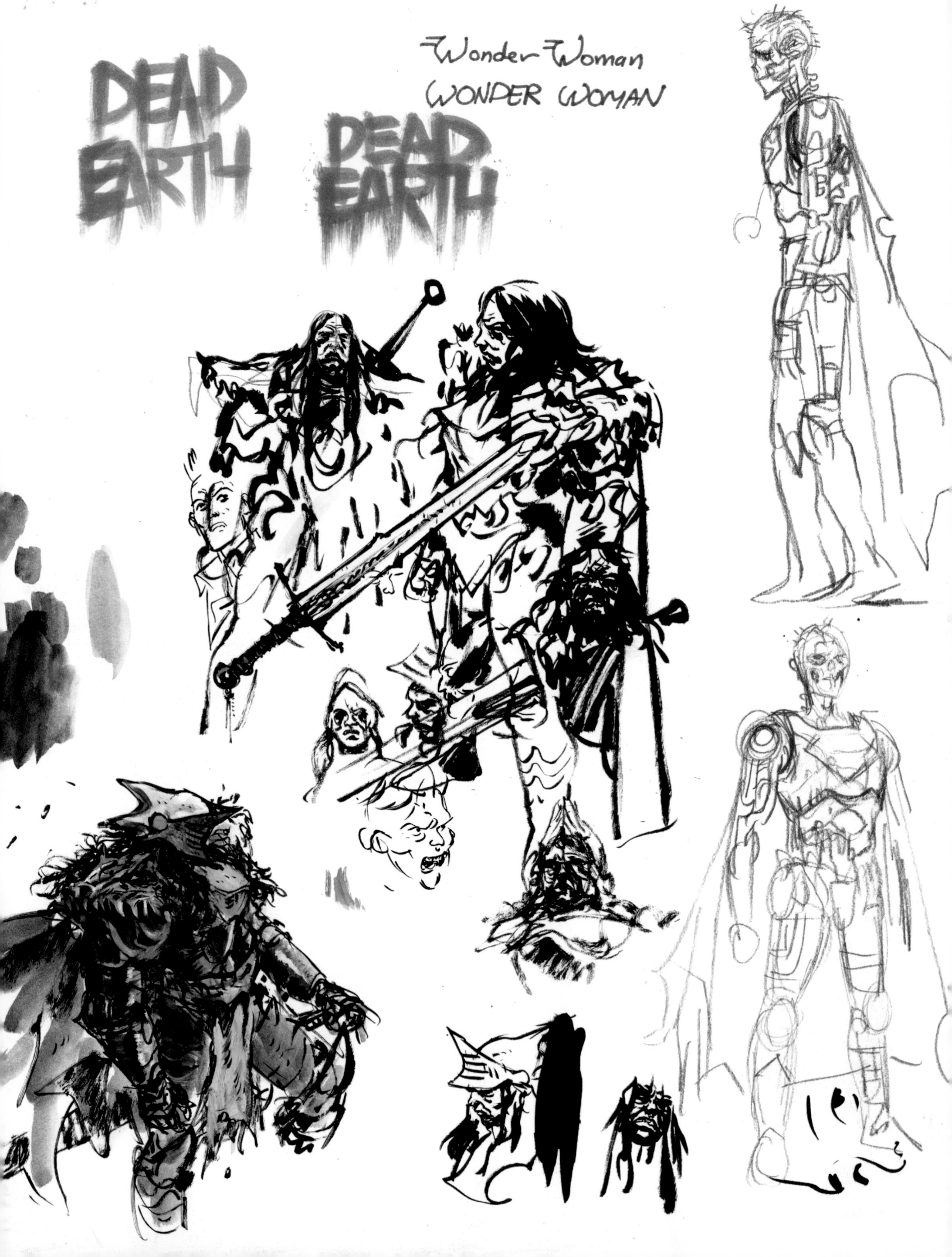
DEAD EARTH
DEAD EARTH
Wonder Woman
WONDER WOMAN

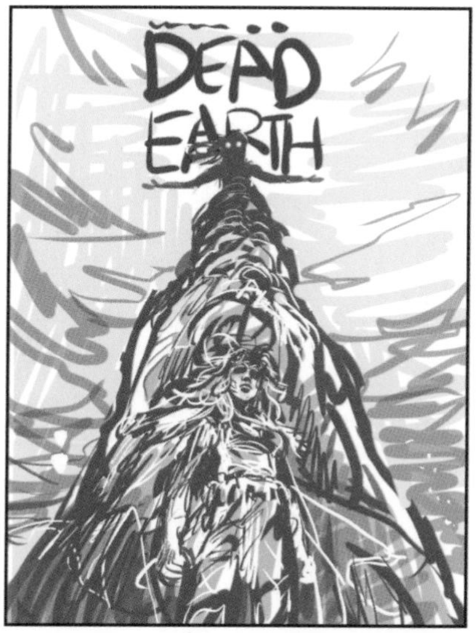
DEAD
EARTH

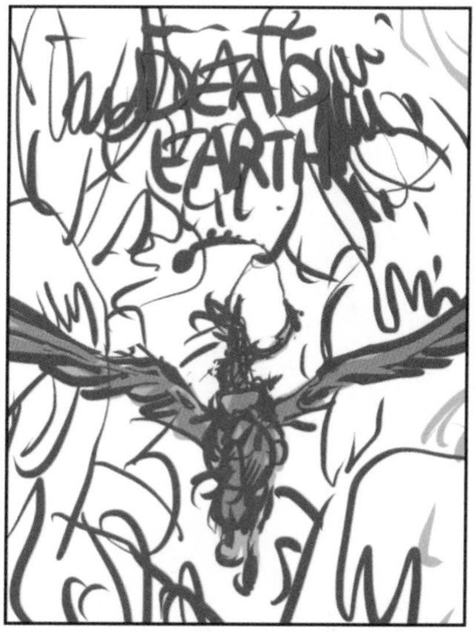
DEAD
EARTH

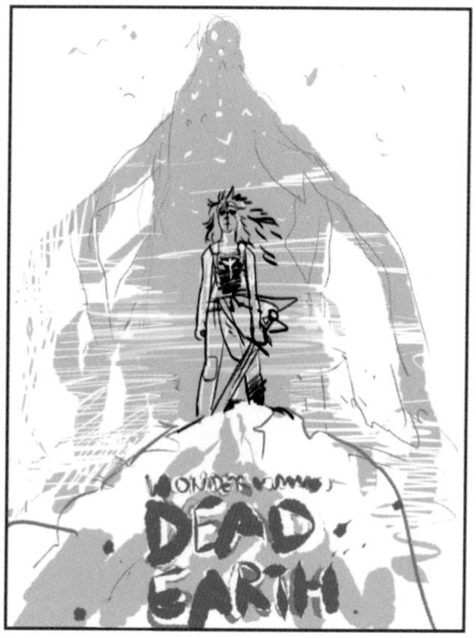
DEAD
EARTH

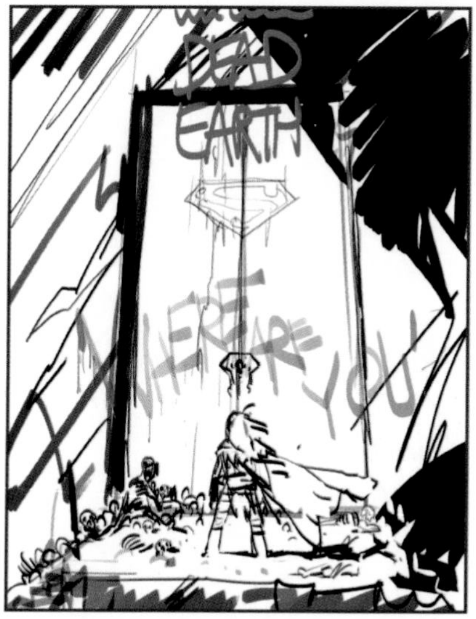
DEAD
EARTH
WHERE ARE YOU

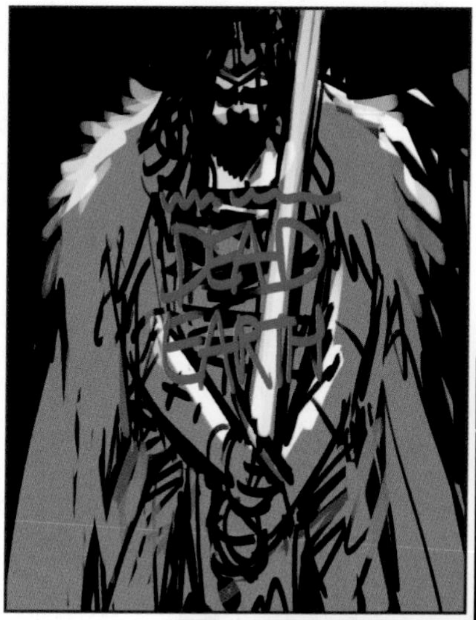
DEAD
EARTH

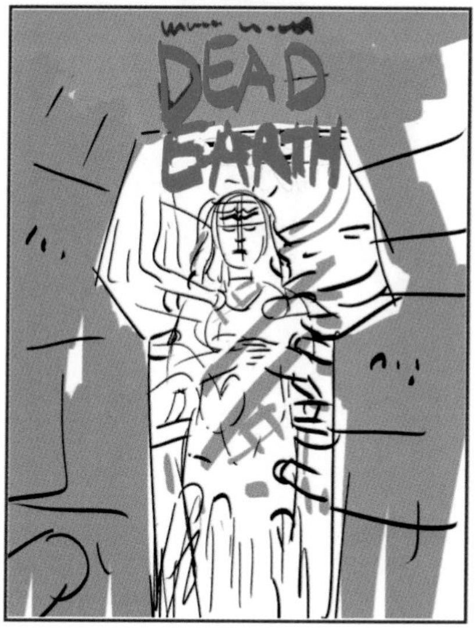
DEAD
EARTH

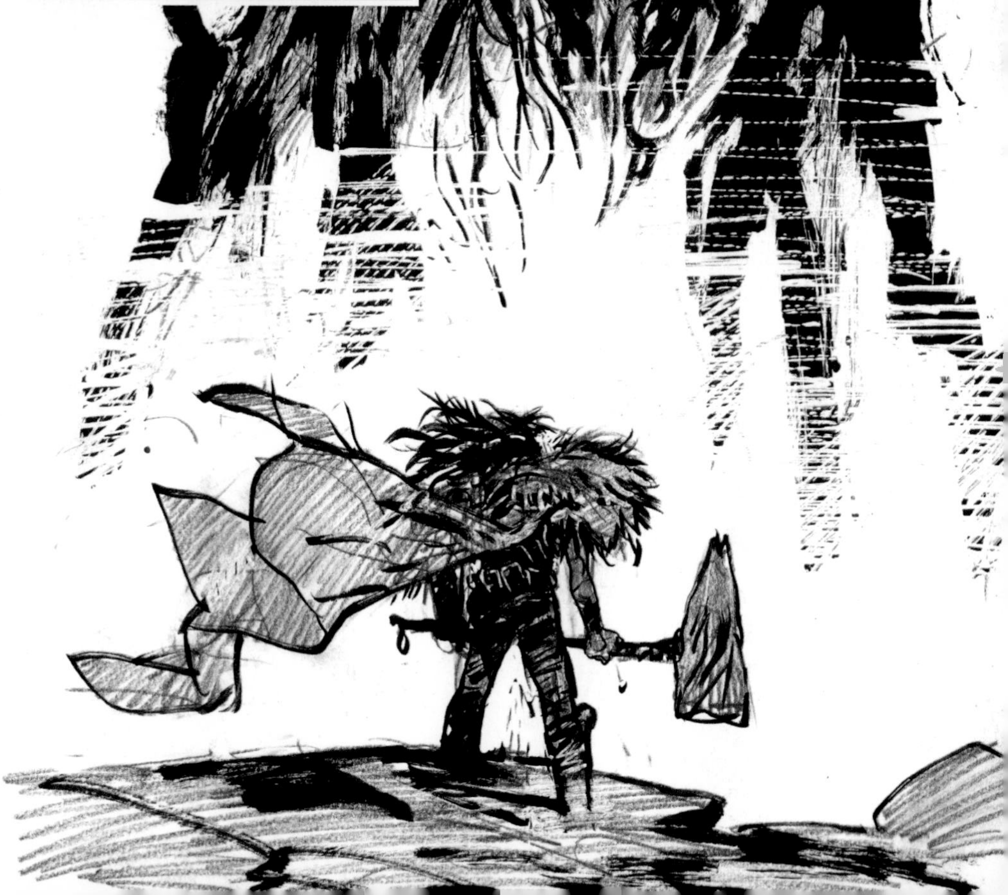

Daniel Warren Johnson is the Eisner Award-nominated writer and artist of *Extremity*, *Space-Mullet!*, and *Murder Falcon*. *Wonder Woman: Dead Earth* is his first project with DC Comics. He lives in Chicago.

Mike Spicer is known for his work on *Silencer*, *Head Lopper*, *Horizon*, *Star Wars: The Last Jedi*, and many more titles from DC Comics, Marvel, Image, Boom! Studios, and nearly every other major American comics publisher. Prior to *Wonder Woman: Dead Earth*, Spicer and Daniel Warren Johnson previously collaborated on the critically acclaimed *Murder Falcon* and *Extremity*, the latter of which was nominated for the Eisner Award for Best Limited Series. Spicer lives in Florida.

Rus Wooton has been lettering comics since 2003, for publishers large and small, across most every genre. He's an artist, designer, and filmmaker holed up in a tiny studio in downtown Los Angeles, subsisting on the wide variety of takeout LA has to offer and lots of coffee.

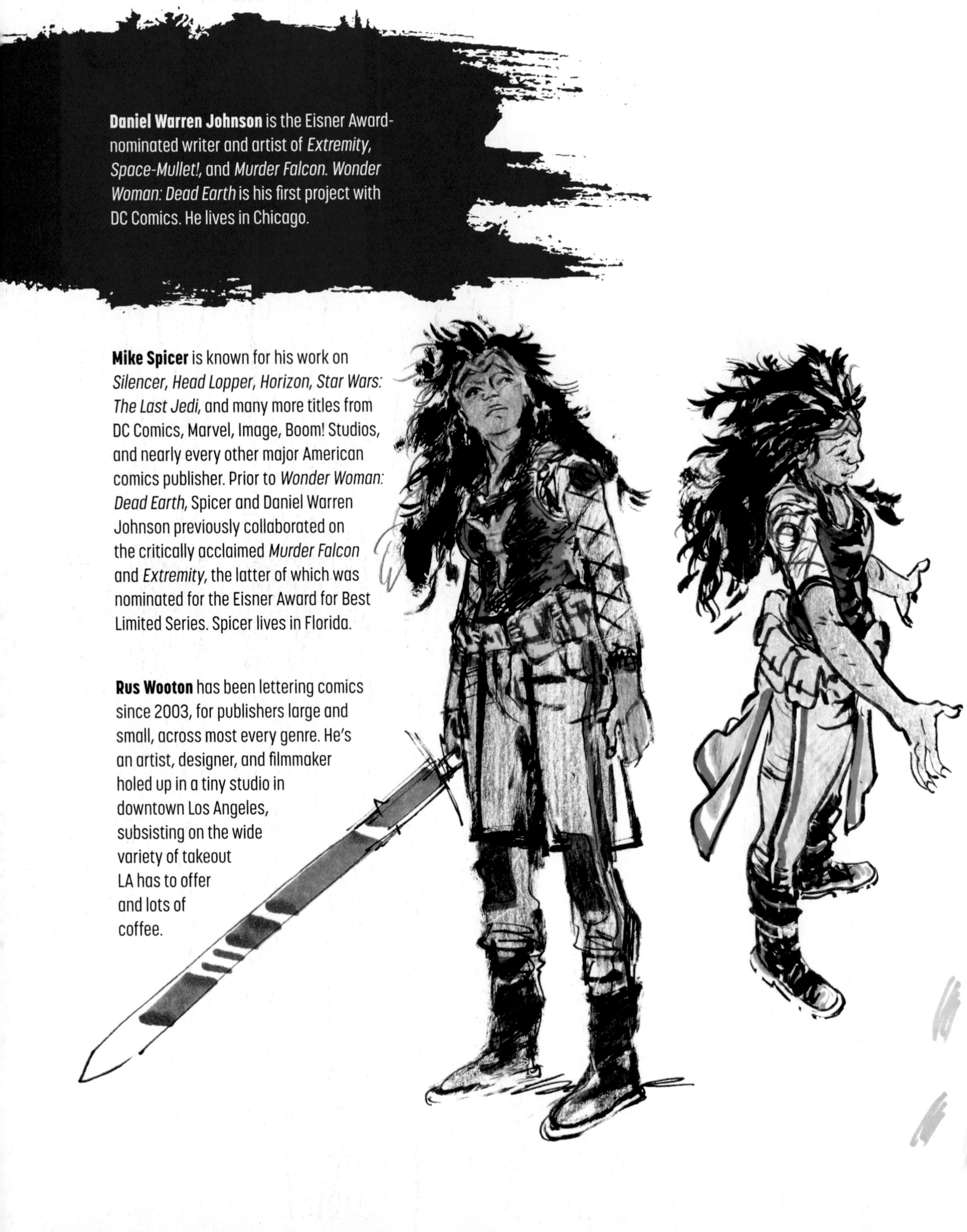